RICOCHET

RICOCHET

SANDRA BROWN

LARGE PRINT PRESS

An imprint of Thomson Gale, a part of The Thomson Corporation

Detroit • New York • San Francisco • New Haven, Conn. • Waterville, Maine • London

LIBRARY OF CONGRESS CATALOGING-IN-PUBLICATION DATA

Brown, Sandra, 1948–
    Ricochet / by Sandra Brown.
        p. cm.
    ISBN 0-7862-8701-2 (lg. print : hc : alk. paper)
    I. Title.
PS3552.R718R53 2006b
813'.54—dc22   20060018097

ISBN 13: 978-1-59413-174-5 (lg. print : sc : alk. paper)
Published in the U.S. in 2007 by arrangement with Simon & Schuster, Inc.

Printed in the United States of America on permanent paper
10 9 8 7 6 5 4 3 2 1

ACKNOWLEDGMENTS

Georgia, not only has some of the best food and most beautiful scenery in the continental United States, its people are the nicest. Among them are Major Everett Regan of the Savannah–Chatham Metropolitan Police Department, who gave of his valuable time to answer myriad questions. Ellen Winters went out of her way to assist me when I was relying strictly on "the kindness of strangers." Without the help of these professionals, getting the necessary details would have been much more difficult.

I'm also indebted to Cindy Moore, to whom Southern hospitality isn't just a catchphrase. She exemplifies it, and then goes above and beyond. Thank you, friend, for opening doors.

And, for exploring with me every square, every street, toting camera gear and risking life and limb to take requested photographs,

without complaining — too much — of the
heat and humidity . . . thank you, Michael.

Sandra Brown

PROLOGUE

The recovery mission was called off at 6:56 P.M.

The grim announcement was made by Chief of Police Clarence Taylor during a locally televised press conference.

His somber expression was in keeping with his buzz haircut and military bearing. "The police department, along with all the other agencies involved, devoted countless hours to the search in hope of a rescue. Short of that, a recovery.

"However, since the exhaustive efforts of law enforcement officers, the Coast Guard, and civilian volunteers haven't produced any encouraging evidence in several days, we've come to the sad conclusion that to continue an organized search would be futile."

The lone drinker at the bar, watching the snowy TV screen mounted in the corner, tossed back the whiskey remaining in his glass and motioned the barkeep for a refill.

The barkeep held the open bottle poised above the highball glass. "You sure? You're hitting it pretty hard, pal."

"Just pour."

"Have you got a ride home?"

The question was met with a menacing glare. The barkeep shrugged and poured. "Your funeral."

No, not mine.

Off the beaten path in a low-rent area of downtown Savannah, Smitty's attracted neither tourists nor respectable locals. It wasn't the kind of watering hole one came to seeking fun and frivolity. It didn't take part in the city's infamous pub crawl on St. Patrick's Day. Pastel drinks with cute names weren't served.

The potables were ordered straight up. You might or might not get a lemon twist like the ones the barkeep was mindlessly peeling as he watched the television news bulletin that had preempted a *Seinfeld* re-run.

On the TV screen, Chief Taylor was commending the tireless efforts of the sheriff's office, canine unit, marine patrol and dive team, on and on, blah, blah, blah.

"Mute that, will you?"

At the request of his customer, the barkeep

reached for the remote control and silenced the TV. "He's dancing around it 'cause he has to. But if you cut through all the B.S., what he's saying is, the body's fish food by now."

The drinker propped both elbows on the bar, hunched his shoulders, and watched the amber liquor sloshing in his glass as he slid it back and forth between his hands across the polished wood surface.

"Ten days after going into the river?" The barkeep shook his head with pessimism. "No way a person could survive. Still, it's a hell of a sad thing. Especially for the family. I mean, never knowing the fate of your loved one?" He reached for another lemon. "I'd hate to think of somebody I loved, dead or alive, being in the river or out there in the ocean, in this mess."

He used his chin to motion toward the bar's single window. It was wide, but only about eighteen inches deep, situated high on the wall, much closer to the ceiling than to the floor, providing a limited view of the outside if one cared to look. It allowed only a slash of semi-light to relieve the oppressive gloom in the bar, and gave only a slim promise of hope to the hopeless inside.

A ponderous rain had been soaking the Low Country of Georgia and South Carolina for the last forty-eight hours. Unrelenting rain. Torrents of water falling straight down out of opaque clouds.

At times the rainfall had been so heavy that you couldn't see across the river to the opposite bank. Low-lying areas had become lakes. Roads had been closed due to flooding. Gutters roiled with currents as swift as white-water rapids.

The barkeep wiped lemon juice from his fingers and cleaned the blade of his knife on a towel. "This rain, can't say I blame 'em for calling off the search. They'll probably never find the body now. But I guess that means it'll forever remain a mystery. Was it murder or suicide?" He tossed aside his towel and leaned on the bar. "What do you think happened?"

His customer looked up at him with bleary eyes and said hoarsely, "I know what happened."

1

Six Weeks Earlier

The murder trial of Robert Savich was in its fourth day.

Homicide detective Duncan Hatcher was wondering what the hell was going on.

As soon as court had reconvened after the lunch break, the defendant's attorney, Stan Adams, had asked the judge for a private meeting. Judge Laird, as perplexed by the request as ADA Mike Nelson, had nonetheless granted it and the three had withdrawn to chambers. The jury had retired to the jury room, leaving only the spectators to question the significance of this unexpected conference.

They'd been out for half an hour. Duncan's anxiety grew with each passing minute. He'd wanted the trial to proceed without a blip, without any hitch that could result in an easy appeal or, God forbid, an

11

overturned verdict. That's why this behind-closed-doors powwow was making him so nervous.

His impatience eventually drove him out into the corridor, where he paced, but never out of earshot of the courtroom. From this fourth-floor vantage point, he watched a pair of tugs guide a merchant ship along the channel toward the ocean. Then, unable to stand the suspense, he returned to his seat in the courtroom.

"Duncan, for heaven's sake, sit still! You're squirming like a two-year-old." To pass the time, his partner detective, DeeDee Bowen, was working a crossword puzzle.

"What could they be talking about in there?"

"Plea bargain? Manslaughter, maybe?"

"Get real," he said. "Savich wouldn't admit to a parking violation, much less a hit."

"What's a seven-letter word for surrender?" DeeDee asked.

"Abdicate."

She looked at him with annoyance. "How'd you come up with that so fast?"

"I'm a genius."

She tried the word. "Not this time. 'Abdicate' doesn't fit. Besides, that's eight letters."

"Then I don't know."

The defendant, Robert Savich, was seated at the defense table looking way too complacent for a man on trial for murder, and much too confident to allay Duncan's anxiety. As though feeling Duncan's stare on the back of his neck, Savich turned and smiled at him. His fingers continued to idly drum the arms of his chair as though keeping time to a catchy tune only he could hear. His legs were casually crossed. He was a portrait of composure.

To anyone who didn't know him, Robert Savich looked like a respectable businessman with a slightly rebellious flair for fashion. For court today he was dressed in a suit of conservative gray, but the slim tailoring of it was distinctly European. His shirt was pale blue, his necktie lavender. His signature ponytail was sleek and glossy. A multicarat diamond glittered from his earlobe.

The classy clothes, his insouciance, were elements of his polished veneer, which gave no indication of the unconscionable criminal behind them.

He'd been arrested and brought before the grand jury on numerous charges that included several murders, one arson, and various lesser felonies, most of which were related to drug trafficking. But over the course of his long and illustrious career, he'd been indicted and tried only twice. The first had been a drug charge. He'd been acquitted because the state failed to prove their case, which, granted, was flimsy.

His second trial was for the murder of one Andre Bonnet. Savich had blown up his house. Along with ATF agents, Duncan had investigated the homicide. Unfortunately, most of the evidence was circumstantial, but had been believed strong enough to win a conviction. However, the DA's office had assigned a green prosecutor who didn't have the savvy or experience necessary to convince all the jurors of Savich's guilt. The trial had resulted in a hung jury.

But it hadn't ended there. It was discovered that the young ADA had also withheld exculpatory evidence from attorney Stan Adams. The hue and cry he raised made the DA's office gun-shy to prosecute again in any sort of timely fashion. The case remained on the books and probably would until the polar ice caps melted.

Duncan had taken that defeat hard. Despite the young prosecutor's bungling, he'd regarded it a personal failure and had dedicated himself to putting an end to Savich's thriving criminal career.

This time, he was betting the farm on a conviction. Savich was charged with the murder of Freddy Morris, one of his many employees, a drug dealer whom undercover narcotics officers had caught making and distributing methamphetamine. The evidence against Freddy Morris had been indisputable, his conviction virtually guaranteed, and, since he was a repeat offender, he'd face years of hard time.

The DEA and the police department's narcs got together and offered Freddy Morris a deal — reduced charges and significantly less prison time in exchange for his boss Savich, who was the kingpin they were really after.

In light of the prison sentence he was facing, Freddy had accepted the offer. But before the carefully planned sting could be executed, Freddy was. He was found lying facedown in a marsh with a bullet hole in the back of his head.

Duncan was confident that Savich wouldn't escape conviction this time. The prosecutor was less optimistic. "I hope you're right, Dunk," Mike Nelson had said the previous evening as he'd coached Duncan on his upcoming appearance on the witness stand. "A lot hinges on your testimony." Tugging on his lower lip, he'd added thoughtfully, "I'm afraid that Adams is going to hammer us on the probable cause issue."

"I had probable cause to question Savich," Duncan insisted. "Freddy's first reaction to the offer was to say that if he even farted in our direction, Savich would cut out his tongue. So, when I'm looking down at Freddy's corpse, I see that not only is his brain an oozing mush, his tongue has been cut out. According to the ME, it was cut out while he was still alive. You don't think that gave me probable cause to go after Savich immediately?"

The blood had been fresh and Freddy's body still warm when Duncan and DeeDee were called to the grisly scene. DEA officers and SPD narcs were engaged in a battle royal over who had blown Freddy's cover.

"You were supposed to have three men monitoring his every move," one of the DEA agents yelled at his police counterpart.

"You had four! Where were they?" the narc yelled back.

"They thought he was safe at home."

"Yeah? Well, so did we."

"Jesus!" the federal agent swore in frustration. "How'd he slip past us?"

No matter who had botched the sting, Freddy was no longer any use to them and quarreling about it was a waste of time. Leaving DeeDee to referee the two factions swapping invectives and blame, Duncan had gone after Savich.

"I didn't plan on arresting him," Duncan had explained to Mike Nelson. "I only went to his office to question him. Swear to God."

"You fought with him, Dunk. That may hurt us. Adams isn't going to let that get past the jury. He's going to hint at police brutality, if not accuse you outright. False arrest. Hell, I don't know what all he'll pull out of the hat."

He'd ended by tacking on a reminder that nothing was a sure thing and that anything could happen during a trial.

Duncan didn't understand the ADA's concern. To him it seemed clear-cut and easily understood. He'd gone directly from the scene of Freddy Morris's murder to Savich's office. Duncan had barged in unannounced to find Savich in the company of a woman later identified by mug shots as Lucille Jones, who was on her knees fellating him.

This morning, Duncan's testimony about that had caused a hush to fall over the courtroom. Restless movements ceased. The bailiff, who had been dozing, sat up, suddenly wakeful. Duncan glanced at the jury box. One of the older women ducked her head in embarrassment. Another, a contemporary of the first, appeared confused as to the meaning of the word. One of the four male jurors looked at Savich with a smirk of admiration. Savich was examining his fingernails as though considering a manicure later in the day.

Duncan had testified that the moment he entered Savich's office, Savich had reached for a gun. "A pistol was lying on his desk. He lunged toward it. I knew I'd be dead if he got hold of that weapon."

Adams came to his feet. "Objection, Your Honor. Conclusion."

"Sustained."

Mike Nelson amended his question and eventually established with the jurors that Duncan had rushed Savich only to defend himself from possible harm. The ensuing struggle was intense, but finally Duncan was able to restrain Savich.

"And once you had subdued Mr. Savich," the prosecutor said, "did you confiscate that weapon as evidence, Detective Hatcher?"

Here's where it got tricky. "No. By the time I had Savich in restraints, the pistol had disappeared and so had the woman."

Neither had been seen since.

Duncan arrested Savich for assault on a

police officer. While he was being held on that charge, Duncan, DeeDee, and other officers had constructed a case against him for the murder of Freddy Morris.

They didn't have the weapon that Duncan had seen, which they were certain Savich had used to slay Freddy Morris less than an hour earlier. They didn't have the testimony of the woman. They didn't even have footprints or tire prints at the scene because the tide had come in and washed them away prior to the discovery of the body.

What they did have was the testimony of several other agents who'd heard Freddy's fearful claim that Savich would cut out his tongue and then kill him if he made a deal with the authorities, or even talked to them. And, since Lucille Jones's whereabouts were unknown, Savich couldn't produce a credible alibi. The DA's office had won convictions on less, so the case had come to trial.

Nelson expected Duncan would get hammered by Savich's attorney during cross-examination that afternoon. Over lunch, he had tried to prepare him for it. "He's going to claim harassment and tell the jury that you've harbored a personal grudge against his client for years."

"You bet your ass, I have," Duncan said. "The son of a bitch is a killer. It's my sworn

19

duty to catch killers."

Nelson sighed. "Just don't let it sound personal, all right?"

"I'll try."

"Even though it is."

"I said I'll try, Mike. But, yeah, it's become personal."

"Adams is going to claim that Savich has a permit to carry a handgun, so the weapon itself isn't incriminating. And *then* he's going to claim that there never was a weapon. He may even question if there was really a woman giving him a blow job. He'll deny, deny, deny, and build up a mountain of doubt in the jurors' minds. He may even make a motion to dismiss your entire testimony since there's no corroboration."

Duncan knew what he was up against. He'd come up against Stan Adams before. But he was anxious to get on with it.

He was staring at the door leading to the judge's chambers, willing it to open, when it actually did.

"All rise," the bailiff intoned.

Duncan shot to his feet. He searched the expressions of the three men as they reentered the courtroom and resumed their places. He leaned toward DeeDee. "What think you?"

"I don't know, but I don't like it."

His partner had an uncanny and reliable talent for reading people and situations, and she had just validated the foreboding he was feeling.

Another bad sign — Mike Nelson kept his head averted and didn't look in their direction.

Stan Adams sat down beside his client and patted the sleeve of Savich's expensive suit.

Duncan's gut tightened with apprehension.

The judge stepped onto the bench and signaled the bailiff to ask the jury to return. He took his seat behind the podium and carefully arranged his robe. He scooted the tray holding a drinking glass and a carafe of water one-half inch to his right and adjusted the microphone, which needed no adjustment.

Once the jury had filed in and everyone was situated, he said, "Ladies and gentlemen, I apologize for the delay, but a matter of importance had to be addressed immediately."

Cato Laird was a popular judge, with the public and with the media, which he courted like a suitor. Nearing fifty, he had the physique of a thirty-year-old and the facial features of a movie star. In fact, a few years earlier he had played a cameo role of a judge

21

in a movie filmed in Savannah.

Comfortable in front of cameras, he could be counted on to provide a sound bite whenever a news story revolved around crime, criminals, or jurisprudence. He was speaking in that well-known, often-heard silver-tongued tone now. "Mr. Adams has brought to my attention that during voir dire, juror number ten failed to disclose that her son is enrolled in the next class of candidate officers for the Savannah–Chatham Metropolitan Police Department."

Duncan glanced at the jury box and noticed the empty chair in the second row.

"Oh, jeez," DeeDee said under her breath.

"The juror has admitted as much to me," Judge Laird said. "She didn't intentionally try to deceive the court, she simply failed to recognize how that omission could affect the outcome of this trial."

"What?"

DeeDee nudged Duncan, warning him to keep his voice down.

The judge looked in their direction, but continued.

"When seating a jury, attorneys for each side have an opportunity to eliminate any individuals who they feel have the potential of swaying the verdict. Mr. Adams is of the opinion that a juror whose family member will soon become a police officer may have a fundamental prejudice against any defendant in a criminal trial, but especially one accused of this particularly egregious slaying."

He paused, then said, "I agree with counsel on this point and am therefore compelled to declare a mistrial." He banged his gavel. "Jurors, you are dismissed. Mr. Adams, your client is free to go. Court is adjourned."

Duncan came out of his chair. "You have got to be kidding!"

The judge's gaze sought him out and, in a tone that could have cut a diamond, he said, "I assure you I am not kidding, Detective Hatcher."

Duncan stepped into the aisle and walked up it as far as the railing. He pointed at Savich. "Your Honor, you cannot let him walk out of here."

Mike Nelson was at his elbow, speaking under his breath. "Dunk, calm down."

"You can retry the case, Mr. Nelson," the judge said as he stood and prepared to leave. "But I advise you to have more solid evidence before you do." He glanced at Duncan, adding, "Or more credible testimony."

Duncan saw red. "You think I'm *lying?*"

"Duncan."

DeeDee had come up behind him and taken hold of his arm, trying to pull him back down the aisle toward the exit, but he yanked his arm free.

"The pistol was real. It was practically smoking. The woman was real. She jumped to her feet when I came in and —"

The judge banged his gavel, silencing him. "You can testify at the next trial. If there is one."

Suddenly Savich was in front of him, filling his field of vision, smiling. "You blew it again, Hatcher."

Mike Nelson grabbed Duncan's arm to keep him from vaulting over the railing. "I'm gonna nail you, you son of a bitch. Etch it into your skin. Tattoo it on your ass. I'm gonna nail you."

His voice rife with menace, Savich said, "I'll be seeing you. Soon." Then he blew Duncan an air kiss.

Adams hastily ushered his client past Duncan, who looked toward the judge. "How can you let him go?"

"Not I, Detective Hatcher, the law."

"*You're* the law. Or rather you're supposed to be."

"Duncan, shut up," DeeDee hissed. "We'll redouble our search for Lucille Jones.

Maybe the weapon will turn up. We'll get Savich sooner or later."

"We could have had him sooner," he said, making no attempt to lower his voice. "We could have had him today. We could have had him right fucking now if we'd had a judge who sides with cops more than he sides with criminals."

"Oh hell," DeeDee groaned.

"Detective Hatcher." Judge Laird leaned upon the podium and glared at Duncan. As though addressing him from a burning bush, he said, "I'm willing to do you a favor and overlook that statement because I understand the level of your frustration."

"You don't understand jack shit. And if you wanted to do me a favor, *Your Honor,* you would have replaced that juror instead of declaring a mistrial. If you wanted to do me a favor, you would have given us an even chance of putting this murderer out of commission for good."

Every muscle in the judge's handsome face tensed, but his voice remained remarkably controlled. "I advise you to leave this courtroom now, before you say something for which I'll be forced to hold you in contempt."

Duncan aimed his index finger at the exit door through which Savich and his attorney

25

had just passed. "Savich is thumbing his nose at you, too, same as he is at me. He loves killing people, and you just handed him a free pass to go out and kill some more."

"I ruled as the law dictates."

"No, what you did —"

"Duncan, please," DeeDee said.

"— is crap on me. You crapped on the people who elected you because they believed your promise to be tough on criminals like Savich. You crapped on Detective Bowen here, and on the DA's office, and on everybody else who's ever tried to nail this bastard. That's what you did. Your Honor."

" 'Hands up.' "

"What?"

"Seven-letter word for surrender."

DeeDee gaped at Duncan as he situated himself in the passenger seat of her car and buckled his seat belt. "Forty-eight hours in jail, and that's the first thing you have to say?"

"I had a lot of time to think about it."

" 'Hands up' is two words, *genius*."

"Still works, I bet."

"We'll never know. I threw the puzzle away."

"Couldn't finish?" he teased, knowing that

it irked her because he could normally finish a puzzle long before she could. He had a knack for them; she didn't.

"No, I threw it away because I didn't want any reminders of your overplayed scene in the courtroom." She left the detention center parking lot and headed toward downtown. "You let your mouth overload your ass."

He sat brooding, saying nothing.

"Look, Duncan, I understand why you want Savich. We all want Savich. He's evil incarnate. But to verbally abuse a judge in his own courtroom? That's crazy. You damaged yourself as well as the department." She shot him a glance. "Of course it's not my place to lecture. You're the senior partner."

"Thank you for remembering that."

"I'm talking as your friend. I'm only saying this for your own good. Your zeal is admirable, but you've got to keep a rein on your temper."

Feeling not at all zealous, he stared moodily through the windshield. Savannah was baking under a fierce sun. The air was laden with moisture. Everything looked limp, wilted, as weary as he felt. The air conditioner in DeeDee's car was fighting a losing battle against the humidity. Already the back of his shirt was damp.

He wiped drops of sweat off his forehead. "I got a shower this morning, but I still stink like jail."

"Was it terrible?"

"Not too bad, but I don't want to go back any time soon."

"Gerard is unhappy with you," she said, speaking of Lieutenant Bill Gerard, their immediate supervisor.

"Judge Laird gives Savich a walk and Gerard is unhappy with *me?*"

DeeDee stopped at a traffic light and looked over at him. "Don't get pissed at what I'm about to say."

"I thought the lecture was over."

"You really gave the judge no choice." In the two years since DeeDee had been bumped up to homicide and made his partner, he'd never seen one iota of maternal instinct in her nature. Her expression now came close. "After the things you said, Judge Laird was practically duty-bound to hold you in contempt."

"Then His Honor and I have something in common. I feel bound to hold him in contempt, too."

"I think he got the message. As for Gerard, he has to toe the company line. He can't have his detectives telling off superior court judges."

"Okay, okay, I acknowledge the error of my ways. I served my time. At Savich's next trial, I promise to be a perfect gentleman, meek as a lamb, so long as Judge Laird, in turn, will cut us some slack. After the other day, he owes us."

"Uh, Duncan."

"Uh, what?"

"Mike Nelson called this afternoon." She hesitated, sighed. "The DA's position is that we didn't have enough on Savich —"

"I don't want to hear this, do I?"

"He said this trial was a long shot to start with, that we probably wouldn't have got a conviction anyway, and that he's not going to try the case again. Not unless we turn up something rock solid that places Savich at the scene."

Duncan had feared as much, but hearing it was worse than the dread of hearing it. He laid his head against the headrest and closed his eyes. "I don't know why I give a damn about Savich or any other scumbag. Nobody else does. The DA is probably more upset with me than he is with the Neanderthal who killed his wife last night over a tough pork chop. He was in the cell next to mine. If he told me once, he told me a dozen times that the bitch had it coming."

Sighing, he rolled his head to gaze out the window at the venerable live oaks along the boulevard. The clumps of Spanish moss dangling from their branches looked bedraggled in the oppressive heat.

"I mean, why do we bother?" he asked rhetorically. "If Savich pops a meth maker like Freddy Morris every now and then, he's performing a public service, isn't he?"

"No, because before that meth maker's body is cold, Savich will have his replacement set up for business."

"So, I repeat, what's the point? I'm all out of that zeal you referenced. I don't give a shit. Not anymore."

DeeDee rolled her eyes.

"Do you know how old I am?" he asked.

"Thirty-seven."

"Eight. And in twenty years I'll be fifty-eight. I'll have an enlarged prostate and a shrunken dick. My hair will be thinner, my waistline thicker."

"Your outlook gloomier."

"You're goddamn right," he said angrily, sitting up suddenly and jabbing the dashboard with his index finger as he enumerated his points. "Because I will have put in twenty more years of futility. There'll be more Saviches killing people. What will it all have been for?"

She pulled to the curb and braked. It hadn't registered with him until then that she'd driven him home, not to the parking lot where his car had been abandoned at the judicial center when he was taken into custody and marched from the courtroom.

DeeDee leaned back against her seat and turned to him. "Granted, we've had a setback. Tomorrow —"

"Setback? *Setback?* We're as dead as poor Freddy Morris. His execution scared the hell out of any other mule who has ever even remotely considered striking a deal with us or the Feds. Savich used Freddy to send a message, and it went out loud and clear. You talk, you die, and you die ugly. Nobody will talk," he said, enunciating the last three words.

He slammed his fist into his palm. "I cannot believe that slick son of a bitch got off again. How does he do it? Nobody's that supernaturally lucky. Or that smart. Somewhere along his body-strewn path, he must've struck a deal with the devil. All the demons in hell must be working for his side. But I swear this to you, DeeDee. If it's the last thing I do —" Noticing her smile, he broke off. "What?"

"Don't look now, Duncan, but you sound full of zeal again."

31

He grumbled a swear word or two, undid his seat belt, and pushed open the car door. "Thanks for the lift."

"I'm coming in." Before getting out, she reached into the backseat for the dry cleaner's bag that had been hanging on the hook on the door.

"What's that?"

"The suit I'm wearing tonight. I'm going to change here, save myself the drive all the way home and then back downtown."

"What's tonight?"

"The awards dinner." She looked at him with consternation. "Don't tell me you forgot."

He raked his fingers through his unruly hair. "Yeah, I did. Sorry, partner, but I'm just not up for that tonight."

He didn't want to be around cops tonight. He didn't want to face Bill Gerard in a semi-social setting, knowing that first thing tomorrow morning, he'd be called into his office for a good old-fashioned ass-chewing. Which he deserved for losing his cool in court. His outrage was justified, but he'd been wrong to express it then and there. What DeeDee had said was right — he'd hurt their cause, not helped it. And that must have given Savich a lot of satisfaction.

She bent down to pick up two editions of

the newspaper from the sidewalk and swatted him in the stomach with them. "You're going to that dinner," she said and started up the brick steps to the front door of his town house.

Once the door was unlocked and they were inside, he made a beeline for the wall thermostat and adjusted the AC.

"How come your alarm wasn't set?" DeeDee asked.

"I keep forgetting the code."

"You never forget anything. You're just lazy. It's stupid not to set it, Duncan. Especially now."

"Why especially now?"

"Savich. His parting 'I'll see you. Soon,' resonated like a threat."

"I wish he would come after me. It would give me an excuse."

"To . . . ?"

"To do whatever was necessary." He flung his sport jacket onto a chair and made his way down the hallway toward the kitchen at the back of the house. "You know where the guest bedroom and bath are," he said, indicating the staircase. "Help yourself."

DeeDee was right on his heels. "You're going to that dinner with me, Duncan."

"No, what I'm going to do is have a beer, a shower, a ham sandwich with mustard hot enough to make my eyes water, and —"

"Play the piano?"

"I don't play the piano."

"Right," she said drolly.

"What I was going to say is that maybe I'll catch a ball game on TV before turning in early. Can't tell you how much I look forward to sleeping in my own bed after two nights on a jail cot. But what I am *not* going to do is get dressed up and go to that dinner."

She planted her hands on her hips. "You promised."

He opened his fridge and, without even looking, reached inside and took out a can of beer, popping the top and sucking the foam off the back of his hand. "That was before my incarceration."

"I'm receiving a commendation."

"Well deserved. Congratulations. You cracked the widow who cracked her husband over the head with a crowbar. Great instinct, partner. I couldn't be more proud." He toasted her with his can of beer, then tipped it toward his mouth.

"You're missing the point. I don't want to go to a fancy dinner alone. You're my escort."

He laughed, sputtering beer. "It isn't a cotillion. And since when do you care if you've got an *escort?* In fact, that's the first time I've ever heard you use that word."

"If I don't have an *escort,* the bubbas will give me hell. Worley and company will say I couldn't get a date if my life depended on it. You're my partner, Duncan. It's your duty to back me up, and that includes helping me save face with the yahoos I'm forced to work with."

"Call up that cop in the evidence room. What's his name? He gets flustered every time he looks at you. He'd escort you."

She frowned with distaste. "He's got a moist handshake. I hate that." Looking thoroughly put out, she said, "It's a few hours of your time, Duncan."

"Sorry."

"You just don't want to be seen with me."

"What are you talking about? I'm seen with you all the time."

"But never in a social setting. Some people there might not know I'm your coworker. Heaven forbid anyone mistake me for your date. Being with a woman who's short, dumpy, and frizzy might damage your reputation as a stud muffin."

He set his beer on the countertop, hard. "Now you've made me mad. First of all, I don't have that reputation. Secondly, who says you're short?"

"Worley called me vertically challenged."

"Worley's an asshole. Nor are you dumpy. You're compactly built. Muscular, because you work out like a fiend. And your hair's frizzy because you perm the hell out of it."

"Makes it easy to take care of," she said defensively. "Keeps it out of my eyes. How'd you know it was permed?"

"Because when you get a fresh one, I can smell it. My mom used to give herself perms at home. Stunk up the whole house for days. Dad begged her to go to the beauty parlor, but she said they charge too much."

"Salon, Duncan. They're not called beauty parlors anymore."

"*I* know that. Mom doesn't."

"Do they know about your jail time?"

"Yeah," he said with some regret. "I used my one phone call to talk to them because they get nervous if they don't hear from me every few days. They're proud of what I do, but they worry. You know how it is."

"Well, not really," she said, using the sour tone of voice she used whenever her parents were referenced, even tangentially. "Do your folks know about Savich?" she asked.

He shrugged. "I downplay it."

"What did they think of their son being in jail?"

"They had to bail me out once when I

36

was in high school. Underage drinking. I caught hell that time. This time, Dad commended me for standing up for what I thought was right. Of course I didn't tell him that I'd used the f-word to get my point across."

DeeDee smiled. "You're lucky they're so understanding."

"I know." In truth, Duncan did know how fortunate he was. DeeDee's relationship with her parents was strained. Hoping to divert her from that unhappy topic, he said, "Did I tell you that Dad's gone high-tech? Prepares his sermons on a computer. He has the whole Bible on software and can access any scripture with a keystroke. But not everybody is happy about it. One old-timer in his congregation is convinced that the Internet is the Antichrist."

She laughed. "He may be right."

"May be." He picked up his beer and took another drink.

"Not that I was asked, but I'd love a Diet Coke, please."

"Sorry." He opened the fridge and reached inside. Then, with a yelp, yanked back his hand. "Whoa!"

"What?"

"I've gotta remember to set my alarm."

DeeDee pushed him aside and looked into

the refrigerator. She made a face, and, like Duncan, recoiled. "What *is* that?"

"If I were to guess, I'd say it's Freddy Morris's tongue."

2

Duncan would take the severed tongue —
now several months old — to the ME in the
morning. For the time being he placed it in
an evidence bag and returned it to his refrigerator.

DeeDee was aghast. "You're not going to
leave it in there, are you? With your *food?*"

"I don't want it smelling up my house."

"Are you going to have the place dusted
for prints?"

"It wouldn't do any good and would only
make a mess."

Whoever had been inside his house, either
Savich or one of his many errand boys —
Duncan guessed the latter — would have
been too smart to leave fingerprints. More
disturbing than finding the offensive, shriveled piece of tissue was knowing that his
house had been violated. In and of itself,
the tongue was a prank. Savich's equivalent
to *na-na-na-na-na.* He was rubbing Dun-

can's nose in his defeat.

But the message it sent was no laughing matter. Duncan had detected the underlying threat in Savich's taunting good-bye, but this wasn't the retribution that threat foretold. This was only a prelude, a hint of things to come. It broadcast loud and clear that Duncan was vulnerable and that Savich meant business. By coming into Duncan's home, he'd taken their war to a new level. And only one of them would survive it.

Although he minimized his apprehension with DeeDee, he did not underestimate Savich and the degree of his brutality. When he launched his attack on Duncan, it would be merciless. What worried Duncan most was that he might not see it coming until it was too late.

He'd hoped the incident would relieve him of having to attend the awards dinner with DeeDee. Surely she wouldn't require him to go now. But she persisted, and ultimately he gave in. He dressed in a dark suit and tie and went with her to one of the major hotels on the river where the event was being held.

Upon entering the ballroom, he took a cursory glance at the crowd and stopped dead in his tracks. "I cannot believe this!"

he exclaimed.

Following the direction of his gaze, DeeDee groaned. "I didn't know he was going to be here, Duncan. I swear."

Judge Cato Laird, immaculately attired and looking as cool as the drink in his hand, was chatting with police chief Taylor.

"I formally release you from your obligation," DeeDee said. "If you want to leave, you won't get an argument from me."

Duncan's eyes stayed fixed on the judge. When Laird laughed, the corners of his eyes crinkled handsomely. He looked like a man confident of the rightness of every decision he'd ever made in his entire life, from the choice of his necktie tonight to declaring Savich's murder trial a mistrial.

Duncan would be damned before he tucked tail and slunk out. "Hell no," he said to DeeDee. "I wouldn't pass up this chance to escort you when you're this gussied up. You're actually wearing a skirt. First time I've ever seen you in one."

"I swore off them once I graduated from Catholic high school."

He made a point of looking at her legs. "Better than decent. Fairly good, in fact."

"You're full of shit, but thanks."

Together they wove their way through the crowd, stopping along the way to speak to other policemen and to be introduced to significant others they hadn't met before. Several mentioned Duncan's days in jail, the sentiments ranging from anger to sympathy. He responded by joking about it.

When they were spotted by the police chief, Taylor excused himself from the group he was speaking with and approached them to extend his congratulations to DeeDee for the commendation she was to receive later that evening. While she was thanking him, someone addressed Duncan from behind.

Turning, he came face-to-face with Cato Laird, whose countenance was as guileless as that of the lead soprano in his dad's church choir. Reflexively Duncan's jaw clenched, but he replied with a civil, "Judge Laird."

"Detective. I hope there are no hard feelings." He extended his right hand.

Duncan clasped it. "For the jail time? I have only myself to blame for that."

"What about the mistrial?"

Duncan glanced beyond the judge's shoulder. Although DeeDee was being introduced to the mayor, who was enthusiastically pumping her hand, she was keeping a nervous eye on him and Laird. Duncan felt like telling the judge in the most explicit terms what he thought of his ruling and where he could shove his gavel.

But this was DeeDee's night. He would hold his temper. He would even refrain from telling the judge about the unpleasant surprise he'd had waiting in his home upon his return.

His eyes reconnected with the judge's dark gaze. "You know as well as I do that Savich is guilty of the Morris hit, so I'm certain you share my misgivings about releasing him." He paused to let that soak in. "But I'm equally certain that, under the circumstances, you ruled according to the law and your own conscience."

Judge Laird gave a slight nod. "I'm glad you appreciate the complexities involved."

"Well, I had forty-eight hours to contemplate them." He grinned, but if the judge had any perception at all, he would have realized that it wasn't a friendly expression. "Please excuse me. My partner is signaling for me to rejoin her."

"Of course. Enjoy the evening."

The judge stepped aside and Duncan brushed past him.

"What did he say?" DeeDee asked out the side of her mouth as Duncan took her arm and guided her toward the bar.

"He told me to enjoy the evening. Which I think includes having a drink."

He elbowed them through the crowd to the bar, ordered a bourbon and water for himself and a Diet Coke for her. Another detective in their division sidled up to them, awkwardly holding a drink in one hand and balancing a plate piled with hors d'oeuvres in the other.

"Hey, Dunk," he said around a mouthful of crab dip, "introduce me to your new squeeze."

"Eat shit and die, Worley," she said.

"What do you know? She sounds just like Detective Bowen!"

Worley was a good detective but one of the "yahoos" that DeeDee had referred to earlier. Never without a toothpick in his mouth, he held one there now, even as he ate from his plate of canapés. He and DeeDee had an ongoing contest to see who could better insult the other. The score was usually tied.

"Lay off, Worley," Duncan said. "DeeDee is an honoree tonight. Behave."

DeeDee was always in cop mode. Having worked with her for two years, Duncan thought that was possibly the only mode she operated in. Even tonight, despite the skirt and the lip gloss she'd smeared on for the occasion, she was thinking like a cop. "Tell Worley what we found in your house."

Duncan described the severed tongue. He indicated a chunk of meat on Worley's plate. "Looked sorta like that."

"Jeez." Worley shuddered. "How do you know Morris was the rightful owner?"

"Just a guess, but a pretty good one, don't you think? I'll take it to the lab tomorrow."

"Savich is pricking with you."

"He's a regular comedian, all right."

"But coming at you where you live . . ." Worley rearranged his toothpick and popped the questionable chunk of meat into his mouth. "That's ballsy. So, Dunk, you spooked?"

"He'd be stupid not to be a little spooked," DeeDee said, answering for him. "Right, Duncan?"

"I guess," he replied absently. He was wondering if, when the final showdown came, he would be able to kill Savich without compunction. He supposed he could, because he knew with certainty that Savich wouldn't hesitate to kill him.

In an effort to lighten the mood, Worley said, "Honest, DeeDee, you look sorta hot tonight."

"Little good it'll do you."

"If I get drunk enough, you might even start to look like a woman."

DeeDee didn't miss a beat. "Sadly, I could

never get drunk enough for you to start looking like a man."

This was familiar office banter. The men in the Violent Crimes Unit gave DeeDee hell, but they all respected her skill, dedication, and ambition, all of which she had in surplus. When the situation called for it, the teasing stopped, and her opinions were respected equally with those of her male counterparts, sometimes more. "Women's intuition" was no longer just a catchphrase. Because of DeeDee's perception, they'd come to believe in it.

Knowing she could fend for herself without his help, Duncan turned away and let his gaze rove over the crowd.

Later, he remembered it was her hair that had first called her to his attention.

She was standing directly beneath one of the directional lights recessed into the ceiling thirty feet above her. It acted like a spotlight, making her hair look almost white, marking her as though she were the only blonde in the crowd.

It was in a simple style that bordered on severity — pulled back into a small knot at the nape of her neck — but it defined the perfect shape of her head and showed off the graceful length of her neck. He was admiring that pale nape when a nondescript woman who'd been blocking his view of the rest of her moved away. He saw her back. All of it. Tantalizing square inches of bare skin from her neck to her waist, even slightly below.

He didn't know jewelry could be worn on that part of the body, but there it was, a clasp made of what looked like diamonds winking at him from the small of her back. He imagined the stones would be warm from her skin.

Just from looking at her, his skin had turned warm.

Someone moved up behind her, said something. She turned, and Duncan got his first look at her face. Later, he thought that maybe his jaw had actually dropped.

"Dunk?" Worley nudged his arm. "You okay?"

"Yeah. Sure."

"I asked you how jail was."

"Oh, just peachy."

The other detective leaned toward him and leered. "You have to fight off any cell mates looking for romance?"

"No, they were all pining for you, Worley."

DeeDee laughed so suddenly, she snorted. "Good one, Duncan."

He turned away again, but the blonde had moved from the spot where he'd seen her.

Impatiently his gaze scanned the crowd, until he located her again. She was talking to a distinguished-looking older couple and sipping a glass of white wine with seeming uninterest in both it and the conversation. She was smiling politely, but her eyes had a distant quality, like she wasn't quite connected to what was going on around her.

"You're drooling." DeeDee had moved up beside him and followed his stare to the woman. "Honestly, Duncan," she said with exasperation. "You're embarrassing yourself."

"Can't help it. I've fallen into instant lust."

"Rein it in."

"I don't think I can."

"Don't want to, you mean."

"Right, don't want to. I didn't know that getting struck by lightning could feel so good."

"Lightning?"

"Oh yeah. And then some."

DeeDee critically looked the woman over and shrugged. "She's okay, I guess. If you're into tall, thin, perfect hair, and flawless skin."

"To say nothing of her face."

She took a noisy sip of her Diet Coke. "Yeah, there's that. I gotta give credit where credit's due. As usual, your sexual radar

48

homed in on the dishiest babe in the room."

He shot her his wicked smile. "It's this gift I have."

The couple moved away from the woman, leaving her standing by herself in the midst of the crowd. "The lady looks lost and lonely," Duncan said. "Like maybe she needs a big strong cop to come to her rescue. Hold my drink." He thrust his glass toward DeeDee.

"Have you lost your mind?" She stepped in front of him to block his path. "That would be the height of stupidity. I will not stand by and watch as you self-destruct."

"What are you talking about?"

DeeDee looked at him with sudden understanding. "Oh. You don't know."

"What?"

"She's married, Duncan."

"Shit. Are you sure?"

"To Judge Cato Laird."

"What did he say to you?"

Elise Laird set her jeweled handbag on the dressing table and stepped out of her sandals. Cato had come upstairs to their bedroom ahead of her. He was already undressed and in his robe, sitting on the side of their bed.

"Who?" she asked.

49

"Duncan Hatcher."

She pulled a pin from her hair. "Who?"

"The man you were talking to in the porte cochere. When I went to pay for the valet parking. Surely you remember. Tall, rugged, in dire need of a haircut, built like a wide receiver. Which he was. At Georgia, I believe."

"Oh, right." She dropped the hairpins next to her handbag and uncoiled the chignon, then combed her fingers through her hair. Facing the mirror, she smiled at her husband's reflection. "He asked if I had change. He needed to tip the parking valet and didn't have any bills smaller than a ten."

"He only asked for change?"

"Hmm." Reaching behind her she tried to undo the clasp of the diamond brooch at the small of her back. "Could you help me here, please?"

Cato left the bed and moved up behind her. He unfastened the clasp, pulled the pin from the black silk with care, then handed her the brooch and placed his hands on her shoulders, massaging gently. "Did Hatcher address you by name?"

"I honestly don't remember. Why? Who is he?"

"He's a homicide detective."

"Savannah police?"

"A decorated hero with a master's degree in criminology. He has brains and brawn."

"Impressive."

"Up till now he's been an exemplary officer."

"Till now?"

"He testified in my court this week. Murder trial. When circumstances forced me to declare a mistrial, he lost his temper. Became vituperative. I found him in contempt and sentenced him to two days in jail. He was released just this afternoon."

She laughed softly. "Then I'm sure he didn't know who I was. If he had, he would have avoided speaking to me." She took off her earrings. "Was the woman with him his wife?"

"Police partner. I don't believe he's married." He slipped the dress off Elise's shoulders, sliding the fabric down her arms, baring her to the waist. He studied her in the mirror. "I guess I can't blame the man for trying."

"He didn't *try* anything, Cato. He asked me for change."

"There were other people he could have asked, but he asked you." Reaching around her, he took the weight of her breasts in his palms. "I thought he might have recognized you, that you might have met before."

Meeting his dark eyes in the mirror, she said, "I suppose it's possible, but if so, I don't remember it. I wouldn't have remembered speaking to him tonight if you hadn't brought it up."

"Untrimmed dirty-blond hair isn't attractive to you? That shaggy, scruffy look doesn't appeal?"

"I much prefer graying temples and smoother shaves."

The zipper at the back of her dress was short. He smiled into the mirror as he pulled it down, following the cleft between her buttocks, then pushed the dress to the floor, leaving her in only a black lace thong. He turned her to face him. "This is the best part of these dull evenings out. Coming home with you." He looked at her, waiting. "No comment?"

"I have to say it? You know I feel the same."

Taking her hand, he folded it around his erection. "I lied, Elise," he whispered as he guided her motions. "This is the best part."

A half hour later, she eased herself from the bed, padded to the closet for a robe, and pulled it on. She paused briefly at her dressing table, then went to the door. It creaked when she pulled it open. She looked back toward the bed. Cato didn't stir.

She slipped from the room and tiptoed downstairs. Her insomnia concerned him. Sometimes he would come downstairs and find her on the sofa in the den, watching a DVD of one of her favorite movies. Sometimes she was reading in the living room, sometimes sitting in the sunroom, staring out at the lighted swimming pool.

He sympathized with her sleeplessness and urged her to get medication to help remedy it. He chided her for leaving their bed without waking him when he might have helped soothe her into sleep.

Recently she had begun to wonder if his concern was over the insomnia, or her nocturnal prowls through the house.

A night-light was left on in the kitchen, but the route was so familiar she could have found her way without it. Whatever else she did when she came downstairs, she always poured herself a glass of milk, which she claimed helped, and left the empty glass in the sink to ensure never being caught in a lie.

Standing at the sink, sipping the unwanted milk, she hoped that Cato would never catch her in the lie she'd told him tonight.

The detective *had* known who she was; he had called her by name.

"Mrs. Laird?"

When she turned, she was struck first by his height. Cato was tall, but Duncan Hatcher topped him by several inches. She had to tilt her head back to look into his face. When she did, she realized that he was standing inappropriately close, but not so close as to call attention to it. His eyes had the sheen of inebriation, but his speech wasn't slurred.

"My name is Duncan Hatcher."

He didn't extend his hand, but he looked down at hers as though expecting her to shake hands with him. She didn't. *"How do you do, Mr. Hatcher?"*

He had a disarming smile, and she suspected he knew that. He also had enough audacity to say, *"Great dress."*

"Thank you."

"I like the diamond clip at the small of your back."

She coolly nodded an acknowledgment.

"Is that all that's keeping it on?"

That was an improper remark. And so was the insinuation in his eyes. Eyes that were light gray and darkly dangerous.

"Good-bye, Mr. Hatcher."

She was about to turn away when he moved a step closer, and for a moment she thought he would touch her. He said, *"When are we going to see each other again?"*

"I beg your pardon?"

"When are we going to see each other again?"

"I seriously doubt we are."

"Oh, we are. See, every judge who finds me in contempt and sends me to jail? I make it a point to fuck his wife."

He made it sound like a promise. Shock rendered her speechless and motionless. So for several seconds they simply stood there and looked at each other.

Then two things happened simultaneously that broke the stare. The woman she now knew was his partner seized Duncan Hatcher by the arm and dragged him toward the car that a parking valet had just delivered. And Cato appeared in her peripheral vision. As he approached her, she turned toward him and managed to smile, although the muscles of her face felt stiff and unnatural.

Her husband looked suspiciously after Hatcher as the woman hustled him into the passenger seat of the car. Elise had feared Cato would confront her then about the brief exchange, but he hadn't. Not until they were home, and by then she'd had time to fabricate a lie.

But she wondered now why she had lied

to her husband about it.

She poured the remainder of the unwanted milk down the drain and left the glass in the sink, where it would be conspicuous. Leaving the kitchen, she returned to the foot of the curving staircase in the foyer. There she paused to listen. The house was silent. She detected no movement upstairs.

Quickly she went down the center hallway and into Cato's study. She crossed the room in darkness, but once behind the desk, switched on the lamp. It cast dark shadows around the room, particularly onto the floor-to-ceiling bookshelves that formed the wall behind the desk.

She swung open the false shelf that concealed the wall safe and tried the handle, knowing already that it wouldn't budge. The safe was kept locked at all times, and even as they approached three years of marriage, Cato had never entrusted her with the combination.

She replaced the shelf of faux books and stepped back so she could study the bookcase wall as a whole. Then, as she'd done many times before, she broke it down into sections, focusing on one shelf at a time, letting her gaze slowly move from volume to volume.

There were countless hiding places in this bookshelf.

On a shelf slightly above her head, she noticed that one of the leather-bound volumes extended a fraction of an inch over the edge of the shelf. Coming up on tiptoe, she reached overhead to further investigate.

"Elise?"

She whipped around, gasping in fright. "Cato! Good Lord, you scared me."

"What are you doing?"

Her heart in her throat, she took the diamond pin from the pocket of her robe, where she'd had the foresight to place it before leaving the bedroom. "My brooch."

"Is that all that's keeping it on?"

It surprised her that her memory would replay Duncan Hatcher's suggestive remark at this moment, when her husband was looking at her curiously, waiting for an explanation.

"I was going to leave it here on your desk with a note so you'd see it before you left in the morning," she said. "I think some of the stones are loose. A jeweler should take a look."

He advanced into the room, looked at the pin lying in her extended palm, then into her eyes. "You didn't mention loose stones earlier."

"I forgot." She gave him a small, suggestive smile. "I got distracted."

"I'll take it downtown with me tomorrow and drop it off at the jeweler."

"Thank you. It's been in your family for decades. I'd hate to be responsible for losing one of the stones."

He looked beyond her at the bookcase. "What were you reaching for?"

"Oh, one of your volumes up there isn't lined up properly. I just happened to notice it. I know how finicky you are about this room."

He joined her behind the desk, reached up, and pushed the legal tome back into place. "There. Mrs. Berry must have dislodged it when she was dusting."

"Must have."

He placed his hands on her upper arms and rubbed them gently. "Elise?" he said softly.

"Yes?"

"Anything you want, darling, you only have to ask."

"What could I possibly want? I don't want for anything. You're extremely generous."

He looked deeply into her eyes, as though searching for something behind her steady gaze. Then he squeezed her arms quickly before releasing them. "Did you have your milk?" She nodded. "Good. Let's go back to bed. Maybe you'll be able to sleep now."

He waited for her to precede him. As she made her way toward the door, she glanced back. Cato was still standing behind his desk, watching her. The glare of the lamp cast his features into stark relief, emphasizing his thoughtful frown.

Then he switched off the lamp and the room went dark.

3

Duncan didn't need the lights on in order to play.

In fact, he liked to play in the dark, when it seemed that the darkness produced the music and that it had no connection to him. It was sort of that way even with the lights on. Whenever he touched a piano keyboard, he relinquished control to another entity that lived in his subconscious and emerged only on those occasions.

"It's a divine gift, Duncan," his mother had declared when he tried to explain the phenomenon to her with the limited vocabulary of a child. "I don't know where the music comes from, Mom. It's weird. I just . . . I just *know* it."

He was eight when she had determined it was time to begin his music lessons. When she sat him down on their piano bench, pointed out middle C, and began instructing him on the fundamentals of the instrument, they discovered to their mutual dismay that he already knew how to play.

He hadn't known that he could. It shocked him even more than it did his astonished parents when he began playing familiar hymns. And not just picking out single-note melodies. He knew how to chord without even knowing what a chord was.

Of course, for as far back as he could remember, he'd heard his mother practicing hymns for Sunday services, which could have explained how he knew them. But he could also play everything else. Rock. Swing. Jazz. Blues. Folk songs. Country and western. Classical. Any tune he had ever heard, he could play.

"You play by ear," his mother told him as she fondly and proudly stroked his cheek. "It's a gift, Duncan. Be thankful for it."

Not even remotely thankful for it, he was embarrassed by his "gift." He thought of it more like a curse and begged his parents not to boast about it, or even to tell anybody that he had the rare talent.

He certainly didn't want his friends to know. They'd think he was a sissy, a dork, or a freak of nature. He didn't want to be gifted. He wanted to be a plain, ordinary kid. He wanted to play sports. Who wanted to play the stupid *piano?*

His parents tried to reason with him, saying it was okay for a person to play sports and also be a musician, and that it would be a shame for him to waste his musical talent.

But he knew better. He went to school every day, not them. He knew he'd be made fun of if anyone ever found out that he could play the piano and had tunes he didn't even know the names of stored up inside his head.

He held firm against their arguments. When pleading with them didn't work, he resorted to obstinacy. One night after a supper-long debate over it, he swore that he would never touch a keyboard again, that they could chain him to a piano bench and not let him eat or drink or go to the bathroom until he played, and even then he would refuse. Think how bad they would feel when he shriveled up and died of thirst while chained to the piano bench.

They didn't cave in to the melodramatic vow, but in the long run, they couldn't force him to play, so he won. The compromise was that he played only for them and only at home.

Although he would never admit it, he enjoyed these private recitals. Secretly he loved the music that was conducted from his brain to his fingers effortlessly, mindlessly, without any urging from him.

At thirty-eight he still couldn't read a note. Sheet music looked like so many lines and squiggles to him. But over the years, he had honed and refined his innate talent, which remained his secret. Whenever an acquaintance asked about the piano in his living room, he said it was a legacy from his grandmother, which was true.

He played in order to lose himself in the music. He played for his personal enjoyment or whenever he needed to zone out, empty his mind of the mundane, and allow it to unravel a knotty problem.

Like tonight. There hadn't been a peep out of Savich since the severed tongue incident. The lab at the Georgia Bureau of Investigation had confirmed that it had indeed belonged to Freddy Morris, but that left them no closer to pinning his murder on Savich.

Savich was free. He was free to continue his lucrative drug trafficking, free to kill anyone who crossed him. And Duncan knew that somewhere on Savich's agenda, he was an annotation. Probably his name had a large asterisk beside it.

He tried not to dwell on it. He had other cases, other responsibilities, but it gnawed at him constantly that Savich was out there, biding his time, waiting for the right moment to strike. These days Duncan exercised a bit more caution, was a fraction more vigilant, never went anywhere unarmed. But it wasn't really fear he felt. More like anticipation.

On this night, that supercharged feeling of expectation was keeping him awake. He'd sought refuge from the restlessness by playing his piano. In the darkness of his living room, he was tinkering with a tune of his own composition when his telephone rang.

He glanced at the clock. Work. Nobody called at 1:34 in the morning to report that there *hadn't* been a killing. He answered on the second ring. "Yeah?"

Early in their partnership, he and DeeDee had made a deal. She would be the first one called if they were needed at the scene of a homicide. Between the two of them, he was the one more likely to sleep through a ringing telephone. She was the caffeine junkie and a light sleeper by nature.

He expected the caller to be her and it was. "Were you asleep?" she asked cheerfully.

"Sort of."

"Playing the piano?"

"I don't play the piano."

"Right. Well, stop whatever it is you're doing. We're on."

"Who iced whom?"

"You won't believe it. Pick me up in ten."

"Where —" But he was talking to air. She'd hung up.

He went upstairs, dressed, and slipped on his holster. Within two minutes of his partner's call, he was in his car.

He lived in a town house in the historic district of downtown, only blocks from the police station — the venerable redbrick building known to everyone in Savannah as "the Barracks."

At this hour, the narrow, tree-shrouded streets were deserted. He eased through a couple of red lights on his way out Abercorn Street. DeeDee lived on a side street off that main thoroughfare in a neat duplex with a tidy patch of yard. She was pacing it when he pulled up to the curb.

She got in quickly and buckled her seat belt. Then she cupped her armpits in turn. "I'm already sweating like a hoss. How can it be this hot and sticky at this time of night?"

"Lots of things are hot and sticky at this time of night."

"You've been hanging around with Worley too much."

He grinned. "Where to?"

"Get back on Abercorn."

"What's on the menu tonight?"

"A shooting."

"Convenience store?"

"Brace yourself." She took a deep breath and expelled it. "The home of Judge Cato Laird."

Duncan whipped his head toward her, and only then remembered to brake. The car came to an abrupt halt, pitching them both forward before their seat belts restrained them.

"That's the sum total of what I know," she said in response to his incredulity. "I swear. Somebody at the Laird house was shot and killed."

"Did they say —"

"No. I don't know who."

Facing forward again, he dragged his hand down his face, then took his foot off the brake and applied it heavily to the accelerator. Tires screeched, rubber burned as he sped along the empty streets.

It had been two weeks since the awards dinner, but in quiet moments, and sometimes even during hectic ones, he would experience a flashback to his encounter with Elise Laird. Brief as it had been, tipsy as he'd been, he recalled it vividly: the features of her face, the scent of her perfume, the catch in her throat when he'd said what he had. What a jerk. She was a beautiful woman who had done nothing to deserve the insult. To think she might be dead . . .

He cleared his throat. "I don't know where I'm going."

"Ardsley Park. Washington Street." DeeDee gave him the address. "Very ritzy."

He nodded.

"You okay, Duncan?"

"Why wouldn't I be?"

"I mean, do you feel funny about this?"

"Funny?"

"Come on," she said with asperity. "The judge isn't one of your favorite people."

"Doesn't mean I hope he's dead."

"I know that. I'm just saying."

He shot her a hard look. "Saying *what?*"

"See? That's what I'm talking about. You overreact every time his name comes up. He's a raw nerve with you."

"He gave Savich a free pass and put me in jail."

"And you made an ass of yourself with his wife," she said, matching his tone. "You still haven't told me what you said to her. Was it that bad?"

"What makes you think I said something bad?"

"Because otherwise you would have told me."

He took a corner too fast, ran a stop sign.

"Look, Duncan, if you can't treat this like any other investigation, I need to know."

"It *is* any other investigation."

But when he turned onto Washington and saw in the next block the emergency vehicles, his mouth went dry. The street was divided by a wide median of sprawling oak trees and camellia and azalea bushes. On both sides were stately homes built decades earlier by old money.

He honked his way through the pajama-clad neighbors clustered in the street, and leaned on the horn to move a video camera-man and a reporter who were setting up their shot of the immaculately maintained lawn and the impressive Colonial house with the four fluted columns supporting the second-story balcony. People out for a Sunday drive might slow down to admire the home. Now it was the scene of a fatal shooting.

"How'd the television vans get here so fast? They always beat us," DeeDee complained.

Duncan brought his car to a stop beside the ambulance and got out. Immediately he was assailed with questions from onlookers and reporters. Turning a deaf ear to them, he started toward the house. "You got gloves?" he asked DeeDee over his shoulder. "I forgot gloves."

"You always do. I've got spares."

DeeDee had to take two steps for every one of his as he strode up the front walkway, lined on both sides with carefully tended beds of begonias. Crime scene tape had already been placed around the house. The beat cop at the door recognized them and lifted the tape high enough for them to duck under. "Inside to the left," he said.

"Don't let anyone set foot on the lawn," Duncan instructed the officer. "In fact, keep everybody on the other side of the median."

"Another unit is on the way to help contain the area."

"Good. Forensics?"

"Got here quick."

"Who called the press?"

The cop shrugged in reply.

Duncan entered the massive foyer. The floor was white marble with tiny black squares placed here and there. A staircase hugged a curving wall up to the second floor. Overhead was a crystal chandelier turned up full. There was an enormous arrangement of fresh flowers on a table with carved gilded legs that matched the tall mirror above it.

"Niiiiice," DeeDee said under her breath.

Another uniformed policeman greeted them by name, then motioned with his head toward a wide arched opening to the left. They entered what appeared to be the formal living room. The fireplace was pink marble. Above the mantel was an ugly oil still life of a bowl of fresh vegetables and a dead rabbit. A long sofa with a half dozen fringed pillows faced a pair of matching chairs. Between them was another table with gold legs. A pastel carpet covered the polished hardwood floor, and all of it was lighted by a second chandelier.

Judge Laird, his back to them, was sitting in one of the chairs.

Realizing the logical implication of seeing the judge alive, Duncan felt his stomach drop.

The judge's elbows were braced on his knees, his head down. He was speaking softly to a cop named Crofton, who was balanced tentatively on the edge of the sofa cushion, as though afraid he might get it dirty.

"Elise went downstairs, but that wasn't unusual," Duncan heard the judge say in a voice that was ragged with emotion. He glanced up at the policeman and added,

"Chronic insomnia."

Crofton looked sympathetic. "What time was this? That she went downstairs."

"I woke up, partially, when she left the bed. Out of habit, I glanced at the clock on the night table. It was twelve thirty-something. I think." He rubbed his forehead. "I think that's right. Anyway, I dozed off again. The . . . the shots woke me up."

He was saying that someone other than he had shot and killed his wife. Who else was in this house tonight? Duncan wondered.

"I raced downstairs," he continued. "Ran from room to room. I was . . . frantic, a madman. I called her name. Over and over. When I got to the study . . ." His head dropped forward again. "I saw her there, slumped behind the desk."

Duncan felt as though a fist had closed around his throat. He was finding it hard to breathe.

DeeDee nudged him. "Dothan's here."

Dr. Dothan Brooks, medical examiner for Chatham County, was a fat man and made no apology for it. He knew better than anyone that fatty foods could kill you, but he defiantly ate the worst diet possible. He said that he'd seen far worse ways to die than complications from obesity. Consider-

71

ing the horrific manners of death he'd seen over the course of his own career, Duncan thought he might have a point.

As the ME approached them, he removed the latex gloves from his hands and used a large white handkerchief to mop his sweating forehead, which had taken on the hue of a raw steak. "Detectives." He always sounded out of breath and probably was.

"You beat us here," DeeDee said.

"I don't live far." Looking around, he added with a trace of bitterness, "Definitely at the poorer edge of the neighborhood. This is some place, huh?"

"What have we got?"

"A thirty-eight straight through the heart. Frontal entry. Exit wound in the back. Death was instantaneous. Lots of blood, but, as shootings go, it was fairly neat."

To cover his discomposure, Duncan took the pair of latex gloves DeeDee passed him.

"Can we have a look-see?" she asked.

Brooks stepped aside and motioned them toward the end of the long foyer. "In the study." As they walked, he glanced overhead. "I could send one of my kids to an Ivy League college for what that chandelier cost."

"Who else has been in there?" DeeDee asked.

"The judge. First cops on the scene. Swore they didn't touch anything. I waited on your crime scene boys, didn't go in till they gave me the go-ahead. They're still in there, gathering trace evidence and trying to get a name off the guy."

"Guy?" Duncan stopped in his tracks. "The shooter is in custody?"

Dothan Brooks turned and looked at the two of them with perplexity. "Hasn't anybody told y'all what happened here?"

"Obviously not," DeeDee replied.

"The dead man in the study was an intruder," he said. "Mrs. Laird shot him. She's your shooter."

Movement at the top of the staircase drew their gazes upward. Elise Laird was making her way down the stairs followed by a policewoman in uniform. Sally Beale was as black as ebony and hard as steel. Her twin brother was a defensive lineman for the Green Bay Packers. Sally's size alone made her physically imposing. It was coupled with a stern demeanor.

But Duncan's gaze was fixed on Elise Laird. Her face looked freshly scrubbed. Her pallor couldn't be attributed to the glare of the gaudy chandelier, because even her lips appeared bloodless. Her features were composed, however, and her eyes were dry.

She had killed a man, but she hadn't cried over it.

Her hair was secured with a rubber band at the back of her head. The ponytail looked mercilessly tight. She wore pink suede moccasins on her feet and was dressed in a pair of soft, worn blue jeans and a white sweater that looked like cashmere. With the outdoor temperature hovering around ninety degrees, the sweater seemed out of season. Duncan wondered if she felt chilled, and why.

When she saw Duncan, she halted so suddenly that Officer Beale nearly ran into her. The pause was short-lived, but lasted long enough to be noticed by DeeDee, who gave him a sharp glance.

When Elise reached the bottom step, her gaze locked with Duncan's for several beats before it slid to DeeDee, who stepped forward and introduced herself. "Mrs. Laird, I'm Detective DeeDee Bowen. This is my partner, Detective Sergeant Duncan Hatcher. I think you two have met."

"Darling, did the shower make you feel better?" The judge came from the living room and quickly moved to his wife, placing his arm around her shoulders, touching her colorless cheek with the back of his finger. Only then did he acknowledge the rest of them. Without so much as a hello, he said, addressing the question to Duncan, "Why did they send you?"

"You've got a dead man in your house."

"But you investigate homicides. This wasn't a homicide, Detective Hatcher. My wife shot an intruder, whom she caught in the act of burglarizing my study, where I keep valuable collectibles. When she challenged him, he fired a pistol at her. She had no choice but to protect her own life."

Standard operating procedure was to keep the witnesses of a crime separate until each had been questioned, so that one couldn't influence the other's account in any way. A criminal court judge should know that.

With consternation, Duncan said, "Thanks for the summary, Judge, but we would prefer to hear what happened directly from Mrs. Laird."

"She's already given an account to these officers." He nodded toward Beale and Crofton.

"I talked to her first," Crofton said. "It's pretty much like he said."

"That's her story," Beale confirmed, slapping her notebook against her palm. "His, too."

The judge took umbrage. "It's not a *story*. It's a true account of what took place. Is it necessary for Elise to repeat it tonight? She's already been traumatized."

"We haven't even seen the victim or the scene yet," DeeDee said.

"Once we've taken a look and talked to forensics, we're certain to have questions for Mrs. Laird." Duncan glanced at her. She'd yet to utter a sound. Her eyes were fixed on a spot in near space, as though she had detached herself from what was going on around her.

Coming back to the judge, he said, "We'll try and keep it as brief as possible. We certainly wouldn't want to contribute to the trauma Mrs. Laird has suffered tonight." He turned and addressed Sally Beale. "Why don't you take her into the kitchen? Maybe get her something to drink. Crofton, you can continue with the judge."

Judge Laird didn't look happy about Duncan's directives, which purposefully kept him separated from his missus, but he consented with a terse nod. Stroking his wife's arm, he said, "I'll be in the living room if you need me."

Sally Beale laid her wide hand on Elise's shoulders, firmly but not unkindly. "I could use a Coke or something. How 'bout you?"

Still saying nothing, Elise went along with the policewoman. DeeDee gave Duncan a questioning look. He raised his shoulders in a shrug and proceeded down the hallway to rejoin the ME. "What about it, Dothan? Does it look like self-defense to you?"

"See for yourself."

Duncan and DeeDee paused on the threshold of the study. From that vantage point, they could see only the victim's shoes. They asked the crime scene techs if it was all right to come in.

"Hey, Dunk. DeeDee." Overseeing the collection of evidence was a small, bookish guy named Baker, who looked more like an antiques dealer than a cop who performed the nasty job of scavenging through the rubble of violent death. "We've vacuumed the whole room, but I don't think he got any farther than where you see him now. He jimmied a window lock to break in." He motioned toward the window.

"We found a tire iron outside under the bushes. We've got casts of the footprints outside the window. Matching prints here inside don't extend past the desk. They were muddy prints, so now they're sorta smeared."

"Why's that?"

"The Lairds smeared them when they

checked to see was he dead."

"Lairds plural?" DeeDee asked.

Baker nodded. "Her, soon as she shot the guy. The judge when he came into the room and saw what had happened. He assessed the situation and immediately called 911. That's what they told Crofton and Beale anyway."

"Huh. How'd the intruder get here? To the house, I mean."

"Beats me," Baker replied. "We've lifted prints off the desk drawers, but they could belong to the judge, his wife, the housekeeper. We'll see. Took a Ruger nine-millimeter out of his right hand." He held up an evidence bag. "His finger was around the trigger. We're pretty sure he fired. Smelled like it."

"I bagged his hands," Dothan Brooks said.

"We pulled a slug out of the wall over there." Duncan and DeeDee turned to look at where Baker was pointing and saw a bullet hole in the wall about nine feet above the floor.

"If he was trying to shoot Mrs. Laird, his aim was lousy," DeeDee remarked, echoing what Duncan was thinking.

"Maybe she startled him, caught him in the act, and he fired too quickly to take aim," Duncan said.

"That's what we figured," Baker said. He motioned toward the photographer, who was replacing his gear in its hard-shell case. "We got pictures from every angle. I made sketches of the room, and took measurements. It'll all be ready when you need it, if you need it. We're done."

With that, he and his crew trailed out.

Duncan advanced into the room. The victim was lying on the floor, faceup, between a desk that was larger than Duncan's car and a bookcase filled with leather-bound books and knickknacks that looked rare, old, and expensive. The rug beneath him was still wet with blood.

The man was Caucasian, appeared to be around thirty-five, and looked almost embarrassed to be in his present situation. Duncan had been taught by his parents to respect the nobility of life, even in its most ignoble forms. Often his father had reminded him that all men were God's creation, and he'd grown up believing it.

He had acquired enough toughness and objectivity to do the work he did. But he never looked at a dead body without feeling a twinge of sadness. The day he no longer felt it, he would quit. If the time ever came when he felt no remorse over a life taken, he would know his soul was in jeopardy. He would have become one of the lost. He would have become Savich.

He felt he should apologize to this unnamed person for the indignity he had undergone already and would continue to be subjected to until they got from him all the answers he could provide. No longer a person, he was a corpse, evidence, exhibit A.

Duncan knelt down and studied his face, asking softly, "What's your name?"

"Neither the judge nor Mrs. Laird claim to recognize him," Dothan said.

The ME's statement jerked Duncan out of his introspection and back into the job at hand. " 'Claim'?"

"Don't read anything into that. I'm just repeating what the judge told me when I got here."

Duncan and DeeDee exchanged a significant look, then he searched the dead man's pockets, hoping to find something that perhaps Baker had overlooked. All the pockets were empty.

"No car keys. No money. No ID." He studied the man's face again, searching his memory, trying to place him among crooks he'd come across during the investigations of other homicides. "I don't recognize him."

"Me, neither," DeeDee said.

Standing, Duncan said, "Dothan, I'd like to know the distance from which the fatal shot was fired. How close was Mrs. Laird when she shot him?"

"I'll give you my best guess."

"Which is usually pretty damn good."

"Baker's reliable, but I'll take my own measurement of the distance between the door and the desk," DeeDee said, pulling a tape measure from her pocket.

"Well, unless y'all need me, I'm off," the ME said, tucking his damp handkerchief into his pants pocket. "Ready to get him out of here?"

"DeeDee?" Duncan asked.

"Sixteen feet." She wrote the measurement in her notebook, then took a look around the room. "I think I'll do my own sketch of the room, too, but you don't have to hang around," she said to the ME.

"Then I'll send in the EMTs." He glanced around, his expression turning sour. "Money sure gets you nice stuff, doesn't it?"

"Especially old money. Laird Shipping was started by the judge's grandfather, and he's the last of the line," DeeDee informed them. "No other heirs," she said, raising her eyebrows.

"This place probably isn't even mortgaged," Dothan grumbled as he turned to leave. "Think I'll find a Taco Bell open this time of night?" He was panting hard as he lumbered off.

As DeeDee sketched in her notebook, she said, "He's going to keel over one of these days."

"But he'll die happy."

Duncan's mind wasn't on the ME's health. He was noting that the victim's clothing and shoes appeared new, but cheap. The kind a con would wear when he was released from prison. "First thing tomorrow, we need to check men recently released from prison, especially those who'd been serving time for breaking and entering. I bet we won't have to dig too deep before we find this guy."

EMTs wheeled in a gurney. Duncan stood by as the unidentified dead man's body was zipped into the black bag, placed on the gurney, and rolled out. He accompanied it as far as the front door. From there he could see that a larger crowd of gawkers had gathered on the far side of the median. More news vans were parked along the street.

The flowers in the vase on the foyer table shimmied, alerting him to Sally Beale's approach. "I had her go through it all again," she said to Duncan, speaking in an undertone. "Didn't falter. Didn't change a word. She's ready to sign a statement."

He surveyed the divided street, trying to imagine it prior to becoming a crime scene. Without the flashing emergency lights and the onlookers, it would be serene.

"Sally, you were first on the scene, right?"

"Me and Crofton were only a couple blocks away when we got the call from dispatch."

"Did you see any moving vehicles in the area?"

"Nary a one."

"Abandoned car?"

"Not even a moped, and other patrol units have been canvassing the whole neighborhood looking for the perp's means of transportation. Nothing's turned up."

Puzzling. Something out of whack that demanded an explanation. "Are the neighbors being canvassed?"

"Two teams are going door-to-door. So far, everybody was fast asleep, saw no one, heard nothing."

"Not even the shots?" He turned to face the policewoman, who was shrugging.

"Big houses, big yards."

"Mrs. Laird showered?"

"Said she felt violated," Beale said. "Asked

would it be okay."

It was a typical reaction for people to want to wash after their home was invaded, but Duncan didn't like it when a bloody corpse was just downstairs. "Did she have blood on her?"

"No, and I was with her the whole time upstairs. All she had on was her robe. I got it from her, gave it to Baker. No blood on it that I saw. But the judge, the hem of his robe had blood on it from when he checked the body. He asked permission to dress. Baker's got his robe, too."

"Okay, thanks, Sally. Keep them separate till we're ready to question them."

"You got it."

He returned to the study, where DeeDee was examining the judge's desk. "All these drawers are still locked."

"Mrs. Laird must have caught the burglar early."

She raised her head and gave him an arch look. "You believe the burglar scenario?"

"I believe it's time we asked just how this went down."

4

"Who first, her or the judge?"

Duncan thought about it. "Let's talk to them together."

DeeDee registered surprise as well as a trace of disapproval. "How come?"

"Because they've already been questioned separately by Crofton and Beale. Sally Beale told me Mrs. Laird's second telling didn't vary from the first and that she's prepared to sign a statement.

"If it really is a matter of her shooting a home intruder, and we continue badgering them, it's going to look like we doubt them, and *that* will seem like reprisal for my contempt charge. The only thing it will accomplish is to piss off the judge. Gerard will have my ass if I have another run-in with him."

"Okay," DeeDee said. "But what if it isn't a case of her protecting herself from a home intruder?"

"We have no reason to disbelieve them, do we?"

He left DeeDee to mull that over and followed his nose until he located the kitchen, where Sally Beale and Elise Laird were seated at the table in the breakfast nook, talking quietly. When he came in, the policewoman, in the manner of a heavy person, pushed herself to her feet. "We're finished here." She closed the cover of her spiral notebook. "I've got it all down."

None of the color had returned to Elise Laird's face. She looked at him inquisitively. He sensed unspoken apprehension.

"We're ready for you in the living room, Mrs. Laird."

He made his way back to the formal room, where Crofton and Judge Laird had been joined by an austere, gray-haired woman who was pouring hot liquid from a silver pot into china cups.

Sally Beale, who had escorted Elise Laird from the kitchen, came up behind Duncan and noticed his curiosity. "The housekeeper," she said in a low rumble. "Something Berry. Blew into the kitchen twenty minutes ago like she owned the place." She chuckled. " 'Bout keeled over when she saw my big black self sitting at the breakfast table."

"So she doesn't live in?"

She shook her head. "Apparently the judge called her to duty and she came running in no time flat. She's prepared to do battle for him."

From over his shoulder, Duncan gave the policewoman a significant look. "For him, but not for Mrs. Laird?"

"All the time she was boiling water and preparing the tea tray, she didn't say boo to the lady of the house. You couldn't melt an ice cube on that one's ass." She raised her shoulders in an indolent shrug. "I call 'em as I see 'em."

The judge stood up and warmly embraced his wife when she rejoined him. They were talking together softly, but Crofton was close enough to overhear, so Duncan reasoned that Judge Laird was only asking his wife how she was faring.

Crofton, trying to balance the dainty teacup and saucer on his knee while jotting something in his notebook, greeted Duncan and DeeDee's appearance with evident relief. "I'll turn it over to the detectives now." He set the china on the nearest table, then left the room along with Beale.

Duncan and DeeDee took the twin chairs facing the sofa, where the judge and his wife sat shoulder to shoulder, thigh to thigh.

Neither had touched the steaming cups of tea in front of them. Laird offered some to Duncan and DeeDee.

Duncan declined. DeeDee smiled up at the sour-faced housekeeper. "Do you have a Diet Coke?"

She left the room to fetch the drink.

"Have they removed it?"

Duncan supposed the judge was referring to the corpse. "Yes. On his way to the morgue."

"Where he belongs," he muttered with distaste.

Elise Laird tipped her head down. Duncan noticed her hands were tightly clasped together and that she had pulled the sleeves of her sweater down over the backs of them as though to keep them warm.

The housekeeper returned with DeeDee's Diet Coke, served over ice in a crystal tumbler on a small plate with a doily and a lacy cloth napkin. To her credit, and Duncan's surprise, DeeDee thanked the housekeeper graciously. Any other time, she would have been breaking up with laughter, or scorn, over such pretentious finery.

At a motion from the judge, Mrs. Berry withdrew, leaving the four of them alone. The judge placed his arm around his wife and drew her closer to him. He looked at her with concern, then focused on Duncan.

"We've told the other officers everything we know. They took copious notes. I don't know what more we could possibly add, although we want to do everything we can to resolve this issue as quickly as possible." His expression was earnest, concerned.

"I hate asking you to retell what happened, but Detective Bowen and I need to hear it all for ourselves," Duncan said. "I'm sure you understand."

"Of course. Let's just get it over with so I can take Mrs. Laird to bed."

"I'll make it as painless as possible," Duncan said, flashing his most reassuring grin. "However, during our questioning, Judge, I'll ask you not to offer a comment or answer unless directly asked. Please say nothing that could influence Mrs. Laird's recollection. It's important that we hear —"

"I understand the procedure, Detective." Although the judge's interruption was rude and his tone brusque, his expression remained as pleasant as Duncan's. "Please proceed."

The man's condescending tone grated on Duncan. The judge was accustomed to running the show. In his courtroom, he was the despotic authority. But this was Duncan's arena and he was the ringmaster. Lest his anger get him into trouble, Duncan thought it best to let DeeDee begin, ease them into it. He'd take over when it got down to the nitty-gritty.

He gave DeeDee a subtle nod and she picked up the cue immediately. "Mrs. Laird?" DeeDee waited until Elise raised her head and looked at her. "Can you lead us through what happened here tonight?"

Before beginning, Elise took a deep breath. "I came downstairs to get something to drink."

"She does nearly every night," the judge chimed in, flouting Duncan's request that he not speak until asked.

Duncan chose to let it pass. Once. "You suffer from chronic insomnia," he said, remembering what he'd heard the judge tell Crofton.

"Yes." She addressed the reply to DeeDee, not to him. "I was on my way to the kitchen when —"

"Excuse me. What time was this?" DeeDee asked.

"Around twelve thirty. I remember looking at the clock shortly after midnight. It was about half an hour later that I got up and came downstairs. I thought a glass of milk would help me fall asleep. Sometimes it does."

She paused, as though expecting someone to comment on that. When no one did, she continued. "I was in the kitchen when I heard a noise."

"What kind of noise?"

She turned toward Duncan, meeting his eyes for the first time since that moment in the kitchen. "I wasn't sure what I heard. I'm still not. I think maybe it was his footfalls. Or him bumping into a piece of furniture. Something like that."

"Okay."

"Whatever it was, I knew the sound was coming from the study."

"You couldn't identify the noise, but you knew where it was coming from?"

The judge frowned at the skepticism underlying DeeDee's question, but he didn't say anything.

"I know that sounds odd," Elise said.

"It does."

"I'm sorry." She raised her hands palms up. "That's how it was."

"I don't see why this couldn't wait until tomorrow morning," the judge said.

Before Duncan could admonish him, Elise said, "No, Cato. I'd rather talk about it now. While it's still fresh in my mind."

He studied his wife's face, saw the determination in her expression, and sighed. "If you're sure you're up to it." She nodded. He kissed her brow, then divided an impatient look between DeeDee and Duncan, ending on him. "She heard a noise, realized where it was coming from, thought — as any rational person would — that we had an intruder."

Duncan looked at Elise. "Is that what you thought?"

"Yes. I immediately thought that someone was inside the house."

"You have an alarm system."

Duncan had noted the keypad on the wall of the foyer just inside the front door. He'd seen a motion detector in the study and assumed that similar detectors were in other rooms as well. Homes of this caliber almost always had sophisticated alarm systems. A judge who'd sent countless miscreants to prison would surely want his home protected against any ex-con with a vendetta in mind.

"We have a state-of-the-art monitored security system," the judge said.

"It wasn't set?" Duncan asked.

"Not tonight," the judge replied.

"Why not?" The judge was about to answer. Duncan held up his hand, indicating he wanted to hear the answer from Elise. "Mrs. Laird?"

"I . . ." She faltered, cleared her throat, then said more assertively, "I failed to set the alarm tonight."

"Are you usually the one who sets it?"

"Yes. Every night. Routinely."

"But tonight you forgot." DeeDee put it in the form of a statement, but she was really asking how Mrs. Laird could forget to do tonight what was her routine to do every night.

"I didn't exactly forget."

These questions about the alarm had made her uneasy. An uneasy witness was a witness who was either withholding information or downright lying. An uneasy witness was one you prodded. "If you didn't forget, why wasn't the alarm set?" Duncan asked.

She opened her mouth to speak. But no words came out.

"Why wasn't it set, Mrs. Laird?" he repeated.

"Oh, for crissake," the judge muttered. "I'm forced to be indelicate, but seeing as we're all adults —"

"Judge, please —"

"No, Detective Hatcher. Since my wife is too embarrassed to answer your question, I'll answer for her. Earlier tonight we enjoyed a bottle of wine together in our

Jacuzzi. From there we went to bed and made love. Afterward, Elise was . . . Let's just say she was *disinclined* to leave the bed in order to set the alarm."

The judge paused for effect. The air in the room suddenly became abnormally still. Hot. Dense. Or so it seemed to Duncan. He became aware of his pulse. His scalp felt tight.

Finally the judge ended the taut silence. "Now, can we move beyond this one point and talk about the man who tried to kill Elise?"

An inactivated alarm system was a significant point in the investigation of a home break-in that had resulted in a fatal shooting. As the lead detective conducting the investigation, that's what Duncan should have been concentrating on.

But instead, he was having a hard time getting past the idea of a bottle of wine and Elise Laird in a tub of bubbles. To say nothing of an Elise Laird in bed, sexually sated to the point of immobility.

And when an erotic visualization of that flashed into his mind, it wasn't Cato Laird who was lying with her.

As though reading his mind, DeeDee shot him a look of reproof, then addressed the next question to Mrs. Laird. "When you

94

heard the noise, what did you do?"

As though grateful for the new direction of questioning, she turned to DeeDee. "I went through the butler's pantry, which is the shortest route from the kitchen into the foyer. When I reached the foyer, I was certain there was someone in the study."

"What made you certain?" DeeDee asked.

She raised her slender shoulders. "Instinct. I sensed his presence."

"*His* presence? You knew it was a man? Instinctually?"

Elise's gaze swung back to Duncan. "I assumed so, Detective Hatcher." She continued to look at him for a moment, then turned back to DeeDee. "I was afraid. It was dark. I sensed someone inside the house. I . . . I took a pistol from the drawer in the hall table."

"Why didn't you run to the nearest telephone, dial 911?"

"I wish I had. If I had it to do over —"

"You would be the one on the way to the morgue." Cato Laird took one of her hands and pressed it between his. He kissed her temple near her hairline.

Duncan interrupted the tender exchange. "You knew there was a pistol in that drawer?"

"Yes," she replied.

95

"Had you used it before?"

She looked affronted. "Of course not."

"Then how did you know it was there?"

"I own several guns, Detective," the judge said. "They're kept handy. Elise knows where they are. I made sure of that. I also insisted on her taking lessons to learn how to use the guns to protect herself in the event she should need to."

She learned well, Duncan thought. She'd shot a man straight through the heart. He was a good marksman, but he doubted he could be that accurate under duress.

To defuse another tense moment, DeeDee prompted Elise. "So you have the pistol."

"I walked toward the study. When I got to the door, I switched on the light. But I flipped the wrong switch and the light in the foyer came on, not the overhead light in the study. They're on the same switch plate. Anyway, I illuminated myself, not him, but I could see him, standing there behind the desk."

"What did he do?"

"Nothing. He just stood there, frozen, looking startled, staring at me. I said, 'Get out of here. Go away.' But he didn't move."

"Did he say anything?"

She held Duncan's gaze for several seconds, then replied with a terse no.

96

He was absolutely certain she was lying. Why? he wondered. But he decided not to challenge her about it now. "Go on."

"Suddenly he jerked his arm up. Like a puppet whose string has been yanked. His hand came up and before it even registered with me that he had a gun, he fired it. I . . . I reacted instantaneously."

"You fired back."

She nodded.

No one spoke for a time. Finally DeeDee said, "Your aim was exceptionally good, Mrs. Laird."

"Thank God," the judge said.

More quietly Elise said, "I got lucky."

Neither Duncan nor DeeDee said anything to that, although DeeDee glanced at him to see if he thought that shot could be attributed to luck.

"What happened next, Mrs. Laird?"

"I checked his body for a pulse."

Duncan remembered Baker saying that the victim's muddy footprints had been smeared, probably by both the Lairds.

"He fell backward, out of sight," she said. "I was terrified, afraid that he was . . ."

"Still alive?" DeeDee said.

Again Elise appeared to take umbrage. "No, Detective Bowen," she said testily. "I was afraid that he was *dead.* When I got up this morning, I didn't plan on ending a man's life tonight."

"I didn't imply that you had."

The judge said brusquely, "That's it, detectives. No more questions. She's told you what you need to know. The law is clear on what constitutes self-defense. This intruder was inside our home, and he posed an imminent threat to Elise's life. If he had survived, you'd be charging him with a list of felonies, including assault with a deadly weapon. Shooting him was justified, and I believe my wife is being inordinately generous by wishing he had survived."

Duncan leveled a hard look on him. "I remind you again, Judge, that this is my investigation. Think of it as my equivalent to your courtroom. I've extended you the courtesy of being present while I question Mrs. Laird, but if you insist on contributing another word without being asked to, you'll be excused and I'll conduct the interview with her alone."

The judge's jaw turned rigid and his eyes glittered with resentment, but he gave a negligent wave of his hand. It wasn't a gesture of concession. He made it appear he was granting Duncan permission to continue.

Duncan turned his attention back to Elise.

"You felt for a pulse?"

She pulled her hand from her husband's grasp, crossed her arms over her chest, and hugged herself. "I didn't want to touch him. But I forced myself. I went into the room —"

"Did you still have the pistol?"

"I had dropped it. It was on the floor, there at the door."

"Okay," Duncan said.

"I went into the study and stepped around the desk. I knelt down, put my fingers here."

She touched her own throat approximately where her carotid would be. Duncan noticed that her fingers were very slender. They looked bloodless, cold. Whereas the skin of her throat . . .

He yanked his eyes away from her neck and looked at the judge. "I overheard you telling Officer Crofton that when you reached the study, you found Elise slumped behind the desk."

"That's correct. She was slumped in the desk chair. I thought . . . well, you can't imagine the fear that gripped me. I thought she was dead. I rushed over to her. That's when I saw the man on the floor. I'm not ashamed of the relief I felt at that moment."

"You had blood on your robe."

He shuddered with revulsion. "There was

already a lot of blood on the carpet beneath him. My hem dipped into it when I bent over the body. I felt for a pulse. There wasn't one."

"What were you doing at this point?"

If DeeDee hadn't asked that of Elise, Duncan would have. He'd been watching her out the corner of his eye. She'd been listening raptly to her husband's account. If he'd said anything contradictory to what she'd experienced, she hadn't shown it.

"I was . . . I wasn't doing anything. Just sitting there in the chair. I was numb."

Too numb to cry. He remembered her eyes being dry, with no sign of weeping. She hadn't shed a tear, but at least she hadn't lied about it.

The judge said, "Elise was in shock. I probably remember more at this point than she does. May I speak?"

Duncan realized he was being patronized, but he let it pass. "Please, Judge," he said with exaggerated politeness.

"I picked Elise out of the chair and carried her from the room. I stepped over the pistol, which was on the floor just inside the study door, as she said. I left it there and didn't touch the body again or anything else in the room. I deposited Elise here in the living room and used that telephone to call

911." He pointed out a cordless phone on an end table. "No one went into the study until the officers arrived."

"While you were waiting on them, did you ask her what had happened?"

"Of course. She explained in stops and starts, but I got the gist of it. In any case, it was rather obvious that she'd interrupted an attempted burglary."

Not so obvious from where I sit, Judge. Duncan didn't speak his thought aloud because there was no point in riling the judge unnecessarily. However, there were some details that needed further investigation and explanation before he was ready to rubber-stamp this a matter of self-defense and close the books on it. Getting an identity on the dead man would be the first step. That could shed some light on why he was in the Lairds' home study.

Duncan smiled at the couple. "I think that's all we need to go over tonight. There may be some loose ends to clear up tomorrow." He stood up, essentially putting an end to the interview. "Thank you. I know this wasn't easy. I apologize for the need to put you through it."

"You were only doing your job, Detective." The judge extended his hand and Duncan shook it.

"Yes. I was." Releasing the judge's hand, he added, "For the time being, the study is still a crime scene. I'm sorry if this poses an inconvenience, but please don't remove anything from it."

"Of course."

"I have one more question," DeeDee said. "Did either of you recognize the man?"

"I didn't," Elise said.

"Nor I," said the judge.

"You're sure? Because Mrs. Laird said she'd turned on the wrong light. The room would have been semi-dark. Did you turn on the overhead light in the study, Judge?"

"Yes, I did. I explained to Officer Crofton that on my way into the room, I switched on the light."

"So, with the overhead light on, you got a good look at the man?"

"A very good look. As stated, he was a stranger to us, Detective Bowen." He softened the edge in his voice by politely offering to see them out. Before leaving Elise, he bent down to where she had remained seated on the sofa. "I'll be right back, darling, then I'll take you up."

She nodded and gave him a weak smile.

Duncan and DeeDee walked from the room with him. When they reached the foyer, DeeDee said, "Judge, before we leave,

I'd like to measure the height of that bullet hole in the wall. It'll only take a sec."

He looked annoyed by the request, but said, "Certainly," and motioned her to follow him toward the study.

Duncan stayed where he was in a deceptively relaxed stance, hands in his pants pockets, staring after his partner and the judge as they moved down the foyer out of earshot.

Beale and Crofton were talking together at the front door. From the snatches of conversation Duncan could overhear, they were discussing the pros and cons of various barbecue joints and ignoring the reporters and curiosity seekers still loitering in the street, waiting for something exciting to happen.

He looked into the living room. Elise was still on the sofa. She had picked up her cup of tea, but left the saucer on the coffee table. Both her hands were folded around the cup. They looked as delicate as the china. She was staring down into the tea.

Quietly Duncan said, "I was drunk."

She didn't move or show any reaction whatsoever, although he knew she had heard him.

"I was also pissed off at your husband."

Her fingers contracted a little more tightly

around the cup.

"Neither excuses what I said to you. But I, uh . . ." He glanced toward both ends of the foyer. Still empty. He was safe to speak. "I want you to know . . . what I said? It wasn't about you."

She raised her head and turned toward him. Her face was still wan, her lips colorless, making her eyes look exceptionally large. Large enough for a man to fall into and become immersed in the green depths of them. "Wasn't it?"

5

Upon seeing Robert Savich for the first time, people were initially struck by his unusual coloring.

His skin tone was that of café au lait, a legacy from his maternal grandmother, a Jamaican who'd come to the United States seeking a better life. At age thirty-four she had given up the quest by slashing her wrists in a bathtub in the brothel where she lived and worked. Her leached body was discovered by another of the whores, her fifteen-year-old daughter, baby Robert's mother.

His blue eyes had been passed down through generations of Saviches, a disreputable lineage no more promising than his maternal one.

Superficially, he was accepted for what he was. But he knew that neither pure blacks nor pure whites would ever wholly accept his mingled blood and embrace him as one of their own. Prejudice found fertile ground in every race. It recognized no borders. It permeated every society on earth, no matter how vociferously it was denounced.

So from the time he could reason, Savich had understood that he must create a dominion that was solely his. A man didn't achieve an egotistic goal of that caliber by being a nice guy, but rather by being tougher, smarter, meaner than his peers. A man could do it only by evoking fear in anyone he met.

Young Robert had taken the dire experiences of his childhood and youth and turned them to his advantage. Each year of poverty, abuse, and alienation was like an additional application of varnish, which became harder and more protective, until now, he was impenetrable. This was particularly true of his soul.

He had directed his intelligence and entrepreneurial instincts toward commerce — of a sort. He was dealing crack cocaine by the time he was twelve. At age twenty-five, in a coup that included slitting the throat of his mentor in front of awed competitors, he established himself as the lord of a criminal fiefdom. Those who hadn't known his name up to that point soon did. Rivals began showing up dead by gruesome means. His well-earned reputation for ruthlessness rapidly spread, effectively quelling any dreamed-of mutinies.

His reign of terror had continued for a decade. It had made him wealthy beyond even his expectations. Minor rebellions staged by those reckless or stupid enough to cross him were immediately snuffed. Betrayal spelled death to the betrayer.

Ask Freddy Morris. Not that he could answer you.

As Savich wheeled into the parking lot of the warehouse from which he ran his legitimate machine shop, he chuckled yet again, imagining Duncan Hatcher's reaction upon finding the little gift that had been left in his refrigerator.

Duncan Hatcher had started as a pebble in his shoe, nothing more than a nuisance. Initially his crusade to destroy Savich's empire had been somewhat amusing. But Hatcher's determination hadn't waned. Each defeat seemed only to strengthen his resolve. Savich was no longer amused. The detective had become an increasingly dangerous threat who must be dealt with. Soon.

The gradual introduction of methamphetamine into the Southeastern states had opened up a new and vigorous market. It was an ever-expanding profit center for Savich's business. But it was a demanding taskmaster, requiring constant vigilance. He had his hands full controlling those who manufactured and marketed meth for him. He was equally busy keeping independents from poaching on his territory.

Any idiot with a box of cold remedy and a can of fuel thought he could go into business for himself. Fortunately, most of the amateurs blew themselves and their makeshift labs to smithereens without any help from him. But as relatively easy as it was to produce, meth was even easier to market. Because of its various forms of ingestion — snorting, smoking, injecting, and simply swallowing — there was something to suit every user.

It was a lucrative trade, and Savich didn't want Duncan Hatcher to bugger it up.

The machine shop on the ground floor of the warehouse was noisy, nasty, and hot, in contrast to the cool oasis of his office suite upstairs. The two areas were separated by a short ride in a clanking service elevator, but aesthetically they were worlds apart.

He'd spared no expense to surround himself with luxury. His leather desk chair was as soft as butter. The finish on his desk was satin smooth and glossy. The carpet was woven of silk threads, the finest money could buy.

His secretary was a homosexual named Kenny, whose family had deep roots in Savannah society and, unfortunately for Kenny, longevity genes. Kenny was waiting impatiently for his elderly parents to die and leave him, their only son and heir, his much-anticipated paper mill fortune.

In the meantime he worked for Savich, who was dark and mysterious and exciting, who was anathema to his stodgy parents for every reason thinkable, and who had won Kenny's undying loyalty by slowly choking to death a violent homophobe who had waylaid Kenny outside a gay bar and beaten him to within an inch of his life.

Their working relationship was mutually beneficial. Savich preferred Kenny to a female secretary. Invariably women got around to wanting a sexual relationship with him, the depth of which depended on the woman. His policy had always been to keep romance and business separate.

Besides, women were too easily swayed by flattery, or even kindness. Cops and federal agents often used this feminine weakness as a means of getting information. They'd once tried that tactic in the hope of incriminating him. It failed when his secretary mysteriously disappeared. She'd never been found. He'd replaced her with Kenny.

Kenny shot to his feet the instant Savich crossed the threshold of the office suite. Although his well-coiffed hair remained well-coiffed as he nodded toward the closed door to Savich's private office, it was apparent that he was in a state of excitability.

"You have a visitor who wouldn't take no for an answer," he said in an exaggerated stage whisper.

Instantly alert to the danger of an ambush — his first thought was *Hatcher* — Savich reached for the pistol at the small of his back.

His secretary's plucked eyebrows arched fearfully. "It's not like *that.* I would have called you if it was like *that.* I believe you'll want to see this visitor."

Savich, now more curious than wary, moved to the door of his private chamber and opened it. His guest was standing with her back to the room, staring out the window. Hearing him, she turned and removed the dark sunglasses that concealed half her face.

"Elise! What an unexpected and delightful surprise. You're always a sight for sore eyes."

She didn't return either his wide smile or his flattery. "I'm glad to hear that because I need a favor."

Duncan's rank as detective sergeant afforded few benefits above those of his colleagues, but one of them was a private office at the back of the narrow room that was home to the Violent Crimes Unit.

Duncan nodded at DeeDee as he walked past her desk. He had a doughnut stuck in his mouth, a Styrofoam cup of coffee in one hand, his sport jacket hooked on a finger of the other, a newspaper tucked under his arm. He stepped into his office, but before he even had a chance to sit down, DeeDee, who'd followed him into the closet-sized office, laid a folder on his desk with a decisive slap.

"His name was Gary Ray Trotter."

Duncan wasn't a morning person. Hated them, in fact. It took a while for him to warm up to the idea of daylight and get all his pistons firing. DeeDee, on the other hand, could go from zero to sixty within a few seconds.

Despite their late night at the Lairds' house, she would have been up and at 'em for hours. Other detectives had straggled into the VCU this morning, looking already sapped by the cloying humidity outside. DeeDee, not surprisingly, was by far the most chipper of the lot and was practically bristling with energy.

Duncan raised his arm and let the newspaper slide onto his desk. He draped his jacket over the back of his chair, set down the coffee, which had grown hot in his hand despite the cardboard sleeve around the cup, and took a bite from the doughnut before removing it from his mouth.

"No 'good morning'?" he asked grumpily.

"Dothan got to work early, too," she told him as he plopped into his desk chair. "He fingerprinted the Lairds' corpse. Gary Ray Trotter was a repeat offender, so I had the ID in a matter of minutes. Lots of stuff on this guy." She indicated the folder lying still untouched on his desk.

"Originally from Baltimore, over the last dozen years he's gradually worked his way down the East Coast, spending time in various jails for petty stuff until a couple of years ago he got brave and expanded into armed robbery in Myrtle Beach. He was released on parole three months ago. His parole officer hadn't heard from him in two."

"My, you've been busy," Duncan said.

"I thought one of us should get a running start, and I knew you wouldn't."

"See, that's why we work so well together.

I recognize your strengths."

"Or rather, I recognize your weaknesses."

Smiling over the barb, he flipped open the file folder and scanned the top sheet. "I thought his clothes looked new. Like a con recently out."

By the time he'd finished reading Gary Ray Trotter's rap sheet he had eaten the doughnut. He licked the glaze off his fingers. "He didn't have a very distinguished criminal career," he remarked as he removed the plastic top from the coffee cup.

"Right. So I don't get it."

" 'It'?"

DeeDee pulled a chair closer to Duncan's desk and sat down. "Burglarizing the Lairds' house seems a trifle ambitious for Gary Ray."

Duncan shrugged. "Maybe he wanted to go out with a bang."

"Ha-ha."

"I couldn't resist."

"He'd never been charged with burglary before," DeeDee said.

"Doesn't mean he didn't commit one."

"No, but from reading his record, he doesn't come across as the sharpest knife in the drawer. In fact, his first offense at age sixteen was theft of a bulldozer."

"I thought that was a typo. It really was a

bulldozer?"

"He drove it from the road construction site where he was employed as a flagman. You know, orange vest? Waves cars around roadwork?"

"Got it."

"Okay, so Gary Ray steals a bulldozer and drives it to his folks' farmhouse, leaves it parked outside. Next morning, the road crew shows up for work, discovers the bulldozer missing, calls the police, who —"

"Followed the tracks straight to it."

"Duh!" DeeDee exclaimed. "How dumb can you be?"

Duncan laughed. "Where was he going to fence a bulldozer?"

"See what I mean? Our Gary Ray wasn't too astute. It's quite a leap from bulldozer theft to breaking into a house with a sophisticated alarm system. It wasn't set, but Gary Ray didn't know that when he went at that window with a tire iron."

Playing devil's advocate, Duncan said, "He'd had years to perfect his craft."

"Wouldn't that include coming prepared? Bringing along the tools of his trade? Let's say Gary Ray had become a crackerjack burglar. Doubtful, but let's say. One who knew how to disarm sophisticated alarm systems, cut glass so he could reach in and unlock windows, stuff like that."

"Your basic Hollywood-heist type with his fancy techno toys."

"I guess," she said. "So, anyway, where was Gary Ray's gear? All he brought with him was that tire iron."

"And a Ruger nine-millimeter."

"Well, that. But nothing to pick locks or crack safes. Nothing he could use to break into a desk drawer."

"Those locks would be simple, the kind you open with a tiny key. Give me a few seconds and I could pick them with a safety pin," Duncan said.

"Gary Ray didn't have even that. And another thing, even if you were the dumbest burglar in history, wouldn't you at least wear gloves to avoid leaving fingerprints?"

None of the points she'd raised were revelations to Duncan. When he'd returned home in the wee hours, he'd made an earnest effort to sleep. But his mind was busy with jumbled thoughts about Elise Laird's account of the events that had left a man dead, and about the judge's urgency for them to accept her account without question.

Every discrepancy that DeeDee had cited, he'd already considered. Even before he knew that Gary Ray was an inept criminal, the break-in seemed ill planned and poorly executed. Failure was practically guaranteed.

Nevertheless, he continued to argue the points. "You're assuming that Gary Ray planned this burglary." He tapped the folder. "According to this, he was a drug user. He started life stupid and then cooked his few good brain cells with controlled substances.

"Supposing he's in bad need of a fix, has no money, sees a house that's bound to have good stuff in it, stuff he can grab quick and fence within a half hour. He could get at least one good toot out of a crystal paperweight or silver candlestick."

DeeDee thought it over for several moments, then shook her head. "Maybe I'd buy that scenario if he'd been in a commercial area. He pulls a crash-and-snatch on an electronics store or something. Even if the alarm is blaring, he could be in and out in a matter of seconds with a goodie in his pocket.

"But not out there in the burbs," she went on. "Especially on foot. No one's found a car attached to him. I checked as soon as I got here this morning. What was he doing in that neighborhood without a getaway car?"

"I wondered about that last night," Duncan admitted. "It's been nagging me ever since. How'd he get there and how did he plan to get out?"

"If he didn't have a car, where'd the tire iron come from?" she asked. "Which, when you think about it, is a pretty clumsy apparatus for a burglar."

The high humidity had upped the frizz factor of her hair. It swept the air like a stiff broom when she shook her head again. "No, Duncan, something's out of joint."

"So what do you think?"

She propped her forearms on the edge of his desk and leaned forward. "I don't think we're getting the straight story from the angel-faced Mrs. Laird."

Dammit, that's what he thought, too.

He didn't want to think it. He'd spent the early morning hours trying to convince himself that Elise Laird was as true blue as a nun, had never told a lie in her life, had never even fudged the truth.

But his detective's gut instinct was telling him otherwise. His master's degree was telling him otherwise. Fifteen years of police work was telling him that something didn't gibe, that the judge's hot tub buddy had intentionally left something out or, worse, made it all up.

Obviously his partner questioned Elise's veracity, and DeeDee didn't even know about the private exchange that he'd had with Elise.

He told himself not to read anything into that, that it was irrelevant, and to forget it. However, in addition to sorting through the elements of the shooting incident that didn't add up, his mind frequently wandered back to that moment when a simple, two-word question had become foreplay.

"Wasn't it?"

Each time he thought about it — the husky pitch of her voice, the expression in her eyes — he had a profound physical reaction. Like now.

For a cop, it was a bad and dangerous reaction to have to a woman who'd fatally shot a man. For a cop who'd criticized fellow officers for having similar lapses in judgment and morality, it was hypocritical.

It was also damned inconvenient, when DeeDee was sitting across the desk, watching him, waiting for his assessment of Elise Laird's story.

"What do you know about her?" he asked in a reasonably normal voice. "Her history, I mean."

"How would I know her history? She and I hardly run in the same circles."

"You recognized her the night of the awards dinner."

"From her pictures in the newspaper. If you read something besides the sports page and the crossword puzzle, you would have recognized her, too."

"She's featured frequently?"

"Always looking sensational, wearing haute couture, attached at the hip to the judge. She's definitely a trophy for His Honor."

"Do some digging. See what you can find on her. I'll go over to the morgue, goose Dothan into giving priority to Gary Ray Trotter's autopsy. We'll compare notes when I get back." He drained his coffee cup. Then, trying not to appear self-conscious, he stood up and reached for his sport jacket.

"Duncan?"

"Yeah?"

"I just realized something."

He was afraid DeeDee would say something like, *I just realized that you're sporting a boner for the judge's wife.*

But what she said was, "I just realized that we're not treating this shooting like it was self-defense. We're investigating it as something else, aren't we?"

He almost wished she'd said the other

thing.

He called the ME from his car and prevailed upon him to put Gary Ray Trotter at the head of the line. Dr. Dothan Brooks had already opened up the cadaver by the time Duncan arrived.

"So far, all his organs are normal size and weight," Dothan said over his shoulder as he placed a hunk of tissue on the scale.

Duncan took up a position against the wall, listening and watching as the ME methodically went about his work. He glanced at the cadaver only occasionally. He wasn't particularly squeamish. In fact, he was fascinated by the information a cadaver could impart.

But his fascination made him feel guilty. He felt like he was no better than people who rushed to the scene of a tragedy in the perverse hope of glimpsing strewn body parts and blood.

The ME finished and turned the human shell over to his assistant to close. After he had washed up, Dothan joined Duncan, who was waiting for him in his office.

"Cause of death was obvious," he said as he huffed in. "His heart was pulp. Exit wound bigger than a salad plate."

"Before I got here, did you see any other

wounds, bruises, scratches?"

"Was he in a fight, you mean? Struggle of some sort?" He shook his head. "Nothing under his fingernails except your common dirt, and there was gunpowder residue on his right hand. He had a broken toe on his left foot, long time ago. No surgical scars. He hadn't been circumcised."

"From how far away would you say he was shot?" Duncan asked.

"Fifteen feet, give or take."

"About the distance between the door of the study and the desk." He remembered that DeeDee had measured it at sixteen feet. "So Mrs. Laird was telling the truth."

"About that." Dothan unwrapped the corned beef sandwich that had been waiting for him on his desk. "Early lunch. Want half?"

"No, thanks. Do you think Mrs. Laird was lying about something else?"

Brooks took a huge bite, but blotted mustard from the corners of his lips with surprising daintiness. He chewed, swallowed, belched, then said, "Possibly. Maybe not. There's the question of who fired first."

"You said Trotter died instantly. Meaning he would have had to shoot first."

"Then you've got to believe he was blind — he wasn't — or the worst marksman in

121

the history of crime."

"Maybe he deliberately aimed high. He was only trying to frighten her with a warning shot."

"Could be," Dothan said, nodding in time to his chewing. "Or maybe she startled him when she appeared in the doorway. Trotter had a knee-jerk reaction, fired a wild shot."

"She didn't startle him. She said she told him to leave. He just stood there, looking at her, then jerked his arm up — that's the word she used — and fired."

"Hmm." The ME talked around a big bite of sandwich. "Then I suppose he was extremely nervous, which would account for his aim being nowhere near her. Another possibility" — he paused to slurp Dr Pepper from a paper cup the size of a small wastebasket — "is that he was in the act of firing when her bullet struck him. His finger reflexively contracted and completed the action that pulled the trigger as he was falling backward." He swallowed. "Now that I think on it, the angle would be right for where the bullet struck the wall."

He acted it out, pretending to fall backward, his index finger serving as the barrel of a pretend pistol. As he went back, his aim moved to a spot high on the wall, far above Duncan's head.

"Could that happen?" Duncan asked. "A reflex like that at the moment your heart is blown to hell?"

Brooks crammed the remainder of his sandwich into his mouth. "I've seen fatal bullet wounds with even more bizarre explanations. You wouldn't believe how far-fetched."

"So what are you telling me?"

"I'm telling you that anything can happen, Detective. But lucky for me, it's your job to find out what actually did."

"I've put them in the sunroom, Mrs. Laird."

"That's fine."

Mrs. Berry had come upstairs to inform her that the same detectives who'd been at the house the night before were downstairs and had asked to see her. "Could you please bring in some refreshments? Diet Coke and iced tea."

The formidable housekeeper nodded. "Shall I tell them you'll be right down?"

"Please."

Elise shut the bedroom door, then stood there, wondering what questions the detectives would be asking today.

Hadn't they believed her last night?

If they had, they wouldn't be back today, would they?

Loose ends, Detective Hatcher had said. The term could cover any number of inconsequential nagging details. Or it could be an understatement for discrepancies of major importance.

She feared the latter.

That's what had prompted her to go see Savich this morning. It had been risky, but she'd wanted to contact him as soon as possible, and using the telephone could have been even chancier than driving to his place of business. She didn't trust that the home telephone would not be tapped, and cell phone calls could be traced.

Cato had got up at his normal time and quietly dressed for work. She'd pretended to be asleep until he left the bedroom. Then, as soon as his car had cleared the driveway, she had dressed quickly and left the house, hoping to complete the errand and return home before Mrs. Berry arrived for the day.

Keeping a watchful eye in the rearview mirror, she'd been confident that no one had followed her. Despite her haste, she had heeded the speed limits, not wanting to be stopped for a traffic ticket that she would have to explain to Cato.

She had returned home only minutes ahead of the housekeeper and had remained in her bedroom ever since, pacing, playing over in her mind the events of the previous night, trying to decide what her next course of action should be.

Detective Bowen and Duncan Hatcher were waiting for her downstairs. She dreaded the interview, but further delay would look suspicious. She went to her dressing table, gathered her hair into a ponytail, considered changing clothes, then decided not to take the time. She picked up a tube of lip gloss, but changed her mind about that, too. Detective Bowen would find fault with her vanity, and Duncan Hatcher . . .

What did he think of her? she wondered. *Really* think of her.

She deliberated that for several precious moments, then, before she could talk herself out of it, did one thing more before leaving the bedroom.

The sunroom was a glass-enclosed portion of the terrace, floored in Pennsylvania bluestone, furnished with wicker pieces that had floral print cushions. Mrs. Berry was better with plants than with people. Ferns and palms and other potted tropicals flourished under her care.

When Elise entered the room, DeeDee Bowen was seated in one of the chairs facing the door. Duncan was standing at the wall of windows looking out over the terrace and swimming pool, seemingly captivated by the fountain at the center of it.

Detective Bowen stood up. "Hello, Mrs. Laird. We apologize for showing up unannounced. Is this an inconvenient time?"

"Not at all."

Upon hearing her name, Duncan turned away from the window. Elise glanced at him, then came into the room and joined Detective Bowen in the sitting area.

"Mrs. Berry will be here shortly with something to drink," she said, motioning Detective Bowen back into her chair, then sat down in one facing it.

"That'll be nice. It's so hot out."

"Yes."

Having exhausted the topic of the weather, they lapsed into an awkward silence. Elise was aware of Duncan, still standing near the window, watching her. She resisted looking in his direction.

Finally Bowen said, "We have a few more questions."

"Before leaving last night you implied that you would."

"Just a few things we'd like to clear up."

"I understand."

"Overnight, did you think of anything you

left out? Something that may have slipped your mind?"

"No."

"That can happen in stressful situations." The woman smiled at her. "I've had people call me in the middle of the night, suddenly remembering a detail they'd forgotten."

"I told you what I remembered exactly as I remembered it."

The soft rattle of glassware announced the arrival of a serving cart, pushed into the room by Mrs. Berry. "Shall I serve, Mrs. Laird?" Her voice was as chilly as the condensation on the ice bucket. Elise wasn't sure if she was disdainful of their guests, or her. Probably both.

"No, thank you." Welcoming a chance to move and get out from under the scrutiny of the detectives, she left her chair and approached the cart. "I believe you prefer Diet Coke, Detective Bowen?"

"Sounds great."

Elise poured the cola over a glass of ice and carried it to her. She accepted it with an easy smile, which Elise instantly mistrusted. Then she turned and looked up at Duncan Hatcher. His eyes were still on her. Unblinking. Intent. "Something for you?"

He glanced at the cart. "Is that tea?"

"It's sweetened. Mrs. Berry thinks that's

the only way to make it."

"That's the only way my mom makes it, too. Sweetened is fine." His smile was as easy as DeeDee Bowen's, but Elise trusted it even less. It never reached his eyes.

She wondered if the decision she'd made before coming downstairs was a foolhardy one.

Of course, it would have been more foolhardy not to do anything.

She poured Duncan Hatcher a glass of iced tea and was passing it to him when Cato strode into the room. "Apparently I didn't receive the memo."

6

"Or did you just happen to be in the neighborhood?"the judge added with less civility.

Yep, he's angry, DeeDee thought. Just as Duncan had predicted he would be once he learned that they'd questioned his wife — or tried to — without his being present. They had the right to, of course, but had agreed to avoid ruffling the judge's feathers if at all possible.

Mrs. What's-her-name, the housekeeper, must have called him immediately upon their arrival, probably even before she went upstairs to tell Elise Laird they were here. It was clear that the domestic's loyalty lay with the judge and that she seemed to have little regard for his missus.

Elise offered to pour her husband a glass of tea.

"No, thank you." He kissed her on the lips, then pulled back and stroked her cheek. "How are you holding up?"

"Fine."

"Still shaken?"

"I think I will be for a while."

"Understandable."

He guided her down onto the settee that was barely wide enough to accommodate both of them, pulled her hand onto his knee, and covered it with his. "What would you like to know?"

DeeDee saw Duncan's jaw tense. He said, "I'd like to know if you want to call a lawyer before we begin. We'll be happy to wait until one arrives."

The judge replied crisply, "That won't be necessary. But to show up here unannounced was a cheap trick and, frankly, beneath you, Detective Hatcher."

"My apologies to you and to Mrs. Laird." Duncan sat down in one of the wicker armchairs facing the couple. "The name of the man who died in your study last night was Gary Ray Trotter."

Like Duncan, DeeDee closely watched their faces for any giveaway sign of recognition. There wasn't so much as a flicker, not in the judge's implacable stare, not in Elise Laird's limpid green eyes.

The judge glanced down at his wife. Reading his silent question, she shook her head. Looking back at them, he said, "We don't know him. I thought we'd made that clear to you last night."

"We hoped the name might jog your memory, remind you —"

"Obviously not, Detective Bowen," the judge said, cutting her off.

"A lot of people have been shuttled through your courtroom," Duncan said. "Trotter was a repeat offender. Perhaps he'd come before your bench."

"I would remember."

"You remember every party to every case you've ever tried?" DeeDee said. "Wow. That's impressive."

He fired another impatient glance at her, then addressed himself to Duncan. "He was a repeat offender? Then what more is there to discuss? This Trotter broke into my house, fired a handgun at my wife, forcing her to protect herself. Thank God her aim was better than his. He died, she didn't. Don't expect me to cry over him."

"I don't expect that at all."

The judge took a slow, deep breath as though to calm himself. "Then I guess I don't understand why you're here today. Why do you feel it necessary to make Elise relive this terrifying event?"

"We have some points that need clarification before we close the case," DeeDee said.

"Elise told you everything she had to tell you last night. As a judge who's heard years of courtroom testimony, I can honestly say that her account of what happened was comprehensive."

"I agree, and we appreciate her cooperation last night," DeeDee said to the couple, smiling at both. "Identifying Gary Ray Trotter has answered some of our outstanding questions, but created others, I'm afraid."

"Such as?"

DeeDee laughed softly. "Well, Judge, he wasn't a very accomplished crook. In fact, he was pretty much a loser, who couldn't even hack it as a criminal."

"So?"

"So Detective Hatcher and I were wondering why he chose your house to burglarize."

"I have no idea."

"Neither do we," DeeDee said bluntly. "Trotter had a criminal history dating back to adolescence. Robbery mostly. But he was a goof. For instance, he once walked into a convenience store with a stick in his pocket in lieu of a pistol and demanded the money in the till. But he paid for the gas he pumped into his getaway car with his sister's credit card."

The judge smiled wryly. "Which I think explains why he failed as a crook."

"I guess," DeeDee exclaimed on a short laugh. "I mean, last night he didn't even bring along gloves or robber paraphernalia of any kind. Can you believe that? Sort of makes you wonder, doesn't it?"

"What?"

Then she dropped her smile. "What the heck Gary Ray Trotter was doing in your study."

After a moment of taut silence, the judge said, "I know one thing he did. He tried to kill my wife."

Duncan pounced on that. "Which is another thing we must clear up, Mrs. Laird."

"What needs clearing up?" the judge asked.

"Are you absolutely certain that Trotter fired first?"

"Of course she's certain."

"I asked *her*, Judge."

"My wife has been through a terrible ordeal."

"And I've got a job to do," Duncan fired back. "That involves asking her some tough questions. If you haven't got the stomach for it, Judge, you can leave."

Elise held up her hand, stopping the judge from saying whatever he was about to say in response to Duncan's angry put-down. "Please, Cato. I want to answer their questions. I don't want there to be any doubt as to what happened." She had addressed her husband by name, but DeeDee noticed that her green gaze didn't waver from Duncan's face, nor his from hers.

"As I told you last night," she said, "when I accidentally switched on the foyer light —"

"Excuse me. Do you mind talking us through it where it happened?"

"In the study?"

"If it wouldn't be too much of an imposition."

"It will be very difficult for Elise to go into that room until it's been cleaned, rid of all reminders of what happened in it," the judge said.

"I realize it won't be easy," Duncan said. But he didn't withdraw the request.

The judge looked at his wife. "Elise?"

"I want to help in any way I can."

The four of them made their way into the foyer. Duncan approached the fancy console table. Beneath the marble top was a slender drawer that ran the width of the table. "You took the pistol from this drawer?"

"Yes, I came out of the butler's pantry through that door," she replied, pointing. "I paused there a moment. I didn't hear anything, but, as I told you last night, I

134

sensed a presence in the study. I went to the table to get the pistol."

Duncan fingered one of the drawer pulls. "Did you make any noise?"

"I don't think so. I tried not to."

"Did you close the drawer?"

"I . . . I don't remember," she said, faltering. "I don't believe I did."

"She didn't," the judge said. "It was open when the first two policemen arrived in response to the 911. I remember pointing it out to them."

DeeDee made a mental note to read the report filed by Officers Beale and Crofton.

Duncan resumed. "You walked from the table to the door of the study."

"Yes."

"Were you wearing slippers?"

"I was barefoot."

"Do you think Trotter heard you approaching?" Duncan asked. "Or did he have no inkling you were there and aware of him until the light came on?"

"If he'd heard me coming toward the study, why didn't he just scramble out the window?"

"That was going to be my next question," Duncan said with a guileless smile.

"Then I must have startled him by switching on the light," Elise said. "When it came on, he froze."

"This is the switch plate?" Duncan flipped one switch, and the overhead light in the study came on. The other turned on a fixture in the foyer directly above their heads. He looked up at the light, then into the study. "DeeDee, would you play Trotter? Go stand behind the desk."

She peeled away the crime scene tape that formed an X in the open doorway, then went into the study and took a position behind the desk.

Duncan said, "Is that about where he was standing?"

Elise replied with a slight nod.

"What was he doing, Mrs. Laird?"

"Nothing. Only standing there looking at me. Staring, like a deer caught in headlights."

"Was he leaning over the desk, like he'd been trying to jimmy the lock on the drawer?"

"It took several seconds for my eyes to adjust to the sudden brightness. Maybe he was bending over the desk drawer, I don't know. The first mental picture I have of him is his standing there behind the desk, looking at me, motionless."

"Huh." Duncan looked toward DeeDee behind the desk as though imagining Gary

Ray Trotter. "And what was it he said?" He came back around to Elise.

She didn't flinch and she didn't hesitate. "He didn't say anything, Detective Hatcher. I told you that last night."

Duncan nodded slowly. "Right. You did. But you spoke to him, correct? You ordered him to leave."

"Yes."

"Did he make a move toward the window?"

"No. He didn't move at all except to raise his arm. Suddenly. Like a string attached to his elbow had been yanked."

"Like this?" DeeDee demonstrated the motion.

"Something like that, yes. And before it even registered with me that he was holding a pistol, he fired it." She placed a hand at her throat as though suddenly finding it difficult to breathe.

The judge moved closer and slid his arm around her waist.

Duncan asked, "Mrs. Laird, is it possible that he was firing a warning shot, meant only to try and scare you?"

"I suppose it's possible."

"Did you feel in mortal danger?"

"I assumed I was. It all happened very fast."

"But not so fast that you didn't have time to 'assume' that you were in mortal danger."

"That's a reasonable assumption, isn't it, Detective?" the judge asked, sounding vexed. "If a man who's broken into your house fires a pistol, even if his aim is lousy, isn't it logical to assume that your life is in danger and to act accordingly?"

"It seems logical, yes," DeeDee said. "But Dr. Brooks had another theory worth considering. He suggested that maybe Trotter was falling backward when he fired his pistol, that reflexively his finger clenched on the trigger. That would explain his aim being so far off."

Duncan was staring hard at Elise. "But that would mean that you had shot at him first."

"But she didn't," the judge said. "She's told you that a dozen times. Why do you keep hammering away at this?"

Duncan tore his gaze from Elise Laird's stricken face and looked at the judge. "Because I've got to have a clear understanding of what happened. I dislike having to put these questions to Mrs. Laird. But I was there this morning when the autopsy was performed on Gary Ray Trotter's corpse. I feel I owe it to him, crook or not, to determine how and why he wound up like that. You're a public official, Judge. You have an obligation to the public to do your duty. So do I. Sometimes it's no fun at all. In fact, most of the time it's not."

He turned back to Elise. "Are you absolutely certain that Trotter fired at you first?"

"Absolutely."

"There. That ends it." The judge's statement was followed by a tense stretch of silence. Finally he said, "I admire your sense of duty, Detective Hatcher. I appreciate your quest for the truth. Elise and I have done everything within our power to help you perform your unpleasant duties.

"Haven't you stopped to consider that we would like a full explanation for what happened here last night, too? We would like that perhaps even more than you and Detective Bowen. Elise has been as straightforward as she could possibly be. Are you now satisfied that it was a break-in that went awry?"

Duncan let the question hover there for at least fifteen seconds before answering, "I believe so, yes."

My ass, thought DeeDee.

The judge said, "Good. Then if that's all, I hope you'll excuse us." He turned, ready to escort them out, when Elise forestalled him.

"I'd like to know . . ." Her voice cracked. She swallowed, tried again. "I'd like to know if Trotter had a family. A wife, children?"

"No," Duncan said. "His closest relative was an uncle up in Maryland."

"I'm glad of that. I would have hated . . . that."

"May I show you out now?" The judge started down the hall, expecting them to follow.

DeeDee came from behind the desk. As she moved past Elise, Elise reached for her hand. "Detective Bowen, I want to echo what my husband said. I know you're only doing your job."

Surprised by the move, DeeDee tried to think of something neutral to say that would be a fitting response, whether Elise was lying or telling the truth. "This can't be easy for you, either."

"It isn't, but if I think of anything to add, I promise to call you."

"That would be helpful."

"Do you have a business card?"

"Right here." Duncan plucked one from the breast pocket of his jacket and passed it to her.

"Thank you, Detective Hatcher." Taking the card, she shook hands with him, too.

■ ■ ■ ■

DeeDee was as bouncy as one of those fuzzy orange dogs that look like manic powder puffs. An ex-girlfriend had owned one. The damn thing had barked nonstop. Most hyper animal Duncan had ever been around. Until today. DeeDee was practically jumping out of her skin.

"She's hiding something, Duncan. I know it. I feel it in my bones."

DeeDee's "bones" were rarely wrong. In this particular case, he hoped they were. He wanted to close this case with dispatch and remain in the judge's good graces. He'd never been a big fan of Judge Cato Laird, believing that often he talked out both sides of his mouth. Tough on crime and criminals one day, favoring the protection of their civil rights the next. His opinions seemed to drift along with the ebb and flow of public opinion, adhering only to the majority rule of the moment.

Duncan couldn't admire a man to whom popularity was more important than conviction, but he supposed in order to win elections, the judge had to practice politics. And he certainly didn't want a superior court judge as an enemy. That's what he was likely to become if he continued hassling the judge's wife because of what his partner felt in her bones.

Unfortunately, his bones were feeling the same thing. Especially after that last interview.

He jerked the steering wheel to the right and crossed two lanes of traffic to the accompaniment of blaring horns and shouted invectives. DeeDee gripped the armrest of the passenger door.

"What are you doing?"

"I'm thirsty." The car jounced over the curb as he came close to missing the entrance to a McDonald's.

"You had sweetened iced tea. 'Mrs. Berry thinks that's the only way to make it,' " she said, batting her eyelashes and mocking Elise Laird's drawl.

"I was *served* iced tea. I didn't drink it. Besides, aren't you overdue a shot of caffeine? Not that you need it," he added under his breath as he leaned toward the speaker to place their order.

"Should we go back and talk to some of the neighbors?" DeeDee asked.

"What good would that do? They were canvassed last night. None reported a recent burglary or break-in. No one saw Gary Ray Trotter lurking around the neighborhood.

Nobody heard anything out of the ordinary last night."

"Maybe Mrs. Laird opened the door and invited him in."

"That's a real stretch, DeeDee."

After picking up their drinks at the window, he got back onto the street and rapidly closed in on the bumper of a soccer mom's van. "What is with everybody today?" he said as he went around the van. "People are driving like there's ice on the road."

"What's your hurry?" DeeDee asked.

He whipped into another lane in order to go around a slow-moving parochial school bus. "No hurry. I just hate this damn traffic."

Heedless of his complaining, DeeDee said, "Okay, so maybe she didn't welcome Trotter like a guest; there's still something wrong with that picture."

"I'll bite. What makes you think so?"

"Generally —"

"Don't be general. Be specific."

"Okay. Specifically, her reaction when you raised the question of her firing her pistol ahead of Trotter. She went whey-faced."

He supposed that "whey-faced" was one way to accurately describe Elise's expression. "I pushed pretty hard. She stuck to her story."

"Most good liars do."

"You think she's lying?"

"Maybe not lying," DeeDee said. "Just not telling the truth, the whole truth, and nothing but the truth."

"You're getting general again. Give me an example."

"I don't know. I can't be specific," she said, matching his irritability. "She just doesn't act like a woman who killed a hapless burglar last night."

"She didn't know he was hapless. Gary Ray Trotter didn't look like a screwup when he was standing in her house, in the dark, firing a weapon at her. Do you think she should have waited to shoot him until after she'd seen his résumé?"

His sarcasm earned him a glare.

"And she was concerned enough to ask if Trotter had a family," he pointed out. "It bothered her to think she might have orphaned some kids."

"I'll admit that was a nice touch."

"Why do you think it was a 'touch'?"

"Why are you defending her?"

"I'm not."

"Sure sounds like it to me."

"Well, it sounds to me like you're doing just the opposite. You think everything she says and does is disingenuous."

"Not everything. For instance, I believe that she was barefoot."

This time, she was on the receiving end of a baleful look.

"All I'm saying," she continued, "is that I believe the sweet remark about Trotter's family was made for your benefit."

"My benefit?"

"Oh, please, Duncan. Wake up. She answers my questions, but whenever she wants to stress a point, such as her truthfulness, she looks at you."

"You're imagining that."

"Like hell, I am. The lady knows on which side to butter her bread."

"Meaning?"

"You're a man."

"Which, in the context of this discussion, is beside the point."

"Right." She used the tone she did whenever he denied knowing how to play the piano. For the next several moments, she was deep in thought, poking at the ice cubes in her drink with her straw. "You know what else? I think suspicion has reared its ugly head to the judge."

"Now I know you're seeing things that aren't there," he said. "He's never more than half a foot away from her, treats her like she's made of porcelain."

"True. He's very protective. Almost as though he's afraid she might need his protection."

"He's her husband."

"He's also a judge who's listened to hours of sworn testimony in his courtroom, as he reminded us today. He commended her comprehensive recall. But you can bet he also knows a lie when he hears one. And he got awfully defensive when we advanced Dothan's theory about Trotter having been shot and reflexively pulling the trigger on his way down. Judge Laird pooh-poohed it without further explanation or discussion. His wife didn't fire first. Period. The end." She paused for breath. "Which leads me to believe that His Honor may be questioning his wife's story."

They arrived at the Barracks. Duncan pulled his car into a slot in the parking lot, but neither of them made a move to get out. He leaned forward, crossed his arms over the steering wheel, and stared through the windshield at the civilians and police personnel going in and out of the Habersham Street entrance.

He felt DeeDee's eyes on him, but he let her be the first to break the weighty silence. "Look, Duncan, I know it's hard to get past that face. That body. Although I know there's been speculation about my sexual orientation from yahoos like Worley, I'm straight. But being straight doesn't make me blind to Elise Laird's appeal. I can appreciate — okay, appreciate and *envy* — the way she looks and the effect she has on the opposite sex. There, I've been honest. Now you, in turn, must be honest with me."

She paused, but when he said nothing, she continued. "Can you honestly, cross-your-heart-and-hope-to-die honestly, be objective when you look at her?"

"I'm a cop."

"With a penis. And that particular organ is notorious for having lapses in judgment."

He turned and looked at her then. "Have you ever, *ever* known me to compromise an investigation?"

"No. With you it's either wrong or right, black or white, no gray areas. That's why as soon as I made detective I petitioned hard to become your partner."

"So where's this coming from?"

"We've never investigated a case involving a woman that you're attracted to. And you were attracted to Elise Laird the instant you saw her at the awards dinner. You can't deny that."

"She was a pretty face in the crowd."

"Who you compared to a lightning strike."

147

"That was before I knew her name. It was for sure as hell before she shot and killed a man."

"So your attraction to her died along with Trotter? No lingering groin tugs in that direction?"

He used his thumb to whisk beads of sweat off his forehead. "The lady is poison, DeeDee. Don't you think I know that?"

Her frown told him that wasn't exactly a direct answer to her question and that she still needed convincing.

"First of all," he said, "she's married."

"To a man you despise."

"Irrelevant."

"I wonder."

"Irrelevant," he repeated with emphasis. DeeDee didn't come back with further argument, but she still looked doubtful. He said, "I've had my share of girlfriends and short-term bed partners."

"An understatement."

"Name one who was married."

She stayed silent.

"Exactly," he said. "I've massaged the issue of sexual morality to fit my lifestyle and to satisfy the urge of the moment, but I draw the line at adultery, DeeDee."

She nodded. "Okay, I believe you. But if she wasn't married —"

"She's still a principal in an active investigation."

DeeDee's face brightened. *"Active.* Does that mean we're not closing the book on it just yet?"

"No," he said heavily. "Not yet. Like you, I sense there's something out of joint."

"It's her. She's . . . what was your fifty-cent word? Disingenuous?"

"The background check you ran on her didn't produce much, did it?"

She ticked off on her fingers the facts she'd learned about Elise Laird. "She has no arrest record, no outstanding debts, and there was nothing printed about her in the local newspaper before she married Laird. She came out of nowhere."

"Nobody comes out of nowhere."

DeeDee thought about it for a moment. "I've got a friend with ties to the society set. Often the best source of information is good old-fashioned gossip."

"Keep the inquiry discreet."

"I won't even have to ask for info. Once I mention Elise Laird's name, I bet I get an earful. This friend thrives on gossip."

They got out, but as they approached the steps of the entrance, Duncan continued down the sidewalk. DeeDee asked where he was going.

"I'm days overdue calling my folks. I can talk to them easier out here than in the office with all the commotion."

She went inside. Duncan followed the sidewalk around to the front of the building that faced Oglethorpe Avenue, walked past the black-and-white 1953 squad car that was parked out front like a mascot, and continued on until he reached the middle of the block, where there was a gated entrance to the Colonial Park Cemetery.

A few stalwart tourists braving the afternoon heat were taking pictures, reading the historical plaques, and trying to decipher the inscriptions carved into the grave markers. He made his way to one of the shaded wood benches and sat down, but he didn't reach for his cell phone to call his parents. Instead he sat there and stared at the leaning headstones and crumbling brick vaults.

He could imagine the ghosts of fallen Revolutionary War heroes staring back at him expectantly, waiting to see what he would do. Would he do what he knew to be right? Or, for the first time in his career, would he violate the dictates of his conscience?

Above the nearby rooftops were the twin spires of St. John the Baptist cathedral, serving as another reminder that to transgress was a matter of choice.

Despite these silent warnings, he reached into his trousers pocket and withdrew the note he'd put there after having it surreptitiously slipped to him by Elise Laird when they shook hands.

He'd felt it immediately, sandwiched between their palms. She'd clasped his hand tightly so the note couldn't fall to the floor and give her away. Her eyes had begged him not to.

Despite her pleading gaze, he should have acknowledged the note right then. If not immediately, then surely as soon as he and DeeDee were alone. He should have told his partner about it, opened it, read it for the first time along with her.

But he hadn't.

Now, it seemed as hot as a cinder lying in his palm. He turned it over several times, examining it. The single white sheet had been folded over twice to form a small square. It weighed practically nothing. It looked innocuous enough, but he knew better. No matter what it said, it meant trouble for him.

If it contained information on last night's shooting, it amounted to evidence, which he was already guilty of withholding.

If it was personal, well, that would be even

more compromising.

The first instance would be a legal matter. The second, a moral one.

It wasn't too late to show it to DeeDee now. He could invent an excuse for not having shown it to her sooner, which she probably wouldn't believe but would readily accept because she would be so curious to read the contents of the note. They would open it, read it, and together analyze its meaning.

Short of that, and almost as honorable an action, he could destroy it and go to his grave wondering what it had said.

Instead, with damp hands, shortness of breath, and a rapidly beating heart, with the spirits of the nation's founders watching with stern disapproval, and the church spires pointing heavenward as though bringing his error to God's attention, he slowly unfolded the note. The words had been written in a neat script.

I must see you alone. Please.

7

Elise was watching a movie on DVD. It was the film version of a Jane Austen novel. She'd seen it at least a dozen times and could practically quote the dialogue. The costumes and sets were lavish. The cinematography was gorgeous. The tribulations suffered by the heroine were superficial and easily solved. The outcome was happy.

Unlike real life. Which is why she liked the story so well.

"I was right," Cato announced as he entered the den, where there was a wide-screen TV and her sizable library of DVDs.

She reached for the remote and muted the audio. "About what?"

He sat down beside her on the sofa. "Gary Ray Trotter was never in my courtroom. As soon as the detectives left, I called my office and ordered that the records be searched. Thoroughly. I never presided over the trial of a Gary Ray Trotter."

"Would you know if he was ever called as a witness in another trial?"

"Determining that would take more man-hours than I'm willing to invest. Besides, I'm almost certain that what I told the detectives is correct. I'd never seen the man before. You said you didn't recognize him either."

"I said it because it's true."

After a beat, he said, "I didn't mean to imply otherwise, Elise."

"I'm sorry. I didn't mean to sound so short."

"You have reason to be." He kissed her gently. When they pulled apart, she asked if he would like a drink. "I'd love one, thank you."

She went to the small wet bar, picked up a heavy crystal decanter of scotch, and tilted the spout against a highball glass.

"Do you know Robert Savich?"

Elise nearly dropped the decanter. "I'm sorry, what?"

"Savich. Ever hear of him?"

She redirected her attention to pouring scotch. "Hmm, the name sounds vaguely familiar."

"It should. He's in the news now and again. He's a drug kingpin. Among other things."

Keeping her expression impassive, she plunked two cubes of ice into his drink, carried it with her back to the sofa, and passed it to him. "I hope it's to your liking."

He took a sip, pronounced it perfect, and kept his eyes trained on her over the top of the glass. "Savich is the reason Hatcher is being so rough on you."

She picked up a throw pillow and hugged it against her chest. "What does one have to do with the other?"

"Remember I told you that I'd found Hatcher in contempt of court and put him in jail?"

"You said he was upset over a mistrial."

"Savich's."

"Oh."

"Detective Hatcher is still holding a grudge against me," Cato said. "You're catching the brunt of it."

She threaded the fringe on the pillow through her fingers. "He's only doing his job."

"I grant that he has to ask difficult questions in any investigation, but he's had you on the defensive from the get-go. His partner, too."

"Detective Bowen doesn't like me at all."

"Jealousy," he said with a dismissive gesture. "She's pea green with it, and one can clearly see why. But she's insignificant."

"That's not the impression I get," Elise murmured, remembering the suspicion with which the other woman had looked at her, last night and today.

"Bowen has earned some commendations, as you know. But Hatcher is the standard by which she measures herself." Chuckling, he rattled the ice cubes in his glass. "And he's a tough yardstick."

"What do you mean?"

"He's smart, and he's an honest cop. Bowen looks up to him. His allies are hers. That goes double for his enemies."

"I doubt he thinks of you as an enemy, Cato."

"Maybe that word is a bit strong, but he has a long-standing gripe with me, and now he's taking it out on you."

"There's more water under the bridge than this recent mistrial?"

"I've heard of his rumblings. He thinks I'm not tough enough." He shrugged as if the criticism didn't concern him. "That's a common complaint from hard-nosed cops."

"He's hardly Dirty Harry."

He smiled at her analogy. "No, he's not *that* hard-nosed. In fact, the man's a contradiction. Once, when he was testifying at the trial of an accused child killer, he got tears in his eyes when he described the crime scene, the small body of the victim. To see him that day on the witness stand, you'd think he was a softie.

"But I've heard that he assumes another personality when he's questioning a suspect, particularly when he knows the suspect is lying or giving him the runaround. It's said he can lose his temper and even get physical." He stroked her hair. "You got a glimpse of that side of him today, didn't you?"

"I never felt physically threatened," she said, only half in jest.

Cato responded in kind. "He wouldn't dare. But the way he was questioning you about who fired first, you or that Trotter character, bordered on harassment." He sipped his drink thoughtfully. "A call to his supervisor, Bill Gerard, or even to Chief Taylor may be in order."

"Please don't."

Her sharp tone surprised him. "Why not?"

"Because . . ." She stopped to think of a plausible answer. "Because I don't want to draw attention to the incident. I don't want more made of it than already has been."

Studying her, he set his drink on the coffee table and curved his hand around her neck. His fingers were very cold. "What are you afraid of, Elise?"

157

Her heart somersaulted, but she managed to form a puzzled smile. "I'm not afraid."

"Are you afraid that the questions Hatcher and Bowen are asking about last night may lead to . . . something? Something uglier than what happened?"

"What could be uglier than a man *dying?*"

He studied her for several seconds, then smiled at her tenderly. "You're right. Never mind. Silly thought." He released her and stood up. "Finish your movie. Would you like Mrs. Berry to bring you something?"

She declined with a shake of her head.

He picked up his highball glass and carried it with him. At the door, he turned back. "Darling?"

"Yes?"

"If you hadn't been downstairs last night, this incident would have been avoided. Trotter may have burglarized us, but that wouldn't have been the end of the world. Everything is well insured. Perhaps from now on, you should confine your strolls through the house in the middle of the night to the upper floor."

She gave him a weak smile. "That's probably a good idea."

He returned her smile and seemed about to go, when he hesitated a second time. "You know . . . another reason for Hatcher's badgering."

"What?"

"It gives him an excuse to look at you." He chuckled. "Poor bastard."

Duncan was in his office, seated at his littered desk, shuffling through telephone messages, trying to look busy for the benefit of DeeDee and the other detectives who were at their desks that afternoon, and wishing like hell that he'd never opened that note.

He couldn't guess at Elise Laird's purpose for passing it to him. But the result was that it had convinced him that her explanation for the shooting of Gary Ray Trotter was bogus. There was more to it than the luck of a dumb crook finally running out. If it had been strictly a matter of self-defense, she wouldn't be slipping a note to the detective overseeing the investigation, asking him to meet her alone.

Which was not going to happen.

It *wasn't*.

He pushed aside the unanswered telephone messages, propped his feet on top of his desk, and reached for a yellow legal tablet on which to jot down thoughts as they came to him.

In addition to the note, there were other

reasons he — and DeeDee — found Elise Laird's story hard to accept. One was the burglary itself. It seemed odd that Trotter was on foot in a classy neighborhood like Ardsley Park. The residential area was demarcated by busy boulevards, but the streets within the area didn't invite pedestrians other than moms pushing baby strollers or people out getting their exercise. A man walking the streets a half hour after midnight would arouse immediate suspicion. A seasoned crook — even an unsuccessful one — would know that and have a getaway car parked nearby.

Also, it was an outlandish coincidence that Trotter had chosen to break into that house on the one night, out of all nights, that Mrs. Laird had forgotten to engage the alarm system.

Okay, so wine and sex could make you lazy. But her satiation hadn't overcome her insomnia. She hadn't drifted off into a peaceful, postcoital slumber. No, she'd gone downstairs for a glass of milk to help her fall asleep. Wouldn't roaming around in the dark house have reminded her that she had failed to set the alarm?

Second, when she heard a noise coming from the study, why hadn't she crept back into the kitchen and used the telephone to dial 911? Why had her first reaction been to grab a pistol and confront the intruder?

Third, Trotter didn't seem like a guy who would brazen it out if caught red-handed. He seemed the type to tuck tail and get the hell outta there. Only a supremely confident burglar would stick around and have a face-off, especially if he was there only to steal something.

Duncan's mind stumbled over that thought. Mentally he backtracked and looked at it again. He underlined *if he was there only to steal something,* then drew a large question mark beside it.

"Hey, Dunk."

Another detective popped his head inside the door. His name was Harvey Reynolds, but everyone called him Kong because of his gorilla-like pelt. Every inch of exposed skin was covered in thick, curly black hair. No one dared speculate on what the unexposed parts of his body looked like.

His apelike appearance was further enhanced by his thick neck, barrel chest, and short legs. Despite his intimidating appearance, he couldn't be a nicer guy. He coached Little League for his twin sons' team and was dotty over his homely wife, believing himself lucky to have won such a prize as she. Duncan, who'd met the lady on several occasions, agreed with Kong. She was a prize. It was clear the couple were nuts about each other.

"Can I bend your ear for a minute?"

Duncan was eager to get back to examining that last niggling thought he'd written down, but he tossed the legal tablet onto his desk and motioned Kong in. "What's the Little League team selling this week? Candy bars? Magazine subscriptions?"

Kong gave him a good-natured grin. "Citrus fruit from the valley."

"What valley?"

"Beats the hell out of me. I'll hit you up for that later. This is business." Kong worked missing persons in the special victims unit, or SVU. Sometimes their cases overlapped. He pulled up a chair and straddled it backward, folding his hirsute arms over it. "Anything cooking on Savich since the mistrial?"

"Not even a simmer."

"Bitch of a turn."

"Tell me."

"He never got nailed for those other two . . . uh . . . Bonnet, wasn't it?"

"Yeah, and a guy named Chet Rollins before him," Duncan said tightly.

"Right. Wasn't ever indicted for those, was he?"

Duncan shook his head.

"I thought you had him for sure this time. Is he gonna get away with doing Freddy Morris, too?"

"Not if I can help it."

"Limp-dick DA," Kong muttered.

Duncan shrugged. "He says he's hamstrung till we come up with something solid."

"Yeah, but still . . . Feds have anything?"

"Not that I've heard."

"They still steamed?"

"Oh, yeah. Breaks my heart. They never call, never write."

Kong chuckled. "Well, anything that I can do to help you nail that son of a bitch Savich . . ."

"Thanks." Duncan hitched his chin at the sheet of paper in Kong's shaggy clutch. "What's up?"

"Meyer Napoli."

Duncan guffawed. "You must have been out overturning rocks today."

Meyer Napoli was well known to the police department. He was a private investigator who specialized in fleecing his clients of huge sums of money by doing practically nothing except making guarantees that he rarely fulfilled.

It wasn't unlike him to work both ends

163

against the middle. If hired by a wife to get the goods on an unfaithful husband, Napoli was known to go to said husband and, for a fee, promise to return to the wife empty-handed. He also usually consoled the broken-hearted wife in a way that made her feel like a desirable woman again.

"Which rock did you find Napoli under?"

Kong tugged on his earlobe, from which a crop of black bristles sprouted. "Well, that's the problem. I didn't."

"Huh?"

"Napoli's secretary called us this morning, said Napoli failed to show up at his office for a meeting with a client. She called his house and his cell phone a dozen times apiece, but failed to raise him. That never happens. He stays in touch, she said. Always. No exceptions.

"So she went over to his place to see if he was dead or something. No trace of him. That's when she called us. She's been calling every hour since, insisting that something has happened to him. Said he wouldn't miss a morning of appointments with clients, no matter what. According to her, he never takes a sick day or vacation, and even if he did, he wouldn't without letting her know.

"She was bugging us so bad, hell, I gave

in. I went over to his office and explained that unless there's evidence of foul play, we don't consider an adult officially missing unless it's been twenty-four hours since he was last seen. She said there was nothing at his house to indicate foul play, but something bad must've happened to him or else he'd be at work."

Duncan figured Kong had a good reason for telling him all this, and he wished he'd get to the point. His stomach had reminded him that it was past suppertime. It had been a very long day after a very short night. He was ready to take home some carry-out chicken, crack a beer, maybe play the piano to help him do some free associating about Trotter, specifically what he was doing in the Lairds' house and why he hadn't made a dash for it when he was caught.

He also needed to think about Elise Laird's note, why she'd given it to him, and why he hadn't shared it with his partner.

Kong was still talking. "I figured Napoli's private office would be sacrosanct. Locked down, you know? But his secretary was so flustered, she didn't notice that I was scanning the paperwork on his desk while she was wringing her hands, wondering where her boss is at."

At this point, Kong produced the sheet of

paper he'd brought in with him. Duncan saw on it a typewritten list of names. "I memorized some of the names I saw on paperwork scattered across Napoli's desk," Kong explained. "Typed up this list soon as I got back to the office so I wouldn't forget them.

"Frankly, I figure Napoli dived underground to avoid somebody he's pissed off, either an irate, dissatisfied client or some broad he was banging. But if the scumbag *has* met with foul play — the secretary's convinced — I figured these names might come in handy. Gives us places to start looking for him."

Duncan nodded, indicating that he followed Kong's reasoning.

"Now, why I bring this up to you . . ." Kong pointed to a name about midway down the list. "Isn't this your guy?"

Duncan read the name. Moving slowly, he lowered his feet from his desk, took the sheet from Kong, and read it again. Then in a dry, scratchy voice, he said, "Yeah, that's my guy."

"It was scandalous. From meeting to altar took less than three months."

It was a short drive from the Barracks to Meyer Napoli's downtown office. DeeDee

166

took advantage of it to share what she'd pieced together about Elise Laird's background.

"Short courtships aren't that unusual or scandalous," Duncan observed.

"Unless a distinguished superior court judge is marrying a cocktail waitress. Riiiiight," she drawled in response to Duncan's sharp look. "Elise worked the bar at Judge Laird's country club."

"Which is?"

"Silver Tide, naturally. Anyway, after meeting her, the judge began playing golf every single day, sometimes two rounds, but spent most of his time at the nineteenth hole."

Duncan parked at the curb in front of the squat, square office building and put a sign in his windshield identifying him as a cop to avoid getting a ticket from one of Savannah's infamous meter maids. He opened his car door and got out, hoping to catch a breeze. The air was motionless, suffocating. The sun had set, but heat still radiated up from the sidewalk, baking the soles of his shoes.

"Want to hear the skinny now or later?" DeeDee asked as they approached the door of the office building.

"Now."

"The judge was a confirmed bachelor who enjoyed casual affairs with widows and divorcées with no intention of getting married. Why share the family wealth? But Elise dazzled him. He fell hard. The gossip is she screwed him silly, got him addicted to her, then refused to sleep with him again unless and until he married her."

"What the hell's taking this elevator so long?" While the air-conditioning inside the building was welcome, it did little to improve Duncan's crankiness, which he blamed on the sultry heat. He punched the up button on the elevator several times, but heard no grinding of gears indicating movement in the shaft. "Let's take the stairs. It's only two flights."

DeeDee followed him up the aggregate steps. Depressions had been worn into them by decades of foot traffic. This wasn't prize real estate. A smell of mildew clung to the old walls.

"The judge's friends and associates were shocked by the engagement," DeeDee said. "The rock he bought her — have you noticed it?"

"No."

"A marquise, reputedly six carats. I'd say that's a conservative estimate."

"You noticed?" Jewelry wasn't something

DeeDee ordinarily paid attention to.

"I couldn't help but notice," she said to his back as they rounded the second-floor landing. "Damn near blinded me this afternoon when we were in the sunroom. Didn't you notice the rainbow it cast on the wall?"

"Guess I missed that."

"You were too busy gazing into her eyes."

He stopped in midstep and looked over his shoulder.

"Well, you were," she said defensively.

"I was questioning her. What was I supposed to do, keep my eyes shut?"

"Never mind. Just . . ." She motioned him forward. He continued climbing the stairs and she picked up her story. "So, the besotted judge throws himself this big, elaborate wedding. Under the circumstances, some thought it the height of tacky and tasteless, and attributed his extravagance to his greedy and demanding bride."

Duncan had reached the third-floor landing. Ahead was a corridor lined on both sides with doors to various offices. Names were stenciled in black on frosted glass. A CPA firm, an attorney, a dentist advertising fillings for the low, low price of twenty-five dollars. All were closed for the night. But one door about midway down stood open, casting a wedge of light into the otherwise dim hallway. He could hear Kong talking to Napoli's secretary. Her voice rose and fell emotionally.

Before joining them, he wished to finish this conversation with DeeDee. He turned to face her, blocking her path. "What 'circumstances'?"

"Pardon?"

"You said circumstances made the wedding tacky and tasteless."

"The bride had no pedigree, no family of any sort. At least none turned up at the wedding. She had no formal education, no property, no trust fund, no stock portfolio, nothing to recommend her. She brought nothing to the relationship except . . . well, the obvious.

"And she wore white. A simple dress, not too froufrou, but definitely white, which some considered the worst breach of etiquette. She did, however, order personalized stationery. Good stock, ivory in color, with the return address in dove gray lettering. She sent handwritten thank-you notes on behalf of her and the judge to everyone who gave them a wedding gift. And she has a very nice script."

Yeah. Duncan had seen her script. Scowling, he said, "Are you making this shit up?"

"No, swear to God."

"Where'd you get your information?"

"The friend I mentioned. We go all the way back to Catholic school. My folks had to roll coins to pay for my tuition. Her family is very well-to-do, but we formed a bond because both of us hated the school.

"Anyway, I called her up, mentioned the shooting at the Lairds' house, which she already knew about, because it's caused such a buzz. Her mom is definitely in the know, plugged into the society grapevine. If you're into this kind of stuff, she's a reliable source."

Duncan ran his sleeve across his forehead. The cloth came away wet. "Is there more? What color was the punch at the reception?"

She frowned at him, but continued. "Mrs. Laird never fails to RSVP to an invitation whether she's accepting or declining. Evidently she picked up a few social graces when she became Mrs. Cato Laird, and she's shown surprising good taste in clothes, but she's still considered *trash* — and that word was emphasized in an undertone. She's tolerated because of the judge, but she's far from accepted. You can forget embraced."

Duncan said, "You know what this sounds like to me? It sounds like Savannah's social set found an easy target for their malice.

Here you have a bunch of snooty, jealous gossips who would give up their pedigree for Elise Laird's looks. They'd sacrifice Great-grandma's pearls in exchange for a chest like hers."

"Funny you should mention that particular attribute." DeeDee took the final steps necessary to join him on the landing. "The judge's circle of acquaintances might have overlooked her other shortcomings, even the fact that she worked in the bar at their country club. After all, it's an elite club, its membership limited to only the 'best people.' But what they couldn't forgive is what she was before becoming a cocktail waitress."

"Which was what?"

"A *topless* cocktail waitress."

8

The crepe myrtle tree was dripping moisture and so was Duncan. Elbows locked, his arms were braced against the smooth tree trunk, his body at an almost forty-five-degree angle from it as he stretched out his left calf muscle.

His head was hanging between his arms. Sweat dripped off his face onto the lichen-covered brick sidewalk in front of his town house. The sidewalk was buckled from roots of live oaks that lined the street and formed a canopy above it. He was grateful for the shade.

Breaking with tradition, he'd gotten up early and had decided to go for a run, before the sun was fully up, before it pushed the temperature from the eighties at six thirty into the nineties by nine. Even so, each breath had been a labored gasp. The air was as dense as chowder.

Most people were sleeping in this Saturday

morning. In the next block a woman was watering the ferns on her porch. Earlier, Duncan had seen a man walking his dog in Forsyth Park. Few cars were on the streets.

He switched feet to stretch his other calf. His stomach growled, reminding him that he'd forgone the carry-out fried chicken last night, opting to come straight home after leaving Meyer Napoli's office. While there, he'd lost his appetite and had skipped supper altogether.

He'd tried to get interested in a baseball game on TV. When that failed, he moved to the piano, but his playing had been uninspired and for once hadn't helped him sort through his disturbing thoughts. He'd slept in brief snatches between long periods of wakefulness. Still restless at dawn, he'd kicked off the annoying bedsheet and gotten up, his mind in as much of a tangle as it had been the previous evening.

"Detective Hatcher?"

With a start, he turned. She was standing no more than three feet away. His heart rate, which during his stretches had returned to a normal, post-exercise rhythm, spiked at the sight of her.

He looked past her, almost expecting someone to be there playing a practical joke on him. He couldn't have been more surprised had there been a rowdy group with balloons and noisemakers having fun at his expense.

But the sidewalk was empty. The woman who'd been watering her ferns was no longer on her porch. There was no sight of the dog and his owner. Nothing, not a single leaf, moved in the thick air. Only his rushing breath disturbed it.

"What the hell are you doing here?"

"Didn't you read my note?" she said.

"Yeah, I read it."

"Well then."

"It's a bad idea for us to meet alone. In fact, this meeting just concluded."

He moved toward the steps of his town house, but she sidestepped to block his path. "Please don't walk away. I'm desperate to talk to you."

"About the fatal shooting at your house?"

"Yes."

"All right. I'm interested to hear what you have to say. I have an office. Give me half an hour. Detective Bowen and I will meet you there."

"No. I need to speak to you privately. Just you."

He steeled himself against her soft-spoken urgency. "You can talk to me at the police station."

"No, I can't. This is too sensitive to talk about there."

Sensitive. A bothersome word for sure. He said, "The only thing you and I have to talk about is a dead and dissected Gary Ray Trotter."

A few strands of pale hair had shaken loose from a messy topknot. The hairdo looked like an afterthought, something she had fashioned as she rushed out the door. She was dressed in a snug cotton T-shirt and a full skirt that hung from a wide band around her hips, the hem skimming her knees. Leather flip-flops on her feet. It was a typical summertime outfit, nothing special about it, except that she was the woman inside, giving shape to the ordinary clothing.

She nodded toward the steps leading up to his front door. "Can we go inside?"

"Not a chance."

"I can't be seen with you," she exclaimed.

"Damn right you can't. You should have thought of that before you came. How'd you get here anyway?"

"I parked my car on Jones."

One street over. That's how she'd managed to come up behind him unheard and unseen until she'd wanted to be. "How'd you know where I live?"

"Telephone directory. I thought the A. D. Hatcher listed might be you. What's the *A* for?" When he didn't respond, she said, "I took a huge risk by coming here."

"You must enjoy taking risks. Like passing me the note practically under your husband's nose."

"Yes, I risked Cato seeing it, and I risked you giving me away. But you didn't. Did you show my note to Detective Bowen?"

He felt his face grow warm and refused to answer.

"I didn't think you would," she said softly.

Embarrassed and angry, he said, "What did you do, sneak out on the judge this morning? Leave him sleeping in your bed?"

"He had an early tee time." She came a step closer. "You've got to help me. Please."

She didn't touch him, but she might as well have for the heat that gathered in his crotch. *"Groin tug,"* he remembered DeeDee saying. Pretty accurate description. He wished he was dressed in something more substantial than nylon running shorts.

"I will help you," he said evenly. "It's my duty as a law officer to help you, as well as to resolve the case involving you. But not here and not now. Give me time to clean up. I'll call Detective Bowen. We'll set a time to meet. Doesn't have to be at the police station. You name the place, we'll be there."

Before he was finished, she had lowered her head and was shaking it remorsefully. "You don't understand." She spoke barely loud enough for him to hear. "I can't talk about this to anyone else."

"Why me?"

She raised her head then and looked up at him meaningfully. Their gazes locked and held. Understanding passed between them. The air shimmered with more than thermal heat.

For Duncan, everything receded except her face. Those eyes, as bottomless as the swimming hole he used to dive into head-first, although he'd been warned that doing so was reckless. That mouth. Shaped as though giving pleasure was its specialty.

Suddenly the front door of the neighboring town house opened, alarming them. Elise slipped into the recessed doorway beneath his front steps where she couldn't be seen.

"Good morning, Duncan," the neighbor lady called as she retrieved her newspaper from the porch. "You're up mighty early."

"Getting in my exercise before it gets too hot."

"My, my, you're disciplined. But, honey, you be careful of this heat. Don't overexert yourself, now."

"I won't."

She retreated into her house and closed the front door. He ducked below the steps into the damp, cavelike enclosure, surprisingly cool and dim. It served as the entrance to a basement apartment that he had rented out when he'd first acquired the town house. His last renter had skipped out, owing him three months' rent. He hadn't bothered to lease it again. He missed the additional income, but rather liked having all four floors of the town house to himself.

Elise stood in shadow with her back pressed against the door.

"I want you away from here," he whispered angrily. "Now. And don't pass me any more notes. What is this, junior high? I don't know what your game is —"

"Gary Ray Trotter came to our house to kill me."

Duncan's rapid breathing sounded loud in the semi-enclosed area. The top of his head barely cleared the low brick ceiling, where ferns sprouted from cracks in the mortar. There was scarcely room enough for two people in the confined space. He was standing close enough to feel the hem of her skirt against his legs, her breath on his bare chest.

"What?"

"I shot him in self-defense. I had no choice. If I hadn't, he would have killed me. That's what he was sent to do. He'd been hired to kill me." She'd spoken in a rush, causing the words to stumble over one another. When she finished, she paused and drew in a short but deep breath.

Duncan stared at her while he pieced together her hurried words so they would make sense. But even after making sense of them, he couldn't believe them. "You can't be serious."

"Do I look like I'm joking?"

"Trotter was a hired assassin?"

"Yes."

"Hired by who?"

"My husband."

His phone was ringing as he ushered — more like pushed — Elise through the front door. He went around her and snatched up the phone, looking directly at her as he raised it to his ear. "Yeah?"

"Are you up?" DeeDee asked.

"Yeah."

"You sound out of breath."

"Just got in from a run."

"I've had some ideas about what we learned last night."

He continued to stare at Elise with single-minded concentration. She was watching him with equal intensity.

"Duncan?"

"I'm still here." He hesitated, then said, "Look, DeeDee, I'm dripping sweat, about to melt all over the living room floor. Let me shower, then I'll call you back."

"Okay, but be quick."

As he disconnected, he realized that he'd made another ill-advised decision. Already he'd placed himself in a dangerously gray area by not telling DeeDee about the note. Now he'd omitted to tell her who was in his living room, making unreasonable claims about a crime they were investigating. In both instances, he had violated police procedure and his personal code of ethics. Somewhere along the way he knew he would be held accountable.

It made him terribly angry at the woman responsible for his misconduct and for the conflicting emotions that assailed him every time he was near her. And even when he wasn't.

As he dropped the phone back onto the end table, she said huskily, "Thank you."

"Don't thank me yet. I'm still a cop with a dead man in the morgue, and you're the lady with a smoking gun in her hand."

"Then why didn't you tell your partner that I'm here?"

"I'm feeling generous this morning," he said, with much more flippancy than he felt. "Especially toward damsels in distress." In a measured tread, he walked toward her. To her credit she stood her ground and didn't back away. "That's the angle you're playing, isn't it?"

"I'm not playing an angle. I came to you because I don't know what else to do."

"Because you see me as a sucker."

"You're a policeman!"

"Who said he wanted to fuck you!"

She was taken aback by his bluntness, but recovered quickly. "You told me that remark had more to do with my husband than with me."

"It did," he said, wondering if she believed that. Wondering if *he* did. He continued forward, forcing her to walk backward. "But when you got yourself in a jam, you remembered it. You killed a man, for reasons yet to be discovered. But, lucky you, the detective investigating the fatal shooting thinks you look good enough to eat."

By now he had her against the wall, and they were standing toe to toe. He planted his hand near her head and leaned in close. "So to turn me all squishy with sympathy and blind to your guilt, you invent this story about a killer for hire."

"It's not a story. It's the truth."

"Judge Laird wants an instant divorce?"

"No, he wants me to *die.*"

The conviction with which she spoke gave Duncan momentary pause. She took advantage of it to step around him. "Maybe you should rinse off."

"Sorry. You'll just have to put up with the stink."

"You don't smell bad, but doesn't the drying sweat itch?"

Reflexively he scratched the center of his chest. The hair there had become matted and salty. "I can stand it."

"I'll be glad to wait for —"

"Why does your husband want you dead?" he asked, speaking over her. "And why is it a big secret you can only tell me?"

She closed her eyes briefly, then opened them and said, "I came to you with this, sought you out personally, because I sensed you would be more —"

"Gullible?"

"Receptive. Certainly more so than Detective Bowen."

"Because I'm a man and she's a woman?"

"Your partner comes across as hostile. For

whatever reason, our chemistry isn't very good."

"By contrast, you think our chemistry is?"

She lowered her gaze. "I felt . . . I thought . . ." When she raised her head and looked at him, her eyes were imploring. "Will you at least listen with an open mind?"

He folded his arms over his chest, fully realizing that it was a subconscious, self-protective gesture. When she looked at him like that, her eyes seemed to touch him, and his physical reactions were as though she actually had.

"Okay, I'm listening. Why does your husband want you dead?"

She took a moment, as though collecting her thoughts. "You and Detective Bowen picked up on the alarm not being set."

"Because you and the judge had sex."

"Yes. After, I tried to get up and set the alarm. But Cato wouldn't let me leave the bed. He pulled me back down and . . ."

"I get the picture. He was horny."

She didn't like that remark. Her expression changed, but she didn't address his vulgarity. "Cato didn't want the alarm to be set that night. He wanted Trotter to get into the house. After I was dead, he could truthfully say that it was part of my routine to set the alarm and that he had prevented me from doing so. He would say that he would never forgive himself, that if only he had allowed me to leave the bed, the tragedy would have been prevented. He would assume responsibility for my murder and, by doing so, win everyone's pity. It's a brilliant strategy. Don't you see?"

"Yeah, I see. But when you were in the kitchen and heard the noise, why didn't you call 911, get help immediately?"

"I didn't know how much time I had." She answered quickly, as though she'd known he would ask that and needed to have a response ready. "My instinct was to protect myself. So I took the pistol from the drawer in the foyer table."

Duncan tugged on his lower lip as though thinking it through. "You wanted the pistol in case Trotter attacked before you could make the 911 call."

"I suppose that's what I was thinking. I'm not sure I was thinking at all. I merely reacted. I was afraid."

She dropped down onto the piano bench and covered her face with her hands, massaging her forehead with the pads of her fingers. This position left the nape of her neck exposed and Duncan's gaze found it, just as it had the night of the awards dinner. He blinked away the vision of kissing her there.

"You were afraid," he said, "but you found the courage to go into the study."

"I don't know where I got the courage. I think maybe I hoped I was wrong. I hoped that what I'd heard was a tree branch knocking against the eaves, or a raccoon on the roof, something. But I knew that wasn't it. I knew that someone was in there, waiting for me.

"I'd been expecting it for several months. Not a burglary, specifically. But *something*. This was the moment I'd been dreading." She pressed her fist against the center of her chest, right above her heart, pulling the fabric of her T-shirt tight across her breasts. "I knew, Detective. I knew." Whispering that, she raised her head and looked up at him. "Gary Ray Trotter wasn't a thief I caught in the act. He was there to kill me."

Duncan pinched the bridge of his nose and closed his eyes as though concentrating hard, trying to work out the details in his mind. Actually, he had to do something to keep from drowning in those damn eyes of hers or becoming fixated on her breasts. He wanted to haul her up against him, kiss her, and see if her mouth delivered as promised. Instead, he pinched the skin between his

186

eye sockets until it hurt like hell. It helped him to refocus. Some.

"Gary Ray Trotter hardly fits the profile of a hired assassin. Mrs. Laird." He tacked on the name to reestablish in his mind who she was.

"I can't account for that."

"Try."

"I *can't,*" she said, her voice cracking.

He crouched down in front of her, and caught himself about to place his hands on her knees. They were face-to-face now, inches apart. From this close, he should be able to detect any artifice. *Should* be able to.

"Judge Cato Laird wants you dead."

"Yes."

"He's a rich and powerful man."

"That doesn't exclude him from wanting to have me killed."

"But he hires a bargain-basement assassin to do it?" He shook his head with skepticism.

"I know it sounds implausible, but I swear to you it's true."

He searched her eyes for signs of drug-induced paranoia or hallucination. None there.

Her husband doted on her, so it was unlikely that she was trying to spice up her mundane existence by creating some excitement.

Schizophrenia? Possibly. Compulsive liar? Maybe.

There was also a chance she was telling the truth, but the odds of that were so slim as to be negligible. Knowing Cato Laird, knowing Gary Ray Trotter, it just didn't gel.

What Duncan suspected, what he believed with every instinct that had made him a good detective, was that she was trying to cover her own sweet ass, and that, because of what he'd said to her the night of the awards dinner, she was trying to use him to do it.

Why her sweet ass needed covering, he didn't know yet. But, based on what he and DeeDee had discovered last night at Meyer Napoli's office, he would soon find out. In the meantime, it pissed him off that she thought he'd be that easily manipulated, and he wanted to tell her so.

For the moment, however, he would continue to play along. "Implausible is precisely the word I would use, Mrs. Laird. I can't wrap my mind around the idea of the judge contracting with someone as inept as Trotter."

"All I know is this. If I hadn't fired the pistol when I did — and I did *not* fire first, no matter how many theories to the contrary you parade out — I would be dead. Cato would have told this story about a burglar caught in the act, and who wouldn't believe him?"

She stood up so suddenly she almost knocked Duncan over. "He's a superior court judge. He's from a wealthy, influential family. It would never occur to anyone that he would hire someone to kill his wife."

"It certainly would never occur to me."

His inflection brought her around slowly to face him.

He shrugged his shoulders. "I mean, he would have to be crazy, wouldn't he?"

"What do you mean?"

"Come on," he said, his voice as taunting as his smile. "What man in his right mind would want to get rid of a wife like you?"

She regarded him closely for several long moments, then said softly, with defeat, "You don't believe me."

His smile vanished and his tone turned harsh. "Not a goddamn word."

"Why?" Her voice had gone thin. If he didn't know better, he would swear she was genuinely perplexed.

To keep himself from falling for it, he gave a sardonic snuffle. "The judge has got himself a live-in topless waitress."

She took a deep breath, the defeat settling on her even more heavily. "Oh."

"Yeah. Oh."

"Because I worked topless, I'm automatically a liar, is that it?"

"Not at all. But it doesn't particularly lend credence to your story, does it. I mean, the judge can look his fill, touch his fill, screw his fill, and he doesn't have to tip. You're every man's wet dream."

She continued to stare at him for several beats, her hurt and bafflement rapidly turning to anger. "You're cruel, Detective."

"I get that a lot. Especially from people who I know are lying to me."

She turned her back to him and marched toward the door. He crossed the room in three long strides and caught her as she was fumbling with the latch. He grabbed her by the shoulders and brought her around.

"Why'd you come here?"

"I told you!"

"The judge hired Trotter to kill you."

"Yes!"

"Bullshit! I've seen him with you. He can't keep his hands off you."

She tried to wrestle herself free of his grasp, but he wouldn't let her.

"You're his prized possession, Mrs. Laird. That six-carat marquise diamond on your left hand took you off the market and bought him whirlpool baths and second helpings in bed. And it's all legal, tied up neat and proper with a marriage license. Now, why would he want you dead?"

She remained silent, glaring up at him.

"Why? If I'm to believe this sob story, I've got to hear a motive. Give me one."

"I can't!"

"Because there isn't one."

"There is, but I can't risk telling you. Not . . . not now."

"Why?"

"Because you wouldn't believe me."

"I might."

"You haven't believed anything else."

"That's right. I haven't. Cato Laird has no motive whatsoever to kill you. You, on the other hand, have an excellent motive for coming here and trying to win me to your side."

"What are you talking about?"

"You don't want me to learn the truth of what went down that night."

"I —"

"Who was Trotter to you?"

"No one. I'd never seen him before."

"Oh, I think you had. I think you knew who was waiting for you in the study, and that's why instead of calling 911, you armed yourself with a loaded pistol, which, by the way, you knew how to fire with deadly accuracy."

He lowered his face close to hers and said in a stage whisper, "I'm this close to booking you for murder." That wasn't true, but he wanted to see what kind of reaction he would get.

It was drastic. She went very still, very pale, and looked very afraid.

"Well, I see that got your attention," he said. "Do you want to change your story now?"

She redoubled her efforts to break his hold. "Coming here was a mistake."

"You're damn right it was."

"I was wrong about you. I thought you would believe me."

"No, what you thought was that if you showed up at my place looking as inviting as an unmade bed, I'd forget all about poor old Gary Ray Trotter. And if one thing led to another and we wound up in the sack, I might drop the investigation of that shooting altogether."

Furious now, she pushed hard against his chest. "Let go of me."

He shook her slightly, demanding, "Isn't that the reason for this secret meeting?"

"No!"

"Then tell me what possible motive Cato Laird could have for wanting to kill you."

"You wouldn't believe me."

"Try me."

"I already did!"

She practically flung the words into his face and met his hot gaze with one equally fierce. Neither of them was moving now, except for the rise and fall of her chest against his. He was dangerously aware of that, damnably aware of every point at which they were touching.

"The only reason I came here was in the hope of convincing you that my husband is going to kill me." Her voice was gruff with emotion, vibrating through her body into his. "And because you don't believe me, he'll do it. What's more, he'll get away with it."

9

"His second tee time was at eleven ten," DeeDee said asshe tossed several Goldfish into her mouth.

She and Duncan were in the bar of the Silver Tide Country Club. It was crowded on this Saturday afternoon. Ralph Lauren's summer line was well represented. Duncan felt conspicuous in his sport jacket, but his shoulder holster and nine-millimeter would have made him even more so.

Among the drinkers were local political figures, private-practice physicians, real estate developers who made a killing off snowbirds who migrated by the thousands to the South's golf course communities each winter, and Stan Adams, the defense attorney who represented a coterie of career criminals, the most notable being Robert Savich. Adams did a double take when DeeDee and Duncan strolled in, then studiously pretended they didn't exist.

Which was just as well, Duncan thought. In his present mood, he wouldn't trust his temper if the lawyer had goaded him about his famous client. Although Savich had kept a low profile since the mistrial, not for a moment did Duncan think he was on hiatus from his criminal activity. He was just smart enough to exercise extreme caution till things cooled down.

Duncan also figured that he was plotting the best time and most effective way to strike at him. He knew Savich would. He'd practically promised it that day in the courtroom. It was only a matter of time before he did. Unfortunately, as a law officer, Duncan couldn't go after Savich without provocation. He had to sit and wait and wonder. That probably tickled Savich no end.

After seeing their badges, the Silver Tide's bartender had served him and DeeDee their drinks gratis. The bar had a nice ambience — dark wood, potted jungle plants, brass lamps, peppy but unobtrusive music. The lemonade Duncan had ordered was hand squeezed. The air conditioner was sufficient to keep the heat and humidity on the other side of the oversized, tinted windows. The view of the emerald golf course was spectacular. It wasn't a bad place in which to spend a sweltering afternoon.

Duncan would rather be anywhere else.

DeeDee dusted Goldfish crumbs off her fingers, remarking, "That must be Mrs. Laird's replacement."

She nodded toward the attractive young woman who was delivering a tray of drinks to a foursome of middle-aged men. They stopped discussing their golf game long enough to ogle and flirt.

"She and the judge have been married nearly three years," Duncan said. "Isn't that what you told me? The club's probably gone through a dozen or so waitresses since Mrs. Laird worked here."

DeeDee turned toward the doorway as another group of men wandered in. Cato Laird wasn't among them. "He played two rounds back to back, starting before seven this morning. If you can believe anybody would voluntarily do that."

"You'd have to hold a gun to my head."

"You don't like golf?"

"Too slow. Too passive. Not enough action."

"Playing piano isn't exactly an action sport."

"I don't play piano."

"Right." She consulted her wristwatch. "The guy at the desk said he should be finishing soon."

At least Elise hadn't been lying about her husband's tee time. She'd said he had an early one.

She'd said a lot of things.

The last thing she'd said was that her husband was going to kill her, and that when he did he would get away with it, and that it would be Duncan's fault because he hadn't believed her.

Then she had squirmed out of his grasp, and with a slam of the front door she was outta there. Her squirming had left him with a doomed erection and respiration more labored than it had been during his five-mile run through the syrupy dawn air. He'd been so angry and frustrated — at her for roping him into her little drama, at himself for allowing her to — he'd actually banged his fist against his front door.

It still hurt. He flexed and contracted his fingers now in an attempt to ease the throbbing ache.

After that burst of temper, he'd gulped a two-liter bottle of water while standing in a cold shower, which had reduced his sweating and deflated his hopeful but disappointed dick. Then he'd called DeeDee as promised.

She had arrived at his town house at the

appointed time, bringing with her a selection of breakfast muffins and two cups of carry-out coffee, because, as she said, "Yours sucks."

She had a plan mapped out for the day. Grouchily, he had reminded her that he was the senior member of the team, the men*tor.* "You're the men*tee."*

"You want to pull rank, fine. What do you think we should do?"

"I think we should confront the judge with what we learned last night. I'm anxious to see his reaction."

"That's what I just said."

"That's why I agreed to let you be my partner. You're smart." Rummaging in the carry-out sack, he frowned. "Didn't you get any blueberry?"

He kept up the familiar, squabbling repartee on purpose, because all the while they were in the town house, he'd been afraid that DeeDee would sense that Elise had been there. The moment he'd admitted his partner through the front door, he'd expected her to stop in her tracks and say, "Has Elise Laird been here?" Because to him, the essence of her was that powerful and pervasive. He could feel it, smell it, taste it.

Halfway through his second muffin, he

suggested that DeeDee call the Silver Tide Country Club.

"How come?"

"It's Saturday. I have a hunch the judge is playing golf."

DeeDee's call to the club confirmed what Elise had told him. DeeDee was informed that the judge was playing his second round. Their plan was to be waiting for him when he finished, catch him relaxed and unaware, spring on him what they'd learned last night, and gauge his reaction.

They'd been waiting now for more than half an hour. Duncan was about to order another lemonade for lack of anything better to do when the bartender approached them. "The front desk just called, said to tell y'all Judge Laird is having lunch on the terrace."

He pointed them through a pair of French doors at one end of the bar that opened onto a loggia. At least that's what the bartender called the open-air walkway enshrouded by leafy wisteria vine. "It'll lead you straight to the dining terrace."

"I hope it's shaded," Duncan muttered.

The tables set up on the terrace were indeed shaded by white umbrellas as large as parachutes, trimmed in braided cotton fringe. Each table had a pot of vibrant pink geraniums in its center. The judge was seated at one, a cloth napkin folded over his linen trousers, a glass of what looked like scotch at his place setting.

He stood up as they approached. They'd been notified that he was on the terrace, but he'd also been notified that the detectives had been waiting on him in the bar. He wasn't surprised to see them, but he didn't appear to be particularly perturbed either.

Of course, he had an audience. Duncan was aware of curious glances cast at them by other diners as the judge shook hands with him and DeeDee in turn and offered them seats at the table.

"I'm about to have lunch. I hope you'll join me."

"No, thank you," DeeDee said. "We had a late breakfast."

"A drink at least." He signaled a waiter, who hastened over. DeeDee ordered a Diet Coke. Duncan switched to iced tea.

"How was your game? Games?" DeeDee amended herself, giving the judge her best smile. The women around her were in sundresses and halter tops, showing off well-tended tans and pedicured toenails. If she was self-conscious of her dark, tailored suit and sensible walking shoes, she gave no outward sign of it. Duncan admired her for that.

The judge modestly admitted to an eighty on the first round, an eighty-four on the second. While she was commending him, he noticed Duncan whisking a bead of sweat off his forehead.

"I realize it's warm out here, Detective Hatcher." He smiled apologetically. "I defer to my wife, who sometimes gets cold in air-conditioning. She prefers the terrace to the sixty-degree thermostat inside."

Duncan was about to point out the obvious — that his wife wasn't there — when he experienced a sinking sensation in his gut that coincided with the judge's brightening smile. "There she is now."

He stood up, tossed his napkin onto the table, and went to meet Elise as she followed a hostess toward the table. Cato Laird embraced her. She removed her sunglasses to return his hug, and over her husband's shoulder she spotted Duncan, standing beside his chair at the table, not even realizing that he'd stood up.

Her eyes widened fractionally, but they shifted away from him so quickly that he thought he might have imagined it. As soon as the judge released her, she replaced her dark glasses.

She was dressed in dazzling white, as though to color-coordinate herself with the umbrellas. It was a simple, sleeveless blouse and a loose skirt. The outfit was tasteful. Correct. Unrevealing.

So why did his mind immediately venture to what was underneath?

He felt like he'd just sustained a kick in the balls. For the second time that morning, the unexpected appearance of Elise Laird had left him feeling untethered, which was an alien emotion for him.

Up till now, his involvements with women were dependent on his mood, his level of interest, and time available. The women's interest was usually guaranteed. He never took undue advantage of his appeal, and had even managed to remain friendly with most of his former girlfriends. On the rare occasion that his interest wasn't reciprocated, he took it in stride and didn't look back. No woman had ever broken his heart.

He'd proposed marriage only once: to a childhood friend with whom he remained very close. The catalyst had been the celebration of his thirty-fifth birthday. He pointed out to his friend that they weren't getting any younger, that both of them had remained single for a reason, and that maybe the reason was that they should be married to each other. He took her "Are you *nuts?"* as a no, and came to realize what she already knew. They loved each other dearly, but they weren't in love.

He'd had more women than some men. Much fewer than others. But *never* a principal in an investigation. And *never* a married woman. Elise Laird was both. Which made this uncommonly strong attraction to her not only unfortunate but absolutely forbidden.

Tell that to his tingling sensors.

The judge escorted her to the table and held her chair. He sat down and replaced his napkin in his lap, then secured his wife's hand, holding it clasped between both of his. "I called Elise and asked if she would like to join me for lunch. I thought it would be good for her to get out." He smiled at her affectionately.

"Obviously I thought so, too. Thank you for the invitation." She returned his smile, then looked across the pot of geraniums at DeeDee. "Hello, Detective Bowen."

"We hate to bust in on your lunch date, Mrs. Laird. But I suppose it's just as well you're here, too. We were about to tell the judge about the latest development."

Elise turned quickly to Duncan. "What development?"

"Something that came up last night." As he said the words, he realized he was assuring her that he hadn't told DeeDee about her visit to his town house. Her evident relief didn't make him feel any better about it.

The waiter arrived with his and DeeDee's drinks, along with a lemonade for Elise. It was like the one he'd had at the bar, except that hers was served with a strawberry as big as an apple impaled on a clear plastic skewer.

The judge ordered another scotch. The waiter asked if they'd like to see menus, but the judge said he would let him know when they were ready. DeeDee requested a straw, and the waiter apologized profusely for not bringing one. These distractions allowed Duncan and Elise time to exchange a long look. At least she was looking toward him. He couldn't see her eyes through the dark shades.

Trickles of sweat were rolling down his torso, and it wasn't only because of the heat. The tension at the table was palpable. Even though they were all going through the motions of being relaxed in one another's company, pretending that this was a casual gathering without agenda, they all knew better.

No one said anything until DeeDee's straw had been delivered. She thanked the waiter with a nod, peeled away the wrapper, and stuck the straw in her glass. "Judge Laird, are you familiar with Meyer Napoli?"

He laughed. "Of course. He's been in my courtroom too many times to count."

"As a defendant?" DeeDee asked.

"Only as a witness," the judge replied unflappably.

"For which side?"

"Depending on the case, he's testified both for the prosecution and the defense."

"Who is he?"

"Sorry, darling." The judge turned to Elise. "Meyer Napoli is a private investigator."

"Had you never heard of him, Mrs. Laird?"

Elise removed her sunglasses and gave DeeDee a level look. "If I had, I wouldn't have asked."

A crease had formed between the judge's eyebrows. "You mentioned a development."

The judge addressed the statement to Duncan, so he responded. "Meyer Napoli has gone missing. It became official this morning. It's been over twenty-four hours since anyone has seen or heard from him. His secretary, who seems to be the person closest to him, is convinced that he's met with foul play."

The judge was hanging on every word. When Duncan stopped with that, he raised his shoulders in a slight shrug. "I hate to hear that. I hope the secretary is wrong, but how does this relate to us? What possible bearing could a private investigator's disappearance have to do with what happened in our home night before last?"

Duncan locked gazes with Elise. "We found Gary Ray Trotter's name among papers on Napoli's desk."

Her lips parted slightly, but Duncan didn't expect her to say anything and she didn't. In fact, no one spoke for a noticeable length of time.

Finally DeeDee cleared her throat. "The detective investigating Napoli's disappearance noticed Trotter's name on a memo. Actually a personalized Post-it. 'From the desk of Meyer Napoli.' The detective thought it coincidental, Trotter being recently . . . deceased. He knew that Detective Hatcher and I would find that interesting, and he was right. We talked to Napoli's secretary last night."

"And?" the judge asked.

"And nothing," DeeDee replied. "Trotter had never made an appointment with the secretary to see Napoli. She doesn't remember anybody by that name coming to the office, but, of course, that doesn't mean that Trotter and Napoli didn't meet somewhere else. Obviously they did. Or had contact of some kind, because the secretary confirmed that the handwriting on the Post-it was Napoli's." She looked back and forth between the judge and Elise.

The judge chuckled. "You've thrown out a lot of assumptions, Detective. Any one of which could be fact. Or none of them. Perhaps Napoli heard through the grapevine that Trotter had died during the commission of a crime. His name rang a bell and Napoli jotted it down to remind himself of it later. Who knows where their paths crossed? Maybe Trotter owed him money." He gave her a gentle, somewhat patronizing smile. "Aren't those as plausible as your assumptions?"

Duncan wouldn't have been surprised if DeeDee had launched herself across the table and knocked him on his condescending ass. He wouldn't have blamed her, either.

Instead she gave the judge an abashed grin. "Detective Hatcher chides me constantly for jumping to conclusions. It's one of my character flaws. However, this time he agrees with me."

The judge looked toward Duncan for elaboration. Duncan nodded him back toward DeeDee, indicating that she still had the floor.

She said, "Meyer Napoli has questionable ethics, but he's reputed to have a mind like a steel trap. He wouldn't need to jot himself a reminder note. He wrote down Gary Ray Trotter's name for a reason."

Elise had been following this exchange silently, but with undivided attention. "Are you implying that . . ." Then she shook her head in confusion and asked, "What are you implying?"

"I think I can answer that, darling," the judge said. "They're implying that there's a connection between Napoli and Trotter, and by association, between Napoli and us. Is that it, Detective Bowen?"

In view of his testiness, she responded with remarkable calm. "We're not implying anything, Judge Laird. But it struck us as coincidental that less than twenty-four hours after he was fatally shot in your home, Trotter's name would show up on the desk of a private investigator who, also coincidentally, has been reported missing. It's strange, to say the least."

"I'm sorry. I can't explain the strangeness of it."

DeeDee continued with her typical doggedness. "Please try, Judge Laird. If there was a connection, no matter how long ago or how remote, it might explain how Trotter chose your house to break into. It seems far-fetched that he chose it at random. That's a quirky element of this case we just can't reconcile. Why did he choose you to burglarize?"

"Unfortunately, Mr. Trotter is in no position to tell us, so I doubt we'll ever know," he said. "He could have heard of us through Napoli, I suppose, if they had a history, even in passing. Beyond that, I can't venture a guess."

"You've never had direct contact with Napoli?"

"Not outside my courtroom. My wife had never even heard of him until a few minutes ago."

"Is that right, Mrs. Laird?"

"That's right. I'd never heard of Napoli. Nor Trotter."

DeeDee sucked the last of her Coke through the straw. "Then I guess we've wasted your time. Thanks for the Coke." She reached for her handbag, and the judge took that as a signal that the interview was over.

"They make an excellent shrimp salad," he said. "I'd be pleased to treat you."

DeeDee thanked him for the offer but declined. The judge stood up and shook hands with each of them. DeeDee smiled down at Elise and told her good-bye.

Duncan was about to walk past Elise's chair, when he hesitated, then extended his hand to her, almost as a dare to himself. First of all, it's not easy to shake hands with a woman who's given you a hard-on, and knows it. And second, he was thinking about what had happened the last time they shook hands. "Good-bye, Mrs. Laird."

She hesitated, then took his hand. Or did she *clutch* it? "Good-bye."

It was more difficult to pull his eyes away from hers than it was to withdraw his hand. He followed DeeDee inside the clubhouse and through the dining room. They waited to speak until they reached the lobby and she had given the parking valet her claim check. "What do you think?"

Before Duncan could answer, Stan Adams strolled up to them. "Well, Detective Sergeant Hatcher, I see that you and Judge Laird have kissed and made up since Savich's trial." He grinned at Duncan, then greeted DeeDee.

"Is this what you do in your spare time?" she asked. "You hang out in the country club until Savich commits another murder?"

The lawyer laughed, but became serious when he turned back to Duncan. "Are you investigating the fatal shooting at the judge's house the other night? What was the guy's name, Trotter?"

Duncan wasn't surprised that Adams knew of the incident. As DeeDee's society friend had said, the story had created a buzz. It also had been reported in the newspaper. Subtly. The judge, who usually basked in the glow of media attention, must have called in a favor with the managing editor.

The story had been buried on page ten and details were practically nonexistent. According to the brief story, Trotter was an intruder who had made an attempt on Mrs. Laird's life, then later died. He could have died of a heart attack or cholera for all the reading public knew.

Stan Adams said, "I thought it was self-defense. How come y'all are on it?"

"Like you, we're always trying to drum up business." Duncan's grin was as affable as the attorney's, but equally insincere.

Adams knew he would get no more information from them. "Well, if it turns out that Mrs. Laird needs a good defense lawyer, I hope you'll recommend me."

He walked away and had reached the double entrance doors, when DeeDee called out to him. "Oh, Mr. Adams, I just remembered. Your dentist called. It's time you had them bleached again." She tapped her front teeth.

The attorney fired a finger pistol at her and said, "Good one, Detective. Good one."

Then he was gone. DeeDee muttered under her breath, "Asshole. Every time I think of that mistrial . . ." She made a snarling sound and clenched her fist.

Duncan was looking at her, but not really seeing her. His mind wasn't on Savich or his oily attorney. It was on the judge. His cream-colored linen trousers, his cool and courteous manner.

"A drink at least. . . . They make an excellent shrimp salad."

He hadn't even broken a sweat.

"Here's the car," DeeDee said and started for the door. Realizing he wasn't following, she turned back. "Duncan?"

But his mind was still on the judge. Tucking his wife's hand into the crook of his elbow. Possessively.

"Tell me what possible motive Cato Laird

could have for wanting to kill you."

"You wouldn't believe me."

Making a split-second decision, Duncan told DeeDee to go on ahead. "I'm going to stick around here for a while."

10

Judge and Mrs. Laird took their time over lunch. Duncan had been spying for — he checked his wristwatch — one hour and twelve minutes.

DeeDee had argued against leaving, reminding him that if she did, he would be on foot. He said he would call a taxi and insisted that she return to the Barracks and see if they'd received the ballistics reports on the two weapons fired in the Lairds' house.

Primarily they'd been interested to learn if Trotter's pistol had been used in the commission of another crime, but had decided, what the hell, while they were at it, it wouldn't hurt also to test the one Elise Laird had fired.

Duncan had also asked DeeDee to check with Kong for any updates on the missing Meyer Napoli. "If Kong's not in today, call his cell phone." It was possible that the PI's secretary was wrong and that her boss was shacked up with a new girlfriend. If so, this case, and by extension Duncan's life, would be made simpler.

After seeing DeeDee off, Duncan returned to the country club's casual dining room and claimed a table that provided an unobstructed view of the Lairds' table on the terrace. The judge had ordered a roast beef sandwich, Elise the recommended shrimp salad. Two parties had stopped at their table to chat briefly, but their exchanges had been mostly with the judge.

There were few lapses in the Lairds' conversation with each other, and both seemed totally absorbed in it. After they finished the meal and were waiting for their plates to be removed, he stroked her bare arm from shoulder to elbow, and once he raised her hand to his mouth and kissed the palm of it.

For the whole seventy-two minutes that Duncan had been observing them, he saw nothing to indicate that the judge wanted her dead. Instead, Cato Laird seemed like a man totally besotted with a woman that he might want to fuck to death, but otherwise had no intention of killing.

When the judge signaled for the check, Elise excused herself and left the table. She didn't see Duncan when she passed through the dining room in which he was seated. He got up and followed into an empty hallway, and saw her go into the ladies' room.

He waited, he paced, keeping a nervous eye on the terrace. The judge signed the tab, pocketed his receipt, and left the table. "Shit!" Duncan hissed. But, fortunately for him, before the judge reached the door, a group of men at another table hailed him and he stopped to chat. Duncan hoped they had a lot of breeze to shoot.

Sensing movement behind him, he turned. When Elise saw him she drew up short, half in, half out the door.

"Trying to decide whether to brave it or slink back into the powder room?"

She stepped into the hallway and let the door close behind her. "I thought you'd left."

"And I thought you might have changed your mind."

"About what?"

"That crock of crap you told me this morning."

"It's the truth."

"Now, now. Is that any way to talk about your husband after he treated you to that romantic lunch?" Her eyes flashed angrily. She tried to sidestep him, but he didn't let her, saying, "I caught your trick with the cherry."

For dessert, both she and the judge had ordered iced coffee drinks with whipped cream on top. The judge had offered his to her.

"I watched you lean in and pull that cherry off the stem with your lips. And I gotta tell you, Mrs. Laird, it was sexy as all get-out. The kind of come-on a man can't mistake. Even with a tinted window between us, I got aroused."

"I have to act as though everything is normal."

"You normally do things for him like sucking that fruit into your mouth?" He snuffled a laugh. "That bastard's got all the luck."

Color spread up from her chest into her cheeks. Whether the blush was from embarrassment or anger, he didn't know, but he suspected she was getting angrier by the moment. She barely moved her lips, pushing the words through her teeth. "Don't you understand? If I tip my hand, I'll be dead."

"Hmm. Okay. Makes sense. And the reason your husband wants you dead is . . . why?"

She remained silent.

"Oh, right." He snapped his fingers. "He's got no motive."

"He has motive."

Duncan moved closer, lowered his volume, but increased the intensity of his voice. "Then tell me what it is."

"I can't!" She looked beyond his shoulder, registering alarm. "Cato."

He turned to see Laird entering the dining room. He spotted them immediately. Coming back around to Elise, Duncan said, "You know, I could just ask him if he wants you dead and why."

He'd tossed that out there just to see her reaction.

Her face drained of the color that had filled it only moments before. The fear looked genuine. Either that, or she was very good.

No. Please.

Reading the soundless words on her lips worked more effectively than if she'd spoken them aloud.

"Detective Hatcher, I thought you'd left hours ago." As he joined them, the judge was smiling, but Duncan could tell that he wasn't pleased to see him. He divided a curious look between him and Elise. "You seemed awfully engrossed in your conversation."

She said, "I bumped into him on my way out of the restroom."

"And I told Mrs. Laird that I needed to talk to you. Alone." Out the corner of his eye, he watched Elise. He saw her breath catch.

"I'm scheduled for a massage," the judge said. "You can follow me to the locker room and talk to me while I change."

"Downstairs?" The judge nodded. "I'll wait for you there. Mrs. Laird."

Duncan looked directly into her eyes, then turned away.

The judge came into the locker room a few minutes later. "She's still not herself," he said without preamble. "On edge. Jittery. I think it will take a while for her to recover from this."

"It was frightening."

"And then some. My locker's over here." He led Duncan down a row of lockers and when he reached his, he began working the combination lock.

Duncan sat down on a padded bench nearby. "Before I forget, I charged my lunch to your account. Club sandwich and iced tea. You know they charge for refills? I also added a twenty-five percent gratuity."

"Twenty-five percent? Very generous of you."

"I figured you would have a soft spot for

the waitstaff here."

The judge gave him a wry look. "You've done some background investigation."

"That's my job."

"So you know Elise's employment history. I suppose you also know what she did before she came to work here at the club." He stated it, he didn't ask. "Do you think less of her for it?"

"No. Do you?"

Duncan's brusque comeback got the judge's ire up. The heavy lock thumped against the blond wood locker when he let go of it. Angrily, he turned toward Duncan. Then, rather than take issue, the fight went out of him. He sat down on the far end of the bench.

He shook his head with self-deprecation. "I'm a cliché, I suppose. Actually, I *know* I am. I knew I would be when I began seeing Elise, not just here at the club, but actually taking her out."

"Sleeping with her."

The judge raised one shoulder in a negligent shrug. "Gossip spread like wildfire among my friends and associates. Our affair became the talk of this club. Then of all Savannah. Or so it seemed."

"That didn't bother you?"

"No, because I was in love. Still am. As

much as possible I ignored the gossip. Then a 'well-meaning friend,' " he said, forming quotation marks with his fingers, "invited me to lunch one day for the express purpose of informing me that the cocktail waitress I was seeing wasn't a suitable companion for a man of my position and social standing. He told me where she'd worked before the Silver Tide. He expected me to be shocked, horrified. But I already knew about Elise's former employment."

"You'd done your own investigating."

"No, Elise had told me herself. She was honest about it from the start, which made me love her all the more. Acquaintances of mine who overtly snubbed her, I consider *former* friends. Who needs friends like that? But it bothers Elise. She thinks I've suffered because of our marriage."

"Have you?"

"Hardly."

"You haven't run for reelection since you married her. Voters may side with those former friends of yours."

"I'm sure anyone running against me will dredge up her past. We're prepared for that. We'll own up to it and dismiss it as irrelevant, and it is."

"Except that it may cost you the election. Will you be okay with that?"

"Which would you choose, Detective? A judgeship, or Elise in your bed every night?"

Duncan realized he was being tested. He held the judge's stare for several beats, then deadpanned, "What's the choice?"

The judge laughed. "My feeling exactly." He raised his hands, palms up. "In the eyes of many, I'm a man to be pitied, a fool for love. I fell in love the moment I saw her, and I'm still in love."

Duncan stretched his feet far out in front of him and studied the toes of his shoes. "I believe that." He waited several seconds, then said, "What I don't believe is that you had no dealings with Meyer Napoli except inside your courtroom." He gave up the study of his footwear and turned his head. "You lied about that, Judge."

Duncan won the staring contest. The initial challenge in the judge's glare slowly evaporated. Finally he sighed with resignation. "You're good, Detective."

"Thanks, but I don't need your compliments. I need an explanation for why you lied."

He took a deep breath, let it out slowly. "So Elise would never know that I had hired Meyer Napoli to follow her."

Duncan had thought it might be something like that. "Why did you?"

"I'm not proud of it."

"That's not what I asked."

"I can't believe I resorted to hiring that —"

"Unscrupulous sleazoid," Duncan said, impatient because he wasn't getting a straight answer. "Napoli didn't come with character references, but you hired him anyway. You hired him to follow your wife. Why?"

"Again, it's a cliché. The oldest reason in the world." He looked sadly at Duncan.

"She was having an affair."

The judge's vulnerable smile was out of character for the man Duncan knew, but he supposed a cuckold was about as humble a creature as there was. "I had my suspicions," he replied. "But before I tell you anything more, I want you to understand that it happened months ago. Last year."

"Okay."

"It's over and has been for some time," he insisted.

"Okay."

Satisfied that he'd made that crucial point, the judge said, "For months I tried to ignore the signs."

"She had a headache every night?"

He chuckled. "No. Even at the height of my suspicion, Elise was as passionate in bed as she'd always been. Our sexual appetite for each other never waned."

Duncan tried to keep his expression impassive, but even if he couldn't, the judge wouldn't have noticed. He was submerged in his recollections.

"It was other things," he said. "Classic signs. Telephone calls she pretended were wrong numbers. Rushing in late for meals without having a good excuse for her lateness. Time unaccounted for."

"Sounds like an affair to me." Duncan was perversely glad to cast doubt on Cato Laird's confidence in his wife's sexual appetite for him.

"I thought so, too. It got so that the thought of her in bed with another man dominated my mind. It's all I could think about. If it was true, I had to know it, and I had to know who he was."

"So you retained the services of Meyer Napoli."

"Which indicates the degree of my desperation. I refused to go to his office. We met late one evening at a driving range. I practiced my swing while he asked pertinent questions. Did I know who her lover was? How long had the affair been going on?"

He shook his head with disgust. "I couldn't believe I was discussing my wife with a man of his caliber. His phraseology, the vulgar terms he used, I couldn't even apply to Elise. It all seemed so wrong, I started to call the whole thing off right then.

"But," he continued with a sigh, "I'd gone that far, and not knowing was making me miserable. So I gave him the required advance on his fee, and left. That's the last time I ever saw him."

Duncan had been following the story, practically anticipating every word the judge was going to say before he said it. It was a familiar story that he'd heard many times over the course of his career. Passion led to possessiveness and jealousy, which spawned all sorts of mayhem, and frequently murder.

But the judge's last statement didn't gibe with the rest of it. "The last time you ever saw him? Napoli didn't come through?"

"No, he came through," the judge said tightly.

"She *was* having an affair?"

"I don't know."

"Sorry, Judge. You've lost me."

"Napoli got back to me," he explained. "He had followed Elise to several clandestine meetings. He identified the man. He had times and places. But . . . but I stopped him there. I didn't want to hear any more. I didn't want it confirmed to me that she was having an affair."

"That's not the usual reaction, Judge," Duncan said slowly. "The husband may be the last to know, but he usually *wants* to know."

"Knowing wouldn't have made a difference in how much I loved her. I wouldn't have left her."

But would you want to kill her over it? Duncan thought. "So you never knew the details of those clandestine meetings?"

Looking pained, the judge shook his head. "No."

"Did she ever know you'd found her out?"

"No. I didn't want her to know I'd stooped so low as to have her spied on. I was ashamed of it. Besides, a few weeks after I dismissed Napoli, it ceased to matter."

Duncan frowned with misapprehension. "She stopped seeing the guy?"

"In a manner of speaking." After a beat, he said, "Elise's rendezvous were with Coleman Greer."

Even at midafternoon, the White Tie and Tails Club was as dark as midnight except for the strobes flashing on the girl dancing onstage, and the pink and blue neon stars that twinkled on the ceiling.

Well ahead of the Saturday night crowd

that would pack the place after nightfall, a handful of customers were seated along the semicircular stage, nursing drinks and enjoying the dancer's performance. Only one was whistling and rowdily applauding the act.

Savich occupied a booth at the rear of the club, far enough from the stage that he could tolerate the volume of the music. He was seated on the banquette against the wall, facing out into the room. He never left his back exposed.

He watched as a hostess in black leather bra and chaps escorted Elise through the maze of empty tables and chairs. When they reached the booth, he indicated that Elise sit down.

"Can I bring you anything, Mr. Savich?" the hostess asked.

He looked at Elise inquisitively. She shook her head. "Are you sure?" he asked. "Pardon my saying so, but you look a bit strung out, like you could use a drink."

"No, thank you."

He waved the hostess off. "We're not to be disturbed."

As she walked away, she put an extra jiggle into her bare buttocks. "She's new. Trying to work her way up to dancer." With a smile, he returned his attention to Elise. "I'm sorry you had to come all this way. Kenny said you sounded urgent."

"Thank you for seeing me on such short notice."

"Speaking of short notice, you haven't given me much time, Elise. You must be in a bigger hurry than you indicated the other day."

"I am."

"Why? What's happened?"

"Nothing. Nothing else. I was just anxious to hear back from you."

He knew she was lying, but he let it pass. He rather enjoyed her vain effort to hide from him that a new development had upset her. Otherwise she wouldn't have called him on a Saturday afternoon, sounding "positively distraught," according to Kenny. She'd been so eager to see him, she had agreed to join him at the topless club where they'd first met. It was miles — and light-years — away from her home, her country club, her present life as Mrs. Cato Laird.

"How does it feel to be back in the White Tie and Tails?"

She took a cursory look around. "It seems like a long time ago since I worked here."

"You're still missed."

"I seriously doubt that. I've seen the new talent."

"But some girls leave a lasting impression." He let the words hover there between them for several moments. Then he leaned back against the padded banquette and reached for his gold cigarette case and lighter.

"Savich, were you able to —"

"Hatcher."

She flinched with surprise. Possibly with something else. "What about him?"

He took his time lighting his cigarette. "Is he still the detective on the case?"

"As of an hour ago."

"Duncan Hatcher, the *homicide* detective," he said. "Why does he continue to investigate the shooting?"

"He said there were loose ends that needed clearing up before he could close the case."

"And you believed that?" he asked, disdainful of her naivete. "He's digging, Elise. He's trying to find fault with your self-defense story."

"He's talking to us, that's all."

"You and your husband?"

"He's talking privately with Cato right now."

"Why privately?"

She took a deep breath, exhaled it along with the words "I don't know."

"Hmm. So that's what got you spooked."

"I'm not spooked."

Her short tone caused him to arch an eyebrow, reminding her that she had petitioned his help, and that she wasn't speaking to him with the deference that a petitioner should. It worked. She backed down.

"Were you able to do what I asked?" she said.

He blew a puff of smoke toward the ceiling. It swirled in the glow of the pink and blue neon stars. "Tell me, Elise, what do you think of Duncan Hatcher?"

"He's tough, just as you warned me he would be."

Lowering his voice, he said, "Maybe a more interesting question would be to ask what Detective Hatcher thinks of *you*, sweet Elise?"

"He thinks I'm a liar."

"Really?" Fixing his steady blue gaze on her, he idly stroked his cheek. "Are you?"

"No."

"Then you've got nothing to be afraid of."

"I'm afraid Detective Hatcher will continue to think I'm a liar."

"Change his mind," he said simply.

"I've tried. He didn't believe me."

"That doesn't surprise me. He can be charming. Or so I've heard. But under those

230

rough-and-tumble Southern-boy, tawny good looks, he's all cop. A fucking cop," he said, letting his enmity toward Hatcher show.

"He won't close your case as long as there's one iota of doubt in his mind that it was self-defense. Hear me well, Elise. He'll leave no stone unturned. And he would delight in finding something nasty beneath one. There's bad blood between him and your husband."

"I know about that. Most recently they clashed over your mistrial."

"Yes, and for that, Hatcher would enjoy embarrassing you and the judge. Publicly if he can. But that's nothing compared to the plans he has for me. He's a man with a mission. He never forgets, and he never gives up."

"I sense that about him."

"You're in a dangerous spot, Elise."

She pulled her lower lip through her teeth. "He doesn't have any evidence to disprove self-defense."

"But Hatcher has been known to build cases out of virtually nothing, and, with the exception of my recent trial, he gets convictions and they stick despite appeals." Sounding almost mystified, he said, "The man actually believes in what he's doing. Right versus wrong. Good versus evil. He's a crusader. True blue. Seemingly incorruptible."

Snagged by his own words, he thought, *Seemingly* incorruptible.

Through the haze of cigarette smoke, he studied his guest. She really was a lovely girl. Classiness and sexiness in one stunning package. A tantalizing combination. Which even a crusader would find hard to resist.

The smile originated with his thoughts and spread slowly across his face. "Sweet Elise," he said, his voice dripping honey, "let's talk about this favor you asked of me. You'll be pleased to know I've already granted it."

11

When the high-pitched warning beep signaled that a main door of the house had been opened, Elise swiftly left her bedroom. She'd reached the top of the stairs when she heard the chirps indicating that the code was being entered. Cato was home.

He appeared in the foyer below her. She called his name. He looked up and saw her poised there at the top of the staircase. "Hello, Elise. You're still awake. Why am I not surprised?" Rather than coming upstairs, he proceeded down the foyer, disappearing from her sight.

Her meeting with Savich had left her shaken. Meetings with Savich always did.

When she'd returned home, the house was empty. Mrs. Berry was off on Saturday evenings, so Elise hadn't expected to find her there. But it surprised her that Cato wasn't. As evening turned to night, she called his cell phone several times but got only his voice mail. He hadn't responded to her messages.

It was uncharacteristic of him not to keep in touch. It was also a bad omen. She passed the entire evening and into the wee hours in a state of high anxiety, wondering what Duncan Hatcher had told her husband.

She quickly descended the staircase. "Cato?"

"In here."

She followed the direction of his voice into the kitchen. As she entered, he turned to face her with a butcher knife in his hand. She looked from the gleaming blade to him. "What are you doing?"

"Making a sandwich." He moved aside, allowing her to see the ham on the countertop, along with fixings for a sandwich. "Would you like one?"

"No, thank you. Wouldn't you rather have breakfast? I could make —"

"This will do." He turned back to carving slices off the ham.

"I've been calling your cell phone all night. Where have you been?"

"Didn't you get the message?"

"No."

"I asked the receptionist at the club to call and tell you that I'd been invited into a high-stakes poker game and that it would be late before I got home."

He reached around her for the telephone, depressing the button that put it on speaker. The static dial tone indicated that no messages were waiting to be retrieved. "Hmm. That's odd. She's usually reliable."

Elise doubted he'd ever made the request to the receptionist. If he'd wanted to assuage her concern, why hadn't he just called her himself?

He built his sandwich and halved it with the butcher knife. "What time did you get home, Elise?"

"Around five, I think. After leaving you at the club, I got a call from the dress shop, telling me that my alterations were ready. I went to pick them up, did some shopping."

That much was the truth. But before going to the boutique where she often shopped, she'd driven to the edge of town to the White Tie and Tails Club to meet Robert Savich.

He put the sandwich on a plate and carried it to the table in the breakfast nook. "Buy anything?"

"A pants suit and a cocktail dress."

He licked a dollop of mayonnaise off his finger. "You can model them for me later."

"I think you'll approve." She sat down across from him, studying his expression, trying to make eye contact, which he was avoiding. "You've never stayed out all night before. Not once since we've been married."

He chewed a bite, blotted his mouth. "Not since we've been married have I had a day like yesterday."

He took another bite, chewed, blotted his mouth again. And he still wouldn't look at her. She was in an agony of suspense.

"My conversation with Duncan Hatcher was most upsetting."

Her throat closed.

"Even Kurt the massage Nazi couldn't work out the tension in my shoulders and back." He took another bite.

"What did he say to upset you? What did you talk about?"

"Our relationship. Yours and mine, not mine and his," he added, flashing a humorless smile.

"Our relationship is none of his business."

Then he did look at her directly. "Maybe he thinks it is."

"Why would he?"

"You tell me."

"I'm sorry, Cato. I don't know what you mean."

"Twice now I've come upon you two with your heads together, lost in conversation. The night of the awards dinner. And again today at the club. I didn't like it either time."

"The night of the awards dinner, he was a stranger asking me for change. Today, when I left the powder room, he was in the hallway, looking for you."

His dark eyes searched hers. "I wasn't that hard to find today. And he could have asked a dozen other people for change that night. He's deliberately putting himself in your path. You must sense why, Elise. You can't be that naive."

"You think Hatcher is interested in me romantically?"

He scoffed. "No romance about it. He'd love to sleep with you only to make a fool of me."

Cato had stayed away all night out of pique and jealousy. She felt her lungs expanding with relief.

"That would be the ultimate payback for my putting him in jail, wouldn't it?" he said. "To seduce my wife?"

Although Duncan Hatcher had said as much to her the night of the awards dinner, she smiled and shook her head. "You're wrong, Cato. He has no interest in me outside his investigation."

"What man could be immune to you?"

She smiled at the flattery.

"But what about you, Elise?"

"What about me?"

"What do you think of the detective?"

"You have to ask?" She placed her hand on his forearm where it rested on the table and squeezed it lightly. "Cato, since the night of the shooting, Detective Hatcher has done nothing but bully me. I dread the sight of him."

His features relaxed. "I'm glad to hear that." Pushing aside his plate, he reached across the table and stroked her cheek. "Let's get in the pool."

"Now? You just ate, and it's nearly dawn. Aren't you too tired to swim?"

"I'm wide awake. Apparently, so are you. And I didn't say I wanted to swim."

He took her hand and they walked outside together. She reached for the switch that turned on the pool light and the fountain in its center. He said, "No, leave them off."

He stripped to the skin. It was evident that he wasn't at all tired. He came to her, untied the belt of her robe, and pushed it off her, along with her slip-type nightgown. He ran his hands over her, possessively and with more aggressiveness than usual.

She responded as expected, but her mind was elsewhere. She was thinking of Duncan Hatcher. He hadn't betrayed her to Cato. Did that mean he believed her? Even a little?

Cato took her hand and pulled her down the steps into the pool. He clasped her around the waist and waded in until she could no longer touch bottom. As her body floated against his, she noticed that here in the center of the pool, the water was deep and dark. Like secrets.

"Duncan?"

He grunted a semblance of a response.

"That's yours."

"Hmm?" He lifted his head from the pillow and opened one eye.

"Your cell phone is ringing."

"Oh. Thanks." He rubbed sleep from his eyes with one hand and reached for his phone with the other. He flipped it open. "Yeah?"

"Guess who they hauled in last night and is still in a holding cell?"

"What time is it?" he grumbled, trying to pull the numbers of his alarm clock into focus.

"Gordon Ballew."

"Who?" How was it that DeeDee didn't sound groggy even on a Sunday morning?

"Gordie," she exclaimed. "Gordie Ballew. One of Savich's boys."

"Got it." With a groan, he rolled onto his back and sat up. The woman who'd been sleeping beside him was already up and across the room, gathering her clothing and pulling it on. "What did he do?"

"Who cares?" DeeDee said. "So long as we can get him in a bargaining mood. Meet you there."

She hung up before he could say anything more. He returned his cell phone to the nightstand and swung his feet to the floor. "Sorry, but I've got to run. Work."

"It's all right," she said as her head popped through the neck of her top. "I've got to go anyway."

He'd met her in one of the hot spots in Market Square last night. She was petite, pretty, and brunette. That was the sum total of what he knew about her. She'd told him some stuff, but the music had been loud, the drinks strong, and he hadn't really been listening anyway because he hadn't been that interested in anything she had to say.

He remembered none of their conversation, not even her name. He didn't specifically recall inviting her back to his place, but he must have. As for the act itself, the only thing he remembered was that he'd made sure to use a condom. Immediately after rolling off her, he'd fallen into a deep sleep.

It wasn't like him to bring home a

stranger, but he'd thought that having sex, even mindless, meaningless sex, would keep him from thinking about Elise Laird.

Silly him.

His distraction must have made itself felt, and that was unfair to any woman. Feeling rotten about it, he said, "Look, you don't have to race out of here just because I do. Stay. Sleep. Make yourself at home. If this doesn't take too long, we could go out for breakfast later."

"No, thanks."

"Well, then, leave your number." He tried to inject his voice with a bit of enthusiasm, but was pretty sure he didn't achieve it. "I'd like to see you again."

"No, you wouldn't, but that's cool." She moved to the door, where she turned back and smiled. "You were a good fuck. Savich said you probably would be."

Gordon Ballew was one of those individuals who'd been doomed before he took his first breath. His mother hadn't been sure who his father was and didn't consider that it mattered much since she didn't keep the baby anyway.

Not even a barren couple desperate for an adopted child wanted one with a cleft palate, so from the delivery room Gordie had

241

become a dependent of the state, shuttled from one foster home to another until he was old enough to exit the system and try and fare on his own.

His entire life had been an endless round of ridicule and abuse because of his deformed mouth, defective speech, and diminutive size. Today, at age thirty-three, he might weigh 120 pounds, sopping wet.

Duncan would have felt sorry for Gordie Ballew, except for the fact that he had never tried to improve his lot, had never attempted to reverse the downward spiral that his life had been since he wormed his way out of the birth canal.

Once he bade his last set of foster parents good-bye, he'd been in and out of penal institutions so many times that Duncan figured Gordie considered a cell block home.

He watched him thoughtfully on the video monitor in the room adjacent to the interrogation room, where a member of the counter-narcotics team had been hammering away at him for several hours, without success.

"Has the DEA been notified?"

Another narcotics officer shook his head and gave a sour harrumph. "They've been such bastards, blaming us 'cause Freddy

Morris got popped, I figure we don't owe them this."

"*Did* we cause Freddy Morris to get popped?" Duncan asked.

"Hell no," the officer answered with soft but angry emphasis.

"Savich got him past you. All of you."

The officer grunted agreement without accepting blame. "I don't see how he coulda done that."

"He couldn't," Duncan said. "Not without help."

The narc looked at him sharply. "From inside? Are you saying somebody on our team ratted us out?"

It was a touchy subject, one that had been broached before to a barrage of protests from both teams. It was something constantly in the back of Duncan's mind, but he dropped it for now.

"Where's Ballew's lawyer?"

"Waived one," the narc told him. "Said he was ready to sign a confession, go straight to jail, do not pass Go."

DeeDee had been practically dancing in place with impatience. "Are we going to get a crack at him, or what?"

"Be our guest," the narc said.

As they moved toward the interrogation room, DeeDee asked Duncan, "Were you good cop or bad cop last time we questioned Gordie?"

"Bad. Let's stick with that."

"Okay."

The narc opened the door to the small, dreary room and told the interrogating officer that he had a phone call. "Besides, homicide has a hard-on for our boy here."

"Homicide?" Gordie squeaked.

The narcotics officer stepped aside to make room for Duncan and DeeDee. "He's all yours. Y'all have fun." He strolled out and let the door swing closed behind him.

"Hi, Gordie." DeeDee took a seat across the small table from him. "How are you?"

"How's it look?" he mumbled.

Ignoring the attitude behind his reply, she introduced herself by name. "Remember us? My partner there is Duncan Hatcher."

"I know you." Gordie cast a wary glance toward Duncan where he was leaning up against the wall, arms folded over his chest, ankles crossed.

"Didn't the narcs get you anything to drink? What would you like?" She moved as though to get up.

"Sit down, DeeDee," Duncan said. "He doesn't need anything to drink."

DeeDee frowned at him with feigned asperity and dropped back into the chair.

"You picked the wrong time to get busted, Gordie. Duncan's pissed. He had plans for this morning, but now he's here with you."

"Don't let me keep you, Detective."

The con's cheeky courage was short-lived. He shriveled under Duncan's hard glare. "Let's stop screwing around," he said to DeeDee, "book him for murder two, and I can be on my way."

"The guy died?" Gordie squealed. "He wasn't bleeding that much. Swear to God it was an accident. I didn't mean to hurt him that bad. He said something about my lip. I was high. It happened before I realized. Oh Jesus. Murder two? I'll confess to assault, but . . . Oh Jesus."

"Relax, Gordie." Duncan's somber tone and the sinister way in which he pushed himself away from the wall and sauntered toward the table didn't inspire relaxation.

Gordie Ballew began to cry, his knobby shoulders bobbing up and down.

"Duncan, he needs a Kleenex," DeeDee said kindly.

"No, he doesn't." Duncan sat down on the corner of the table.

Gordie wiped his running nose on his sleeve and looked up at him with patent fear. "He *died?* I barely swiped him with that broken bottle."

"The guy you assaulted last night was treated and released."

Gordie sniffed loudly. He gaped up at Duncan, then looked at DeeDee, who nodded encouragingly. "Then how come y'all're talking murder two?"

"Another case, Gordie. Freddy Morris."

His face, flushed with anxiety moments before, turned pale. He licked snot off his misshapen upper lip. His eyes began to dart between them, wild with fear. "You're crazy, Hatcher. I didn't have nothing to do with Freddy Morris. Me? You kidding?"

"No. I'm not kidding. You want to change your mind about that lawyer?"

Gordie was too upset for that to register. "I . . . I never shot nobody. I'm scared of guns. They make me nervous."

"That's why we're not charging you with first degree. We don't believe you made poor Freddy lie down in that marsh, cut out his tongue, and then popped him in the back of the head with a forty-five." He pretended to fire a pistol and made a loud noise with his mouth.

Gordie flinched. "I gotta go to the bathroom."

"You can hold it."

"Duncan," DeeDee said.

"I *said,* he can hold it."

She looked at Gordie with sympathy and raised her shoulders in a helpless shrug.

"Look, Gordie," Duncan said, "we know, those narcs outside know, the Feds know, we all know you gave Freddy Morris over to Savich."

"Are you nuts? *Savich?* He scares me worse than guns. If Freddy had been smarter, he would have been scared of him, too, and kept his trap shut."

Duncan looked over at DeeDee with a complacent grin, as though expecting her to congratulate him for scoring a point. Too late, Gordie realized that he'd given himself away. Immediately he tried to rectify it. "At least that was the word on the street. I heard that Freddy Morris, uh, you know, was in conversation with y'all. I didn't have personal knowledge of it."

"I think you did, Gordie," Duncan countered smoothly.

"No," he said, shaking his head adamantly. "Not me. Un-unh."

He squirmed in his chair. He wiped his damp palms on the thighs of his grimy blue jeans. He blinked hard as though clearing his vision.

Duncan let him stew for a moment, then said, "Tell me about Savich."

"He's a tough customer. So I hear. I only

know him by reputation."

"You work for him. You cook and sell meth for him."

"I peddle some dope now and then, yeah. I don't know where it comes from."

"It comes from Savich."

"Naw, naw, he's a mechanic, ain't he? Makes machines or something?"

"You think I'm queer, Gordie?" Duncan asked angrily.

"Huh? No!"

"Is that what you think?"

"No, I —"

"Then stop jerking me around. You're not clever enough to outsmart me. You're one of Savich's most reliable mules. We've got schoolkids who testified at your last trial, Gordie, remember? They said under oath that they go to you for a sure score."

"I admitted to dealing every now and then. Didn't I?" He turned to DeeDee, frantically seeking her backing. "Didn't you hear me just admit that?"

"You're far too humble, Gordie," Duncan said. "Savich depends on you to make addicts, future customers, out of children. You've introduced them to meth. You've got them raiding their folks' medicine cabinets for boxes of Sudafed. You're an asset to Savich's operation."

The little man swallowed hard. "Far as I know, his operation is that machine shop."

"Are you afraid that if you talk about him to us, you'll wind up like Freddy Morris did?"

"What I heard? I heard . . . I heard Freddy bought it over some woman. A guy, I don't know who, did Freddy on account of he was banging his old lady. That's the story I got."

Duncan spoke softly, but with menace. "You're jerking me around again."

"I ain't gonna say nothing about Savich," the convict cried out, his voice tearing. He tapped the tabletop with a dirty, chipped fingernail. "You'll never get me to say anything, neither. Not now, not ever."

He appealed to DeeDee, whining, "Where's the confession? Those first cops that arrested me? They said it would take a while to draw up the paperwork. Left me waiting here, and in come those narcs, harassing me. Now y'all. Just let me sign a confession saying I went at that guy last night with a broken beer bottle. Lock me up. I'm ready to take my punishment."

"We could make a deal —" DeeDee began.

"No deal," he said with a stubborn shake of his head.

"We could make this assault with a deadly

249

weapon charge disappear like that." Duncan snapped his fingers an inch away from Gordie's flat nose. "Or we could lay several others on you. We might even ratchet this charge up to attempted murder. You'd do more time."

"Fine. You do that, Hatcher," he said, calling Duncan's bluff. "I'd rather go to jail than . . . Nothing," he finished in a mumble.

"Than wind up like Freddy Morris?" DeeDee asked.

But even her seeming gentleness didn't make a dent. She and Duncan continued with him for another half hour. He would not incriminate Savich. "Not even for spittin' on the sidewalk," he avowed.

They left him alone, not showing their weariness until they were out of the room. DeeDee slumped against the wall. "I've never had to try so hard to be nice. I wanted to wring it out of the little jerk."

"You were convincing. Even I thought you were turning soft." Duncan was teasing, and she knew it, but neither was in the mood for levity.

"Y'all did the best you could," said one of the narcotics officers gazing morosely at the video monitor, where Gordie could be seen gnawing at a bleeding cuticle. "Can't say as I blame him. Freddy Morris had his tongue cut out. Savich got to Chet Rollins in prison. Somebody crammed a bar of soap down his gullet. He died slow. And that Andre . . . what was his last name?"

"Bonnet," Duncan supplied.

"No sooner had the DEA struck a deal with him to testify against Savich than his house blows up, his mother, his girlfriend, and her two kids in there with him."

"Savich got a hung jury and that screwup ADA ruined us for a retrial," Duncan said. "He got away with killing five people. The baby was three months old."

"We thought we had Morris locked down tight," the narc said, taking out his frustration on his chewing gum. "That Savich is one smart sumbitch."

"He's not that smart," Duncan growled. "We'll get him."

"Doesn't look like we're going to get him with Gordie Ballew's help," the second narc said.

"Even if he made a deal with us, Gordie isn't a good candidate." They all looked to Duncan to elaborate on his statement. "First off, he's scared shitless of Savich. He'd give himself away before you could set up the sting. Secondly, he's resigned to spending most of his life behind bars.

"In fact, I think he wants to. Why would

he risk dying violently by ratting out Savich, when he can be guaranteed three squares a day and a home where everybody else is just as bad off as he is? For someone as pathetic as Gordie, that's about the best deal available."

They all muttered agreement of sorts. Duncan and DeeDee left the others to wrap up getting Gordon Ballew's confession to the assault charge.

"Who do we know I could get to sweep my house for electronic bugs?"

By tacit agreement, Duncan and DeeDee had regrouped in his office. She was opening a can of Diet Coke when he asked his surprise question, nearly causing her to spill the drink.

"You think your house is *bugged?*"

He told her about his overnight guest.

She listened, her mouth slack with disbelief. "Duncan, you stupid —"

"I know, I know." He raised his hands in surrender. "I was an idiot. I confess. But it happened. Now I've got to do some damage control."

"She could have killed you."

"Savich is saving that particular honor for himself. This was just another taunt, his way of letting me know how vulnerable I am."

"Was she worth it?"

"I don't even remember," he admitted. "I didn't know anything until you called and woke me up. When she dropped that bombshell, I bounded out of bed and chased her downstairs. She struck off down the sidewalk at a run. I would've gone after her, but realized I was bare-assed, unarmed, and that possibly that was the plan. Savich could be waiting out there in the bushes, ready to pop me the minute I appeared. So I went back in, got my weapon, and searched the house, thinking he might be inside. He wasn't, of course. Far as I can tell, nothing was disturbed."

"Except her side of the bed."

"You couldn't resist, could you?"

"Did she take anything?"

"I don't think so. I didn't notice anything missing. But while I was asleep she might have planted some kind of surveillance equipment in my house. I want it checked as soon as possible."

Within half an hour, they'd run down a surveillance expert who sometimes did contract work for the department. He promised to do the sweep later that morning. Duncan gave him the location of his hidden key as well as the code of his alarm system, which he'd changed before leaving the house.

As he concluded the call, DeeDee stacked her hands atop the mass of steel wool that passed for hair, and sighed with resignation. "What am I going to do with you?"

"Send me to my room?"

"Did you at least use a condom?"

"I did."

"Well, that's something. And you're being conscientious about setting your house alarm. That's good. But from now on, get references before you take a woman to bed, okay? If Savich is —"

"Cato Laird lied to us."

She dropped her hands from her head. "I thought we were discussing Savich."

"Now we're discussing the Lairds."

"You learned something yesterday after sending me away from the country club, didn't you? You fibbed when you told me nothing came out of your locker room chat with the judge. Waste of time, you said."

He'd called her on his cell phone from the taxi he'd taken from the club to his town house. "Yeah, I fibbed."

"How come?"

"Because I wanted to take an evening off."

"Look how that turned out," she said drolly.

"I knew if I even hinted that I'd learned something potentially important, neither of us would have had a night off, and in my estimation, both of us needed one."

"I could kill you," she snarled. "But not before you tell me what you found out."

"He lied to us about Meyer Napoli."

He recounted everything Judge Laird had told him about hiring the private investigator to follow Elise. "He's so crazy in love, he doesn't care that their marriage has cost him the respect of friends and associates. Possibly even his next reelection. They share a passionate sexual appetite for each other. Even though she had an affair, he loved her too much to confront her with it. It's over. History. The marriage remains intact. Everyone's happy."

"She doesn't know that he hired Napoli?"

"He says she doesn't."

"So the lady was telling the truth when she claimed she'd never heard of him."

"I guess."

"And the judge is convinced the affair is over?"

"Oh, it's over, all right."

DeeDee looked at him quizzically.

"Mrs. Laird's lover was Coleman Greer."

12

They went to breakfast in a downtown coffee shop near the Barracks. DeeDee ordered an egg white omelet with fat-free cheese, fresh tomatoes, and whole wheat toast. Duncan had two eggs over easy, fluffy grits with melting butter, sausage links, and biscuits with gravy.

"That's so unfair," DeeDee remarked as she watched him dunk a piece of sausage into the gravy. "I'm having a voodoo doll made of you. Every time I have to eat low-cal, I'm going to poke a needle into it."

"It'll catch up with me one of these days."

"I doubt it," she muttered. "It's genetic. One of God's meanest jokes on the human race is that you get to see what you're going to become. Have you seen my mother's butt? Broad as a barn."

"But she's not wrinkled."

"Because her face is as round as a pie plate. I'm seeing them today." Visits with her parents always put her in a bad and self-critical mood.

"You'll eat well there."

"But not until we've gone to the cemetery and paid homage to precious Steven." Then she placed her palm against her forehead and rubbed it hard. "Listen to me. My brother is dead, I'm alive, and I'm resenting *him?* What kind of person does that make me? A terrible person, that's what."

"Look, if you'd rather have this conversation with yourself alone, I can leave and come back later."

She shot Duncan a wry smile. "Sorry. But you know how I hate those pilgrimages to Steven's grave. Mom sobs. Dad turns as silent as the headstone. As we leave, he looks at me and I know what he's thinking. He's thinking why, if he had to lose one of his children, it had to be Steven."

"That's not what he's thinking."

"Oh, yeah? Then why does he make me feel like I'm a colossal disappointment?"

"He just doesn't know how to show you how proud he is. He loves you." This is what Duncan always told her, but he knew she didn't believe it. He wasn't sure he believed it himself.

DeeDee's brother had been killed in a car accident a week before his high school graduation. DeeDee, several years younger, had taken it upon herself to fill her brother's shoes, or try. Two decades after the tragedy, her parents were still mourning him and she was still trying to make up for their loss and win the love they had lavished on her dead sibling, their fair-haired child.

Her father had been a career military man. So straight out of college DeeDee had joined the Marines. She'd had a perfect service record, but it had failed to impress her father. She declined to reenlist when her stint was up and signed on with the SPD instead. Working her way up through the ranks, she'd made detective in record time, asked for VCU, and got it.

She had a natural aptitude for police work, and seemed to thrive on it. But Duncan often wondered if her career choice was yet another attempt to prove to her parents that she could do a difficult job as well as, or better than, any man. As well as, or better than, Steven could have.

Her goal-setting and overachieving were admirable. But the quest for excellence that made her a good cop also made her a discontented individual. Never satisfied with her performance, she was constantly striving to do better. She worked to the exclusion of everything else. She had few friends and took even fewer occasions to socialize. She scorned the very idea of a romantic relationship, saying that it wouldn't be worth the effort required to make it work, and if by some miracle it did work, it wouldn't coalesce with her career.

Many times Duncan had pointed out how lopsided her life was and urged her to give it some balance. But obsession was a tough adversary to argue against. Once a person became that grafted to something, it ruled her life, governed her decisions, and ultimately could lead to calamity.

His mind stumbled and fell over that last thought.

Whose obsession had he been thinking about? DeeDee's or his own? He'd been dangerously close to obsessing over Savich. Now, Elise Laird.

"Duncan?"

DeeDee jarred him out of the disturbing introspection. "Huh?"

"I said let's talk about Elise Laird's affair with Coleman Greer."

Swell.

"That hunka hunka burning love," she said, in tune to the Elvis song.

"I didn't know you were such a fan."

"Duh."

"Good ballplayer."

"Good? All-Star, Duncan. For the three seasons he was with the Braves."

"I know the statistics. Better than you, I bet," he added, wondering why he was suddenly feeling so cross with the world, and with DeeDee in particular. Could it be because she thought Coleman Greer was a hunka hunka burning love, and, apparently, so had Elise?

"What are your thoughts on their affair?" DeeDee asked.

Stalling, he signaled the waitress to refill his coffee cup. The question went unanswered until their plates had been cleared away and he was sipping the fresh brew.

"It hasn't been confirmed that they had an affair." Even as he said that, he knew DeeDee's reaction would probably be volatile. It was.

"Oh, please! Give me a break. A woman has secret meetings with Coleman Greer, and you don't think they were doing the nasty thing? What else would they have been doing?"

He couldn't think of a plausible alternative to the nasty thing.

She said, "Let me tell you what I think."

"I never doubted that you would."

"I think the chances are very good that Mrs. Laird lied when she said she'd never heard of Meyer Napoli. No, let me finish," she said when she saw that he was about to interrupt. "She copped that innocent act for our sake as well as for her husband's. I think she somehow discovered that Napoli was following her. She figured it had to have been her husband who hired him to do so. And she confronted Napoli."

"You're outdoing yourself, DeeDee. Jumping to conclusions without having anything to back them up. Zilch. Zero."

"Hear me out."

He shrugged and indicated for her to continue.

"She confronts Napoli, who, we know, has the morals of a maggot. She pays him more than her husband does. He returns to Cato empty-handed. . . . What?" she asked when Duncan began shaking his head.

"Laird told me that Napoli brought him evidence of the affair, but he refused to hear it or see it, remember?"

She gnawed on that for a moment, then said, "Okay, then maybe Napoli went to her. Later. After the judge had dismissed him. He shows her pictures, video, some kind of proof of her cheating. Tells her that maybe her husband is no longer interested in the material, but others would be. Media, perhaps. Coleman Greer is news, et cetera.

He blackmails her. It's not beyond Napoli to double-dip like that."

"No, but where does Gary Ray Trotter factor in?"

"Messenger boy."

"She shot the messenger?"

"Something like that."

Duncan was reluctant to admit that all day yesterday, after his conversation with the judge, his thoughts had clicked along the same track. Cato Laird had lied about knowing Meyer Napoli outside the courtroom. Elise could have lied just as easily, and perhaps more convincingly.

"Your scenario isn't without merit," he said. "But as long as we're being creative and playing make-believe —"

DeeDee made a face at him.

"— let's look at it from another perspective. Let's say that Napoli had been blackmailing the judge. He's got the goods on the judge's wife and her famous baseball-player lover. The judge may not want to know the lurid details, but you can bet the public does."

"To avoid exposure, the judge pays Napoli to keep his wife's affair a family secret," DeeDee said.

"Exactly. His Honor is playing both ends against the middle. He doesn't want the dirt on his wife to become public, and he doesn't want his wife to know he's got the dirt." He closed his eyes to better concentrate.

"What?" DeeDee said after a time.

The scenario he'd constructed moved him only a hair's breadth away from believing Elise's allegation. But he had to be very careful how he presented it to DeeDee. "What if . . ."

"What?" she pressed.

"What if Judge Laird isn't quite as forgiving and forgetful of the affair as he wanted me to believe? What if it's been eating at him? A cancer on the marriage, on his love for his wife, on his ego and manhood?"

DeeDee frowned. "He'd have to be one damn fine actor. He seems to worship the ground on which she treads."

"I'm only playing 'what if?' " he said irritably.

"Okay. Go on."

"The night of the shooting, he kept her in bed, didn't let her set the alarm."

"We don't know that he *kept* her in bed."

He did. At least that's what Elise had told him. "Let's assume."

"Wait," DeeDee said, holding up her hand like a traffic cop. "Are you saying . . . ? What are you saying? Where are you going with this? That Trotter wasn't simply Napoli's go-between? That he was there for a more nefarious purpose?"

Duncan shrugged as though to say it was possible, wasn't it? "He had a pistol, which he fired."

"Gary Ray Trotter? An enforcer? Some kind of hired gunman sent to put pressure on Judge Laird?"

"Or Mrs. Laird."

"I hate to speak disrespectfully of the dead, but, Duncan, come on. Gary Ray Trotter, hired assassin?"

"You don't think that idea has legs?"

"Not even stumps."

Actually, neither did he. The more he thought about it, the less likely it seemed that a man of Cato Laird's intelligence and resources would hire a chronic screwup like Trotter to do his killing for him. Elise Laird was playing him for a chump. He just didn't know why. And he was furious with himself for giving her any credence at all.

But why would she make up a story like that? *To protect herself from prosecution, stupid.*

Why would she come to him with it? Even stupider. He had lust in his heart and she knew it.

But, dammit, she'd seemed genuinely scared when he said he might simply ask

Cato what motive he could have for wanting his wife dead. Was that motive her affair with Coleman Greer?

"Shit!"

"What?" DeeDee asked in response to his expletive.

"I don't know what. I've gone round and round on this thing and still all we've really got is a fatal shooting that doesn't add up. It's . . ."

"Hinky."

"For lack of a better word. But the deeper we go, the less —"

"It looks like self-defense."

"But nothing we have contradicts self-defense."

"Then why are we spending so much time on it?"

"I don't know."

"Yeah, you do."

Yeah, he did, but he wasn't yet willing to tell DeeDee about Elise Laird's note, her visit to his town house, and her allegation that her husband had hired Gary Ray Trotter to kill her.

"We're not closing the book on it because of our intuition. We both feel we're missing something," she said. "And that something could mean the difference between A: a woman protecting herself from a home intruder."

"Or B: a homicide."

"A significant difference." She watched the waitress serve another diner a slice of coconut cream pie. "If Elise Laird eats like that, I'll kill myself."

"You don't like her, do you?"

"I hate her," she said bluntly. "Isn't it enough that she looks like Helen of Troy and lives a life of luxury in a frigging mansion? It's just too much to take that she also got to see Coleman Greer naked."

"That's not hate, that's jealousy."

"Before, it was jealousy," she said. "It's graduated to hate now that I know about her and Coleman Greer."

"We need to confront her about that." Duncan swore to himself that his interest in Elise's affair with the baseball player was strictly business. It could be integral to their investigation. He needed to see her reaction when Greer's name was mentioned. But *only* because her reaction could be telling and therefore important to the case. Honest.

"I couldn't agree more," DeeDee said. "We need to ask her about it, let her know that we know." Her eyes narrowed the way they did when she was at the shooting range, taking aim at a target. "I particularly want to know if she was responsible for his suicide."

13

Shortly after noon on Monday, DeeDee bounded into Duncan's office. "I just got off the phone with her. She'll be here in five minutes."

"That soon?"

"That soon. I got her on her cell. She was out running errands, said she'd come straight here."

After breakfast, they had decided to give themselves, as well as Elise Laird, a free Sunday. DeeDee had gone to her parents' home for dinner. She called it "paying penance."

He'd gone to his gym in the afternoon and worked out, including fifty laps in the pool. He spent the remainder of the day at home, which the electronic surveillance guy had told him was bug-free. He was only mildly relieved to hear it.

Savich hadn't sent the woman to plant any bugs, but to send a message: Savich could get to him whenever he was good and ready, and, as Duncan had feared, he probably wouldn't see it coming.

He'd watched TV, worked a crossword puzzle, played the piano. These pastimes didn't require one to be armed with a lethal weapon. Nevertheless, he'd kept his pistol with him. He'd slept with it.

He'd thought about Elise. More than was good for him.

When he and DeeDee arrived at the office this morning, they'd discussed how they were going to handle the upcoming interview with Elise. It would be tricky to question her about her affair with Coleman Greer without revealing that they'd learned of it through her husband. Duncan didn't want to incur the judge's wrath if he could avoid it.

"Did she ask what we want to talk to her about?" he asked DeeDee now.

"I told her it was a delicate subject and that we wanted to protect her privacy as much as possible."

"Huh. She didn't pursue it?"

"Nope."

"She say anything about the judge?"

"Only that she intended to ask him to join us."

"Shit."

"But I dissuaded her, again hinting that she would want to keep this confidential."

"He'll have our hides if he finds out about it."

DeeDee said, "I'm banking she won't be the one to tell him. If Judge Laird is right, she never knew that he had knowledge of her affair. Why would she confess it to him now?"

"It may be the lesser of two evils. She may own up to the affair if she's faced with an indictment."

"Admit to committing adultery, but deny murdering Trotter."

"Not a tough choice," he said. "Especially if your husband has already forgiven you."

"Hubby also knows the ins and outs of murder trials," DeeDee said. "He knows the best defense attorneys, and price wouldn't be an issue. The judge could save her skinny tush."

But would he? Duncan wondered. Not if Elise's claim that he wanted to kill her was true.

"We could clear up a lot of this if we could talk to Napoli," DeeDee remarked, breaking into his thoughts.

"Kong says he's got no leads. They can't even locate his car. No airline ticket or bus ticket."

"Boat rental?"

Duncan shook his head as his desk phone buzzed.

"Maybe Napoli was raptured, taken straight to heaven."

"That was going to be my next guess." He answered the phone and was informed that Mrs. Laird had arrived and was in the lobby. He covered the mouthpiece. "Where should we do this? Interrogation room?"

"Let's keep it as friendly as possible," DeeDee suggested. "How about right here?"

He told the receptionist that Detective Bowen would come down and escort Mrs. Laird to the VCU. While DeeDee was gone, he wedged another chair into his cramped office, then caught himself checking his shirttail and straightening his necktie. What the hell? he thought querulously. He didn't have a date with her; this was an interrogation.

DeeDee was chattering like a magpie, making friendly small talk as she led Elise down the space that separated the detectives' desks. Elise, on the other hand, didn't say anything until she reached the open door of his office. "Hello, Detective Hatcher."

"Thank you for coming on such short notice."

He offered her a chair. DeeDee took the other. He sat down at his desk. "We —"

"Should I call a lawyer?"

"If you like," he replied.

She glanced at DeeDee, then back at him. "Before you ask me a question, I have one for you."

"Fair enough."

"Why are you investigating the shooting at my home as though it's a homicide?"

"We're not," DeeDee said.

But Elise's gaze didn't waver from his. "What do you know, or think you know, that prevents you from accepting that I shot that man in self-defense?"

"If you polled the murderers in prison, Mrs. Laird, probably ninety-nine percent of them would claim they killed in self-defense. We can't simply take their word for it."

"Nor mine, it seems."

The softened pitch of her voice hinted that she was referring to more than just the question of self-defense. He hadn't taken her word about Cato Laird wanting her dead, either. "Nor yours," he said.

She took a steadying breath. "Why did you ask me to come here today?"

"What about the attorney?" DeeDee asked.

"First, tell me what this is about."

"Coleman Greer."

Caught completely off-guard, she breathed out in a gust. *"What?"*

"You knew the late Coleman Greer, All-Star first baseman for the Atlanta Braves."

She darted a look toward Duncan, then addressed her nod to DeeDee. "I knew him well. We were friends."

"Friends?"

"Yes."

No one said anything for several moments. Duncan and DeeDee waited to see if she would elaborate, but she appeared shell-shocked. Finally she looked at Duncan. "What about Coleman?"

Before he could answer, DeeDee said, "He was an amazing athlete."

"He was very talented."

"Were you a fan?"

"More his friend than a fan. I don't follow the sport that closely."

"How did you two meet?"

"We grew up together." Seeing their surprise, she continued. "Junior high. High school. We were from the same small town in central Georgia."

"Were you high school sweethearts?"

"No, Detective Bowen. Friends."

"Did you maintain this friendship after high school?"

"That was difficult. Coleman got a baseball scholarship. After college he was drafted into the minors. I'm sure you know all this," she said to Duncan.

"I know about his baseball career. I don't know about his personal relationships. That's what we want to know. About your relationship with him."

"Why? What relevance does it have?"

"That's what we're trying to determine."

"There's nothing to *determine*," she said. "How did you even know that Coleman and I were friends?"

"We have our ways."

It was such an inane statement that Duncan echoed the look of derision that Elise shot DeeDee. He said, "You lost contact with him while he was in college and the minor leagues?"

"Playing baseball consumed all his time. We sent birthday cards, Christmas greetings. But beyond that, we didn't stay in close contact."

"When was the last time you saw him?"

She looked away, said quietly, "A few days before he died."

"Before he killed himself," DeeDee said bluntly.

Head lowered, Elise nodded.

"Did he give you any indication that he

planned to end his life?"

She raised her head and glared at DeeDee. "If he had, don't you think I'd have done something to stop him?"

"I don't know. Would you?"

DeeDee's harsh question left her dumbfounded. She stared at DeeDee for several beats, then turned to Duncan. "I don't understand this. Why are you asking me questions about Coleman?"

"They're painful for you?"

"Of course."

"Why?"

"He was my friend!"

"And lover."

"What?"

"I need to repeat it?"

"No, but you're wrong. We weren't lovers. We were friends." DeeDee made a snorting sound of disbelief, but Elise ignored it. Her attention was focused on Duncan. "I thought this was about Gary Ray Trotter. What does Coleman have to do with that? With anything?"

"When did you reestablish contact with him? More contact than birthday cards and such."

"He called and invited me to come see him in Atlanta."

"Was your husband included in this re-union?"

"No, this was right when Coleman started playing for the Braves. I hadn't even met Cato. Later, after I was married, I invited Coleman to our home for dinner. Cato is a Braves fan, so he was delighted to learn that Coleman and I were friends."

"They liked each other?"

"Very well."

"Except for that one dinner, did they ever socialize?"

"Coleman arranged for us to sit in a box at one of the home games. We met him afterward for dinner. As far as I know, those are the only two occasions he and Cato were together."

Duncan got up from his chair and sat on the corner of his desk, so he'd have the advantage of height and would be looking down at her. "You know very well that they never saw each other again, because it would've been messy to have your husband and your lover —"

"Coleman was not my lover."

"You never saw him alone, without your husband?"

She faltered. "I didn't say that."

"So you did see him alone."

"Sometimes."

"Often?"

"Coleman's schedule was —"

"Often?"

Relenting to his pressure, she nodded. "Whenever our schedules allowed it."

"Where did you meet?"

"Usually here in Savannah."

"Where, here in Savannah?"

"Different places."

"Restaurants? Bars?"

"Coleman tried to avoid public places. Fans wouldn't leave him alone."

"So you met in places that afforded you privacy?"

"Yes."

"Like hotel rooms?"

She hesitated, then nodded.

"What did your husband think of these rendezvous in hotel rooms?"

She didn't respond.

"He didn't know about them, did he?" Duncan continued. "You didn't inform him when you were going to meet a popular, good-looking superstar like Coleman Greer in a hotel room, did you? Because he wouldn't have liked it one bit."

She shot up from her chair. "I don't have to listen to this."

Duncan placed a hand on her shoulder. "You can listen to it here and now, alone, or you can listen to it later with a lawyer and your husband present."

He could feel her body heat radiating into his hand. Her breathing was rapid and light, agitated. "Coleman and I were friends. Only friends."

"Who had secret meetings in hotel rooms."

"Why don't you believe me?"

"Because nothing you've told me is credible." His eyes speared into hers. *"Nothing."*

"I've told you the truth."

"About you and Coleman Greer?"

"About everything."

"How long did these cozy get-togethers last? One hour? Two? Longer?"

"It varied."

"Ballpark. No pun intended."

"An hour or two. Usually no longer."

"Depending on how long you could sneak away."

She released a slow breath. "You're correct about that. Cato didn't know about these visits with Coleman."

"Ah."

"But it wasn't what you're thinking. It wasn't an affair."

"Hotel rooms are used for two things. One of them is sleeping. I don't think you met with Coleman Greer to sleep."

"We talked."

"Talked."

"Yes."

"That's it?"

"Yes."

"With all your clothes on?"

"Yes!"

"Do you honestly expect me to believe
—"

"It's the truth!"

"— that you were in a hotel room with a
man —"

"A *friend.*"

"— and didn't get fucked?"

She inhaled a quick breath. She seemed about to speak, then thought better of it. Her lips compressed.

Duncan smirked. "That's what I thought."

Until she shrugged off his hand, he didn't realize that it had been clamping her shoulder all this time. "Are you arresting me, Detective Hatcher?"

"Not yet."

She retrieved her handbag and stormed out.

Her sudden departure left a vacuum in the small room. Duncan, staring at the empty doorway through which she had passed, raked his fingers through his hair and mumbled a stream of swear words.

Long moments later, he realized DeeDee was still there, watching him, parallel frown lines between her eyebrows.

He raised his shoulders. "What?"

"What was that all about?"

"What?"

"The . . ." She sawed her hand back and forth, as though forming a connection between her chest and an invisible point in space. "That thing between the two of you."

"What thing?"

"Tension. Something. I don't know. Whatever it was, it was crackling."

"You're imagining things. Talking about Coleman Greer naked got your sap running."

"If you let this woman cloud your judgment, you're the sap."

He pounced on that. "Tell me how I exercised poor judgment."

"By letting her sail out of here."

"We don't have anything to justify holding her, DeeDee," he said, rather too loudly. "Without any evidence, how could I? I wanted to detain her, God knows."

Before walking out, she fired a parting shot. *"Detain?* Is that a new word for it?"

For the remainder of the afternoon, DeeDee stayed at her desk, cleaning up paperwork on another case. Duncan stayed at his desk, too, thinking about Elise and wondering if she was an accomplished liar or telling the truth, but ostensibly running his trotlines on Savich.

Going through the motions, he placed a call to his contact at the DEA. "He's been quiet," Duncan said. "Makes me nervous."

He learned from the agent that after getting a tip from an informant, they'd raided one of Savich's trucks. All they'd found was machinery and the proper shipping invoices that matched the cargo, right down to the correct serial numbers.

Duncan wasn't surprised. Savich wouldn't use his company trucks to ship drugs along Interstate 95. While the truck was being stripped down and searched, family vans and nondescript sedans loaded to the gills were headed for the lucrative markets along the eastern seaboard.

He consoled the agent over the failed mission. "I couldn't get him for Freddy Morris, either."

"You still dry?"

"As a bone," Duncan admitted. "Lucille Jones has gone underground, and the DA won't try the case again without something substantial, like the knife Savich used to cut out Freddy's tongue. He'd prefer it to still be dripping blood."

"Not gonna happen."

"One can dream."

Duncan's frustration matched that of the federal agent. He suspected that Savich was having information fed to him, probably by one of the department's own paid informants. Although, maybe not. Savich had infallible sensors that had served him well over the course of his criminal career. He may only have sensed Freddy Morris's betrayal and, taking no chances, acted with dispatch to eliminate him.

Ready to put an end to the unproductive Monday, Duncan left for home early. On his way out, he stopped at DeeDee's desk. "What's your gut feeling?"

She didn't look up. "On?"

"Laird. Do we sign off on it? It was self-defense. Case closed."

"Is that what you want to do?"

"If we could talk to Napoli —"

"But we can't."

"And that's like an itch I can't scratch," he said. "The whole Napoli-Trotter-Laird connection."

"It would be useful to know what Napoli had on Mrs. Laird. How damaging was it?"

He stared out the window for a moment, then said decisively, "Let's keep working it.

Give it a few more days. Maybe Napoli will surface."

She looked up at him then, her smile bright. "See you tomorrow."

However, less than an hour later, she called him on his cell phone. "What are you doing?"

"Buying groceries," he replied.

"Groceries? You don't cook."

"So far I've got toilet paper and beer."

"Essentials, for sure."

Relieved that they were friends again, he asked, "What's up?"

"We've been summoned to appear at the Lairds' house at eight o'clock."

"Tonight?"

"Yep."

"What for?"

"I don't think it's for dinner."

"Meet you there."

At thirty seconds to eight, they met on the walkway leading up to the front door of the stately residence. "Any ideas?" he asked.

"He just said to be here at eight, and here we be."

"Why'd he call you?"

"I was the one still in the office." DeeDee punched the doorbell and they heard the chime inside the house. "We probably shouldn't count on getting a full confession."

"To what?"

"To anything."

Mrs. Berry answered the door and regarded them as though they smelled like raw sewage. "They're waiting for you."

She led them as far as the arched opening into the living room. Cato Laird was standing with his back to the fireplace and the painting with the dead rabbit lying among the fresh vegetables. Elise was seated on the sofa. Both wore solemn expressions, but his voice was cordial enough when he thanked them for coming and asked them to take seats. There was no offer of refreshments on this visit.

The judge sat down beside his wife on the sofa. He took her hand and patted it reassuringly. "Elise told me about her interview with you earlier today. My initial reaction was to call Bill Gerard and raise hell. You placed my wife at a terrible disadvantage."

Prudently, Duncan and DeeDee remained silent.

"But on second thought, I changed my mind about filing a complaint. You deserve a dressing-down for pulling a stunt like that, but I didn't want to put any additional stress on Elise.

"And, actually, I was more angry with myself than with you. It's my fault that she had to undergo that unpleasant interrogation. I couldn't live with that." He glanced at her, then came back to them. "So I confessed to her that I'd hired Meyer Napoli to follow her."

Duncan's gaze moved to Elise. She was regarding him with palpable hostility.

The judge said, "I felt that Elise should know everything that was said during our conversation in the locker room the other day, Detective Hatcher. I'm not proud of myself for lying to you and Detective Bowen when I said I'd never had personal dealings with Napoli. I deeply regret my business with him, especially if it resulted in the shooting of Trotter, no matter how roundabout the connection was."

"That was our thinking when we talked to Mrs. Laird today," DeeDee said. "That Trotter's break-in was somehow related to Meyer Napoli."

"My business with him was so short-lived," the judge said, "I still hold firm to my theory that Trotter was acting alone, and that any connection he had to Napoli was coincidental. But looking at it from the perspective of an investigator, I'll admit it warranted closer examination, particularly if Napoli had proof of an affair between Coleman Greer and my wife.

"So," he went on, "I felt we should clear the air. Hopefully by explaining a couple of outstanding issues, we can put this regrettable incident behind us once and for all. Now that there are no lingering secrets between Elise and me, we can be perfectly frank with you. Fire away."

DeeDee plunged right in. "Mrs. Laird, *does* Napoli have proof of an affair between you and Coleman Greer?"

"No such proof exists, Detective Bowen. There was no affair."

Reading the skepticism in DeeDee's face, the judge said, "You will believe her after she explains the nature of their relationship."

"She told us they were friends," DeeDee said.

"I told you we were *close* friends. To have something ugly made of our friendship offends me deeply." As she said this, she shot Duncan a drop-dead look. "It pains me to have to talk about him at all, but since you give me no choice . . ." She paused and took a deep breath. "He and I dated a few times in high school, but it was always platonic, never sexual, not even romantic. We were pals, confidantes."

286

DeeDee asked, "If you were so close, why didn't you know he was contemplating suicide?"

"I knew that Coleman was depressed, but I didn't realize the depth of his depression. I wish I had."

"He was at the top of his game," Duncan said. "What did he have to be depressed about?"

"His heart was broken."

The simple statement took him and DeeDee aback. He said, "That begs for an explanation, Mrs. Laird."

"Coleman's lover was leaving him."

"But you weren't that lover."

"No," she said firmly. "I was not."

"So all those times that you met him secretly, you —"

"I provided him a shoulder to cry on."

"You didn't have a carnal relationship."

"How many times must I repeat it, Detective Hatcher?"

The judge said, "They still don't believe you, darling. They won't believe you until you tell them what you told me."

She gave Duncan a long, measured look, as though willing him to accept what she was about to say. "Coleman didn't have a sexual relationship with me or any woman. His lover was Tony Esteban. His teammate."

14

Even so far inland, Atlanta was as sultry as Savannah.

The heat sucked the breath out of Duncan as he exited the airport to hail a cab. The driver was friendly and talkative, keeping up a lively chatter as he negotiated the expressway traffic toward Buckhead, where Tony Esteban owned the penthouse of a high-rise condo.

Duncan had woken up early, knowing he was going to come to Atlanta. He didn't tell anybody, not even DeeDee, who would have wanted to come with him. He figured the Braves' Puerto Rican treasure would be reluctant to discuss his sex life with cops, but that one would be less intimidating than two.

Besides, he was grateful to have a break from DeeDee. After leaving the judge and his wife last night, they'd driven separately to a restaurant, where Duncan ate a late supper, and DeeDee imbibed Diet Coke by the quart and railed endlessly against Elise Laird and her lies.

"I can't believe she had the nerve to say that Coleman Greer was gay! That's what she wants us to believe? As if!"

"It goes against stereotype, but that doesn't mean —"

"Coleman Greer was *not* gay."

She wouldn't listen to any argument to the contrary and rebuked both Duncan and the judge for giving any credence to it whatsoever. "She's got her husband by the dick. He'll believe it because he wants to. She's so damn clever. She told him the one lie where he could save face. She let herself off the hook *and* salvaged his wounded pride. That takes talent. She's a player, Duncan. The likes of which I've never seen."

When he could work in a word edgewise, he'd said, "Even if what she claims about Greer is false, that only makes her guilty of adultery. We're no closer to having evidence that she plugged Gary Ray Trotter for any reason other than self-defense."

"It's still murky, Duncan."

Yes, it was. Murky enough for him to make the short flight from Savannah to Atlanta, paying his own way. He would try to get reimbursed later. Even if he wound up financing the trip himself, it would be worth the price of the airfare to get to the truth. Was Elise Laird a manipulative liar? If so, the investigation into the fatal shooting would continue. If not, her own life was at risk.

Either way, he had to know.

The driver pulled the taxi into the porte cochere of the high-rise and remarked on its swankiness. Duncan agreed. He paid the man and walked into the marble lobby, which embraced him with refrigerated air, the scent of lilies, and soft music. The reception desk was manned by a uniformed concierge.

"Good morning, sir. Can I help you?"

"Morning. I'm here to see Mr. Anthony Esteban." He reached for his ID wallet, and in doing so made certain the man could see the holster beneath his sport jacket.

The concierge cleared his throat. "Is Mr. Esteban expecting you?"

Duncan flashed him a wide smile. "I didn't want to spoil the surprise."

"I'll have to buzz him."

"Whatever. No rush."

Belying his nonchalance, he leaned forward over the tall desk and watched with interest as the concierge raised a telephone receiver to his ear, then pressed the call button for the penthouse. "Mr. Esteban, I hate to disturb you. There's a gentleman here, asking to see you. A Mr. . . . uh . . ."

"Detective Sergeant Duncan Hatcher, Savannah–Chatham Metropolitan Police Department." The city and county departments had officially merged a year ago. Duncan rarely used the full name. For one thing, it sounded stupid. For another, it was too long. In the time it took you to identify yourself to a felon, you could get killed. He really only used it when he wanted to look like a big shot.

The concierge repeated what he'd said, listened, then asked the baseball player to hold on. "He wants to know in regards to what."

"Elise Laird and an incident at her house last week."

Again, he repeated Duncan's words into the telephone receiver. After a brief pause, he said, "Mr. Esteban says he doesn't know an Elise Laird."

"Coleman Greer's friend."

The concierge's mouth formed a small, round O, then he passed along the message to Esteban. "Of course, Mr. Esteban." He hung up. "Go right up. The elevator bank is behind this wall."

"Thanks."

The elevator was so fast, Duncan's ears popped on the express ascent. The doors opened into a sizable foyer. Tony Esteban was waiting for him outside his front door. He was several inches shorter than Duncan, solidly built, and, Duncan knew, had arms that could knock the stitches out of a baseball. He was wearing nothing except a pair of workout shorts and a chunk of gold suspended from a half-inch-wide chain around his neck.

"Hatcher?"

"It's a pleasure, Mr. Esteban."

"Call me Tony," he said, extending his hand. "Come in." He spoke with only a trace of a Spanish accent.

"The proverbial glass house," Duncan remarked as he stepped into the penthouse and took a look around. Floor-to-ceiling windows afforded almost a 360-degree view of the city.

"You like it? Cost a fucking fortune."

"You make a fucking fortune."

He grinned the grin that had made him vastly popular with fans and the media. "You want something to drink?" He led Duncan across what seemed to be an acre of sparsely furnished living space to a wet bar. He pushed a concealed button that opened the mirrored doors behind the bar to reveal its stock. "Whatever you like. Scotch, bourbon, a milk shake? I got everything."

"How about a glass of ice water?"

He looked disappointed, but said okay. Duncan expected him to step behind the bar, so he was surprised when he hollered, "Jenny!"

Within seconds Jenny appeared. All six feet of her, most of it sleek, tanned legs that looked like they'd been airbrushed to perfection. Her hair was the color of a sunset, her breasts were huge, and she was gorgeous. She was wearing a miniskirt, high-heeled sandals, and a tank top no bigger than a slingshot, which left absolutely nothing to the imagination. "Jenny, this is Mr. Hatcher."

"Hi, Mr. Hatcher."

Duncan found his voice. "How do you do, Jenny."

"Fine. Are you in baseball?"

"Uh, no."

"He's a cop from Savannah and he's thirsty. Fix him some ice water. Do me one of those protein shakes."

"Berries and yogurt?"

"Yeah, all that health stuff."

She went behind the bar to do his bidding. Esteban motioned Duncan toward one of the low white leather sofas in a grouping of similar pieces. The end tables were hammered metal and glass.

Once they were seated, Esteban asked, "You a baseball fan?"

"Yes."

"Braves?"

"Of course."

"Good." He beamed. "You ever play?"

"Some. Mostly football."

"Pro?"

Duncan smiled and shook his head. "I maxed out in college."

They filled the time it took Jenny to prepare their drinks talking about sports and the Braves' season so far. "Show him your ring, honey," Esteban said to her after she'd served their drinks. She extended her left hand toward Duncan, who praised the diamond, since it seemed that was expected.

"Almost ten carats," Esteban told him, though he hadn't asked.

"Wow." He smiled up at Jenny. "Is it an engagement ring?"

"He proposed in a hot air balloon," she simpered.

"In Napa," Esteban added. "One of those wine country things."

"Sounds romantic."

"It was," said Jenny.

"Have you set a date for the wedding?"

"Thanksgiving weekend. It can't be during the season."

"Right."

"Wedding, wedding, wedding is all she talks about. Flowers. Dresses. Shrimp cocktails. All that shit. Go on now, honey."

"It was nice to meet you, Mr. Hatcher. Bye."

"Bye."

Esteban affectionately smacked her heart-shaped butt as she strutted away, her heels tapping on the marble floor. As she disappeared through a set of double doors, he said, "She's something, huh?"

"She's amazing."

"I'm crazy about her. Have you ever seen a body like that?"

"Not that I can recall."

"She had some added to the top. I paid. She wanted them bigger, and I thought, what the hell? The bigger the better, right?"

"That's always been my motto." His wryness escaped the other man, who was too egotistical to hear anything except the sound of his own voice.

"She's a sweet kid. Goes through money like it was water, but it keeps her happy. And she keeps me happy. I'm telling you — and this is no exaggeration." He leaned in closer. "She could suck your eyeballs out through your dick."

"Impressive."

"You don't know the half of it." He took a drink of his shake and glanced at his wristwatch. "I got practice in an hour. How can I help you?"

"I'm investigating a fatal shooting."

"Fatal means somebody died, right?"

"Right. It took place last Thursday evening at the home of Judge Cato Laird and his wife, Elise."

"Yeah, I remember Elise. Now that you reminded me who she is. She's dead?"

"No." Duncan filled him in on the facts. He tried to avoid using words with more than five letters. "It seems Elise fired the fatal shot in self-defense. I'm just clearing up a few points."

"Like what?"

"I understand she had a close personal relationship with Coleman Greer."

He grimaced with obvious regret. "King Cole, we called him. What a fucking thing to do. You know, they think he'd been dead for a couple days before someone went to his place and checked on him. I heard it was a mess."

He'd blown the top of his head off. That could be messy, all right.

"What do you know about his relation-ship with Elise?"

"They went way back. Fuck buddies, you know? When there's nobody else around to fuck?"

"I'm familiar with the phrase."

"They were that kind of friends."

Duncan took a drink of his ice water and tried to look and sound casual. "When did you meet her?"

"He brought her to a Braves party, not long after he signed with the team. Knocked us all for a loop, 'cause she was such a babe and Cole had never said nothing about her. But he was low-key like that. Not a wild party guy."

"Are you a wild party guy?"

He laughed. "I do my share."

"Will marriage cramp your style?"

Esteban bobbed his eyebrows. "What happens on the road stays on the road. Know what I mean?"

"Gotcha."

Esteban held out his fist. Duncan bumped it with his, forming a male pact of silence. "So, King Cole brings Elise to a Braves party and she's a babe."

"Yeah."

"And?"

"And nothing." Esteban reached for his

shake and took a slurp. "That's it."

"Really."

"Never saw her again and, as I said, Cole didn't talk about stuff like that. So, I guess that's all I can tell you."

Duncan leaned against the stiff leather back of the sofa and propped one ankle on the opposite knee. "Know what Elise told me? She told me that you and Coleman Greer were the fuck buddies, and that you were breaking it off, and that's why he put the barrels of that shotgun in his mouth and pulled the trigger."

Esteban's jaw went slack. He leaned forward, then back. He opened his mouth to speak but found he had no words. Finally he shook his head and said, "That bitch. That lying bitch!"

"It's not true?"

"Fucking A, it's not true." He bounded off his seat and began to prowl the marble floor, flinging deprecations in rapid-fire Spanish.

"Why would she say such a thing?" Duncan asked.

Esteban bore down on him. "Why? I'll tell you why. You want to know why?"

"Why?"

"Okay, it was like this. That night at the party?"

"The one where you said there was 'and nothing'?"

"I didn't want you to think I was a jerk, the kind of guy who would —"

"What happened at the party, Tony?"

"Cole got wasted. He passed out. That girl, that Elise, comes on to me. And I mean, man, she was hot for it. Hot, you know?"

"Okay."

"She's all over me. Made me nervous."

"Nervous?"

"Yeah, I didn't want my new teammate pissed at me over this chick, but she said it wasn't like that between her and Cole. Said they were friends and that he would want her to have a good time at the party. She was saying stuff like that all the time she's got her hand inside my pants. So I gave her what she wanted. Coupla times. I mean, she's great-looking. Why not, you know?"

Duncan made a guttural sound of acknowledgment.

Esteban sat back down. "She was good, man. I wouldn't have minded having some more of that, but the next morning, she's writing down all her phone numbers, asking when I'm gonna call, stuff like that.

"Every day after that, she's calling me, asking when she's going to see me, why haven't I called, didn't I like her, how dare I use her and then dump her like she was nothing."

He stopped suddenly. "You see that movie *Fatal Attraction?* That's what she was. That broad. That psycho bitch from hell. I expected to come home one day and find a fucking bunny boiling on my kitchen stove."

"Did you ever see her again?"

He shook his head. "I don't need that shit, man. I guess she gave up. She finally stopped calling."

"What did Coleman have to say about this?"

"He didn't know. At least, I didn't tell him. Don't know if she did." He frowned with disgust. "Man, I knew she was one twisted chick, and she swore she would pay me back for dumping her, but I didn't figure on her making up something like I'm gay. Gay? Jesus!" Then he chortled a laugh. "It's funny when you think about it."

"You took it upon yourself to go to Atlanta and see Tony Esteban?"

"Yes."

No sooner had Duncan cleared the door of the Barracks than he'd been summoned into Bill Gerard's office. Captain Gerard was a good cop with nearly forty years with the department. He was a fair supervisor who kept himself up to speed on all the cases the VCU was investigating, and he dispensed advice when asked for it. But he trusted the detectives under his supervision to do their jobs without having to be micromanaged.

However, when necessary, he could chew ass effectively. Duncan braced himself for a good one.

"The Braves management office called," Gerard said, stacking his freckled hands on his thinning ginger-colored hair. "They were steamed you didn't go through them to interview Esteban."

"I wanted to catch him unaware."

"Apparently you did, because after you left, he had second thoughts. He went whining to the team's PR people about a cop from Savannah asking him about a woman he barely knows who's involved in a fatal shooting. He was scared the media would get wind of it, blow it out of proportion, he'd wind up the cover story of *The National Enquirer.*

"The nervous PR people called Chief Taylor, who called me and wanted to know what the hell was going on." He spat into his dip cup and peered at Duncan over the top of his reading glasses. "I'd sorta like to know that myself, Dunk. What the hell's going on?"

"I'm not convinced the fatal shooting of Gary Ray Trotter was self-defense."

"Aw, shit."

Gerard liked to hunt and fish, read books about the Civil War, and make love to the wife he'd been married to since the night after his high school graduation. He was looking forward to enjoying those pastimes in retirement, which was only two years away. Until then, he wanted to do his job well, meeting its demands, but avoiding the snares of bureaucratic politics so that he could exit the police department gracefully and enemy-free.

"You think the judge's wife wasn't just protecting her life?"

"I think she may have been protecting her life*style.*"

"Shit," he repeated. "This isn't going to sit well with Cato Laird."

"I realize that, Bill. Believe me, I deliberated on it all the way back from Atlanta. He's chief judge of superior court. He presides over felony cases. The last thing a police department wants is a judge with a grudge against cops who bring those felons to court. This places the department in an awkward position. I understand and appreciate that. But it's my duty —"

Gerard held up his hand. "None of my detectives has to explain himself to me, Dunk. I trust you. Trust your instincts even more."

He wouldn't trust him so well if he knew the secrets Duncan had been keeping recently, the ethics he'd violated. Elise's note. His private encounter with her at his house. He wouldn't trust him so well if he knew how hard Duncan had struggled with his decision to pursue the case against her.

"What did Esteban say that implicated her?" Gerard asked.

"Is Kong here?"

Gerard looked at him with puzzlement. "I don't know, why?"

"I'd like for him and DeeDee to be in on this. That way I only have to tell it once."

"I'll go take a leak. You get them in here."

They reconvened five minutes later. DeeDee came in with a can of Diet Coke and an attitude. She was miffed at Duncan for going to Atlanta without her, or even telling her about the trip beforehand. He didn't let her pouting bother him. She'd get over it. Soon, unless he missed his bet. She'd suspected Elise of an ulterior motive all along, and he was about to provide one.

Kong was his hairy, sweaty, but affable

self. "What up?" he asked Gerard.

The captain pointed to Duncan. "This is his meeting."

Duncan began by saying, "First of all, I'm giving notice here and now. When I grow up, I want to be a professional baseball player." His description of Tony Esteban's penthouse was designed to have them smiling, relaxed, and listening by the time he got down to the nitty-gritty.

"There was this red metal sculpture standing in the center of the room. It looked like an instrument of torture, or maybe a swan. And just like in the movies, he pushes a button, these smoky mirrored doors slide open, and there's a bar stocked with every conceivable potable."

They were raptly attentive by the time he got to Jenny. "Hugh Hefner never had it so good. Legs that went on forever. Tits out to here." He gestured with both hands, holding them away from his chest. "Right there on display beneath this tight tank top, and I'm talking —"

"We get it, Duncan," DeeDee said. "She had big tits. What did Esteban have to say?"

He gave the men a look that said there would be a more detailed description of Jenny's chest later, then recounted for them his conversation with Esteban.

When he finished, Gerard asked for clarification on a few points. "It was Mrs. Laird who told you Coleman Greer was gay?"

"Last night at their home," Duncan replied. "DeeDee and I were summoned there. Mrs. Laird was reluctant to destroy the myth —"

"It's no myth," DeeDee said.

"— of Coleman Greer's machismo, but she told us that after their high school romance, which was platonic —"

"Like hell," mumbled DeeDee.

"— he confessed to her what he'd never told another living soul. He was attracted to men."

" 'As God is my witness.' " DeeDee dramatically placed her hand over her heart. "Á la Scarlett O'Hara, she swore it."

"Jeez, I can't believe it," Kong said. "My boys would be crushed. I mean, not that there's anything wrong with it. Live and let live, I say. But . . . well, you'd rather your baseball heroes be straight." He looked around as though polling them. "Wouldn't you?"

"According to Esteban, Coleman Greer was straight."

"Correction, Bill," Duncan said. "According to Esteban, *he's* straight. He couldn't speak for Coleman Greer, and doesn't know with absolute certainty, but Esteban seriously doubts he was gay. How could he have been gay and nobody know? How could he have kept that hidden when he lived and traveled in the company of men half the year? He doesn't believe Coleman Greer was gay. But he *knows* that *he* 'ain't no fucking fag.' "

"Which blows a big hole in Elise Laird's story," DeeDee said. "I'm positive she invented that lie because it was the one her husband would grab on to with both hands. During all those trysts, she wasn't screwing her baseball player. No, she was consoling him over his gay love affair gone awry." She snuffled with scorn. "Priceless. Your affair is exposed by a PI your husband has hired to follow you. You need a lie, and quick. Voilà! Your lover isn't your lover. He doesn't even like girls."

"PI?" Kong said. "Here's where my missing person comes in, right? The PI was Napoli?"

Duncan said, "Anything?"

"Nothing. Not a hair off his greasy head."

"The judge hired *Napoli?*" Gerard said, his dismay showing.

"He said he was desperate to know if his wife was having an affair or if it was his imagination," Duncan explained. "He admitted to us that Napoli came through with something, but at the last minute he changed his mind, didn't want to learn what that something was."

"And Kong found Gary Ray Trotter's name among papers on Meyer Napoli's desk."

"That's right, Bill," Duncan said.

"Now I see where you're going with this," the captain said.

"Napoli had proof of Mrs. Laird's affair. The judge got cold feet, didn't want to know the truth after all, turned it down. But Napoli got greedy and took the proof to Mrs. Laird. He blackmailed her with it. Whether to protect herself, or Coleman Greer, or both of them, she agreed to a big payoff. Gary Ray Trotter was the drop man." He paused, then added, "This is all speculative, but it fits."

They sat in silence for a moment, pondering Duncan's summary. Kong was the first to speak. "But how'd she know Trotter would break in that particular night?"

"It could have been prearranged." Duncan told Gerard and Kong about her insomnia, her habit of going downstairs for milk. "Trotter may have been about to leave the goods, as instructed —"

"But she popped him first," DeeDee said.

307

"Maybe he was firing his pistol in self-defense, not her."

"Maybe," Duncan said, tugging thoughtfully on his lip. "But if that's the way it went down, where are the goods? Supposing he had an envelope with him, what did she do with it?"

"Lots of places to hide it in that study," DeeDee said. "She could have stuck it between two law books before the judge got downstairs. Or in a credenza drawer. It could have looked innocuous enough. She went back for it later."

"I guess."

"If Trotter was coming through with the promised goods, why'd she shoot him?" Kong asked.

"To tie up a loose end. This is one cold gal," DeeDee replied.

"Funny," Duncan said, "Tony Esteban described her as hot."

"I guess it depends on your point of view."

"I guess it does," Duncan said, matching the bite in DeeDee's voice.

Gerard said, "The key to all this is Napoli. If he sent Trotter to the Lairds' house, and Mrs. Laird was expecting him, we've got ourselves a case of premeditated murder."

"Or," Duncan countered, "it was a burglary gone bad and a matter of self-defense as she claimed." Or, he thought, there was another scenario. The one in which Elise was supposed to die, not Trotter. But he had only her say-so for that, and after his conversation with Esteban, it seemed even more unbelievable than it had before.

"What about ballistics on the two weapons?" Gerard asked.

"I got the report this afternoon," DeeDee said. "Both clean as a whistle. The judge purchased his seven years ago."

"Long before he'd even met Elise," Duncan remarked.

"Trotter's has never been attached to a crime," DeeDee said. "Dead end."

Addressing Kong, Bill Gerard said, "Napoli needs to be found."

"I've got every cop on the force with his eyes peeled and an ear to the ground. Right now, looks like he's pulled a Jimmy Hoffa."

Then the captain turned to Duncan. "What's your next move?"

He thought about it for a moment. "I suppose I go back to Mrs. Laird and tell her that Esteban categorically denied being Coleman Greer's lover. See what she says."

"She'll say he's lying." That from DeeDee.

Gerard spat into his cup. "You're frowning, Dunk. What's on your mind? Something tells me you're not convinced."

He stood up, walked over to the window, and gazed out thoughtfully. A horse-drawn carriage loaded with tourists was clopping past. The tour guide was pointing out the architectural features of the Barracks, giving them its history.

"Convinced?" Duncan said. "Good word, Bill. Because I've been wondering if maybe Esteban was trying to convince me that he's heterosexual. Everything he said, his posturing, it was almost overkill. His Barbie-doll fiancée with an engagement ring bigger and heavier than an anchor. Her jumbo-sized breasts, which he paid for. Eyeballs through his dick."

"Excuse me?"

He turned back into the room and smiled at Kong. "You had to be there. The point is, he wanted there to be no doubt in my mind that he was a superstud, a man who liked women."

"He's that way all the time," Gerard said. "You ever see him when he wasn't strutting his stuff?"

"He's cocky as hell," Kong agreed.

"Yeah, the swagger and boasting may just be elements of his personality." Duncan returned to his chair, but didn't sit down. He braced his arms against the back of it. "But let's say, for the sake of argument, that

Esteban and Coleman Greer *were* lovers. Who's the one person in the world who might know about it and could expose it?"

Gerard supplied the answer. "Coleman's longtime friend and confidante, Elise Laird."

"Right. When the concierge of Esteban's building announced me, I said I was there to talk to him about Coleman Greer's friend Elise Laird. Maybe he panicked. Maybe he thought right then and there that the jig was up, that his homosexuality was about to be exposed. So everything he said and did was calculated to contradict anything she might have told me about his relationship with his teammate."

"Or maybe her lie was payback for him dumping her, just like he said," DeeDee argued.

"He's an egomaniac. That whole story about her coming on to him could have been a lie."

She made a snorting sound. "You just don't want her to be guilty of murder."

"And you do," he fired back.

"No," she said slowly. "But just because she's got a doll face and a figure to match doesn't mean she's innocent."

"It doesn't mean she's guilty, either."

"Why don't you push her the way you do

other suspects?"

"Up till today she hasn't been a suspect."

"Only because you didn't want to think so," DeeDee retorted angrily.

"Hey!" Bill Gerard interrupted the heated exchange. "What's with you two?"

"Duncan goes calf-eyed every time he sees Elise Laird."

"You're pissing me off, DeeDee." He spoke quietly, his lips barely moving to form the words. "Name one thing I've failed to do." She continued to stare at him without speaking. *"Name one thing I've failed to do,"* he repeated angrily.

She looked across at Bill Gerard and sighed with resignation. "He hasn't failed to do anything. He's conducted a thorough investigation."

"Thank you," Duncan said stiffly. "Have I been cautious? More tentative than normal? You're goddamn right I have. Because we're about to go after a superior court judge's wife. Before we do, I think we should explore every possibility. Because if we're wrong on this, we're gonna be butt-fucked and then we're gonna be unemployed."

A long, tense silence ensued. Kong broke it by saying, "Ouch."

Everyone relaxed, chuckled. But Duncan wasn't quite ready to forgive DeeDee, and when he looked at her, he didn't smile.

"It comes down to this, Dunk," Gerard said. "One of them is playing you. Either Mrs. Laird or Tony Esteban. Who do you think it is?"

That's the question he'd asked himself a thousand times since leaving Esteban's penthouse. Did he believe the cocky baseball player or the woman who had killed a man last week?

Quietly he said, "Elise Laird." He glanced at DeeDee, then addressed his captain. "Too many things about that shooting just don't add up, Bill. It doesn't *feel* right. I think we should get her in here tomorrow, put her in an interrogation room with a court reporter, make it official. Hammer her pretty hard. See if we can shake something loose."

Gerard nodded, but he looked unhappy. "Shit's gonna fly. I'll notify Chief Taylor tonight, because I'm sure he'll get an earful from Judge Laird tomorrow." No one disputed that. "Kong, let them know soon as you get anything on Napoli."

"Will do."

DeeDee was the only one in the room who looked happy. She stood up and dropped her empty soda can in the wastebasket, saying to Duncan, "I'll be at my desk, if you want to go over the plan for tomorrow."

"Fine."

On his way out, Kong nudged Duncan and said in an undertone, "I still want to hear about that eyeball thing."

Duncan was left alone with Gerard, who was using his necktie to polish his reading glasses. "What your partner said, is it true? Do you go moony over this lady?"

"I'd have to be a eunuch not to notice her, Bill. And so would you."

"I've seen her. I understand. So I gotta know. Can you put blinders on and be objective?"

"She's married."

"Not what I asked, Dunk."

"She's a principal in an investigation."

"Again."

"We've got no solid evidence on which to build a murder case against her. Yet. But upon my recommendation we're moving forward on the investigation, and if we find that needed evidence, I'll get an indictment."

Gerard replaced his eyeglasses and reached for a stack of paperwork on his desk. "All I needed to hear."

15

"Elise?"

She spun around, knowing she looked guilty. Knowing she was. "Cato," she said, laughing breathlessly. He was standing in the open doorway, carrying a shopping bag. "You scared me. When did you get home?"

"Just now. What are you doing?" As he came into the study, his expression was curious, a shade suspicious.

"This room still makes me jumpy."

"Then why come in here?"

"I was checking the repair."

She indicated the wall that had been patched after the bullet from Trotter's pistol was removed. Yesterday policemen had taken down the crime scene tape and told them they were free to use the room again. Cato had people standing by to restore his study to its pre-incident perfection.

The bloodstained rug had been rolled up and hauled out, with his instructions that it be destroyed. He didn't want it back. Then the entire room had been cleaned and sanitized by professionals.

"I wasn't satisfied with the workmanship and knew you wouldn't be, either," Elise said now. "I was looking in your desk for the plasterer's business card. I wanted to call him first thing tomorrow."

"Mrs. Berry has his business card."

"Oh."

"I'll ask her to reschedule him."

"I think you should. You want the job done right. I know how much you enjoy this room."

"It's sweet of you to care." He smiled. "Join me for a drink before dinner?"

"I'd like that." She came from around his desk and glanced down at the bag. "What's that?"

"A present."

"Hmm." She reached into the pink tissue paper sticking out the top.

"It can wait." He set the bag on the floor, slid his arms around her waist, and tried to kiss her, but she pulled away. "I intended to freshen up before you came home. I rested this afternoon as you suggested, and actually managed to nap. I haven't even brushed my teeth yet."

"I don't mind."

"But I do. I'll go upstairs and make myself presentable. You mix the drinks."

"Even better, I'll mix the drinks and bring them upstairs."

"That is better." She disengaged herself and moved toward the door.

"Here, take the bag with you." He picked it up and passed it to her.

"Can I peek?"

He laughed. "I think you will whether or not I give my permission, so go ahead."

Matching his lightheartedness, she left the room, calling over her shoulder, "Vodka and tonic, please. Lots of lime, lots of ice."

She jogged up the staircase and went straight into their bedroom. As soon as she closed the door, she leaned against it, breathing hard, her heart pounding. She was trembling. She'd come awfully close to getting caught.

Following his confession about hiring the private investigator, Cato had been tender and loving, frequently asking if she had forgiven him for his mistrust. She assured him that he had her forgiveness. Her responses to him were warm and affectionate. On the surface, nothing seemed amiss.

She brushed her teeth and quickly changed into the new outfit wrapped in tissue inside the shopping bag. She was spraying herself with fragrance when he entered the bedroom carrying two drinks. He looked at her and nodded approval.

"The difference was worth the wait."

"Thank you."

"Fit okay?"

"Perfect." Holding the full skirt out at the sides, she did a pirouette.

"Nothing fancy," he said, "but I saw it and liked it."

"So do I. Very much. Thank you."

He had removed his suit jacket and tie. The top two buttons of his shirt were undone. Giving her a meaningful look, he closed the bedroom door. She glanced at her wristwatch. "Mrs. Berry will be waiting to serve dinner."

"I told her to keep it warm, so we can take our time."

He crossed the room and handed her the drink. He clinked his glass of scotch against it. "To forgetting the shooting and its unpleasant aftermath."

"I'll drink to that."

They both took a sip of their drinks, then he pulled her toward the bed, sat down on the edge of it, and guided her to stand between his spread thighs. He set his drink on the nightstand and placed his hands at her waist. "I'm not sure I can wait till you finish your drink."

She took several sips from the glass, then set it on the nightstand beside his.

He moved his hands lightly up and down her rib cage. "Are you still angry with me, Elise?"

"About the private investigator? No, Cato. I've told you time and again. What else could you think? All the signs pointed to an affair. It was silly of me not to explain Coleman's situation to you."

"Even if you had, I wouldn't have approved your meeting him in hotel rooms."

"I didn't inflame his desire," she said with a light laugh. "I tried to when we were in high school. It was a disaster. He didn't want me that way."

"Then he wasn't only gay. He must have been dead, too."

The telephone rang. He glanced at it, but saw that the light for the kitchen extension was on, indicating that Mrs. Berry had answered. He curved his hand around the back of her neck to draw her head down to his.

Through the intercom, Mrs. Berry said, "Judge Laird, I apologize for the intrusion. That Detective Hatcher insists on speaking to you."

Cato held Elise's gaze for several seconds,

then removed his hands from her and picked up the receiver. He depressed the blinking red button on the telephone's panel. "Detective Hatcher?"

Elise reached for her drink, noting that her hand was shaking, hoping that Cato didn't notice.

"I see," he said. The conversation lasted only a few more seconds. "I'll adjust my schedule accordingly. We'll be there." Slowly he replaced the receiver and continued staring at the phone, saying nothing.

She was unable to contain her anxiety. "What did he want? You said we'll be there. Where?"

"The police station. Ten o'clock tomorrow morning."

"Why?"

He looked up at her then. "We have a problem, Elise. Or rather, the police have a problem."

"With what?"

"Your relationship with Coleman Greer. They don't believe you."

Duncan's car crawled along the street as he checked addresses until he found the one he sought. He pulled to the curb and stopped in front of the house. It was a dangerous, high-crime neighborhood that could accurately be called a slum. Every house on the street showed decades of disrepair and neglect, but this one was particularly ramshackle.

The darkness may have been playing tricks on his eyes, but the clapboard structure appeared to be listing several degrees. Nothing was growing in the yard except for a lone live oak that was hosting too much Spanish moss. The tree itself appeared to have been sucked dry.

He turned off the car's engine and slid his service weapon from its holster. With the pistol secure in his right hand, he got out of the car and took a careful look around. The street appeared to be deserted. Or perhaps "abandoned" would be a more accurate word. A few houses on the block had lights on inside, but most were dark and seemingly vacant. The few streetlights that still had globes intact provided feeble light and served only to deepen the shadows.

The sidewalk was uneven. Weeds grew up through the wide cracks in it. Concrete crumpled into dust beneath Duncan's shoes as he walked to the edge of the yard and studied the house. It was entirely dark.

He questioned the advisability of being here. At the very least, he shouldn't have come alone. He knew that, acknowledged it. It was reckless and stupid and, to some extent, self-serving.

"It's about Savich. Come alone."

That and this house address had been the sum total of the message left in his cell phone mailbox by a husky female voice. When he checked the call log, he saw that the call had come in at 10:37 P.M. Instead of a number, it had said "Private Caller."

No shit.

He'd thought immediately of the woman Savich had set him up with last Saturday night. Was he using her again? Would Savich be that blatant? It didn't sound like something Savich would do, but if you tried to predict Savich, you'd be wrong nine point nine out of ten times.

Cautiously he took the walkway up to the porch of the house. He looked over both shoulders, but saw no movement on the street, heard no sounds. Old boards groaned beneath his weight as he crossed the porch to the door.

He realized chances were excellent that he was walking into a trap that would spell his doom. He had figured that Savich would launch a surprise attack. Had he been wrong? Had Savich decided on a face-to-face showdown instead?

Or maybe, inside this house, Savich had

another gory surprise waiting for him. The corpse of Lucille Jones, perhaps. The prostitute who'd been pleasuring Savich following the murder of Freddy Morris was still at large and, consequently, unable to be questioned by police. Possibly Savich had silenced her forever and left her body here for Duncan to find.

Gordie Ballew also crossed his mind. Had Savich heard that they'd tried to strike a deal with Gordie to turn snitch? Lucky for Gordie, he was safely behind bars in the county jail.

Whatever this old house held in store for him, the moment of truth had arrived. Duncan moved aside the rusty screen door that was hanging by one hinge, then took hold of the doorknob. It turned in his hand. He had to apply his shoulder to get the moisture-swollen door to open, then he stepped across the threshold into the house. The air inside was stifling hot, and had the musty smell of old, vacant houses. But not of decaying flesh, he noted with relief.

Listening intently for any sound, he took a moment to orient himself. It was a traditional Southern house, built before air-conditioning, when cross-ventilation was necessary for cooling during the brutal summers. At one time, maybe a century ago, it would have been a lovely house.

Ahead of him stretched a hallway with a staircase at one end and rooms opening off it on both sides. He crept forward and guardedly looked into the first one on his right. It was empty. Wainscoting and several generations of faded, tearing wallpaper. A hole in the ceiling where a chandelier had once hung. Probably designed to be a dining room.

He crossed the hallway to the opposite room, which was a parlor. Different wallpaper, but also torn. Ragged sheer curtains looking as fragile as spiderwebs hanging in the windows. The room was furnished, but sparsely.

Elise Laird was standing in the center of it.

His heart did something funny. But he raised his gun and pointed it at her.

"You're here." Her voice was barely a whisper. The same whispering voice that had left the message on his cell phone. He wondered why he hadn't recognized it as her voice.

Or had he?

Had he known, despite the mention of Savich, precisely who would be waiting for him here in this dark and deserted house? Had he refused to acknowledge that it was her voice, because if he had, he couldn't have come here with a clear conscience? Savich provided him justification for coming. She didn't.

"What the hell?" he asked angrily.

"I used that criminal's name to get you here."

"How did you know it would?"

"Cato told me about your history with him."

He studied her for long, ponderous moments, then lowered the nine-millimeter. But he left a bullet in the chamber and he didn't return it to the holster. He moved so that his back would be to the wall and not to the open doorway.

Sensing his wariness, she said, "There's no one else here, if that's what you're thinking. I had to see you alone."

"Whose place is this?"

It was the first time he'd seen her with her hair hanging loose rather than pulled back. It brushed her shoulders when she moved her head. "It belongs to a friend."

"Your friend should consider refurbishing."

"He's been away for a long time. He gave me permission to use the house if I needed to, in exchange for airing it out occasionally."

Duncan nodded as though that explained everything, when actually it explained nothing. It generated more questions, but those would have to wait. Already, there was enough to talk about.

"Okay, I took the bait and you got me here. What do you want?"

"It's not a matter of what I want, Duncan. It's what I need. Your help. I'm desperate."

Hearing her say his name was like getting a punch in the gut. He tried to ignore the sensation, but couldn't, and that made him angry. "I assume you sneaked out on your husband."

"I didn't have to. Your phone call upset him. He went to the country club." Reading his surprise, she explained. "A lot of his colleagues, even the DA, are in a poker tournament. They were playing tonight. Cato knew word would circulate that I was being questioned by police again tomorrow. He wanted it to seem that he wasn't worried. He didn't tell me that. I just know how he thinks. Anyhow, he went. I waited for Mrs. Berry to go home, then called you."

"And lured me here to Boo Radley's house. Why?"

"Would you put the gun away?"

"No."

"You've got nothing to fear from me."

Only losing my job, he thought. My career. My integrity.

"I'm the one who should be afraid." Saying that, she took several steps toward him.

He caught a whiff of perfume. It was light, floral. Intoxicating. She was dressed similarly to how she'd been when she showed up at his town house. Skirt, sandals, a tank top. Not nearly as skimpy or revealing as Esteban's fiancée's had been. But skimpy enough to make Duncan aware of the shape of her breasts. Uncomfortably aware.

"I know what these little games of yours are about, Mrs. Laird. They're to keep me off track, to divert me from the investigation, to keep me from arresting you for the murder of Gary Ray Trotter."

There. That sounded good. He was the investigator; she was the suspect. That's the way it was, and that's the way it had to be, even if he was aching to put his hands on her.

"Why don't you believe I shot Trotter in self-defense? Why don't you believe me about Cato? About Coleman?"

He paused for effect, then said, "I'm glad you brought him up. I went to Atlanta to see Tony Esteban today."

Her reaction showed how surprised she

was to hear that. "You talked to him?"

"Oh, yeah. We had a friendly chat."

"What did he say?"

"You're not his favorite person."

"Nor he mine."

"In fact he called you a psycho bitch and worse."

"He doesn't even know me. I only met him once at a party."

"Where Coleman Greer passed out from too much drink, and you and his friend Tony got nekkid and held a private party."

"What?"

"I'll spare you the embarrassment of recounting the juicy details. Suffice to say, you were the initiator. You and Esteban had a real good time while your fool of a date, Coleman Greer, was incapacitated.

"But next morning, you turned into every man's nightmare. Got possessive and clingy. Kept calling Tony on the phone. Wouldn't go away, and when it became obvious that he wanted nothing more from you than those couple of hot-hot tumbles, you swore to get even with him someday, which turned out to be yesterday when you told Detective Bowen and me that he was Coleman Greer's gay lover."

She looked at him aghast. "You believe all that?"

"More than I believe your version."

She groped behind her for the padded arm of the sofa, one of the few pieces of furniture in the room, and slowly sat down on it. For several minutes she stared into space.

Eventually she looked across at him. "He's lying," she stated simply. "He's *lying*. Yes, Coleman invited me to a Braves party. I told you that. And there, he introduced me to Tony Esteban. Coleman did get drunk that night. But he did so because Tony was flirting with me. Coleman was already infatuated with him, and Tony had led him to believe that his interest was reciprocated."

Duncan remained silent and skeptical.

"Tony Esteban is a fraud and a liar," she said with emphasis. "Even if he weren't homosexual, or bi, or whatever he is, I would never be attracted to him. He's obnoxious. An egomaniac. I had nothing to do with him that night or any other time."

"Are you accusing him of the same thing he accused you of? Are you saying he told me all this stuff just to get back at you for rejecting his advances?"

"I don't give a damn what his motives are. I care even less what he thinks of me," she said. "But he's lying about his relationship with Coleman. Tony broke my friend's heart. He was afraid they were going to be found out, so he refused to see Coleman alone anymore.

"Coleman anguished over the breakup for months. That's when he and I were meeting often. He was in pain and needed someone he could talk to openly about the love affair, someone he trusted implicitly. He was devastated by Tony Esteban's rejection and eventually killed himself over it. That is the truth. I swear it."

Duncan took off his jacket and used his shirt sleeve to wipe sweat from his forehead. He was hot and agitated, and dangerously close to believing her, so he argued vehemently against it. "Esteban has got a red-headed bombshell for a fiancée. She performs for him like a trained seal. He bought her a boob job and a diamond ring, and it's a tie which is bigger. They're getting married this fall."

"Of course he has a girl like her. He always does. That was a point of contention between him and Coleman. Whenever Tony boasted of his sexual conquests to their teammates, or squired around his latest squeeze, it wounded Coleman.

"But all Tony's machismo swagger is for show, Duncan. The marriage will be a sham. Don't you see that he's putting on this act as a cover? The redhead is a smoke screen. Within a year she'll probably be having a child. He'll make certain of it."

Duncan had thought along a similar track, but he wasn't yet ready to concede it.

"Tony treated Coleman horribly," she said. "He would lavish him with affection one day, ignore him the next. He ran hot and cold and made Coleman miserable."

"Then why was Coleman so blindly in love with him?"

She didn't speak for a moment, then said quietly, "I don't believe we get to choose who we fall in love with. Do you?"

Suddenly it seemed the room became darker, smaller, airless. Duncan's skin was clammy; his body was humming like a tuning fork. He looked away from her.

He said, "I don't know who's gay, who's straight, or who was screwing who, and frankly it doesn't matter. What does matter is that Meyer Napoli had something on you. The judge paid him off, but Napoli is an enterprising man and saw a way to make another buck.

"He came to you and threatened to make public whatever your dirty little secret was unless you paid him off. You agreed, and told him to meet you in your husband's study late one night. Napoli said okay, whatever, but he's no fool. To protect his own ass, he subcontracted dumb, hapless Gary Ray Trotter to be his drop man just in case you weren't playing straight with him.

"By the way, what did Trotter bring with him that night? Photos, tape recordings, X-rated videos? Maybe you truly weren't screwing Coleman Greer. Maybe you were actually protecting your best friend's privacy and public image.

"That doesn't matter, either. Whatever Napoli had on you, it was damaging not only to you, but to your friend, and — most importantly — to your husband. And above all else, you wanted to safeguard your position as Mrs. Cato Laird.

"You go into the study, as prearranged, expecting Napoli. But there's Trotter. He said something to you. I know goddamn well he did, although you've denied it. After you shot him, you secured the goods, then made it look like you caught a burglar. You may have even planted that tire iron, you may have broken the window yourself.

"Enter Cato. Weak at the thought of how close he came to losing his beloved. You've got him coddling you like he's never coddled you before. He swallows the self-defense story whole, and Trotter ain't talking." His eyes narrowed on her. "What must really be haunting you now is, where's Meyer Napoli? Except for him, you're clear. He's the only person who can ruin this for you."

Her shoulders slumped forward and she bowed her head.

Duncan strode over to her, placed his hand beneath her chin, and yanked her head up. "Isn't that the way it went down?"

"Yes." Surprising him, she surged to her feet and thrust her hands toward him, the insides of her wrists pressed together. "Handcuff me. Arrest me. Put me in jail. At least there I'll be safe."

"From your husband?"

"Yes!"

"Because he's going to kill you?"

"Yes! No," she said, shaking her head. "Not him. He wouldn't do it himself. He's not that foolish. He had his chance the other night in the swimming pool. I thought he might drown me and be done with it. But he didn't kill me then, and he won't. He'll just make certain that I die."

"Why?" Duncan fired at her.

"He . . ."

"Why?"

"I can't tell you why."

"Because there is no *why.*"

She shook her head violently. "Just please trust me."

"Trust you?" He laughed. "Not on a bet."

"What do I have to do for you to believe me? Turn up dead?"

"That would be a start."

She drew in a shocked breath and fell back a step.

"In the meantime," he continued in the same cold voice, "I'll see you at the Barracks. Tomorrow. Ten o'clock."

He turned away from her and headed for the center hall. She came after him, caught his arm, and brought him around. "I don't have anyone else who can or will help me. I'm afraid. Cato knows . . ."

"What?"

"He knows, or at least suspects, that I know what he's trying to do. That's why he told you about Napoli. So he would look like the cuckolded husband, win your sympathy against the unfaithful wife. He let you draw the connection between Napoli and Trotter and ultimately to Coleman to make me look guilty. It's all a part of his grand scheme."

"All right," Duncan said. "If that's the way it is, make that your official statement. Go on the record with it tomorrow during the interrogation."

"I can't. How could I? I would be as good as dead for sure." Her grip on his arm tightened. "Please, Duncan."

"What is it exactly you're asking me to do?"

"Stop investigating *me*. Start investigating Cato, and why Trotter came to our house that night."

"Which was to kill you?"

"Yes."

"How would a bungler like Trotter know that you wander around the house in the middle of the night?"

"Cato would have told him. He would have told Trotter to wait in the study until I came downstairs, which was inevitable."

"Cato kept you in bed so the alarm wouldn't be set and Trotter could get in."

"Doesn't that sound plausible?"

It did, yes. He saw the hopefulness in her expression, and it tempted him to believe her. "Tell me why your husband wants you dead."

"I can't," she said in an anguished whisper. "Not until I know, without doubt, that you believe me. Completely."

"Then you're shit out of luck."

Before he could turn away, she placed her hands on his shoulders and moved in close. "You want to believe me."

He reached up to remove her hands. "Don't," he said, but her hands stayed on his shoulders and his hands stayed on hers.

"I know you do." She came up on tiptoe and brushed her lips across his, breathing against them. "Believe me, Duncan. Please."

Groaning with anger and frustrated desire, he dropped his jacket and pistol to the floor and grabbed a handful of her hair. He yanked her head back. He might have released her and walked out if only she had returned his glare, if her eyes had held even a trace of triumph or defiance. Instead, they closed.

"Damn you," he whispered. "Damn me."

His mouth came down hard on hers. He pushed his tongue inside as his arm curved around her waist and drew her up flush against him. The feel of her body along his, her scent, the taste of her mouth all combined to snuff out the last flicker of conscience. Desire such as he'd never experienced pulsed through him.

She folded her arms around his neck and drove her fingers up through his hair. Her mouth was responsive, closing seductively around his tongue and making him crazy with wanting more of it, more of her, all of her.

He walked her backward until she was against the wall, then raised the hem of her tank top. There was nothing beneath it but

Elise. He continued pulling up the tank until her arms were raised above her head, the shirt gathered on her forearms. He took both her wrists in one hand and held them pressed against the wall high above her head.

Later, he would regret that he hadn't paused then to study her stretched torso, taken time to gaze at what he'd fantasized about since the first time he'd seen her at the awards dinner. He would regret that he didn't treat his fingertips to the feel of her skin, that he didn't touch her breasts or caress them with his mouth.

But at that moment, he was driven by a primal hunger to have her. He reached under her skirt and palmed her ass, encountering nothing but skin. Growling profanities, or maybe desperate prayers, he lifted her against him and carried her to the sofa.

As she stretched out along it, she pulled off her tank top and tossed it aside. Impatiently he shrugged off his shoulder holster and dropped it on the floor. He planted one knee on the sofa and raised her skirt as far as her waist. He dragged the thong panties down her legs and focused on the patch of soft hair between her thighs. His breathing was a harsh thrashing sound in the otherwise silent room as he grappled with belt buckle and zipper, then he pushed apart her thighs and thrust himself into her.

Sheathed by her, he sank his fingers into her hair and buried his face in the hollow of her neck. He took a precious few seconds to celebrate how damn good that alone felt, just to be inside her, surrounded by her, possessing her.

Then he started moving. His hard, deep strokes were born of frustration almost as much as passion. They drew from her small choppy sounds. Even if she was faking them, he didn't care. He liked them. They urged him on.

Sliding his hands beneath her hips, he angled her up and held her in place as he thrust into her with escalating force, the tempo increasing, the friction growing hotter, until he shattered with pleasure. His climax was long and intense and left him replete.

He settled on her heavily, his breath sighing loudly, humid against her throat. He could have lain there forever, with her beneath him, in that state of blissful lethargy. But even before he had regained his breath, he levered himself up and tried to pull away.

"No." She clutched at him. "No."

Her body was taut. A shallow frown had

formed between her brows. Her eyes were closed and her breathing was rapid. She wet her lips then rolled them inward.

Sliding her hands under his wet shirt, she dug her fingers into the sweat-slick flesh of his back. She mashed her pelvis against his in a gentle grind. The increased pressure caused her breath to catch. He forgot about leaving her, and instead bracketed her hips between his hands and nudged his body against hers. She murmured a low, wanting sound.

He rubbed himself against her while holding her hips even tighter against him. He felt the bite of her nails into his flesh. He made the slightest of rocking motions, but it was sufficient. More than enough. With a soft cry, her back arched off the sofa and her thighs squeezed his hips tightly. He felt her orgasm from the tip of his cock, buried deep inside her, to the back of his throat.

When it receded, she lay panting beneath him. A streetlight shone through the window, casting a shadow upon her breasts in the lace pattern of the tattered curtain. A tear rolled from the corner of her eye into the damp hair at her temple, where a vein pulsed. Her hair was a riot of pale silk behind her head. Her lips looked swollen and bruised.

He wanted very badly to lie with her. He wanted to kiss her, wetly but softly and gently. But that would send him to hell for sure. He'd lost his head and responded to a carnal impulse he could later blame on biology. But he would have no excuse for lingering tenderness. He was in full command of his faculties now, and the enormity of his folly crashed down on him.

She opened her eyes and gazed up at him. Murmuring his name, she lifted her hand toward his cheek. Before she could touch him, he pulled away from her and stood up. Keeping his back to her, he readjusted his trousers and haphazardly buckled his belt. He left his shirttail out. He picked up his holster, but didn't put it on.

He'd gone up against some of the most brutish criminals in Savannah's history, but the most courageous thing he'd ever had to do was turn around and look at this woman.

To his relief, she had sat up. Her skirt was back in place. She hadn't put on her tank top yet, but she was modestly holding it against her chest. That classically feminine, protective pose was seared into his brain for later recall, when remembering how vulnerable she had looked at that moment would cause his heart to ache.

But that was later.

Now, he walked as far as the hallway, where he bent to retrieve his sport jacket and service weapon from the floor. Over his shoulder he said, "Ten o'clock. Have your lawyer with you, and don't be late."

16

Elise awoke, sitting bolt upright, gasping for breath, heart racing. One second, she'd been in a deep sleep, the next it was as though an alarm had sounded loudly in her head, awakening her with a jolt. Frantically she looked around, and although she was surrounded by darkness, she remembered instantly where she was, and why, and what had happened.

When Duncan had walked out, she'd been so distraught, she'd wept until she cried herself to sleep. She'd *slept?* She, the chronic insomniac, had fallen into a dreamless sleep? For how long? Half an hour? Longer? Even as she pulled on her tank top, she tried to read her wristwatch, but it was too dark to see the hands. Cato! What would she tell him?

Sweat had dried on her skin, making it feel tight and dry. She wiped her cheeks and felt the salty tracks of tears. She groped along the floor for her underwear. As she stepped into the panties, she realized that she needed to bathe before she saw Cato.

She grabbed her handbag and within seconds of waking up was feeling her way through the dark house, moving as quickly as possible. She must get home ahead of Cato. Otherwise how would she explain her absence? How would she explain her appearance?

There was only one explanation for that. If he looked at her, he would know instantly what she'd done.

God, please let him still be playing cards.

Whatever his mood, she must deal with it. Since Duncan had made plain his intention to follow through with his investigation, she had no choice now except to continue the pretense with Cato that their relationship was one of matrimonial bliss.

She let herself out the back door through which she had come in. The yard was a hardscrabble landscape of wild grass and weeds that chafed her bare legs as she crossed it in a run.

A gate in the cyclone fence at the back of the yard opened into the alley. It was a rutted, unpaved path lined with garbage cans and the detritus of an uncaring community — rusted-out appliances, old tires, discarded furniture, toys, tools, and trash.

The route back to where she'd left her car led her between the two houses that backed up to the one that Duncan had described as Boo Radley's house. He didn't know it, but *To Kill a Mockingbird* was one of her favorite movies. When she was a kid, she had watched it every time it came on TV. She'd probably seen every movie ever aired on television. Comedies, dramas, mysteries, she loved them all. They had been her escape from the grim reality of her life.

This neighborhood boasted several Boo Radley houses. The ones on either side of her were dark, nothing to indicate that she was being watched from behind shuttered windows. But just when she thought she would get past undetected, a cat jumped out from a scrawny hedge, causing her heart to leap. The cat hissed and bowed his back, then darted back into the shrubbery.

Her car was parked halfway down the block. She was relieved to see that none of the windows had been smashed and that the hubcaps were still there. Having her car vandalized would have been tough to explain to Cato.

Passing under a streetlight, she checked her wristwatch again, and when she saw the time, she almost stumbled on the uneven sidewalk. She'd been asleep for hours!

Frantic with anxiety, she dug into her purse and pulled out her cell phone. If it had rung, it hadn't awakened her. She looked at the readout. Good! No missed calls had been logged.

When Cato had announced his plan to go to the country club, she had told him she was going to take a sleep medication and hopefully get some rest in preparation for the interrogation in the morning. At the risk of disturbing her much-needed sleep, he had said he wouldn't call.

Well, at least he hadn't called her cell phone. But he might have called the house.

She considered calling his cell phone to see where he was. If she caught him still at the club, she could say she was just checking on him. But if he was at home, he would demand to know why she wasn't there, tucked in safe and sound. He would want to know what she was doing out at this hour when she was supposed to be enjoying a medicated sleep. Then what? What would she tell him?

No, better not to call than to risk being put on the spot like that. Her best chance of not being found out was to get home ahead of him. Toward that end, she jogged the remaining distance to her car.

She unlocked it with the remote. It chirped and her headlights flashed once, momentarily relieving the darkness along the deserted street, and reminding her of the strobe lights that had been pulsing during her most recent meeting with Savich.

She opened the car door, tossed her handbag into the passenger seat, and slid in behind the wheel. She hit the automatic lock button as soon as she had closed the door, then quickly started the car and drove away.

Best-case scenario: Cato was still at the club and had done as he said he would and left her to sleep undisturbed. He had played cards into the wee hours last Saturday. Perhaps he had again tonight. *Hopefully* he had.

A slightly more bothersome scenario: He was still at the club, but had been calling the house to check on her. If that was the case, she could explain that she'd taken two tablets of over-the-counter medication. Stronger than she thought, the sleep aid had knocked her out and she'd slept through his calls.

Worst-case scenario: Cato was at home angrily awaiting her return.

To explain her absence, she could say that despite the sleep aid, her insomnia had been so bad she'd gone out for a drive. That was lame, but at least credible.

But how would she explain the unmistakable signs of lovemaking? Duncan hadn't been gentle. Neither had she.

"I don't believe we get to choose who we fall in love with. Do you?"

He hadn't said anything in response to her question. He hadn't needed to. His expression had told her what she'd needed to know. What she already knew.

Once triggered, his passion had been explosive and mindless. It had left marks. Unless she was able to make repairs before she saw Cato, he would surely notice her tangled hair and wrinkled skirt, the whisker burns around her lips.

Checking to see if the abrasion was as visible as it felt, she glanced into the rearview mirror.

A face grinned at her from the backseat.

She cried out in shock and fear, and reflexively stamped hard on the brake pedal.

"Mrs. Laird. We've never actually met. Allow me to introduce myself." With a flourish, the man proffered a business card, holding it between his index and middle fingers. "Meyer Napoli."

After leaving Elise, Duncan had driven

347

around aimlessly for a while. In search of what, he couldn't say. Redemption, perhaps.

But it wasn't going to be found driving the streets of the city, or in a bar, or the gym, or a movie theater, all of which he considered. He ended up at the Barracks.

Only one other detective was in the VCU. When Duncan came in, the officer made a joke of the late hours they were keeping. Duncan said something suitable in reply, then went into his office and closed the door, signaling that he didn't want conversation.

In the back of his mind, he supposed he was thinking that if he was working on the case — actually seated at his desk reviewing the contents of the case file — then he could rationalize his private meeting with Elise.

Even after all that double-talk speculation about Savich, when he'd seen who was waiting for him inside that house, he could credibly say that he'd stayed *only* because he was in pursuit of the truth, a confession, new evidence. Something.

If he could convince himself of that, he could almost excuse himself for what had happened. For several hours he tried. But eventually he gave up the pretense. He'd stayed in that house because he'd wanted to be with her, not to make headway on the case. What had taken place on the dusty sofa could not be classified as police work.

Admitting it was liberating to some extent. But not entirely. He still had to grapple with the guilt.

As long as he was wallowing in his culpability, he'd rather do it in the comfort of home. He left the Barracks and drove the few blocks to his town house. By now it was as close to dawn as to midnight, but as soon as he got inside, he sought refuge in his piano.

He played rock and roll, country, and classics, but every tune had a funereal beat. The music didn't salve his soul as it usually did. He soon quit trying to find comfort in it and lay down on his couch, placed his forearm across his eyes, and gave way to the remorse he'd been trying to outrun since leaving Elise.

It landed on him like an anvil.

On a professional level, there was no justification for what he'd done. He had been intimate with a suspect, probably the primo, numero uno no-no of law enforcement.

DeeDee and his fellow detectives would scorn him. His superiors would discipline him if not outright fire him. But no matter how severe their condemnation, it wouldn't be as harsh as he deserved, or as severe as his self-condemnation. He had compromised an investigation. There was no forgiveness for that.

And even if that were forgivable, there was the other thing — Elise was married.

He'd been the typical preacher's kid, out to prove that he was no holier than the other kids. Growing up, he'd habitually gone looking for mischief and usually found it.

During adolescence, he'd developed a real wild streak. The worst punishment he'd ever received was having to sit through two Sunday morning services so hungover from a Saturday night drinking binge that he'd wanted to cry. He'd had to leave the sanctuary three times to throw up a rancid blend of bile and apple-flavored wine cooler.

His dad had hoped the punishment would teach him a lesson. The experience had only taught him how to choose his liquor more wisely, how to avoid a hangover, and how to handle one if the avoidance tactics didn't work.

Much to his loving parents' despair, he was determined not to be different just because they were in the ministry, which made him even more adventurous than most teenagers. That applied especially to sexual exploration. He started early, and some of the most memorable of those experiences had occurred on church grounds. While the deacons were discussing the purchase of new pews or hymnbooks with his father, he was coaxing kisses from their daughters in the choir room closet, where the robes were stored.

He copped his first feel of a breast at church camp. It was after the evening service, on the walk through the woods from the tabernacle back to the cabins. Two summers later, he lost his virginity in a similar fashion. The next morning when prayers of thanksgiving were said, possibly his was the most sincere.

He'd had some pretty crazy escapades during his college years, but who hadn't? Maturity had made him more cautious and careful — last Saturday night being an exception.

He'd evolved from the horny college kid out to nail any coed who would say yes to a more responsible man who had a genuine liking and respect for women. No matter how long a relationship lasted, or didn't, he tried to conduct himself honorably.

That included never poaching on another man's claim. It most certainly meant never having carnal knowledge of another man's wife.

For over forty years his parents had enjoyed a loving, stable, and happy marriage. There was no doubt in his mind that they were still madly in love and sexually active. The sanctity of the institution was a familiar theme of his dad's sermons.

Duncan supposed, as hell-raising as he'd been, that particular moral lesson had stuck. Adultery was one commandment you didn't break. You just didn't go there. He'd never even been tempted.

But now, he'd taken a married woman, and he was ashamed of himself for it.

The real shame, however, was that, despite everything, he still wanted her.

That would be his punishment, knowing that he could never have her.

No matter how the investigation into the Trotter shooting was ultimately resolved, he would *never* have Elise.

And the investigation wouldn't be left to him to resolve.

He wouldn't be at that ten o'clock interrogation session. Because at nine thirty, he would be in Captain Bill Gerard's office, admitting that, in regards to Mrs. Laird, he hadn't been as objective as he'd claimed to be. Not even as objective as he wanted to be. He would make a full confession to Gerard, taking sole responsibility for what had happened, leaving Elise blameless.

He would ask Gerard not to tell Cato Laird why he was removing himself from the case, and Gerard would probably grant that request, not to spare him, but to spare the judge, Elise, and the police department a public scandal.

Gerard would take some disciplinary action, possibly even demand Duncan's badge. Tomorrow at this time, he might be out of a job. It was no less than he deserved.

There was one other person to whom he must confess. DeeDee. Other coworkers would speculate on why he was no longer serving in his capacity, and probably a few would guess correctly. But DeeDee needed to hear the truth from him. He owed her that. As his partner, and as his friend. Because as both partner and friend, she had warned him against letting his personal feelings for Elise interfere with their investigation. He doubted she would say "I told you so," but even if she did, she'd earned that right.

Having resolved what he would do, he left his couch and trudged upstairs. Before he talked to DeeDee, it seemed only proper, and symbolic, that he wash away all vestiges of Elise.

In his bathroom, he reached into the

shower stall and turned on the faucets, then took off his clothes. Surrendering to a moment of weakness, he held his shirt against his face. He inhaled the essence of her, which seemed woven into the fabric. Then he impatiently stuffed the garment into the hamper before he talked himself into saving it as some kind of romantic souvenir.

He stepped into the shower beneath the spray.

He had looked at what he'd done from a practical, professional, and moral standpoint, forcefully keeping his emotions at bay, fearing that they would prevent him from making the right decisions.

But the warm water of the shower dissolved his control. Moaning, he leaned against the tile wall and pressed the heels of his hands into his eye sockets. The ache inside his chest *was* guilt. He *was* suffering the torment of conscience. Regret *had* sunk its sharp teeth into him.

But he still wanted Elise with every breath he drew.

He couldn't turn it off, this all-encompassing desire. Both tenacious and urgent, it was unlike anything he'd felt for any other woman. It had gripped him the instant he saw her, and tonight, having had her, it was even more acute than before.

Tomorrow he would atone. "I swear I will," he vowed in a ragged whisper.

But tonight . . .

He closed his eyes tightly and let the recollections flow through his mind as freely as his blood surged through his veins. He remembered every detail, vividly. He relived every sound, smell, taste, every touch, every sensation he'd experienced. That first turbulent kiss. Discovering her wet for him. The last sweet ripple of her orgasm.

A raw groan escaped his tight throat. The warm water rained down over his body as a tide of sensation coursed through him, inexorably and uncontainably. As it spilled from him, he shuddered and permitted himself to say, with all the emotion he felt, what he hadn't allowed himself to say before. "Elise. Elise."

Towel around his waist, he walked from his bathroom into his bedroom and sat down on the bed. He was physically exhausted, but knew he wouldn't be able to rest until he'd unburdened himself to DeeDee. This couldn't keep till daylight.

He picked up his cell phone, took a deep breath, and before he could talk himself out of it, speed-dialed her number.

She answered on the first ring. "How'd

you hear so fast? Did Worley call you, too?"

"Huh?"

"You know about Napoli, right?"

"Napoli? No. What about him?"

"They found him on the Talmadge Bridge, deader than a hammer. I'm ten minutes from you." She clicked off before he could say anything else.

For several seconds, he stared at the phone in his hand, wondering if the bizarre conversation had actually taken place or if he'd imagined it. Then, having assimilated what she said, he bounded off the bed and dressed hastily. He finger-combed his wet hair and jogged downstairs, only barely remembering to set the house alarm before leaving.

He was pacing the sidewalk in front of his town house when DeeDee turned the corner onto his street. He jogged to meet her. She stopped only long enough for him to scramble in, then sped away.

"You were farther than ten minutes out."

"I stopped for coffee, Grumpy. Please don't bother to thank me for being kind and considerate enough to guarantee that you get your minimum daily requirement of caffeine."

She had a Big Gulp of Diet Coke wedged between her thighs, but he was too grateful for the coffee to remark on it.

"Are we still mad at each other?" she asked, looking at him out the corner of her eye.

He took a sip of coffee. "I wasn't mad at you."

"You were mad."

"We had a difference of opinion. It happens. Even between people of like minds."

"Well, I was mad at you." He looked over at her. She shrugged. "First for sneaking off to Atlanta without me."

"You wouldn't like Tony Esteban. Trust me on this."

"Then I was mad because you were being so mulish about Elise Laird. For a while there, I was afraid you'd gone round the bend. I was relieved when you decided to bring her downtown tomorrow. Or today, actually."

"Wait, DeeDee. Before you give me too much credit, which I don't deserve, there's something I've got to tell you." He hesitated, trying to find the words for his confession that wouldn't send her into orbit. "Tonight I —"

"From the minute we walked into the Lairds' house the night of the shooting, I've felt that something was out of joint," she said. "I still do. Now this."

" 'Now this'? What do you mean?"

She took the entrance ramp of the bridge too fast. Duncan, never entirely comfortable on the bridge, gripped the armrest and tried to keep from spilling hot coffee in his lap.

From just about any point in downtown Savannah, you could see the Eugene Talmadge Memorial Bridge. That was especially true at night, when its well-lighted struts dominated the northern skyline of the city. Tonight, it was even more visible. At its crest, the flashing colored lights of several emergency vehicles had it lit up like the Fourth of July.

"Forensics is already here. Good," DeeDee said, noticing their van. She brought the car to a halt and opened her door.

Duncan reached across the console and stopped her from getting out. "What did you mean by 'now this'?"

She stuck out her hand, palm up. "I'm betting a hot fudge sundae against an egg white omelet that our dead Meyer Napoli is somehow connected to our dead Gary Ray Trotter."

Duncan looked down at her open palm then reluctantly slapped it.

She was out of the car like a shot.

His confession would have to wait.

Meyer Napoli didn't look as dapper in death as he had in life.

Vain as he was, Napoli would have hated making such a bad-looking corpse. His olive complexion had faded to the color of biscuit dough. It looked even paler in the flash of the crime scene photographer's camera.

"Bled quarts on the inside, I bet," Worley remarked around his toothpick and stepped aside to give Duncan and DeeDee a better view into the car, which was parked on the shoulder of the inbound lane.

Napoli was in the driver's seat. His chin was resting on his chest; he had died gazing at the bullet hole in his upper abdomen and possibly wondering how a wound that small could wreak such havoc.

His hands were lying in his lap, palms up. They'd provided a reservoir for the blood that had trickled from the fatal wound. Perhaps he'd tried to contain the internal hemorrhage by pressing on the bullet hole, until he'd become resigned to the inevitable.

"Bullet must've passed through several organs," Worley told them. "Bursting them like water balloons. He bled out."

"Is that what Dothan said?"

"He hasn't got here yet," Worley replied,

"but I've seen enough men gut shot to know what it looks like."

"Did you find a weapon?"

"Not yet."

"Have you looked?"

Worley removed his toothpick and sneered at DeeDee. "No, Detective Bowen. I'm a damn rookie. Would never occur to me to look for a weapon at a shooting."

Duncan jumped in before they got into one of their verbal skirmishes. "No weapon rules out suicide."

"Correct. Besides, this asshole was too conceited to off himself. But I'm guessing he may have been shot with his own pistol. He always carried a Taurus twenty-five in an ankle holster, with a bullet in the chamber."

"Trusting guy," DeeDee said.

"He bragged about it. One time I personally saw him pull up his pants leg and show it off." Worley bent down and raised the cuff of Napoli's left trouser leg with the tip of a ballpoint pen. A holster was strapped to his ankle with Velcro. It was empty.

"Shell casing?" Duncan asked.

"No sign of one yet. And I've looked," he added for DeeDee's benefit. "Along with forensics. They checked under the car seat. Nothing."

DeeDee said, "Time of death?"

"Dothan will have to nail that. But the blood isn't quite congealed, so I'm guessing not too long ago. Besides, it couldn't have been too long because he would have been discovered sooner."

"Crazy that he was shot here on the bridge," Duncan said. "It's brighter than a shopping mall on this damn thing. Anybody passing would have witnessed the shooting."

"Struck me as strange, too," Worley said. "I guess it was a crime of passion. Unplanned. The act of a moment. This time of morning, traffic's light. Whoever plugged him got lucky. Shot him then boogied outta here before the next car came along.

"Of course, anybody driving past could have thought he was just broken down or something. He's sitting up. No blood visible. It was actually a highway patrolman who found him. He stopped to tell him to get his car moving." Signs were posted at regular intervals prohibiting standing, stopping, or parking on the bridge.

"You questioned the patrolman?"

Worley nodded. "He said, 'What you see is what you get.' "

"Was the car door closed?"

"It was. Patrolman did a cursory check of the area after calling it in. No one else was around or near the car, he said. He didn't see anything, and he didn't touch anything except to open the door and he used a hankie to protect prints."

Duncan looked at the corpse and noted something else. "Have you ever seen Napoli with a hair out of place?"

"Yeah, looks like there might have been a tussle," Worley said. "He used that goo, you know, that kept every hair on his head plastered down."

Napoli's hair was still greasy, but it looked like it had been hit by a hurricane-force wind. His necktie was askew. And yet he was sitting perfectly straight behind the wheel, both feet near the pedals.

Worley, never known for his sensitivity, said around a chuckle, "He'd hate having his picture taken looking like this, wouldn't he?"

"Any other signs of a struggle?" Duncan asked.

"Heel marks over there by the railing. Might or might not be his. We won't know until we can get his shoes off and compare, but Baker and his crew have roped off the scuff marks to check later, just in case."

Duncan wasn't fond of heights. He didn't get nauseous and dizzy like someone with severe acrophobia, but he kept to the inside lane when driving over high bridges and overpasses, and he never went out of his way to hang suspended or to peer into deep gorges.

But he walked toward the wall of the bridge now, where forensics had placed orange traffic cones and yellow crime scene tape to form a perimeter around an area about fifteen feet square. Avoiding that, he stepped to the wall and looked down at the Savannah River two hundred feet below.

The tide was out, so the river was flowing toward the ocean. At high tide, it flowed in the opposite direction, something that puzzled tourists and newcomers until the phenomenon was explained to them. At the tidal mouth of the river, fresh water mixed with seawater to form an estuary. The direction of the river current was dependent upon the tide. Because of all the crosscurrents, this stretch of the river, which was used as the shipping channel, was treacherous.

Duncan walked back to the others. "Attempted carjacking?" There had been a rash of them in the city. Often either the victim or the thief wound up dead.

"Here on the bridge where a pedestrian would be immediately suspect?"

"DeeDee's right, Dunk," Worley said, "this

is something else. This isn't even Napoli's car." He grinned and shifted his toothpick to the other side of his mouth. "That's why I called y'all. This car is registered to Cato Laird."

17

Duncan felt as if the bridge had given way beneath him and he was falling through thin air. He stared at Worley. "Did I hear you right?"

"You heard him right," DeeDee said, grinning. "You owe me a hot fudge sundae." Then she asked Worley if he'd been in contact with the judge yet.

"No one answered their house phone, but Captain Gerard had the judge's cell number on account of the Trotter thing. Found him at Silver Tide Country Club, where he was playing poker with some of his legal eagle buddies."

Duncan had thought it preposterous when Elise had told him about it earlier. Apparently DeeDee thought so, too. "He's out playing poker the night before his wife is interrogated about a fatal shooting?"

Worley shrugged. "He must be confident of her innocence. Or cocksure of his influence. He was playing ante-up with the DA. Anyhow, he confirmed the car is his, said it's the one his wife drives."

Duncan's heart had been ranging from a dead stop to full-out ramming speed. He continued to experience the sensation that he was falling.

"Mrs. Laird's purse was in the passenger seat," Worley told them. "We've bagged it as evidence."

"Of what?" DeeDee asked.

"Of whatever."

Duncan needed to sit down. He needed to vomit. But he had to keep it together, had to appear personally detached, interested only insofar as he was a homicide detective and Elise Laird was a key player in a fatal shooting.

Now two.

He managed the language sufficiently to ask Worley if anybody had seen or heard anything of Mrs. Laird.

"Negativo. Last time the judge saw her was between nine thirty and ten. He said she was gonna take a sleeping pill and go to bed."

But she hadn't taken a pill and gone to bed. She'd met Duncan. He'd seen her since her husband had, tear tracks on her cheeks, holding her tank top against her breasts, looking ravished.

"Soon as Gerard notified the judge of this," Worley was saying, gesturing toward the body, "he tried to reach her at home. When he didn't get an answer, he called the maid, asked her to go to their house, see if the missus was all right. He, the maid, Gerard — who told me all this by phone — converged at the judge's house. The lady of the manor wasn't there, and her bed hadn't been slept in."

"Cell phone?" DeeDee asked.

"It was still in her purse," Worley said. "So either she got separated from it before she was called, or she didn't answer when it was called." Looking beyond DeeDee and Duncan, he said, "Here's Dothan."

As the medical examiner approached, he was breathing heavily from the exertion of walking up the gradual incline from where he'd left his car. Sweat was rolling in wide streams down his fat face. "Napoli's turned up, huh?"

They moved aside and gave him room to inspect the body, although he could barely wedge his bulk into the open car door. "Bullet's well placed. Probably bled out."

"Told you," Worley said, casting DeeDee a smug glance.

"I never said he didn't."

"Hard to tell until we move him, but I don't think there's an exit wound," Worley reported. "No blood leaking around the seat behind him."

"Bullet must've ricocheted off a rib in the rear," the ME observed. "Got the stomach for sure. Could have also hit the liver, spleen, and an artery or two. No telling what all was nicked or busted."

"His pistol is missing from his ankle holster and there's no shell casing," Duncan said.

Brooks took a flashlight from his pocket and directed it toward Napoli's bloody hands, then bent down and sniffed both of them.

"Looks like you're giving him a blow job," Worley remarked.

"You're a pimple on a pig's ass, Worley," DeeDee said.

The ME ignored them. "Don't smell gunpowder, so he didn't shoot himself. Was he in a fight?"

"A struggle of some sort, we think."

"I'll bag his hands. He could have tissue underneath his fingernails."

"That would be a break," Worley said, "if we could nail Elise Laird with a DNA test."

"Hey, y'all?"

The shout came from Baker of forensics.

He was standing near the wall of the bridge, quite a distance from the car. He motioned toward something on the pavement. Duncan was the first to reach him, but when he saw the object, he stopped suddenly, forcing Worley and DeeDee to eddy around him.

DeeDee knelt down. "My gosh. Duncan, do you recognize this?"

He shook his head, but he was lying. A few hours ago, the sandal had been strapped to Elise's right foot.

"I do." DeeDee stood up and faced him. "Mrs. Laird was wearing a sandal like this the other day when we interviewed her and the judge in their sunroom. I remember the turquoise stones. I started to ask her where you can buy sandals like that, but figured it wasn't any place I could afford."

The three detectives moved aside so Baker's photographer could take his pictures of the sandal before it was placed in an evidence bag.

"What do you make of it, Dunk?" Worley asked.

He roused himself from his daze. "Don't know."

"You think she did Napoli?"

"Have you ever known a perp who gut-shot a man, then left her recognizable sandal behind?"

While Worley and DeeDee were mulling that over, sirens signaled the speeding approach of a police vehicle in the opposing lane. When it was even with Elise Laird's car, the souped-up SUV came to an abrupt stop next to the concrete median that divided the inbound and outbound lanes of the bridge.

As soon as the vehicle was braked, doors opened. Bill Gerard stepped from the driver's seat. Judge Cato Laird was riding shotgun. Duncan had never seen him looking so disheveled. He and Gerard stepped over the low wall and crossed the two inbound-traffic lanes at a brisk clip, reaching the car on the shoulder just as the trio of detectives returned to it.

"Okay for us to approach?" Gerard asked Worley, fairly barking the question at him.

"Yes, sir. Forensics is done with the car."

"What about it, Dothan?" Gerard asked.

The ME gave them a brief summary of his findings. "I doubt he lasted long."

"I don't give a damn how long he lasted." Laird elbowed Gerard aside and bore down on Dothan Brooks. "What about my wife?"

"I don't know anything about your wife." The ME removed a handkerchief as large as a tablecloth from his hip pocket and wiped his sweating face with it.

Gerard turned to the detectives. "What do you know?"

He was uncharacteristically curt, probably because his responsibilities in the VCU were now mostly administrative. It had been a long time since he'd attended the scene of a murder, and no matter who'd been killed, even a nasty character like Napoli, it was never a pleasant experience.

But mostly, Duncan guessed, his boss was feeling pressure from the judge to get answers quick.

Worley removed the toothpick from his mouth and gave a concise account of the facts. "A few minutes ago, we found a shoe, a sandal with turquoise stones. Way over there." He pointed to where the photographer was still taking photographs.

"Oh, Jesus." Laird dragged his hand down his face. "Elise owns a pair of sandals like that. I want to see it." He struck off in that direction.

"You may be tempted to pick it up, Judge. Please don't touch it."

He glared at Worley. "I'm not an idiot."

Duncan looked after him, and despite his dislike of the man, he sympathized with his situation. If circumstances were different, vastly different, he would be behaving exactly as the judge. He would be frantic with worry, anguishing over possibilities, desperate for answers.

But he wasn't Elise's husband. He wasn't even her friend. He wasn't her anything except the detective who would probably have to hand her over to the DA for indictment. He couldn't give vent to the uncertainty and fear raging inside him. He had to do his job.

"Chief Taylor called me," Gerard was saying, speaking to his subordinates in an undertone. "Ordered me to personally oversee this investigation, which takes precedence over everything else we're working right now. Give the judge anything he wants, he said. Taylor wants everybody sharp on this. Understand?"

"Excuse me," DeeDee said. "Is Mrs. Laird considered a *victim?*"

"Until we know otherwise." Gerard left them then to rejoin the judge.

"So our investigation just got political," Worley muttered. "Fucking fabulous."

Dothan Brooks walked up to them, wheezing. "Can I have him?"

Duncan left the ME with DeeDee and Worley to discuss transporting Napoli's corpse to the morgue. Slowly he walked back to the cones that sealed off the heel marks on the roadway and squatted down

372

to study them more closely. They might turn out not to be Elise's heel marks at all, but interrupted tire tracks or someone else's heel marks. Any number of things could have made those black smudges on the pavement of a highly trafficked bridge that merged with several major boulevards of downtown Savannah on one end, and with South Carolina state highway 17 on the other.

He looked back at the car, gauging it to be about fifteen feet away from the marks. The sandal had been found at the wall, still farther away. All were within the narrow shoulder of the roadway. Duncan stood up and retraced his footsteps to the car, searching the pavement carefully.

"What're you looking for?" Worley asked, noticing him.

"Blood."

"He was shot in the car."

"Maybe. Or maybe he was shot during a struggle, over there where the scuff marks are. He staggered back, managed to get into the driver's seat and close the door."

"Thinking maybe he could drive himself away."

"He could have been gushing blood on the inside, but there was only a trickle on the outside," Duncan said. "He didn't drip any, especially if he was clutching the wound, as the smears on his hands and shirt indicate."

"He could also have been shot right where we found him behind the steering wheel of Mrs. Laird's car."

"Dammit!" Duncan said, acknowledging that what Worley said was true. "What was a slug like Meyer Napoli doing behind the steering wheel of Mrs. Laird's car?"

"Beats me," Worley said.

The ambulance had been motioned forward. The driver wove it between squad cars that had the inbound lanes of the bridge temporarily blocked to traffic, which at this time of morning was light. Worley wandered back to where DeeDee was conversing with Dothan Brooks.

Left alone, Duncan returned to the area blocked off by the traffic cones and cautiously peered over the nearby wall of the bridge. He didn't look at the flowing river this time, however, but at the bridge itself.

Spanning two thousand feet, it had been built to replace a drawbridge that had become inefficient in handling the traffic on the river as Savannah's importance as a seaport increased.

Duncan had driven across the bridge a thousand times, but because of his aversion

374

to heights and suspension, he'd kept his eyes on the road. He'd never studied the structure of the bridge. He'd certainly never been this up-close and personal with its awe-inspiring construction and massive proportions.

He leaned as far over the wall as he dared and studied the infrastructure. As he was mentally gauging the height of the nearest tower, which supported the struts, he noticed a descending metal ladder that connected to a piece of machinery — he didn't even know what to call it — on the underside of the bridge. And on the floor of that thingamajig, he spotted something fluttering, something that didn't belong.

He jogged toward the tower, keeping his eyes trained on the spot, hoping that what had captured his attention wouldn't disappear before he could determine exactly what it was. When he was directly above it, he leaned over the wall and looked down onto the mechanism below.

What he'd seen was a piece of cloth. Light-colored, soft-looking, out of place on this brutally masculine structure of iron and steel and concrete.

Napoli's body was being transferred from the car to a gurney. Worley and DeeDee had been cleared by forensics to investigate the interior of the car. They were busy with that. Gerard was catching an earful of abuse from Judge Laird, who was punctuating his tirade with jabs of his index finger.

"Why are your detectives concentrating on what happened to Napoli?" Duncan heard him say. "They need to be searching for my wife."

Duncan returned to his study of the piece of machinery attached to the underside of the bridge and to the ladder that connected it to the level on which he was standing. Trying to stave off the dizziness assailing him, he switched his focus to the giant tanker gliding beneath the bridge on its way out to sea. However, the movement of the vessel only made his vertigo worse.

Nevertheless, he threw his leg over the wall, stepped onto the small platform at the top of the ladder, and started down. The metal rungs were enclosed by bars that formed a small cylindrical cage, but those bars were widely spaced and he wasn't sure they would hold him if he was to slip and fall backward against them.

He was about halfway down when he heard Gerard exclaim, "Dunk! What the hell are you doing?"

He glanced up. A mistake. He was blinded by the lights on the top of the tower, shining down on the bridge. In the direction of Gerard's voice, he shouted up, "There's something down here."

"Are you crazy?"

That from DeeDee, practically screeching.

"Probably," he said under his breath.

"Get back up here!"

Ignoring her, he continued down. Thankfully he had put on sneakers when he'd quickly dressed. Their rubber soles gave him a better grip than dress shoes would have. He had pulled on a pair of latex gloves as soon as he and DeeDee had arrived at the scene. Inside them his hands were wet with nervous perspiration. He didn't dare look down at the swift current of the river, now churning in the wake of the tanker.

"Bill?" he called up. "Do you know anything about this thing under here?"

"The carrier?"

"I guess."

"There are three of them. One for each section of the bridge. They connect to tracks on each side of it. They roll along the underside of the bridge so workers have access to the navigational lights. They can do maintenance, conduct inspections. Like that."

"So no one except maintenance workers

would come down here, right?"

"And damn fools!" he heard DeeDee shout.

Maintenance workers didn't wear clothes made of soft fabric that could flutter when there was no wind and only a negligible breeze.

He risked glancing down and was relieved to see that he had only three more rungs to go. He took them with relative speed and stepped onto the carrier. Solidly built, it was an impressive example of ingenuity and engineering, but he was glad that someone else had the job of working on it. To him, it seemed a hell of a long way to the other side of the bridge. And beyond that, empty air. He didn't want to think of the nothingness directly beneath him.

Instead he stayed focused on the area immediately surrounding him. The fixtures lighting the bridge from its underside were as bright and eyeball-searing as suns. He tried to avoid looking directly into them as he went down on his haunches. The piece of fabric was snagged on a bolt that secured the ladder to the floor of the carrier.

One edge of the printed material was hemmed. The other had obviously been ripped from a garment . . . which in this case was the skirt Elise had been wearing that night.

Pinching the fabric between two gloved fingers, he carefully worked it free from the metal on which it had become snagged, then placed it in a brown paper evidence bag. Slowly, he stood up and returned the bag to his pocket.

His colleagues were shouting questions down to him. He was no longer in their sight so they were concerned about his safety. They wanted to know if he was all right. They were admonishing him to be careful. He heard Worley ask if he'd found anything.

Tuning them out, he forgot his acrophobia and stared into the river far below him, where the water at this point was over forty feet deep. He looked at the slow-moving tanker, a floating city, now gliding past the restaurants and bars lining River Street and, on the far side, the docks at the Westin Resort.

His throat became uncommonly tight as he realized the implication of finding only one of Elise's sandals and this scrap of fabric ripped from her clothing.

Chances were very good that she hadn't made it off this goddamn bridge alive.

18

Judge Laird paced the limited square footage of the SVU office, wearing a path in the ugly maroon carpeting and muttering affirmations to himself that his wife was alive. He also launched into periodic tirades about the sluggish pace and general ineptitude with which the police investigation was being conducted.

He demanded immediate answers to questions to which no one had answers. He refused to accept honest replies such as, "We don't know, but we're doing all we can to find out."

Unfortunately DeeDee had been put in charge of him.

After cordoning off a larger section of the bridge to include the carrier and the ladder leading down to it, DeeDee had accompanied Bill Gerard and the judge back to police headquarters, while Duncan and Worley stayed behind to coordinate the investigation, which would involve several other law enforcement agencies.

She resented that they'd have all the fun, while she'd been assigned what amounted to baby-sitting duty. But Captain Gerard had issued the order, and he'd been in no mood for argument.

Actually she would have felt sorry for Judge Laird, had he not been such a total bastard. Rarely did he address a question directly to her. Any unsolicited conjecture or suggestion she made was ignored. He tolerated her, barely, and only because he must.

The Cato Lairds of the world, good ole boys that custom-tailored suits couldn't disguise, underscored the insecurity that had been instilled in her by her parents, particularly her father. The judge's disdain reduced her achievements to mediocrity and insignificance. He made her feel as her father had, like a tinfoil star trying to replace the solid-gold one her older brother had been.

It also had fallen to her to question the judge about his activities before being notified of Napoli's murder in his wife's car, and to ask what he knew of her activities during that same time period.

That was the shittiest aspect of this shit detail.

He was frenetic. He could sit still for only a few minutes at a stretch. He was easily distracted by anyone who came into or left the unit. Every time a telephone rang, which was often, his reflexes went into overdrive.

When she did manage to hold his attention, he either answered her questions with dramatized resignation or took umbrage, although she went out of her way to be tactful.

"When was the last time you saw Mrs. Laird?"

"About nine thirty or so. We'd had dinner. Elise wanted to turn in early. That being the case, I asked if she would mind if I went to the country club. A poker tournament had commenced last Saturday night. I knew some of my friends would be playing last night."

"Given her insomnia, it's unlike Mrs. Laird to go to bed early, isn't it?"

"She'd bought a sleep aid that she hoped would help her rest."

"Do you usually play poker on a work night, so to speak?"

"No, but we were both upset and needed something to take our minds off the interrogation that was scheduled for the morning."

"Why was the prospect of that upsetting?"

"Detective Hatcher advised us to bring our attorney with us. He made it sound as though Elise was a criminal."

"We had more questions about her relationship with Coleman Greer."

"Elise gave you a full explanation of their relationship."

For the time being, DeeDee let that pass and moved on. "Did you speak with Mrs. Laird by telephone, or have any contact with her, after you left the house yesterday evening?"

"No. In the hope that the sleep medication was working, I didn't want to disturb her by calling."

"I doubt she took that medication, Judge. We know she didn't sleep." She didn't let his fulminating look prevent her from pressing on. "What was she wearing when you last saw her?"

"A skirt and sleeveless top. You know this, Detective Bowen. I recognized the scrap of fabric that your partner found on the carrier. It was from Elise's skirt."

"You're sure? Most husbands wouldn't notice or remember —"

"I'm not most husbands," he said icily.

"The skirt was new. I'd just brought it home to her as a gift. She had tried it on for me."

"Did she have on the sandals with the turquoise stones?"

"She was barefoot."

"For dinner?"

"We had dinner on trays in the bedroom."

"I see. Mrs. Berry served you there?" He nodded. "What time did she leave?"

"I heard her tell Captain Gerard that she left around ten thirty."

"After you, then."

"Correct. She wanted to make certain that Elise didn't need her."

"Sometime after Mrs. Berry left, your wife put on her shoes and left the house in her car."

"We don't know the circumstances under which she left," he said. "She could have been forced from the house."

"Maybe, but according to Captain Gerard, who was at your house, there was no sign of a struggle, forced entry, nothing like that. We can rule out robbery because Gerard said you'd found her jewelry, wedding ring, and ear studs — sizable diamonds in both — on her dressing table."

"That's right."

"So it looks like she dashed out in a hurry, doesn't it? I mean, not even remembering to put on her wedding ring. And that's a ring you wouldn't likely leave behind unless you were really rattled."

The judge stayed stonily silent, while DeeDee tapped her pencil against the legal pad on which she'd been jotting down notes. "Do you have any idea where your wife might have gone, Judge?"

"If I did, don't you think I'd be looking for her there?"

"Does she have friends or family —"

"No."

"Nobody she might have decided to go visit, even on the spur of the moment?"

He shook his head. "Not without telling me."

She didn't tell you about her visits with Coleman Greer, DeeDee thought peevishly. Tired of all the pussyfooting around, she cut to the chase. "Do you think she had an appointment with Meyer Napoli tonight?"

He leaned in close to her, his features rigid with rage. "Is this the way you solve crimes, Detective Bowen? You hound a victim's loved ones with silly questions and draw asinine conclusions?"

Probably he didn't expect an answer, but she gave him one. "Sometimes. You'd be surprised what witnesses know that they don't know they know. I toss out possibilities to see if anything sticks. Often something does, and it can be that seemingly unimportant, silly fact that ultimately solves the case."

He looked around impatiently as though searching for someone to come to his rescue. Gerard had disappeared; DeeDee assumed he was in his office. A few other detectives were milling around, trying to look busy, but actually drawn to the excitement as moths to a flame.

The judge said, "I know the importance of being thorough and precise, Detective Bowen. After all my years on the bench, I realize that crime-solving nuggets can be pried from the memory of a witness. But I know only what I've told you. *Repeatedly,*" he stressed.

She flipped back a sheet of the legal tablet so she would have a fresh page on which to take notes. "May I continue?"

And so it had gone for a grueling hour and a half. Finally, believing he had nothing else that he was able or willing to tell her, she released him to do his pacing and haranguing.

She used a phone outside the SVU to place a call to the manager of the Silver Tide Country Club. She woke up his wife, who woke him up after DeeDee identified herself and conveyed the urgency of the call. From him she got phone numbers for the club's parking valet and bartender who'd been on duty that night.

She called them at their respective residences. Neither was happy to be called at this hour, especially after having worked a long shift. But both confirmed to her that the judge had arrived at the club shortly before ten o'clock and joined a spirited poker game. He hadn't left until he was notified by police that Mrs. Laird's car had been found on the narrow shoulder of the Talmadge Bridge with a dead man inside.

"When he was told that there was no sign of her, he freaked," the bartender told DeeDee.

"I can imagine." She asked the names of those with whom the judge had been playing cards all evening. It was a star-studded lineup of movers and shakers, including the district attorney.

If indeed it turned out that Elise Laird had met Meyer Napoli for no honest purpose, while the judge was enjoying a night of poker and single-malt scotch, he would have a lot to live down. He would look even more a fool for love than before. Some political enemies, and possibly even loyal supporters, might question whether such a fool should be chief judge of superior court.

The professional repercussions of this situation might account for some of his crankiness.

Gerard reappeared to check on how the judge was holding up, and also to ask DeeDee to notify Napoli's secretary of her boss's demise and see about contacting his next of kin.

Upon hearing the news, the secretary lapsed into hysteria. It surprised DeeDee that Napoli could evoke that much emotion — except perhaps fury or repulsion — from another human being. Once she had calmed down, the secretary explained that Napoli had no relatives that she knew of and agreed to go to the morgue in the morning to identify his body.

She also demanded to know what was being done to track down the "monster" who'd shot him. DeeDee assured her that homicide detectives were on the case to do just that.

The sky was turning gray with approaching dawn and DeeDee was on her third six-pack of Diet Coke when Duncan and Worley trudged in. Worley looked exhausted and glum. Duncan looked like something dug up from Colonial Cemetery next door.

They'd barely cleared the doorway when

Laird pounced on them. "Well?"

"Get us some coffee, will ya?"

DeeDee was about to remind Worley that fetching his coffee wasn't in her job description. But she took a closer look at Duncan's haggard face and realized that he needed a pick-me-up, and needed it in a hurry. She went to pour two cups of coffee, but kept her ears tuned to what was being said.

"The GPA and DOT have agreed to give us the outside lane of the bridge for a while longer," Worley said, referring to the Georgia Port Authority and the Department of Transportation. "They're not happy about it. It'll create a bitch of a traffic problem come morning rush hour, but we want that scene for as long as we can have it. Something may show up in daylight that we missed tonight."

He gratefully took the Styrofoam cup of coffee from DeeDee. Duncan didn't seem to notice the cup she extended to him until she nudged his shoulder. He looked at her blankly for several seconds, then reached for the coffee.

"Never mind the traffic jam," Laird said. "What are you doing to locate Elise?" He addressed the question to Duncan.

"The canine unit has all the dogs out. They're combing both banks of the river and Hutchinson Island."

"That's very limited. What about the other islands between here and the ocean?" the judge asked. "Are those being searched?"

No one wanted to tell him that rarely did a person make it as far as the mouth of the river. For all the accident victims and jumpers who had gone off the bridge, DeeDee knew of only one who had survived the fall. Usually a body surfaced within a few days, depending on the time of year and the temperature. It would show up somewhere along River Street or near the Corps of Engineers' dock on Hutchinson Island, which divided that stretch of the river into two channels.

"We'll expand the ground search as needed, Judge," Gerard said diplomatically. "What else, Dunk?"

"An APB was issued with a physical description of Mrs. Laird, so that engages state troopers, this department, the sheriff's office. The marine patrol is searching every channel of the river. The Coast Guard has already launched one craft," he said. "It's cruising the Atlantic coastline, but . . ."

But, again, rarely did a body make it that far before reappearing, DeeDee thought. If it got that far, it would probably be lost forever.

"Coast Guard will also have search-and-rescue teams in choppers," Duncan said. "They're being mobilized as we speak. We've had the department's helicopters airborne almost since you left the bridge and came back here." The update seemed to have sapped what energy Duncan had left. He paused to sip his coffee.

"I've heard that the main switchboard has been lit up with incoming calls," Gerard said. "People have seen the helicopter searchlights moving along the river, want to know what's going on."

"I don't care who it inconveniences," Laird said. "Keep those helicopters in the air."

"Of course." Gerard looked frazzled and annoyed. The judge's imperious attitude had worn thin. "I tell you this only because if citizens want answers, you can be sure the media does. Sooner or later we're going to have to address the reporters who've assembled downstairs."

"We had to fight our way through them when we came in," Worley said. "Didn't tell them anything, of course."

"I've fielded a half dozen calls myself that have come into the unit here under the pretense of having information on Mrs. Laird," Gerard continued. "The press knows it was Meyer Napoli who got popped on the bridge. Reporters also know that Mrs. Laird is somehow involved, but they don't know how or to what extent. You should be thinking about how you want to handle that, Judge."

Laird deflated and sat down heavily in the nearest chair. In a matter of seconds, the fight went out of him and he acquired the lost, vulnerable, and defeated bearing of a victim. He slumped forward and stared at the floor.

They gave him those moments. No one said anything. For once, even Worley was sensitive enough to keep his crude mouth shut.

Finally Judge Laird raised his head and looked at Duncan. "Did you find *anything?* Any clue to her whereabouts?"

"That scrap of fabric." Duncan cleared his throat and combed his fingers through his hair. By the look of it, that wasn't the first time it had been thoughtlessly pushed back in that manner. "You, uh, you said you thought it came from a skirt belonging to Mrs. Laird."

"I don't think, I *know.*"

DeeDee said, "We covered that. The skirt was new as of today. A gift from him."

DeeDee couldn't imagine why that would

make Duncan look so pained, but it did. He actually winced. "We don't know how it came to be on the carrier," he said. "Forensics dusted the rungs of the ladder for prints, but with all the workers who've gone up and down it . . ." He let the sentence trail, again seeming to have run out of steam.

"Any trace of the other sandal?"

Duncan shook his head. "No sign of it or of anything else belonging to her. As soon as it's light, the department's dive team will . . . will begin their search."

The sound that came from the judge was very much like a dry sob.

DeeDee saw Duncan glance at Worley, who had become busy engraving a pattern onto his Styrofoam cup with his fingernail, his way of relinquishing this unpleasant duty to Duncan.

"What came to our attention that we didn't notice earlier," Duncan continued, "is that her sandal probably wasn't removed voluntarily. The strap was still buckled."

DeeDee said, "The sandal could be slipped on and off without unbuckling the strap. I'm almost sure."

He nodded. "But the heel strap was torn out of the sole."

Gerard asked, "How could that happen, Dunk?"

He rolled his shoulders as though they ached. "It would have taken some force, I think." It wasn't much of an answer, but it said enough, more than any of them wanted to address.

Duncan seemed to be finding it difficult to speak. DeeDee never remembered that happening before, not even when he'd had to notify a crime victim's next of kin that the most horrendous fate imaginable had befallen his or her loved one.

"We're checking the marks on the pavement against the heels on Napoli's shoes," he said, "but what it looks like is that he and Mrs. Laird engaged in some sort of struggle near the wall." He spoke directly to the judge. "Maybe he stepped on the back of her sandal, causing the strap to break. Just because I found that piece of fabric on the carrier doesn't mean that's where it was ripped from her skirt. It could've drifted down there after being torn off during a struggle on the bridge."

"Maybe over possession of the weapon," Worley said, finally making a contribution. Everyone's attention shifted to him. "We haven't found Napoli's pistol, but we're working under the assumption that he was shot with it. However, Judge, if you'd inventory your guns as soon as you get home, we would appreciate it."

The judge bristled. "Are you suggesting that Elise left home, armed with a pistol, for a meeting with Meyer Napoli?"

"She was trained in how to use a handgun," DeeDee remarked, since it seemed she was the only cop in the room with balls enough to mention that. "Isn't that what we were told?"

The judge turned to her, his eyes fierce with anger. "Yes, that's what you were told. You were also told that she agreed to the training at my insistence. She didn't like handling guns. She wouldn't have taken one from home."

"If you can account for all the handguns you own," Duncan said, "and I'm betting you can, then we could rule out that Napoli was shot with a weapon belonging to you. In the meantime, we're going on the assumption that it was his gun that killed him."

"During a struggle over it outside the car, near the wall of the bridge?"

"That's one theory," Worley said in reply to Gerard's question. "It's only conjecture at this point."

"Conjecture," the judge said heatedly.

"But you have *no* idea what actually happened, do you?"

"One thing we know," Worley said, matching the judge's testiness, "is that at some point one or both of them were in the backseat."

"The backseat?"

Worley was too busy looking smug over the point he'd scored to reply, leaving Duncan to explain. "Baker's guys collected grains of some compound from the floorboard carpet. Driver's seat, passenger seat, backseat."

"What the hell are you talking about? What compound?"

"We can't be positive till we get the lab to confirm it, but it looks like ordinary cement," Worley said. He rubbed his fingers together. "Ground up to dust, like. We called the morgue and asked Dr. Brooks's assistant to check Napoli's shoes. He confirmed there were traces of some gray stuff on the soles. Looks like gritty powder with chunks in it.

"And the same stuff was on the sole of Mrs. Laird's sandal," he went on. "Meaning, as I said, that one or both of them were in the backseat as well as the front." He paused for effect. "If the lab can determine for sure what this stuff is, and give us a guess as to its origin, it might point us to where Napoli and Mrs. Laird linked up."

Duncan dragged a hand down his face, catching DeeDee's attention. She'd never seen him this shaken, not even after they'd left the most horrible of horrible homicides. She wondered, not for the first time, about the depth of his attraction to Elise Laird.

He wasn't comporting himself like an objective policeman investigating a case. Naturally he would be concerned about the fate of any citizen who had disappeared from a crime scene where another individual had died. But he seemed to be inordinately upset by this crime scene in particular.

She stared at him long enough for him to sense it. When he looked over at her, she mouthed, *Are you all right?* He mouthed, *Just tired,* and went back to listening to Worley as he addressed Laird's exception to his terminology.

"When I said 'linked up,' I wasn't implying anything illicit, Judge. It was just a figure of speech."

"Elise would not have agreed to meet that man. Especially alone. I'm sure he forced his way into her car."

"Possibly," Worley said behind a dry cough. "The car seems to be in perfect running condition. No flat tire, nothing like that. So we don't know why they pulled over and stopped at the highest part of the bridge, when there are signs against parking posted every few yards. And then there's the question of why they were headed back into the city, indicating that they'd been somewhere else and were returning. Any idea?"

"None."

Worley continued, unfazed by the judge's curtness. "We'll ask for any possible eyewitnesses to come forward. Anyone who drove across the bridge ahead of that highway patrolman could have seen something. We can't predict what an appeal to the public like that will yield. Ordinarily, it's not much, but maybe this time will be an exception."

Duncan said, "Detective Worley and I agree that at some point they got out of the car and were standing near the wall, but we don't know why."

"He was sitting on his business card," DeeDee said. She explained to Judge Laird and Gerard that they'd found Napoli's business card in the driver's seat when his body was removed. "It's unlikely he would have been sitting on it unless he'd got out, then got back in."

Duncan nodded. "We don't know why they got out, but if we're reading the signs right, an altercation of some sort took place there along the wall. This theory is borne out by the broken sandal, the fabric ripped from Mrs. Laird's skirt, and the scuff marks on the pavement."

"You're thinking that Napoli was holding her at gunpoint?" Gerard said, asking for clarification.

"Again it's conjecture, Bill, but that's a distinct possibility," Duncan said. "If we're able to find Napoli's weapon and determine that it fired the fatal shot, then it becomes an even greater possibility."

"How so?"

"Indications are that the pistol was fired from close range directly into his stomach, so more than likely he was facing the individual who shot him. But he was found sitting face forward behind the steering wheel of the car. In order to get a shot like that, the shooter would have had to reach around him from the side. That would be an awkward, to say nothing of inconvenient, angle for anyone either standing in the open door of the car or sitting in the passenger seat. That's why we think maybe — and I emphasize *maybe* — that he was shot outside the car."

"Was there an exit wound?" Gerard asked.

"No. First thing Dothan looked for when

he removed the body. That's why there was so little blood and Napoli caught most of it in his hands." He paused, then summarized. "Worley and I think it's possible that while they were wrestling over the pistol, it discharged. Clutching his wound, Napoli managed to get back into the car before he died."

"But that doesn't explain where Elise is," the judge said, looking around wildly. "If . . . if it was as you described, then she was trying to protect herself, fighting for her life. Right? Maybe he was trying to push her. . . ."

Worley coughed behind his hand again. "Possibly."

Duncan looked ready to hurl chow.

The judge fell apart. "Oh Jesus! Where is she? What did he do to her?"

Given his emotional state, no one was brave enough to venture a guess. After a moment, Gerard walked over to him and laid a comforting hand on his shoulder. "I urge you to go home, Judge. Wait there for further word."

"I can't leave. Something could turn up at any moment."

"It could, and you will be notified immediately when it does. In the meantime, there's nothing you can do here. The detective work from this point gets tedious. We'll go over everything again among ourselves, but basically we'll be waiting, too. Every law enforcement agency in the state is in on the search. As soon as she's found —"

"Stop bullshitting me, Bill," the judge said, angrily throwing off Gerard's hand. "You think he pushed her from the bridge. You think she's dead, don't you?"

Gerard kept his expression impassive. "I go by what I *know,* not by what I *think,* and right now, we know precious little. I won't consider her dead until I see her body. It could be that Mrs. Laird was traumatized by whatever happened on that bridge. She could be wandering around in a daze. Given everything that's taken place this week, starting with Trotter, that would be understandable. When she's found, or comes to her senses, she'll return home. You want to be there if she finds her way back."

That argument seemed to penetrate when no others had. Laird nodded absently and came slowly to his feet. He let himself be guided toward the door. "I'll walk you down and have an officer drive you home and stay there with you," Gerard said.

"Unnecessary."

"No argument. Napoli had a lot of enemies, so most won't be sorry he's dead. But it's possible he had an ally or two. In the unlikely event that he did, I'm taking no chances and neither is Chief Taylor. You'll have police protection until we sort all this out." He hesitated, then said, "It goes without saying that if you hear anything from Mrs. Laird, you'll contact us without delay."

The judge stopped and turned to him with a frown of consternation. "I would protect Elise with my own life," he said. He made eye contact with each of the detectives in turn. "But I would also do the right thing."

19

"Like hell he'd do the right thing," DeeDee muttered after the judge and Gerard were out of earshot. "He lied to us about Napoli in order to protect her. He may be lying now. He may know exactly what happened on that bridge."

"I don't think so." Duncan was almost too weary to speak. He was certainly too exhausted to go toe to toe with DeeDee, who was wired and fidgety, partly from guzzling caffeine. She was also juiced over the startling events of the past night. Her eyes were unnaturally bright and restive as she looked over at him. "You don't think he's lying?"

"He may be lying about some aspects of this, but I don't think he knows what happened on that bridge."

"Who the hell does, except Napoli and the broad." Worley had gnawed his toothpick into splinters and was patting down his pockets in search of the cigarettes he'd quit smoking two years ago. In times of stress, he reverted to the conditioned motions if not to the habit. "One of them is dead and the other one's disappeared."

"Which doesn't distinguish it from most of our cases," DeeDee remarked. "Name me one time we've found the doer standing over the do-ee with the weapon at his feet and his hands in the air."

"Yeah, but in this case . . ."

Worley let the rest of his thought go unspoken as Gerard returned, saying as he came in, "Judge Laird is on his way home. Unhappily, but obediently."

"What about the media?"

"They swarmed us. TV, newspaper, the whole shebang is outside. We gave them the standard 'no comment,' but soon we'll have to make some kind of statement."

"Will you clear that statement with Judge Laird and the chief?"

Gerard nodded. "In fact, Chief Taylor will probably want to conduct the press conference himself. Judge Laird is a respected community leader, high-profile public servant, a man with strong convictions and an unimpeachable reputation for fairness. He has the support of every law enforcement agency, and those agencies are working round the clock to locate Mrs. Laird." He finished with a sigh. "So forth."

"What will he say about Mrs. Laird being in the company of a disreputable character like Napoli in the middle of the night?" DeeDee persisted.

"Don't have the vaguest," Gerard replied. "It'll be the public information office's problem to give that particular element the right spin. My problem — *our* problem — is locating Mrs. Laird so we can solve this thing."

"Mrs. Laird or her body," Worley said.

Duncan's heart constricted. Thankfully DeeDee jumped on Worley's statement, freeing him of having to comment immediately. "Are you sold on the scenario you laid out for the judge?"

"Not entirely," Worley admitted.

"I'm glad to hear it," she said. "Because I think that if Napoli had been shot during a struggle over the pistol, Mrs. Laird would have dropped it in horror and called for help. I mean, wouldn't you? Even if you were in a struggle for your life, and the other guy wound up getting shot, wouldn't you try to get aid immediately and explain the circumstances under which he was shot?"

"That's what she did with Trotter," Duncan observed quietly. "We didn't believe her story. Maybe she's twice shy."

"Which brings me to point B," DeeDee said, undeterred. "If a person is involved in an accidental fatal shooting once in a lifetime, it's bizarre, a quirk of fate, damned rotten luck. It's happened to this lady *twice* in one *week?* Give me a break."

"Dunk is talking out both sides of his mouth, DeeDee," Worley said. "Your conclusion is the one we drew, too. We talked about it before we got here. Dunk and I agree that if Mrs. Laird was able to call for help after Napoli was shot, she would have called."

" 'Able' meaning what, exactly?" she asked.

" 'Able' meaning alive," Worley replied. "Or 'able' meaning innocent of any wrongdoing."

"Option one would indicate that Napoli pushed her off the bridge at the exact instant she shot him." DeeDee's frown dismissed that as a remote possibility. "I'll go with option two. Mrs. Laird gained control of the pistol, backed Napoli into the driver's seat of the car, and plugged him in the stomach for all the trouble he's caused her in recent months. She then fled on foot —"

"One foot," Duncan interjected.

"— taking the pistol with her. Or throwing it in the river."

"She commits murder and leaves a shoe behind for evidence?" Duncan said, angrily coming to his feet. "She 'fled' without taking her handbag, credit cards, cash?"

"Well, what do you think, then?" DeeDee fired at him.

"I —"

He closed his mouth with a soft click of his teeth. He didn't know what he thought.

He didn't want to think of Elise being so coldhearted that she had fatally shot two men in the space of a week to protect her marriage and lifestyle with Cato Laird.

But it was even worse to think of her foundering in the river before being dragged under by the wake of an oceangoing vessel.

Neither could he endure thoughts of her pleading for his help, and his refusing it, hours before she died by one violent means or another.

If they thoroughly analyzed that scrap of fabric from her skirt, they would find human skin cells, and at least some of them could belong to him. He recollected grabbing handfuls of that soft fabric and bunching it up around her waist, out of his way.

If they checked his shoes, they'd find gritty gray powder on the soles. He could tell Worley exactly where to find a sidewalk in such disrepair that it was crumbling into dust.

The matching gray residue found on Napoli's shoes was proof that he had also been in that neighborhood last night. No way did Duncan believe that to be a coincidence. But what was eating at him was this: Did Elise have an appointment to meet Napoli after her interlude with him in the abandoned house? Or had Napoli abducted her when she returned to her car, and forced her to drive to the middle of the bridge?

The car was in the *inbound* lane. Where had they been?

Was she an innocent victim? Or guilty of double murder?

These questions warranted some serious brainstorming with his colleagues. Knowing Elise's actions before she met with Napoli was the kind of clue-worthy information that he often wrung from material witnesses who were reluctant to disclose it, fearing either retribution or exposure of their own misdeeds.

Now, he was that material witness. He was withholding pertinent information. His coworkers were watching him, Gerard and Worley with puzzlement, DeeDee with dangerous perception.

He should tell them about him and Elise now. He should come clean, as he had resolved to do. He should admit to what had happened mere hours before Napoli died bloody and Elise pulled a vanishing act.

But if he did, *if he did,* he would be immediately removed from the case. He would probably be fired and possibly jailed, but by one means or another, he would be banished from the police department. Confession would amount to abandoning Elise.

He couldn't do that, not now, not after last night. Whether she was already dead or still alive, he had to learn what had happened to her. If she was the perpetrator, the killer of two men, he would see to it that she was brought to justice, and own up to his own guilt as well. If it was determined that she was the victim, he wouldn't stop looking for her until she was rescued, or her body was recovered.

But in order to carry out either pledge, he must remain at the epicenter of the investigation. That was essential.

The others were waiting for an answer. He plopped down into a swivel chair, grumbling, "I don't know what to think."

In lieu of a cigarette, Worley put a fresh toothpick in his mouth. DeeDee took a sip of room-temperature Diet Coke. Gerard was the one to break the charged silence.

"I've been thinking about the timing," he said. "The housekeeper left Mrs. Laird at home around ten thirty. Dothan called a while ago to tell me that he places the time of Napoli's death somewhere between two thirty and three. Where were he and Mrs. Laird for that four hours in between, and what were they doing?"

Well, Duncan could account for an hour of her time.

Had she met Napoli immediately after he'd left her in the abandoned house? Or later?

"If we knew where they were returning from, we might know how they'd filled that time," DeeDee said.

"I've got a problem with his being shot outside the car," Worley said. "The highway patrolman told me that the car door was closed. He remembers that clearly because he knocked on the driver's window before he took a closer look inside and saw that Napoli was dead."

"Okay," DeeDee said. "What's your point?"

"Who closed the car door?"

"Napoli," she returned.

"He couldn't have," Duncan said, real-

410

izing what Worley was getting at. "There was no blood on the door handle or the panel."

"Right," Worley said. "Napoli's hands were bloody."

"So he was shot inside the car, and either the shooter closed the door, or the shooter was inside the car with him," Gerard said.

"Either way leaves us with yet another mystery," Worley said. "Why did savvy, ass-saving Napoli just sit there and let the shooter reach around him to put a bullet square in the spot where it would do the most damage?"

"Especially when a shot to the head would have been much easier and just as deadly," Duncan said.

"But that would also have been messy," DeeDee said. "People driving by would have seen the gore on the windows."

"Besides, a shot to the head is quick, probably painless." They all looked toward Worley for elaboration. "What I mean is, when you go for a gut shot, you're going for a fatal wound, but a slow one. You want to give your victim time to think, Holy shit, I'm gonna fucking die!"

"I think our lady is capable of that," DeeDee said. When nobody responded, she looked first at Worley. "Worley?"

He shrugged. "Don't know her, but I trust your instincts. Dunk, what do you think?"

"If she did him, how'd she get Napoli to just sit there and let her do it, when he outweighed her almost a hundred pounds?"

"She was whispering sweet nothings in his ear?" DeeDee said.

None of the men smiled, especially Duncan. "Okay. Then why in her own car? Why did she leave so many clues behind? The sandal. The scrap of fabric from her clothing. How could she run, and where to, without taking the cash from her wallet? According to Baker, there was several hundred dollars in it."

"All of which seems as unlikely as Napoli tossing her over the bridge railing at the same instant she pulled the trigger, discharging the fatal shot," Worley said, frowning. "I don't know what we've got here."

"Third party?" DeeDee ventured.

"No evidence of one," Worley said.

"There is one other possibility," Gerard said quietly.

Duncan knew what Gerard was going to say. That one other possibility also had occurred to him, but he had stubbornly refused to acknowledge or accept it.

"I think it's safe to say that Mrs. Laird had gotten herself into trouble over Coleman Greer. Whether he was gay or bi or whatever, first Trotter, then Napoli, threatened her with a nasty scandal. Her life went from sugar to shit in a very short period of time. The incident with Trotter could be explained away as self-defense. Plausibly, I believe.

"But no matter how this business with Napoli went down, it was ugly, and she was stuck with a second dead man. That was going to raise questions as well as eyebrows, and possibly incriminate her. Even if she didn't go to jail, the scandal would have ruined her husband's career and, more importantly, her way of life.

"Maybe the fear of all that fallout was overwhelming." He let that statement reverberate for a moment, then concluded, "Elise Laird may have jumped from the bridge because she wanted to die."

Promising to write up his report first thing when he returned, Duncan left the office ahead of everyone else.

Or tried.

DeeDee fell into step with him as he left the building and forged past reporters. "Duncan, are you all right?"

"Yes."

"No."

413

"Yes," he repeated insistently. "I'm exhausted, that's all."

"I don't think so. What's going on with you?"

"Nothing!"

"Stop yelling at me!"

"I'm not yelling, I'm emphasizing a point. I'm okay except for all the . . . ambiguity."

"Ambiguity?"

He unlocked his car door then turned to face her. "Think about it. The last two cases we've investigated haven't been clear-cut homicides. I wish we'd draw one where we looked at the corpse and said, 'This was your textbook, old-fashioned, honest-to-God malice-with-aforethought, thou-shall-not-kill murder.' "

"I have thought about it," she said. "And you know what? I think that's exactly what we've got. Honest-to-God, thou-shalt-not, et cetera, murders. Doesn't it strike you funny — and I don't mean funny ha-ha — that in those same two *ambiguous* cases, the victims died looking at Elise Laird?"

He opened the car door and climbed in. "See you later." DeeDee caught the door before he could close it. He frowned up at her. "We'll pick this up later, DeeDee. I'm so beat, I can't even think right now, much less concentrate."

"You're more than tired. I've seen you tired. This isn't tired."

"Take a good look. This is tired." He pulled on the door until she let go. "See you later."

As he drove away, he watched her in his rearview mirror. She stood staring after him, frowning with concern, before turning and walking back toward the building. As soon as she was out of sight, he kicked up his speed by twenty miles an hour.

A few minutes later, he was back in the neighborhood where he'd met Elise last night. Ordinarily, the pastel glow of early daylight softened the appearance of even the most hostile environment. Not these streets. They appeared as malevolent this morning as they had the night before.

He drove past the house slowly, looking for any sign of activity inside and finding none. He recalled now that when he'd arrived last night, there had been no evidence of anyone being inside then either.

Where had Elise parked her car?

When she'd ambushed him at his town house, she'd parked on another street to prevent her car from being seen. Deducing she might have used that same technique last night, he turned at the next corner and drove around the block.

The houses on this street were in no better condition than their neighbors behind them. He parked in front of the house that backed into the one belonging to Elise's unnamed friend, although he wondered if there was such a person.

Before getting out, he took a flashlight from his glove box. He welcomed the weight of his service weapon tucked beneath his arm, although, unlike last night, he wasn't worried about Savich right now.

Breakfast smells wafted from a few of the houses. A television was playing inside one, tuned to morning cartoons. Basically, however, he had the street to himself. He walked up and down it on both sides, going several blocks in each direction, searching for anything that might indicate that Elise had parked along the curb. He found nothing except the same crumbling sidewalk as on the next street.

He returned to his car. From there, he followed the hedge between the two houses. Both were shuttered and silent, seemingly vacant. Nothing challenged him except sticker patches, the uneven ground, and a cat with a nasty disposition that hissed at him for trespassing.

As he moved along, he searched the ground carefully. At one point he found a small, circular depression in the dirt that might have been made by the short heel on Elise's sandal. But he was no expert tracker. It could have been made by something else just as easily.

He crossed the alley. The house where they'd met looked even more dilapidated from the rear. He vaulted the unstable chain link fence and jogged through the tall weeds of the backyard. The screen door squeaked when he pulled it open. He froze, held his breath, and listened. Hearing nothing after several moments, he wedged himself between the screen door and its solid counterpart and tried the knob. It was locked, but the lock was old and flimsy, and with the help of his pocketknife, he had it open within seconds.

The door opened directly into the kitchen. He switched on his flashlight and shined it around the dim room. There was no sign that anyone had been there in a long while. He crossed the cracked and curling linoleum floor and pushed through the swinging door leading into the long central corridor. His flashlight cut through the gloom, catching nothing in motion except dust motes.

When he called her name, his voice echoed eerily. He moved swiftly toward the living room, and when he reached it, he realized he was holding his breath in anticipation.

Except for the scent of her, of them, the room was empty.

He'd been called to the scene of Napoli's murder shortly after three o'clock. Almost five hours ago. And during all that time, while he'd been investigating the crime scene, trying to reconstruct what had taken place and surmising Elise's fate, he had clung to the slender hope that he would find her where he'd last seen her, perhaps disoriented by trauma, cowering in fright, or eluding capture. In whatever condition he might have found her, at least she would have been alive.

Now he expelled a sigh of profound disappointment, and despair settled over him like a mantle of chain mail. A desultory search of the other rooms on the first floor yielded nothing. He forced himself to climb the creaky staircase and check the upstairs rooms, but they were all empty save for one of the bedrooms that contained a rusty iron bedstead with even rustier springs.

He returned to the living room. Although he realized it was pathetically maudlin, he sat down on the sofa and ran his hand over the nap of the upholstery, imagining it to be still warm from the heat their bodies had generated.

What had happened here after he walked out? *What?* What had she done next?

Even if he hadn't confessed to the sexual encounter, perhaps he should have told his colleagues about his meeting with Elise in this house. It was material to their investigation.

It wasn't too late. He could call DeeDee now, give her this address. She would make record time getting here. He could give her a condensed version of what had transpired in this room last night. Telling her about it would be a relief, would make his burden of guilt lighter.

But DeeDee would do the right thing. No question of that. She would go straight to Gerard. Gerard might think that his clandestine meeting with Elise was reason enough to take him off the case, put him on suspension.

He couldn't let that happen. So for the time being, it would remain his secret, and he was stuck with carrying his guilt.

He had a lot to feel guilty about. Elise had implored him to believe her. She was in desperate fear for her life. She had begged for his help. He had refused. By doing so, he had either caused her to kill Napoli, or he had handed her over to Napoli to be killed, or, rejected by her last hope for help, she had thrown herself off the bridge and killed herself.

"Christ." He covered his face with his hands and fell against the back of the sofa.

When he was seven years old, the family cat had given birth to a litter of kittens. His parents had said that he could choose one to keep. The others they would give away.

He knew immediately the one he wanted. It was the cutest of the litter by far. Around the clock, he kept vigil over the box of kittens. He asked every day when he could take his kitten to his room to live.

His mother told him repeatedly, "As soon as he's weaned, Duncan."

That became a little too long. He was afraid that one of the adopting families would lay claim to that kitten before he could establish his ownership of it. One night after his parents had gone to bed, he sneaked into the kitchen and took the newborn from its mother. He placed it in bed with him. The frightened kitten was still mewling when Duncan drifted off to sleep.

The following morning, it was dead.

He cried for days and couldn't be consoled. Even though his mistake hadn't been malicious, even though his parents didn't scold him, he blamed himself and couldn't get over what he'd done. He had wanted that kitten more than anything in the world. He had loved it with the unrestrained passion of a seven-year-old. But his selfishness had killed it.

For more than an hour, he sat in abject misery where, only hours before, he had known ecstasy. He should be wishing that he'd never met her. Short of that, he should be wishing that he'd never gone near her, never touched her. Instead, he wished he had taken more time to touch her. He wished his touch had been gentler. He wished they had shared at least one tender kiss.

But if he had taken more time and shown her more tenderness, would that have alleviated the heat of this personal hell, or made it worse?

And, despite the angry roughness with which they'd coupled, had she sensed his yearning for it to be different? Had she been aware of the emotion he wanted to express, but couldn't? Had she?

He would never know.

20

Shortly before noon Duncan returned to the VCU.

"We caught a break," Worley informed him as soon as he cleared the doorway.

He stopped in his tracks. "You found her?"

"I said a break, not a miracle."

Duncan had left the abandoned house and gone home, ostensibly to sleep for a few hours. He lay down, but he remained awake, half in dread, half in anticipation of a telephone call telling him that Elise had been found . . . one way or the other.

He'd finally given up trying to sleep. In between a shower and shave, he'd placed a dozen or more telephone calls, phoning every agency taking part in the search. As lead investigator, he'd insisted on talking to the individual in charge. None had anything substantial to report, nor had he expected to hear of a breakthrough. As soon as there was one, he would know of it. But he gave all of them a pep talk, reminding them of Judge Laird's standing in the community and the priority that Chief Taylor had given Mrs. Laird's disappearance.

The Coast Guard had several choppers in the air, flying low along the coastline. The beaches were being patrolled. Search-and-rescue craft were patrolling offshore. These activities looked and sounded good, but no one actually expected Elise to reach the Atlantic.

Exhausted dogs and their trainers were still searching the riverbanks and marshes. Police boats were searching the river and all its tributaries. Chatham County SO and state troopers were assisting any way they could. The dive team had been in the shipping channel since daylight.

Local TV stations frequently interrupted their programming to recap the story and update viewers on the search. These news bulletins reported nothing except that there was nothing new to report.

"Pardon my saying so, Dunk," Worley said now, "but you look like shit."

"And here I was about to tell you how fresh and handsome you look today."

Worley continued to regard him with concern. "Have you had anything to eat?"

"Grabbed something on my way here,"

Duncan lied. "What kind of break?"

Worley went to the door and shouted down the hallway, "Hey, Kong? Dunk's here."

Kong appeared carrying an insulated drinking cup and wiping powdered sugar from his mouth with the back of his hairy hand. "Hey, Dunk. You don't look so good."

"So I've been told."

"Yeah, well, heard y'all had a late night. Found my guy for me. Just for the record, I'd have preferred him alive."

"So would I. What's the break?"

Duncan's tone must have conveyed that he wasn't in the mood for chitchat. Kong said, "Ever since Napoli went missing, we've been looking for his car. Turned up this morning."

"Where?"

"A church parking lot."

"Last place we'd think to look for Napoli," Worley said around a chuckle.

Duncan headed for the door. "Let's go take a look."

"DeeDee's already on it."

"Oh."

"But that's not all of it," Worley said. "I figured that Napoli hadn't gone to the church to pray. I think he just dropped his car there 'cause it was a convenient place to leave it — and probably because it was the last place we'd look."

They'd come to the conclusion last night that if Meyer Napoli was blackmailing either of the Lairds, his so-called disappearance of the last few days had been voluntary.

"I checked all the taxi services in the city and guess what?"

Duncan was no more in the mood for Worley's guessing games than he was for chitchat, but he guessed anyway. "Napoli called a taxi to pick him up at the church."

"At twelve sixteen in the A.M.," Worley declared with satisfaction. "The driver dropped him at his destination at twelve twenty-six."

"Short trip," Kong remarked.

"A few miles."

"What was his destination?" Duncan asked.

Worley consulted his small spiral notebook and read off the address.

Duncan knew the street; he'd been walking up and down both sides of it just a few hours ago looking for a trace of Elise or her car. "That's a rough neighborhood," he said, hoping his voice sounded neutral.

"Well, it wasn't the street Napoli was interested in," Worley said. "It was the car parked *on* the street. The car that didn't fit

425

the neighborhood and stuck out like a sore thumb. The taxi driver said Napoli didn't want to be let out at any particular house number and tipped him real good to forget he'd ever seen him.

"But when the guy saw Napoli's picture on TV this morning, he figured what the hell? What was Napoli going to do to him if he told about it now? So when I called, he was eager to talk. Driving around a murder victim hours before he got popped has made this guy a celebrity among his coworkers."

Worley straddled the nearest chair and asked Kong if he had any more doughnuts. Kong apologized for having eaten the last one.

Duncan asked, "Did the cabdriver describe the car parked on the street where Napoli was dropped?"

"Elise Laird's," Worley replied as he frowned at Kong for hogging the doughnuts. "He didn't get the license number or anything, but he described it to a T. So, I guess that solves the mystery of where they linked up. Oops. Don't tell His Judgeship I used that 'vulgar' phrase again." He explained to Kong how Judge Laird had jumped him for suggesting that his old lady's meeting with Napoli had been prearranged.

"We haven't confirmed that it was prearranged," Duncan reminded him.

"No," Worley replied a shade irritably. "That hasn't been *confirmed,* but what else would Mrs. Laird be doing in that neighborhood?"

Screwing a cop, Duncan thought.

He had left Elise around eleven forty, eleven forty-five. Had she stayed there, waiting for Napoli to join her at twelve twenty-six? Why? To enlist his help, since Duncan had refused his? Or to solve her problem once and for all? If it hadn't been a prearranged meeting, how had Napoli known where to find her?

Struck by a sudden thought, he asked, "Where's her car now?"

"In the pound."

This time he made it to the door, saying over his shoulder, "Call me as soon as anything else breaks."

An hour later Duncan upended the brown paper evidence bag and dumped the small, round object onto Bill Gerard's desk. "A transponder."

"Duncan found it under Mrs. Laird's car," DeeDee explained.

She and Duncan had met at the car pound. She had accompanied Napoli's car when it was towed from the church parking lot to the garage. Duncan had given her a Cliffs' Notes rendition of Napoli's taxi ride.

"So what are you doing here?" she'd asked.

"Looking for a tracking device."

Napoli had been sloppy about hiding it, and in under a minute Duncan had found it. He'd wasted no time getting it back to the Barracks.

"She didn't *meet* him there," he told Gerard, DeeDee, and Worley, who were grouped around the captain's desk looking at the transponder as though it were a specimen of some foreign matter. "He tracked her there."

"How'd he get this gizmo on her car?" Worley asked.

"He did stuff like this for a living. You can order surveillance equipment off the Internet. He could have put it on her car while she was parked outside the hairdresser's. He could have got a flunky like Trotter to do it while she was having lunch with her husband. It wouldn't have been hard. Couple of seconds and the deed was done."

"Okay, that bug is pretty incriminating. Napoli was tracking Mrs. Laird. But what was our esteemed judge's wife doing in that run-down neighborhood last night?" DeeDee tossed out the question, but no one picked it up, especially not Duncan.

Finally Worley said, "The first thing we need to do is ask the judge was he having his wife followed again."

"Even if he was, he'll deny it," DeeDee said. "And how can we prove it now?"

"Is the neighborhood being canvassed?" Gerard asked.

"As we speak," Worley said. "I've got two uniforms working it."

DeeDee said, "Maybe you should have used plainclothesmen."

"In that neighborhood it wouldn't matter," Duncan said. "Whoever we sent would be marked for cops."

Without saying it, the three veterans knew that the canvass would be a waste of time and manpower. In that part of town, anyone who was friendly with cops today could be the victim of a seemingly random drive-by shooting tomorrow. No one was going to talk to two uniforms going door-to-door asking questions.

Gerard's desk phone rang. He answered with a brusque, "Gerard." He listened for a moment, then said, "I'll tell 'em, thanks." He hung up and said, "Dothan's ready to perform the autopsy on Napoli."

"I'll go," Duncan offered. If Napoli's corpse produced any of his assailant's DNA, he wanted to be the first to know. Carefully he picked up the transponder and returned it to the evidence bag. "I'll drop this at forensics."

Gerard said, "Worley, let's get the names of residents for each address on the street where Mrs. Laird's car was found. See if we can connect her to anyone."

"I'll get somebody on it. Then I'll pay the judge a visit. Tell him about the transponder, hint that in all probability his old lady was being followed by Napoli, see what his reaction is."

"Good. Take DeeDee with you. She's good at reading people." Gerard paused, then added, "It wouldn't hurt to check out resident names on the surrounding streets in that neighborhood, too."

As they filed out, Duncan was hoping that the unnamed owner of the ramshackle house where he'd met Elise wouldn't easily be flagged as an acquaintance of hers.

One good thing, running down information like that was tedious and time-consuming. It could take days before a comprehensive list of homeowners and current lessees was compiled, especially in that neighborhood, where aliases were as commonplace as cockroaches. Finding the connection to Elise would take even longer.

Weeks, perhaps.

Surely she would be found before then.

Surely.

But one week crawled by. The fervor with which everyone began the search for Elise Laird waned a little each day that passed without uncovering a single clue to her whereabouts.

Napoli's autopsy proved the initial guess correct: he had died of internal hemorrhage due to the puncturing of several major organs. "Even if he'd made it to a trauma center alive, I don't think a surgeon could've saved him. Blood loss was too quick and too significant," the ME told Duncan. "The shooter knew where to aim to make it deadly."

Just like Gary Ray Trotter's shooter.

Lost in that thought, Duncan almost missed Dothan telling him that the bullet he'd removed was from a .22-caliber pistol.

"You mean a twenty-five," Duncan said.

"I mean a twenty-two."

"Napoli carried a twenty-five."

The medical examiner shrugged as he handed Duncan the evidence bag containing the bullet. "Not my job."

"What about his hands? Did you scrape anything from under his nails?"

"They were clean as a newborn's."

Back at the Barracks, Duncan shared these two discrepancies with DeeDee and Worley. She said, "I was hoping for some tissue for DNA testing later, if it was needed."

"None there," Duncan said.

"Damn! I was sure he'd been shot with his own twenty-five," Worley said.

"Well, he wasn't."

They were stockpiling questions without answers.

They plodded through several more unproductive days.

The public information office issued periodic statements to the press, but only after they were approved by the chief of police and Judge Laird. In every news story printed or broadcast, Elise Laird was portrayed as the victim, Meyer Napoli as her armed abductor. Suggested motives for his forcing her to stop her car on the Talmadge Bridge included extortion, kidnap for ransom, rape, and vengeance for an unnamed grievance.

Worley and DeeDee questioned the judge at length about keeping Napoli on retainer to follow his wife. He denied it. Then Duncan had a heated session with him. Duncan used every interrogation maneuver he knew to try to shake Cato Laird, but at the end of the session, the judge remained steadfast: His dealings with Napoli had ended months earlier, and if Napoli had continued to follow Elise, he had been doing it on his own, and obviously with criminal intent.

"There's something else," Duncan said at the conclusion of the taxing interview with Cato Laird. "We requested an inventory of your gun collection."

"All are accounted for except an old twenty-two-caliber pistol." Reading Duncan's reaction, he said hastily, "I'm sure it's only been misplaced."

"When do you remember last seeing it?"

"A while back. It was in a box of outdated hunting gear I put up in the attic." Becoming increasingly agitated, he said, "Surely you don't think . . . Look, Detective, Elise didn't even know I owned that gun."

"Okay," Duncan said, feeling anything but okay about this development. "Let me know if you run across it."

In addition to the department's press releases, the judge called a press conference nearly every day. They were brief and emotional. His appeals for information into his wife's disappearance produced nothing except the usual crank calls and chronic confessors.

Then, toward the end of the first week, he surprised the media as well as the PD by offering a fifty-thousand-dollar reward for information that would lead to his wife's rescue. That increased the number of nuisance calls into the VCU, but yielded nothing useful.

By day seven the investigation had completely stalled.

Then two things happened that recharged it.

Early that morning a maintenance man working on the dock of the Westin Resort spotted Elise's missing sandal among flotsam sloshing against the pilings.

He recognized it for what it was, because the sandal found on the bridge had been described in detail in every press account. He fished it from the water with a wire coat hanger, but had sense enough not to handle it and called the police immediately.

Duncan and DeeDee felt they should personally convey this portentous news to the judge. He'd been staying at home, within reach of the telephone, surrounded by friends and supporters, waited on by the vigilant Mrs. Berry.

It was she who answered the door. Duncan asked her to notify the judge that they were there and that they needed to see him immediately and in private. She led them into the study where Gary Ray Trotter had died two weeks earlier. Duncan noted that the bullet hole in the wall had been patched. There was a new rug on the floor. Nothing else in the room had changed except for the unopened mail stacked on the judge's desk.

Cato Laird rushed into the room, breathless and anxious. Their somber expressions brought him to an abrupt standstill. He frantically searched their faces for a hint of why they were there, but he couldn't bring himself to ask.

"As far as we know your wife is still alive," Duncan said, eliminating his primary fear. "We don't have any news of her whereabouts." Then he told him about the workman finding the sandal.

"Where was it?" Cato Laird's mellifluous voice sounded raw.

When Duncan told him, his face drained of color. "That's where . . . last year . . . that fisherman who fell out of his boat into the river . . ."

The man had drowned in the current even as people watched helplessly from the riverbank. His body had disappeared, then surfaced a few days later near the resort's dock.

"It's only a sandal," DeeDee said quietly.

"That doesn't necessarily mean that Mrs. Laird was in the river when it came off her foot."

Duncan cleared his throat, but it still hurt to say the words. "Nevertheless, the search-and-rescue operation has been reclassified. It's now a . . . a recovery mission."

The judge lowered himself onto the nearest chair, his expression bleak. "Meaning that they're now searching for her remains."

Duncan stood mute. DeeDee nodded and murmured, "I'm sorry."

Laird covered his face with his hands and began to sob. DeeDee and Duncan turned him over to the people hovering in the magnificent foyer of his home and let themselves out the front door. To reach DeeDee's car, they had to battle their way through a throng of reporters who for a week had kept vigil in the Washington Street median in front of the judge's home.

"Give me a break, Hatcher," one of them shouted at Duncan. "What's the new development?"

"Go fuck yourself."

"Can I quote you?"

"Please." Duncan climbed into the front seat and slammed the car door. "Get the hell out of here," he said to DeeDee as she clambered into the driver's seat.

They rode back to the Barracks in virtual silence. DeeDee must have sensed his mood, or maybe she had been subdued by the judge's apparent grief. In any case, she remained blessedly and uncharacteristically mute.

But the day was far from over.

No sooner had they entered the VCU office than Worley sidled up to them. Bobbing a toothpick in his mouth, he said to Duncan, "Get ready for the hard-on of your life, my friend."

"Bad timing, Worley," DeeDee snarled. "We're in no mood for one of your dirty jokes."

"No joke."

"Then what?" Duncan asked brusquely.

"While you were out, we got a tip. Someone who saw Elise Laird."

Duncan's heart began to race. "When?"

"Last week. What? Oh, you thought I meant like today?" Worley shook his head. "Naw. Last week. Before his arrest."

"Arrest? Whose arrest?"

"Gordie Ballew's."

"Gordie Ballew!" DeeDee exclaimed, underscoring Duncan's disappointment.

"He demanded a meeting with his public defender," Worley said. "He's changed his mind and wants to deal. Says he saw Elise

Laird the same day he was arrested. Earlier in the day."

Duncan made a scoffing sound. "Why's he suddenly remembering this?"

"His lawyer mentioned time served and Laird's reward of fifty grand."

"Every lowlife within a hundred miles of Savannah is laying claim to that reward," Duncan said. "And the lowest of them is Gordie Ballew. Tell him I said to find himself a sweetheart among the cons and enjoy his stay in prison." He turned toward his private office, but Worley hooked his elbow and pulled him back around. "I'm not yanking your pod, Dunk, and neither is Gordie. This could be a legitimate break."

Crossly, he pulled his elbow free. "I doubt it, but okay. What did Gordie have to say?"

"Guess who he claims was with Mrs. Laird."

DeeDee, sharing Duncan's impatience, asked, "Who?"

"Robert Savich." Worley grinned and jabbed Duncan in the gut. "You hard yet?"

21

Savich's secretary, Kenny, recoiled from DeeDee's coiffure with unconcealed horror. "I can recommend a product that will help control that."

"Control what?" she asked, flashing him her badge.

"Oh dear."

Duncan didn't know if his lament was over DeeDee's frizzy hairdo or the police being there to question his boss.

As they entered Savich's office, he smiled from behind his desk and politely motioned them to sit in the matching chairs facing him. "I've been expecting you."

"Why's that?" Duncan asked.

"Because whenever you've got a murder without a suspect, you come to me. I'm flattered, Detective Hatcher. Truly I am. But being your fall guy on a regular basis is testing my patience."

"What do you know about Elise Laird?"

His startling blue eyes shifted to DeeDee, who'd posed the question without preamble. "In what context?"

"In the context that she's been missing for a week."

"Well, in that context, I know nothing except what I've read in the newspaper or heard on television." Dismissing DeeDee, he returned his unblinking gaze to Duncan. "Did Kenny offer you some refreshment?"

"Just days before she went missing, you met with Elise Laird in a topless bar called White Tie and Tails."

Savich formed a steeple with his fingers and mused aloud, "Do you think the name of that club has racial implications?"

"The meeting, Savich."

Duncan's impatience made him grin. "Someone's pulling your leg, Detective Hatcher."

"Detective Bowen and I are very busy these days. Please don't waste our time. Tell us the purpose of your tête-à-tête in that dark booth with Elise Laird."

"There was no such tête-à-tête."

"Someone told us otherwise."

Savich remained unruffled. "Let me guess. That 'someone' is after the fifty-thousand-dollar reward her husband has offered."

"That someone is a reliable source,"

DeeDee said.

Gordie Ballew was about as reliable as a snake oil salesman's verbal guarantee, but Duncan nodded his agreement to DeeDee's lie.

Savich said, "He's lying."

"I didn't say it was a he."

Savich gave a negligent wave of his hand. "He, she, whatever. Your snitch is lying."

"I'd put my money on you being the liar," DeeDee said. "We have the time and the place of the meeting, plus a witness willing to testify to it. Now, think real hard, Savich. Concentrate. Are you sure you didn't have a meeting last week with Elise Laird?"

Savich assessed her while idly drumming his fingers on the polished surface of his desk. After several moments, he said, "I bet you eat pussy, don't you?"

She would have lunged from her chair if Duncan hadn't clotheslined her across the chest to keep her in her seat. Her angry reaction was exactly what Savich was after. Duncan had learned that lesson the hard way and had spent two days in jail as a consequence.

Before they arrived, he'd reminded DeeDee to beware of Savich's manipulations and warned her against reacting to them. Savich would push whatever buttons

441

he could to distract them.

Duncan gave DeeDee a warning look, then went back to Savich. "You're lying about that meeting. We know it took place. So, why not just give it up sooner rather than later and tell us what you know about Elise Laird."

"I know that she's a lovely girl," he said. "Or was the last time I saw her."

"When was that?"

"Hmm, it's been a long time. Certainly before she got married, and how long has that been?" Focused on Duncan now, he said silkily, "But she's not a woman you easily forget, is she? I met her while she was working at the White Tie and Tails. I remember the first time she . . . entertained me. I was captivated by her."

He laughed out loud. "Ah, I see by your expression that you're not immune to her charms, Detective Hatcher. How reassuring. It's nice to know that you have the same base appetites as the rest of us mere mortals."

Duncan was seething inside but kept his expression schooled.

Savich snickered, then continued. "As alluring as Elise was, I suggested it would further her career if she got breast implants. She didn't embrace the idea. Actually, that's an understatement. She was quite opposed to it."

He opened a silver box on his desk and took a long, black cigarette from it. "Either of you care for one?" When neither deigned to answer, he fit the cigarette into an ivory filter and lit it with a gold lighter, snapping the lid closed with a decisive click that snuffed out the flame. He inhaled deeply and directed a plume of smoke toward the ceiling.

"In retrospect," he said, "I believe Elise was right to reject my suggestion. Her breasts are very soft and sexy in their natural state."

Duncan wanted to yank the cigarette from Savich's smiling lips, grind it out against his eyeball, and then push the smooth-talking son of a bitch through the plate glass window behind his desk.

Stiffly, he asked Savich if he'd known Meyer Napoli.

"I knew who he was, of course."

"Did you ever retain his services?" DeeDee asked.

"What an absurd notion, even for you, Detective Bowen."

"Why absurd?"

"Why would I hire a private investigator with limited resources and skills?"

"When you have people on your payroll who do that kind of dirty work for you."

Savich said nothing.

DeeDee said, "We can question everyone who was in the club that afternoon. Someone will remember that meeting between you and the judge's wife."

Savich smiled at her veiled threat. Balancing his cigarette in a crystal ashtray, he opened his lap drawer and withdrew a business card, then slid it across the desk toward her. "There was no such meeting. Your snitch is lying. However, if you insist on wasting everyone's time, I can guarantee the full cooperation of the manager of the White Tie and Tails.

"That's his card with his phone number, fax number, and e-mail address. Kenny also has his private cell phone number. You can ask for it on your way out." Having called her bluff, he stood up. "Now, you'll have to excuse me. I'm late for a business meeting."

Neither of the detectives moved. Finally DeeDee turned her head. "Duncan?"

He was engaged in a staring duel with the criminal. "Meet me outside."

She stood up, but hesitated. "Are you —"

"I'll be right there."

She hesitated a moment longer, then reluctantly walked out. Kenny said something to her; she responded, matching his bitchy tone.

Duncan didn't break eye contact with Savich. "I'll find out, you know. What that meeting with Elise Laird was about. I'll find out."

Savich's eyes glittered as coldly as the diamond in his earlobe. They didn't change, not even when his lips slowly formed a wide smile. "You seem to have a real fire in your belly for this case, Detective. Even more so than usual. I wonder why that is. Could it be . . ."

His eyes narrowed to slits. "Do I detect a crack in your armor of righteousness? Could a mere woman have caused that breach? Is snatch your weakness, Detective Sergeant Hatcher?" He made a tsking sound. "How disappointingly ordinary. And how very sad for you that the object of your affection is feared dead."

He laughed long and loud at Duncan's expense. Then, leaning across his desk, he whispered, "Happy hunting."

Later that afternoon the detectives went to the Chatham County Detention Center and were granted twenty minutes with Gordie Ballew. While his court-appointed attorney stood by, Duncan, feeling the aftereffects of his infuriating meeting with Savich, hammered him with questions about what he'd seen at the topless bar.

Duncan had to learn what business Elise had with Savich. It was important to their investigation, certainly. It was possibly even more important to him.

He bore down on Gordie Ballew. "What were they doing?"

"Talking."

"Just the two of them?"

"Yeah. Private." The more nervous Gordie got, the more noticeable his speech impediment became. "In a booth. Like I told you. Like I've told you a hunnerd times already."

He claimed not to have known the blond woman's identity or realized the significance of her meeting with Savich until he saw Elise Laird's picture on the front page of the newspaper. "I recognized her right off."

"Why didn't you notify us immediately?"

"Took five days to get his sorry ass over here to see me!" Gordie exclaimed, casting a disparaging glance toward the lawyer, who yawned in response.

"You know how bad I want Savich for Freddy Morris and others," Duncan said.

"Yeah. So?"

"So I think you reconsidered the offer you turned down last week. You made up this bullshit story so you'd have something juicy to bargain with."

Gordie looked wildly at DeeDee and the lawyer, neither of whom offered him an escape hatch. Coming back to Duncan, he said, "It ain't like that."

"Cross your heart and hope to die?"

"I saw her with Savich," the small man insisted, his nasal voice rising in pitch.

"That's not the club where you were arrested later that night for assault."

"Right. I left the White Tie and went to that other place."

"Savich see you at the White Tie?"

That possibility made him visibly fearful. He squirmed in his seat. "He wasn't paying no attention to me. I was on the other side of the club, watching the show, one of them girls getting it on with a brass pole."

"You were skulking in a dark strip joint —"

"What's skulking?"

"Were you drunk?"

"No."

"Gor-dee," Duncan said.

"Okay, okay, I was getting there, but I wasn't drunk yet."

"High?"

His eyes darted about evasively, but then he said, "I may have had something. I don't

447

remember."

"But you remember the blonde Savich was in conversation with."

"Yeah."

"From across a dark nightclub. While you were high and drunk. And days later you conveniently recognized her as Elise Laird."

Gordie bobbed his head emphatically. "That's right. What you just said, Hatcher. That's it in a nutshell."

Duncan stood up and shoved his chair beneath the table. "You're full of crap."

"No! I swear I'm not! Not this time."

"Why should this time be any different? Oh, wait." Duncan snapped his fingers. "The reward. That's the difference."

"That fifty grand's got nothing to do with it."

"Do I look like I was born yesterday?" Duncan shouted. "You heard about the fifty-thousand-dollar reward. You know I want Savich. Bingo. You've made up this story and wasted my time, which I have precious little of these days. I have even less patience with lying, sniveling lumps of maggot shit like you, Gordie."

"Okay, Hatcher, maybe I have lied to you a few times before," he said, his voice cracking. "But not this time. I swear it, I . . . Where are you going?" he squealed in panic as Duncan headed for the door.

"We'll get back to you," Duncan said over his shoulder as he and DeeDee walked out.

Worley was waiting for them on the other side of the door. "What do you think?"

Duncan expelled a long breath as he thoughtfully watched through the small window as Gordie was escorted from the room by guards. "He's a habitual liar. But either he's gotten exceptionally good at it, or he's telling the truth this time. He's stuck to his story without changing a word. Let's give him overnight to fret about it, then come at him again. In the meantime, let's take this to the judge. See what —"

"Ixnay." Worley poked a fresh toothpick into his mouth. "No can do, Dunk. Orders from above."

"What the hell?"

"I knew you'd be pissed. That's why I put off telling you until after you'd had a crack at Savich and Gordie here, but Captain Gerard said we're not to confront the judge about his wife's alleged meeting with Savich."

DeeDee sputtered, "Are you serious?"

"As death and taxes," Worley said. "Gerard bounced Gordie's story off the chief, who practically bounced Gerard out of his office. Through this whole ordeal, they've managed to keep a lid on Mrs. Laird's history as a topless dancer. You can imagine the field day the media would have with that. But an association with Savich would make her G-string days look like Sunday school."

DeeDee said, "If memory serves, it was Chief Taylor himself who ordered us to use every resource available to solve the mystery of Mrs. Laird's disappearance, right?"

"I'm only telling you what Gerard told me," Worley said. "Gerard said that Chief Taylor said that this business about her and Savich was a story from a con trying to create a better bargaining position for himself, and that the judge didn't need to be made aware of it until we had indisputable proof. He asked what were the chances of Mrs. Laird having anything to do with a criminal like Robert Savich."

"What were the chances of her having anything to do with Meyer Napoli?" DeeDee really didn't expect an answer and none was forthcoming. She divided a look between Worley and Duncan, landing on Duncan. "Well? Our hands having been tied, what do we do from here?"

We find Elise so I can demand to know what the fuck she was doing with Savich. That's what Duncan was thinking, but that's not what he said. "We keep looking for her."

No sooner had the words left his mouth than a loud clap of thunder rattled the windows.

The thunder preceded the rain that began that afternoon and fell relentlessly over the next forty-eight hours. It made the recovery mission more problematic, and literally dampened the spirits of everyone involved, so that by the third consecutive day of rain without any sign of letup, the mood in the VCU was funereal.

Even though it was Saturday, no one was taking a weekend off. The detectives were gathered in Duncan's office, going over what they knew, speculating on what they didn't. The ballistics report was back on the bullet the ME had removed from Napoli — no match for it on any of the national crime databases. Dead end there.

Worley gnawed his toothpick. "If she went into the river, whether she was pushed or jumped, how come she hasn't popped up yet? Usually doesn't take this long. Ten days?"

"Maybe she was never in the river," Duncan said.

"Maybe she was never on the bridge." The men turned to DeeDee, who expanded her thought. "Napoli was driving back into the city. He could've dumped her body in South Carolina somewhere. Miles of marsh, forests. Lots of places to hide remains."

"What about her sandals?" Worley asked.

"He realized he had them, stopped on the bridge to get rid of them —"

"And the Wicked Witch of the West flew in on her broom and shot him."

"It was just a thought, Worley," she said snidely.

To her further irritation, she lost the coin toss and had to go out in the downpour to pick up lunch. She had just returned and was passing out the sandwiches when Cato Laird surprised them by walking into the office unannounced.

He looked like he'd lost at least a pound for each of the ten days his wife had been unaccounted for. His golfing tan had turned sallow. His eyes were sunk deep into their dark sockets. His shoulders were stooped. He hadn't bothered with an umbrella. His clothes and hair were wet, adding to his ragged appearance. His unexpected arrival silenced everyone in the unit. All eyes were on him as he approached Duncan, who was trying to work up enough enthusiasm to take a bite of the sandwich that DeeDee had foisted on him.

"Detective Hatcher, we need to talk."

Duncan motioned for the judge to follow him into his tiny office. Once they were seated, the judge laid a manila envelope on Duncan's desk, then glanced toward the open door. "I suppose they should be in on this, too."

"DeeDee, Worley," Duncan called, knowing they were well within hearing distance. They appeared almost immediately.

"Captain Gerard, too," the judge said. "Is he here?"

"We're all working overtime. I'll get him." DeeDee wheeled about and went to summon Gerard.

"Can I get you some coffee? Water?" Duncan wasn't being hospitable. He extended the offer merely to postpone hearing whatever it was the judge was about to tell them regarding the manila envelope lying on his desk. It looked ordinary enough, but he had a bad feeling about it. If it contained anything hopeful, the judge wouldn't be acting like the end of the world was nigh.

"Judge Laird?" Gerard squeezed into the room and shook hands with him. "Detective Bowen said you wanted to see us."

Nodding, the judge reached for the envelope. The metal clasp remained closed, but the seam at the top had been slit open.

"This morning, in an attempt to get my mind off Elise, I decided to attack the mail that had piled up since her . . . disappearance.

"I found this. I don't know when it was delivered, but it's postmarked the day of . . . the day Meyer Napoli died and Elise disappeared." He glanced around at his raptly attentive audience. "I think this will explain . . . Well, you'll see."

And with that, he slid the contents of the envelope onto Duncan's desk. There were about a dozen eight-by-ten black-and-white photographs. The grainy quality of some indicated that the pictures had been taken through a telephoto lens. Elise and Robert Savich were together in each of them, obviously unaware that they were being photographed.

"As you can see, the venues are different." Cato Laird spoke haltingly, his voice fractured by apparent pain and dismay. "So is their clothing. That indicates several meetings over a period of time, wouldn't you think?"

The detectives were studying the photographs, handling them carefully to avoid smudging any fingerprints that might be on them. Duncan hadn't touched them, but he picked up the business card that had been

454

sent with them in the envelope. It was engraved with Meyer Napoli's name, business address, and several numbers where he could be contacted, exactly like the card they'd found at the scene of his murder.

Gerard said, "Napoli was blackmailing your wife."

The judge sighed heavily. "So it would appear. And since he sent these to me, I suppose he intended to blackmail me also."

"You didn't know Mrs. Laird was acquainted with Robert Savich?"

DeeDee's question sparked his imperious nature. "Of course not."

In every shot, the two were fully clothed. All but a few of the photos had been taken outdoors, although the close-up framing made it impossible to determine the location. The pair didn't appear to be intimate, merely comfortable with each other and engrossed in whatever it was they were discussing. There was nothing lewd, or even compromising, about the photographs, except that a superior court judge's wife was in the company of a notorious criminal. That in itself was explosive.

"If I were to guess . . ."

"Please, Judge," Gerard said, encouraging him to continue when he faltered.

"If I were to guess, I think perhaps Napoli

stumbled across this . . . this . . . acquaintanceship when he was following Elise for me. When he saw her with Savich, her visits with Coleman Greer became of secondary importance." He glanced at the photographs, then quickly away. "Napoli would have realized that these photos could be far more damaging to both of us. He was trying to cash in on his bonanza."

"Trotter was his messenger boy," DeeDee said.

The judge winced. "I suppose. Whether accidentally or intentionally — naturally I prefer to believe the former — Elise foiled that plan."

"Between the time you heard the shots fired and when you reached the study, did she have time to hide a set of these photographs?"

He gave a small nod. "She could have stashed them somewhere, intending to retrieve them later. In fact, I've caught her in the study several times recently, startling her when I came in. Guilty reactions, I realize now." He dwelled on that for a moment, then said, "She probably destroyed the set of photos Trotter delivered. But Napoli, being Napoli, would have had a backup set. This set."

"The night of the bridge incident, Napoli

told her that he had mailed these pictures to you," Gerard surmised.

"I suppose she became enraged and . . ."

"And used your missing twenty-two to kill him," DeeDee said, finishing for him.

The judge covered his face with both hands and began to weep.

"Is there someone you'd like us to call?" Gerard asked quietly.

He shook his head, but he didn't lower his hands from his face, and he didn't speak.

Gerard indicated the door and the detectives shuffled out. "I think he deserves a few minutes of privacy," the captain said to his subordinates once they were outside Duncan's office.

"He's got some heavy shit to absorb," Worley said. "Napoli's one thing, but *Savich?* Jeez. But how does he factor in?"

Duncan had no answer for him, but he'd been trying to stave off a most disturbing thought. Was it even remotely possible that Savich had sent Elise to him? He recalled the smug manner in which Savich had taunted him about his evident interest in her. Had she been Savich's secret weapon, the one Duncan had feared he wouldn't see coming? The one that would destroy him?

Breaking into his thoughts, Gerard said, "I'll clear it with the chief first, but I think it's time we had another go-around with Gordie Ballew." He asked DeeDee to call Gordie's pro bono lawyer and make the arrangements. "We want to talk to him as soon as possible," Gerard told her as she moved away to make the call. "Tonight. Make sure he understands that."

"Got it."

"Looks like for once the little weasel is telling the truth," Worley remarked. "Who'd have thunk it possible?"

Judge Laird emerged from Duncan's office, his eyes red-rimmed and watery. "I feel I should inform Chief Taylor of this myself. Will you come along with me, Bill?"

"Certainly."

"I would appreciate that."

"It's going to get ugly for you, Judge, once all this gets out," Gerard said.

"I'm aware of that. However, the only thing the photographs really prove is that Elise and Savich are speaking acquaintances. They're doing nothing criminal in them. They're not sexual. And perhaps I'm wrong about the timing of them. For all we know, they could have been taken years ago, before she even met me."

Gerard glanced at Duncan, effectively assigning him the job of dispelling that myth. "Actually, Judge, someone has come forward. He claims to have seen Mrs. Laird with Savich at the club where she used to work. This meeting took place only days before she disappeared."

The judge took a staggering step backward. "What? That recently?"

"So he says."

"Who is this individual?"

"A guy presently in jail on an assault charge," Duncan replied.

"How long have you had this information? Why wasn't I told?"

Gerard jumped in. "This man is a repeat offender with a long record. Chief Taylor figured he was only after the award, maybe a reduced sentence. He asked that we not bother you with his story until we had corroboration."

"However," Duncan said, "he's been questioned at length and swears he's telling the truth. If he is . . ." He paused to swallow the bile that filled the back of his throat. "If he is, then it's possible Savich was somehow connected to your wife's disappearance."

"This man in jail . . . what's his name?" the judge asked excitedly, showing more animation and hopefulness than he had in recent days.

"Gordie Ballew."

"If he's acquainted with Savich, maybe he knows more than he's telling. Maybe he knows where Elise is."

The man's renewed optimism was almost more heartbreaking to witness than his earlier despair. Even if they found his wife alive, she would be charged with Napoli's murder. He seemed to have forgotten that. Or else he didn't care, so long as she was alive.

Gerard tried to match his hopefulness. "If anybody can wring information from Ballew, it's Duncan. You're welcome to observe when he questions him again."

"He won't be questioning him again." Though DeeDee had addressed all of them as she approached, she was looking at Duncan. "About an hour ago, Gordie Ballew opened his carotid artery with the tine of a plastic fork. He's dead."

DeeDee's announcement had the effect of a death knell. Worley moved to his desk and began rifling drawers in search of a forbidden cigarette, which he saved for emergencies.

Gerard sat down on the corner of a desk and despondently stared at the floor.

The judge didn't seem to understand the impact of Gordie Ballew's suicide. "You can still implicate Savich, can't you? Why don't you question him directly?"

Duncan had begun to feel that he would suffocate in this room. First the photographs of Savich with Elise. Then his gnawing suspicion that his seduction had been orchestrated by Savich. Now the loss of Gordie Ballew.

Although he'd felt like ranting over each of these disclosures, somehow he had managed to function with the cool detachment that was expected. But the judge's inane question caused his anger to erupt.

"Why don't we question Savich? Don't you think we have?" he shouted, his voice quaking with wrath. "Gordie Ballew is dead. So Savich's meeting with your wife might just as well never have happened. It's been deleted. Like that." He clapped his hands together as though squashing a mosquito between them.

"And isn't it just a little late for you to be gung-ho to nail Savich? You let him go! If not for you and your damned mistrial, he would be behind bars, not out destroying people. Destroying lives."

"Duncan." That from Gerard. He spoke softly, but the admonishment couldn't have been more effective.

Every cell in Duncan's body throbbed

with fury. He felt like hitting something, hurting something, but he clamped his jaws shut to keep from saying anything more.

DeeDee cleared her throat and said diplomatically, "Savich denied any such meeting with your wife took place, Judge. It's unlikely that anyone else will come forward now."

The judge exhaled a shuddering sigh and sat down heavily in the nearest chair. "The photographs explain a lot. Elise was leading a double life. It culminated with her killing Napoli. Then she jumped from the bridge." He made eye contact with each of them, as though hoping someone would dispute the hypothesis. None did. "All this time we've been searching for her and hoping we'd find her alive, she's been dead, hasn't she?" His voice gave out and he sobbed. "I guess it's over."

"Wrong," Duncan said. "It's not over until her body is found."

He stormed out of the VCU and was halfway to the detention center before he even realized where he was headed. Mistrusting what he might say or do if he stayed a moment longer in the office, he'd been intent only on escape.

But subconsciously he must have resolved

that Gordie Ballew's death would not go unnoticed. He was the latest of Savich's victims, as surely as if Savich himself had dug into his neck with that fork.

Somehow Savich had gotten to Gordie Ballew and persuaded him that even a bloody suicide was a far more graceful way out of this life than the violent exit Savich had planned for him.

Jail bars would have been no barrier. Savich had tentacles everywhere, in every field of commerce, every branch of local government, every law enforcement agency. His influence was far-reaching and pervasive. If he wanted to get a message to Gordie in jail, he could have done so with shocking ease.

But Duncan was going to make it harder for him to get away with it.

Unmindful of speed limits, he cut by half the drive time from the Barracks to the jail. He parked and got out, then strode toward the entrance. His plan was to spend some quality time with the guards, whose inattention had allowed Gordie Ballew to commit suicide. At least one of them had to be on Savich's payroll.

Just then, as though his thoughts had conjured him up, he spotted Savich, strolling coolly through the lobby of the building on his way toward the exit.

Duncan reached the doors first, barged through them, and blocked the man's path. Savich's surprise over his sudden appearance was momentary. He smiled pleasantly. "Well, hello, Detective. Fancy meeting you here."

Duncan's hands formed fists at his sides. "Did you come to see for yourself that Gordie Ballew is good and dead?"

"Oh, so you've heard about poor Gordie. He'd had such a tragic life, and true to form, it ended badly. I came to claim his body, give it a decent burial."

"Bullshit. You came to make sure he'd done what you told him to."

"I have no idea what you're talking about." He tilted his sleek head and gave Duncan a critical once-over. "You're flushed. Are you that upset over this? I didn't realize that you and Gordie were that close."

"Did you dip your finger in his blood?"

"What a revolting thing to say."

"You had to make certain that Gordie was silenced forever and no longer a threat to you. You wouldn't trust the newspaper story of a jail cell suicide. You had to check it out for yourself, see if that plastic fork did the trick."

Savich rolled his eyes. "You've topped

yourself, Detective Hatcher. This is your most fanciful invention yet. I'm here out of charity for a former employee. Nothing more. Now if you'll excuse —"

He made to go past Duncan, but Duncan hooked his hand around Savich's biceps and flung him against the wall, then planted himself in front of him. Bringing his face close, he said, "Did you send her to me?"

"The girl you picked up in the River Street bar? She's awfully good, isn't she?"

Duncan placed his forearm across Savich's throat. "Elise," he growled.

"Ah, the judge's fair wife." Because of the pressure Duncan was applying to his windpipe, his face was turning duskier, but he was smiling. "So I was right. Your interest in her wasn't entirely professional."

"Hey, guys?"

Out the corner of his eye, Duncan saw two security guards coming toward them, looking wary. He said, "I'm Hatcher, Savannah PD, homicide."

"Yeah, uh, we know who you are, Detective. Need any help here?"

"No. Back off." He pressed his arm harder against Savich's throat and lowered his voice so that only Savich could hear him. "Did you send her to me?"

"I'm not a matchmaker. Well, except for

that one time. I thought you deserved a Saturday night of fun and frolic."

Duncan blinked against a red mist of rage that clouded his vision. *"Did you send Elise to me?"*

"Why would that even occur to you? Or don't you have any confidence in your own sex appeal?"

The guards were edging closer. One had unsnapped the leather holster on his hip and had his hand on the grip of his pistol. "Detective Hatcher," he said, "if you need assistance —"

"Are you arresting this man?" the other guard asked. "If so —"

"I said back off!" Duncan shouted.

Because of the pressure to his throat, Savich's laugh was a low gurgle. "You really are unraveling, aren't you? Poor man. You're defeated at every turn. And, as if that weren't bad enough, you're now enamored of a ghost." Barely above a whisper, he added, "Take heart, Detective. Maybe Napoli made it quick."

Duncan's fist connected with Savich's cheekbone with the impetus of a pile driver. He saw the skin split, saw blood, saw Savich's grimace of pain. His satisfaction, however, was short-lived. The guards surged forward, joined now by two others. Together the four of them dragged him away from Savich, who had calmly taken a handkerchief from his pocket and was using it to stanch the bleeding cut on his cheekbone.

Duncan didn't struggle with the guards. He let himself be hauled away. But his eyes speared into Savich's. "Get ready for me. I'm coming for you."

Only moments before, Savich had been amused. Now his eyes glittered with malice. He hissed, "I look forward to it."

22

The barkeep wiped lemon juice from his fingers and cleaned the blade of his knife on a towel. "This rain, can't say I blame 'em for calling off the search. They'll probably never find the body now. But I guess that means it'll forever remain a mystery. Was it murder or suicide?" He tossed aside his towel and leaned on the bar. "What do you think happened?"

Duncan looked up at him with bleary eyes and said hoarsely, "I know what happened."

Smitty's barkeep scoffed. "Sure you do, pal. Sure you do."

Following his altercation with Savich, Duncan had come straight to the tavern. He'd been escorted out of the detention center by the guards, who advised him to go somewhere and cool off before coming back. He didn't blame them. They'd only been doing their job. He supposed he should be glad that Savich hadn't pressed charges for assault.

He'd left peacefully and didn't return, having realized the futility of confronting the jail guards about Gordie Ballew's suicide. He hadn't been in the proper state of mind to conduct an inquiry that important. He'd also figured it would be a waste of time. No one working as a mole for Savich was going to give him up. Not with Gordie's blood still fresh.

He'd sought solace in Smitty's, where whiskey and heartache were undiluted. Against his will, his eyes gravitated once again to the silent TV set behind the bar. The press conference dragged on. In the words of the barkeep, the body was fish food by now. Why not just sum it up with that? Why not conclude the thing and return to *Seinfeld?*

The discovery of Elise's missing sandal had ended all hope that she had survived her plunge from the bridge, whether voluntary or not. Now even the search for her remains had been canceled. End of case. Tomorrow everybody would pick up where they'd left off ten days ago.

Everybody but him.

Suddenly the door was hauled open, admitting a gust of rain and a customer. Standing on the threshold, she pulled the door closed, then turned around. Duncan groaned and reached for his drink.

DeeDee took a moment to let her eyes adjust to the darkness, then spotted Duncan at the bar and made her way to it. She shrugged out of her rain slicker and shook water off it. As she sat down on the bar stool next to his, she gave her head a hard shake that flung rainwater off her hair and onto him.

He frowned and made a show of brushing drops off his shirt sleeve. "They have these cool things now, called umbrellas."

"I left mine in your car this morning."

"Out for a stroll? You just happened to be passing by and got thirsty?"

"I ran out of options and finally deduced that you might be here."

"How did you deduce that?"

"You came here only one other time that I know of. The time the murder we were investigating involved a mother and baby who'd been decapitated."

He saluted her with his glass. "Thanks for the reminder. Just what I needed to cheer me up."

"On that occasion you told me that this was a good place for getting drunk." She looked around with distaste. "I guess." To the barkeeper she said, "Diet Coke." When he served it, she nodded down at Duncan's highball. "How many of those has he had?"

"Let's just say I'm glad you're here to drive him home."

"That many?"

"Go away, DeeDee," Duncan mumbled.

"Hey, I'm the one with a right to be pissed, not you," she said angrily. "You haven't been driving around in the rain for hours looking for you. I have. I went to your house, your gym, everywhere I could think of."

"I'm touched by your concern."

"Why did you just split like that without telling anybody where you were going? Why didn't you answer your cell phone?"

"Hint, hint: I didn't want company tonight."

"Too bad. You've got it." She unwrapped a straw, stuck it in her Coke, drew hard on it.

"If you're hoping to lift my spirits and make me feel better about things, you're wasting your time," he said. "No matter what, I'm not going to feel better."

"Then why are you bothering to get tanked?"

"Because I fucking want to," he snapped.

DeeDee maintained eye contact for several

beats, then looked up at the television where Chief Taylor was still silently waxing poetic. He was flanked at the podium by Bill Gerard and Cato Laird.

"You heard that the recovery mission was officially canceled?"

He nodded.

"That was decided after the judge and Gerard talked to Chief Taylor. Those pictures of Mrs. Laird and Savich sort of changed the complexion of the situation." She paused to allow Duncan to comment. He didn't, only continued to stare morosely into his highball. "The judge won't be saying anything or answering any questions tonight, but he insisted on being present at the press conference when the announcement was made.

"They, uh, they also agreed not to publicly address Mrs. Laird's connection to Savich unless and until they're forced. Which isn't right, but it's certainly . . . cleaner. For everyone." DeeDee took another pull on her straw. Still Duncan said nothing. After a time, she asked, "Have you eaten today?"

He shook his head.

"You should eat something."

"I should eat. I should get some sleep. I should refocus on other cases. I get it, DeeDee," he said testily. "God knows you've harped on me enough the last several days. Stop mothering me. Get out of here. Go home. Leave me alone."

She was hurt by his rejection of her help and concern. It also made her angry. "What is it with you these days? Where is this coming from? Tell me, Duncan. Is it about her?" She looked at him with consternation. "It is, isn't it? She got to you, didn't she? I mean *really* got to you. From the very start."

He planted his elbows on the bar and rested his forehead on the heels of his hands, curling his fingers up into his disheveled hair. "Yeah," he said gruffly. "She got to me from the very start."

She had sensed this coming from the night of Gary Ray Trotter's fatal shooting. Or maybe Duncan had been doomed the first time he saw Elise Laird at the awards dinner. Gordie Ballew's sad fate had been the proverbial last straw, but the judge's deceitful wife was at the crux of her partner's misery. Once his path had crossed Elise Laird's, his slide into this pit seemed inevitable.

"I'll have a refill," he said, sliding his glass toward the bartender.

"Duncan —"

"I asked you nicely to leave me alone."

"What happened, happened, Duncan.

There's nothing you can do about it now."

"Wrong. I can get drunk."

DeeDee threw up her hands. "Okay, fine." She motioned the bartender to pour him another shot.

She noticed that the press conference had ended. An anchorwoman now appeared to be solemnly summarizing the story. Then the screen returned to *Seinfeld.* They watched the muted TV for several moments, then he said, "She begged for my help."

DeeDee looked at him in profile, the flickering light of the television set playing across his careworn features. "Elise Laird?"

"She came to me twice. And twice I refused to help her."

DeeDee dreaded what she was about to hear, but she couldn't stop herself from asking for details. "What are you telling me, Duncan? That she came to you in private?"

"First she passed me a note, asking to see me alone. I didn't respond. Then she surprised me by showing up at my house. Early on that Saturday morning when we later went to the country club. The table on the terrace. White umbrellas."

"I remember."

"Early that morning you called my house suggesting we confront the judge about Napoli's connection to Trotter. Elise was in my living room when you called."

She imagined Duncan carrying on a telephone conversation with her while their suspect was within earshot. She must have sounded like a fool, prattling on about the case they were building against Elise Laird while she and Duncan were eyeball to eyeball. DeeDee hated nothing worse than being made to look a fool. "Why didn't you tell me?"

"I'm telling you now," he said shortly.

"You hustled her out of your house before I got there, then played out that little farce on the country club terrace, pretending for the judge and me that . . . that . . ."

"That we hadn't been alone together earlier that day."

DeeDee had to forcibly tamp down her rising anger. If they quarreled, she might never hear all this, and she needed to hear it. Moreover, Duncan needed to confess it. If he didn't, it would continue to eat at him and he might never recover. "What happened when she came to your house?"

"What difference does it make now?"

"If it makes no difference, then tell me."

"We were coming at her like she was a suspect."

"She was."

"She had another story."

"I'm sure she did. Did you believe it?"

His defensiveness slowly ebbed. DeeDee watched the tension in his shoulders relax. Softly he said, "Not a word of it."

She sat quietly for a moment, considered ordering another Coke, but decided not to because she didn't want to distract Duncan. "You said she begged for your help *twice.*"

"The second time, she called my cell phone, left a time and place on my voice mail."

"Presuming you would meet her."

"She didn't have to presume a damn thing. I knew it was wrong not to tell you about it. I knew it was wrong to go and meet her alone. But I went anyway. Oh, I justified it. I talked myself into believing that the call had come from Savich, that he was setting me up. But deep down I think I knew it would be Elise who was waiting for me."

"Where did this meeting take place?"

He snuffled a bitter laugh. "It wouldn't have mattered, DeeDee. It could have been anywhere, and I still would have gone. Nothing would have stopped me from going to her. See, I went with the clear understanding that she would try to compromise me. I went *hoping* she would try."

"Why?"

"Because I knew what she would use to barter." He turned his head and looked at her in such a way that she couldn't mistake his meaning.

She swallowed hard. "I see."

"She knew what I wanted, so that's what she offered."

"And you accepted?"

"Yeah." He closed his eyes and repeated huskily, "Yeah."

With a detached part of her mind, DeeDee wondered what it must be like to hold that much sway over another human being, how heady it must feel to have the power to make someone sacrifice his integrity, his life's work, for a few minutes of sexual gratification.

He drained his glass. "After we . . . Well. I welched on the bargain. I left her with tears on her face, begging me for help."

"To do what?"

"Help her out of her mess. The details don't really matter now. Hours after I walked out on her, Napoli was dead and we were searching for her body." He plowed his fingers up through his hair again and held his head between his hands. "Christ help me."

This explained his despair. He had compromised their investigation and violated his personal codes of morality and ethics, and he would never forgive himself for those transgressions.

Years before, while she was still a beat cop, two SPD officers had been accused of sexual misconduct with a female suspect. They had claimed that the woman was the initiator and a willing participant — which turned out to be true. Nevertheless, DeeDee remembered that Duncan was incensed over the officers' refusal to admit their fallibility and accept blame. In his view, they'd had the choice, as well as the responsibility, to do what was right, no matter how strong the temptation. Now he had made a similar misstep, and to him that would be indefensible.

But flaws and all, Duncan Hatcher was DeeDee's hero. To see him so reduced by guilt filled her with compassion, not condemnation. That she reserved for Elise Laird, for whom she had the utmost contempt. She'd be damned before she let that conniving woman's ghost destroy Duncan.

"You made a mistake," she said gently. "But you've acknowledged it. Put it away. It's over."

"Not for me, it isn't. I'll never forget the way she looked at me when —"

"Duncan, she was a player!" she exclaimed, loudly enough for the bartender to glance their way. "She knew you were attracted to her and she used that. What better way to protect herself from prosecution than to screw the cop who's trying to incriminate her?"

"I know that, DeeDee. Goddamn it, don't you think I know all that? But knowing it doesn't make me any less culpable. Three people are dead, not even counting poor Trotter, who started all this. Napoli, Gordie Ballew, and Elise. If I had done the right thing, they wouldn't have died."

"You don't know that. No one can know that. One way or another it was bound to end tragically." She leaned toward him so he had no choice but to look at her. "The lady was poison. You said so yourself when we started investigating this case. You lusted after her body, but that didn't blind you to her character. I know that for a fact. You trusted her no more than I did.

"She lied at every turn, she lied to everyone, and that night on the bridge all those lies caught up with her. Frankly, I don't regret whatever happened between her and Napoli. I'm glad she became history before she had a chance to destroy your career. Before she had a chance to destroy *you.*"

She rarely touched him, never wanting their working relationship to be jeopardized. But now she laid her hand on his arm and gave it a no-nonsense squeeze. "Put this behind you, Duncan. Forgive yourself for being male, for being human. Make a conscious decision to forget her. Refocus. Tomorrow we start fresh trying to nail Savich." She pushed the highball glass out of his reach. "For that, you need to be stone cold sober."

Duncan let himself be led out of the bar and into the deluge. By the time they reached DeeDee's car, he was drenched. He didn't care.

"What about my car?" he asked as she herded him into the passenger seat of hers.

"I'll pick you up in the morning and drive you back here to get it."

He didn't argue, having no interest whatsoever in any aspect of tomorrow.

It was a short distance to his town house; they covered the blocks in a matter of minutes. DeeDee cut her engine and was reaching for the door handle when he stopped her. "Don't come in."

"I'm coming in."

"I'll be fine. I won't drink any more. I swear," he said in response to her skeptical expression.

"All right, I believe you. But are you sure you don't want company?"

"Positive."

"Go play the piano for a while."

"I don't play the piano."

"Right." She grinned.

He forced one in return, but it felt like an unnatural stretching of his lips.

"Try and get some rest. See you in the morning."

He scowled. "Not too early." With that, he opened the door and got out.

The gutter had turned into a rushing creek. He stepped over the swift current and onto the sidewalk. Then he climbed the steps to his front door and unlocked it. He turned to wave good-bye to DeeDee. She tooted her horn as she drove away through the rain.

Inside, Duncan switched on a table lamp and, out of habit, walked toward the kitchen. When he got there, he couldn't think of a single thing that sounded appetizing. He wasn't hungry. He wanted nothing more to drink even though Smitty's whiskey hadn't had the desired mind-numbing effect. His head was all too clear.

Heedless of the rainwater he was dripping onto the rugs and hardwood floors, he made his way back into the living room, then stood in the center of it like a stranger, looking about for something familiar with which to make an emotional connection. For the first time ever in his life that he could remember, he felt utterly alone.

He could call his parents, who had always been there whenever he needed them, ready with an embrace, with a prayer and words of encouragement, with unqualified love. But he couldn't talk to them about this. Not yet.

DeeDee would come back in a heartbeat. She'd even offered to stay with him tonight. But he couldn't drag her down with him into this morass of guilt and self-loathing. Besides, he hadn't been completely honest with her.

He had confessed making love to Elise.

He hadn't confessed falling in love.

He glanced at the piano with complete indifference, but the piano bench was a painful reminder of the morning Elise had sat on it, looking up at him with imploring eyes that entranced and ensnared as facilely as they lied.

Irresistibly drawn to it, he sat down where she had sat. He was haunted by the possibility that nothing she had said or done had been true. Nothing. And worse, he feared that she'd been coached by Savich, that she had operated strictly under instructions from him. That when she was moving against Duncan on that shabby sofa, every touch, every expression, every sigh had been calculated.

Actually, it was treachery worthy of Savich. If Savich had shot him execution-style as he had Freddy Morris, it would have been too obvious, and Savich might have been easily captured.

Besides that, a bullet to the head wouldn't have been poetic. How much more satisfying to Savich to place Elise in his path, then sit back and watch with glee as Duncan came under the spell of her allure, compromising every ethical code to which he adhered, sacrificing his integrity, his career, his self-respect, everything that was valuable to him, slowly but inexorably bringing about his own downfall.

A brilliant plan.

He bowed his head lower and tried to compose a prayer of contrition, but the only sounds that issued from his raw throat were harsh, dry sobs. He longed to cry, but what would he be crying over? His squandered morality? Or Elise? What right did he have to cry over losing something that was never his to lose? Elise was lost to him forever.

He was simply lost.

He sat there a long time, but he never touched the keyboard. Eventually he got up, switched off the lamp, and started upstairs, feeling his way in the dark. The rain-streaked skylight cast a watery shadow on the wall of the staircase that made it appear to be weeping. He paused on the landing to watch the mournful trickles reflected on the wallpaper, then entered his bedroom, switching on the light as he passed through the door.

She was backed into the corner between his bed and the window.

He cried out in disbelief, shock, outrage. And *joy.* She was alive!

Acting instinctively, he whipped his pistol from its holster and crouched, aiming the barrel directly at her. "Drop the coat and face the wall, hands above your head."

"Duncan —"

"Fucking do it!" he shouted. "Do it or so help me God, I'll shoot you."

Elise dropped the rain slicker that she'd been holding folded over her arm and turned toward the wall, hands raised.

It took a conscious effort to close his mouth and control his rapid breathing. There was nothing he could do to slow down his racing heart. "Do you have the twenty-two?"

"The what?"

Keeping his pistol aimed at her, he came up behind her and hastily patted her down, running his hand down both her sides from armpit to ankle, up the inseam of her jeans and around the waistband. Satisfied that she wasn't armed, he sidestepped across the floor and picked up the telephone on the nightstand. She turned around as he fumbled with the rubberized digits on the phone.

She held up a hand, palm out. "Don't call anyone. Not until I've had a chance to explain."

"You'll explain, all right."

"Duncan —"

"Don't call me that! I'm not Duncan to you. I'm not anything to you except the cop that's gonna haul your ass to jail."

"I don't believe that."

"Believe it."

"You don't have to hold a gun on me."

"I'm sure you said that to Trotter and Napoli, and look what happened to them. How'd you get in here?"

"I heard you downstairs. Were you crying?"

"How did you get in?" he repeated, enunciating the words.

"A back window on the ground level

wasn't locked. I guess you forgot to set your alarm. Why were you crying?"

Again, he dodged that question. "Armies of men and women all over the Southeast have been busting their butts looking for you. There's been much ado over your disappearance off that bridge. You enjoyed all that attention, I'm sure."

She spread her arms at her sides. "Do I look like I enjoyed it?"

She had a point. She looked like hell. "What happened to your hair?"

"When you fake your suicide, the first thing you do is change your appearance."

Her hair looked like it had been sawed off with a dull butcher knife. It was short and spiky and stuck up in random spots like a punk rocker's. And it had been dyed a dark brown.

She wasn't dressed in the quality stuff she usually wore. The jeans and shirt were too large and looked like rejects of a yard sale. On her feet were plain canvas sneakers. No turquoise stones on these shoes. They were also wet and muddy.

Her face was gaunt, the thinness emphasized by the extreme haircut. Her eyes were outlined in dark makeup that had been applied with a heavy hand. When she saw that he noticed it, she said, "To cover up a black eye, compliments of Meyer Napoli."

"Who put up the fight? Him or you?"

She extended her arm and pushed up the long sleeve of her shirt. From wrist to elbow her arm was mottled with bruises in a range of colors. "I don't think he expected me to fight back."

The cordless telephone felt heavy in Duncan's hand. So did the pistol, but he didn't lower either of them. "He was waiting for you in your car?" She gave him an odd look, and he said, "That much we figured out. Napoli took a taxi to where you'd left your car."

"While I was with you."

"While you were favoring me with the motherlode of fucks."

She lowered her gaze but only for a moment. When she looked at him again, her eyes were bright with anger. "Don't you get it yet?"

"Apparently not."

"I was desperate," she cried out. "I would have done anything to enlist your help."

"But you didn't do *anything.* You did that."

"Because I knew . . ." Again her gaze faltered, but only for a moment before it locked with his. "Because I knew that's what you wanted."

It was almost verbatim what he'd said to

DeeDee a half hour earlier, but hearing it from Elise made his blood run hot with fury.

"I even knew that's what you expected me to do," she continued. "Detective Bowen, too. She would have expected me to play the whore. So I guess I proved you both right."

"Well, it was a wasted effort."

"I know. You didn't believe me."

"Not then, and for damn sure not now."

"I hoped you might have changed your mind."

He didn't allow himself to be taken in by her wounded look. "What happened on the bridge?"

She shook back long hair that was no longer there, a reflexive gesture Duncan recognized as what she did when collecting her thoughts. Or fabricating lies. "After you left, I fell asleep."

"Oh, right. You the insomniac." She really was a priceless liar. She would like for him to believe that she had drifted off following their lovemaking, when she'd been unable to sleep after sex with her husband. Lest he fall for the manipulation, he yanked his mind back to what she was saying.

"I slept for over two hours. When I woke up, I panicked, knowing Cato would be looking for me. I rushed back to my car.

Napoli was waiting for me in the backseat."

"As arranged."

"No."

Trying to trap her in a lie, he said, "But you recognized him immediately."

She shook her head emphatically. "I'd never seen him before. He introduced himself, even gave me his business card."

Duncan had wondered why, if their meeting was prearranged, there'd been any need for the transponder and why Napoli's card had been in the seat of her car. He'd raised those questions once with DeeDee and Worley, but they'd shrugged them off as insignificant details.

"Okay," he said, "Napoli's in your car. Then what?"

"He held a gun to my head and told me to drive to the middle of the Talmadge Bridge. I did as he said, but when we topped the bridge I called his bluff and kept going. He dug the barrel of his pistol into my temple and threatened to pull the trigger unless I turned around. So as soon as we reached the other side, I made a U-turn."

That explained why the car had been in the inbound lane. But she could have heard that in the news reports.

"This time, when I reached the crest, I stopped. He told me to leave the key in the ignition, get out, and walk to the wall. I kept stalling, asking him what he wanted, offering him money. He said he'd already struck a deal for more than I could ever pay him."

"With who?"

"Who do you think?"

"Don't dare say your husband. The man's been shattered by this."

"You're wrong."

"And you're lying," he fired back. "For ten days I've watched him. I've seen him disintegrate bit by bit. He's devastated."

"That's what he wants you to think."

"He's faking it?"

"Yes."

"You're sticking to that story?"

"Yes."

He started pressing digits on his phone.

"Wait! Duncan, I beg you. Listen to me."

He stopped dialing, but kept his thumb poised over the buttons.

She clasped her raised hands in a gesture of appeal. "Gary Ray Trotter failed, so Napoli had to finish the job himself. He gave me the choice of jumping off the bridge, or of being shot. Either way was fine by him, he said. I wouldn't survive the two-hundred-foot fall into the river. People would think I'd killed myself. If he shot me, it would look like another carjacking. Either way, I'd be dead and he would be richer, courtesy of Cato."

"Why would your husband pay a creep like Napoli to get rid of you?"

She hesitated; Duncan laughed shortly. "We never get further than that, do we?" He pressed another of the digits on the telephone. "Motive trips you up every time. But you had plenty of motive to shoot Napoli, didn't you?"

"Yes. No."

"Well, which is it?" he shouted.

She put her hand to her butchered hair. "You're confusing me."

"Welcome to the club, lady. I've been a little confused myself lately."

"I had motive to shoot him, but I didn't. I got away from him and ran. He chased me. He stepped on the heel of my sandal and it snapped off. I stumbled, fell. Napoli hauled me up by my arm. He wrenched it hard and I screamed. That startled him. I took advantage of his surprise and grabbed for the gun. I yanked it out of his hand and threw it into the river. He hit me in the face." She pointed to her eye. "I swatted at his head, grabbed his hair, and pulled hard. He fell back, and I took off running again."

"At some point you shot him in the stomach with your husband's old twenty-two."

"I don't know anything about a twenty-two," she cried. "In any case, I didn't shoot Napoli."

"Well, somebody plugged him in the gut."

"Savich."

His breath came out in a gust of disbelief, almost amusement. *"Savich?"*

"That's right."

He laughed. "What a convenient scapegoat. First you used his name to get me to the old house for our secret meeting. Now you're trying to —"

"It's the truth!"

"You watched Savich shoot Napoli."

"Yes."

"And he let you get away?"

"He didn't see me."

Laughter as well as patience deserted him. Giving her a hard look, he said, "Try again."

She took a deep breath as though ready to launch into a long and complicated story. "I was running from Napoli —"

"On second thought, save your breath. I'm sick of your bullshit. You killed Napoli. Otherwise you would have notified the police."

"I couldn't."

"Couldn't?"

"I knew everyone would think that I had killed him. Like Gary Ray Trotter. No one would have believed me."

He didn't. Certainly not this crap about Savich, especially now, knowing what good friends they were. But for the time being, he played along. "Okay, so you ran and miraculously escaped Savich. Where have you been for the last ten days? How'd you live? What did you do for money? We've had cops up and down the East Coast from Miami to Myrtle Beach checking hotels and motels, from the ritziest to the sleaziest. Bus stations, airports, boat rentals and charters, car rental companies. Anything that moves, we've checked. Bicycles, motorcycles, and pogo sticks," he finished angrily. "How did you manage to disappear? Did you have help?"

"Help? No. I had a contingency plan to disappear. For months I'd been preparing for it. I had some money stashed away, a credit card in another name, a fake ID, a place to go."

"You didn't go to the house where I met you."

She tilted her head. "You went back there to look for me?"

"Yeah, I went back."

"Alone? Or with your partner?"

He avoided that. "You hid out until to-night when the search was called off. Now, nobody's looking for you or your remains. So why'd you come back? Why'd you come to *me?* Why didn't you just stay dead?"

It was a vicious thing to say and she reacted accordingly. But he let the question stand.

Finally she said softly, "I came back because I have unfinished business."

"Yeah, I know about that. You've got a smooth operation going with Savich." Reading her shock, he moved toward her in a measured tread. "I saw the pictures. The ones Napoli was using to blackmail you."

"Blackmail me? What are you talking about? What pictures?"

The thought of hitting a woman was repugnant to him, but remembering the photographs with her and Savich raised the level of his frustration and brought him close to slapping her. At the very least giving her a hard shake to dislodge the phony perplexity in her expressive eyes.

He also wanted to touch her, to crush her against him and inhale the scent of rainwater coming off her, just to reassure himself that she was real and warm, not a figment of his cruel imagination, just to see if she felt as good against him as he remembered.

Duty and desire were warring again, and he hated her for it.

"I curse the day I first saw you," he said, meaning it. "God damn you for dragging me into your scheme, whatever the hell it is. I wish to heaven —"

The telephone in his hand rang, startling them. They both looked at the instrument as it rang a second time.

"Don't answer, Duncan. Please."

"Shut up."

Using the pistol, he motioned her to back away from him then raised the phone to his ear. "Hello?"

He listened for about thirty seconds, his gaze never wavering from her face. He ended the call by saying, "Sure. I'll be right there." Even after disconnecting, he held her stare.

Her chest rose and fell anxiously. She wet her lips. "What?"

"Earlier tonight a woman's body was pulled out of the river," he stated slowly. "Judge Laird has just identified it as you."

23

"She's pretty much a mess." Dothan Brooks spoke in a reverential undertone. "You know what a floater looks like, and she's been in the water." He looked Duncan up and down. "You're not much drier than she is."

His hair and clothes were wet. "I'd been out in the weather when I got the call. Didn't want to take time to change."

He'd reached the morgue as quickly as possible, having to first jog from his town house to the parking lot of Smitty's to retrieve his car. He and the ME were standing a discreet distance from the judge, granting him time alone with the corpse on the gurney. The body was entirely covered by a sheet, save for the right hand, which the judge held clasped between his as he wept unabashedly.

The body had been discovered by a tugboat crew beneath a pier where the tugs docked. The Talmadge Bridge was well within sight.

"How come she didn't surface sooner?" Duncan asked.

"Got hung up on something under the pier is my guess. Fish have had at her. She was a feeding ground. She finally shook loose of whatever was holding her down, and up she came."

"If she looks that bad, how did he make the ID?"

"Birthmark. Lower abdomen, part of it under her pubic hair. Only a husband or lover would know about it. I told him we could wait on a positive ID until we obtained her dental records, but he insisted on looking at her. Nearly tossed his cookies when he saw her face, or lack thereof. Said no way was that his beautiful Elise.

"But then he saw that birthmark, and I'm here to tell you, he fell apart. Would have collapsed if I hadn't caught him." Dothan took a package of peanut M&M's from his pants pocket and ripped it open. "Want some?"

"No, thanks. Any signs of her struggle with Napoli?"

Dothan chewed a handful of the candies, crunching them noisily between his teeth. "Not readily apparent, but they wouldn't be, considering. I'll take a closer look during the autopsy. But no bullet wounds or anything like that, if that's what you mean."

"Cause of death was drowning?"

"If so, there'll be water in her lungs."

"What was she wearing?"

Dothan motioned him over to a sterile table on which lay a wristwatch with a narrow leather strap and three articles of badly stained and sodden clothing. They were filthy, but recognizable. The ME said, "According to the judge the watch belonged to her and the clothes match what she was wearing the last time he saw her."

"He should know. He bought them for her."

Duncan left the ME with his snack and approached the gurney, moving to the left side of it so that he was facing Judge Laird across it. He pretended to be contemplating the still form beneath the sheet but actually he was studying Elise's seemingly bereft husband.

He wiped his eyes with the back of his hand, looked up, and nodded a greeting. "Detective."

"Everyone working the case extends their condolences."

"Thank you."

Mentally he braced himself and lifted the top corner of the sheet. Dothan had understated the damage. His stomach lurched. The organic destruction to the features made them practically indistinguishable as such. However, one ear remained intact. He noted that it was pierced, but there was no earring in the hole. The hair was wet and matted with God knows how many varieties of river matter, but it was the approximate color and length of Elise's. He lowered the sheet. "It must be very difficult for you to see her like this."

The judge squeezed his eyes shut. "You have no idea how painful."

"Are you sure it's your wife?"

His eyes popped open and he looked at Duncan with reproach. "Of course."

"I'm not trying to pick an argument with you, Judge. It's just that people have made false identifications before. You wouldn't be here if the situation wasn't already traumatic. You come down here scared, emotionally and physically drained. Under those circumstances, mistakes have been made before."

"There's no mistake. Did Dr. Brooks tell you about the birthmark?"

"Yes."

"I couldn't possibly mistake that."

"I'm sure. All the same, we'll rely on dental records."

"Of course. Whatever Dr. Brooks needs, I'll make available to him tomorrow." He gazed at the draped body. "I wish with all my heart that I was wrong. But it's Elise." He bent over the hand he was holding. It was a ghastly color, and Duncan knew it must be cold and repugnant to the touch. The judge kissed the back of it. As he straightened, he said, "In times of personal crisis, it's very difficult to be a public official."

"You're in the spotlight even as you're grieving," Duncan said, following his thought.

"I understand there's already press outside."

"Your wife's disappearance has been a big story. This is the final chapter."

"I can't cope with the media right now. Besides, I want to stay with Elise for as long as possible before turning her over to Dr. Brooks for the autopsy." He voice cracked and he covered his eyes with his hand.

Duncan walked around the gurney and stood beside him. "I'm sure Dr. Brooks will give you all the time you want, Judge. And we'll have officers outside to protect you from the press when you leave. Until you're ready, let our department's PIO deal with them."

As he made to go, the judge detained him. "We got off to a rocky start, Detective Hatcher, and we've had some cross moments. But generally speaking, you've been extraordinarily sensitive to my distress during all this. I want you to know how much I appreciate everything you did for me and my wife."

Duncan shook the hand extended to him, but as he looked into the judge's tearful eyes, he was thinking, You wouldn't appreciate everything I did for your wife, you lying, cocksucking son of a bitch.

She was sitting on the bathroom floor where he'd left her, handcuffed to the plumbing pipe beneath the sink. She'd fought him like a wildcat as he wrestled her into the bathroom and put the handcuffs on her. He left her pleading with him not to leave her there like that. He'd told her it was for her own protection, but the truth was that he didn't trust her not to pull another vanishing act.

He didn't trust her not to be in cahoots with Savich, either. Before leaving, he didn't neglect to set his house alarm. And even though the LED didn't register a disturbance when he disengaged it upon his return, he climbed the stairs with pistol drawn.

She was alone, just as he'd left her, although she no longer looked angry. Either that or she was simply too exhausted to rail at him as he knelt down to unlock the handcuffs. He helped her to her feet.

"What happened?" she asked. He gave her a few seconds to massage circulation back into her wrists before reaching for her hands again. "Oh, please don't," she begged as he replaced the cuffs. "Why?"

"My peace of mind."

"You still don't trust me?"

He opened his closet and pulled out a duffel bag, tossed it on the bed, and unzipped it. "Did you bring anything here with you except the rain slicker?"

"No. Did you see Cato?"

"Yeah, I saw him."

"Where?"

"At the morgue."

"And he identified *my* body?"

"She was wearing your wristwatch."

"Napoli made me take it off and give it to him."

"It wasn't in the car when we found him."

"Then Savich must have taken it."

"Must have." There was much to learn, but not before they were safely away from here. "Where have you been staying all this time?" he asked as he rifled bureau drawers

502

and began throwing items of clothing into the duffel bag.

"In a house on Hilton Head. I paid a year's rent on it six months ago, but I hadn't used it until this past week."

"How'd you get to the island?"

"A while back I bought a used car and kept it parked in a paid lot, so I could leave in a hurry if I needed to. That night I walked to it from the bridge."

He stopped what he was doing and looked at her. "And then drove back across?" One route to the island meant crossing the Talmadge Bridge.

"No, I took the interstate."

"Going back to the bridge would have been audacious, even for you," he said bitterly. He resumed packing. "How did you manage to come by a house, car, et cetera when your husband had Napoli following you?"

"I guess I wasn't under constant surveillance."

Or Napoli had deliberately withheld some information to use to bait the judge later, up the ante, make more profit. "Where's the car now?"

"Same place. This evening, as soon as I heard on the news that the search had been called off, I drove from Hilton Head. I left the car in the paid lot and walked from there to here."

"A rental house and a car purchase. That's a paper trail a mile wide. A blind man could follow it."

"Then how come nobody discovered it while I was missing?"

"Good point," he said wryly. "But I don't want to take any chances. You've got to stay invisible."

"For how long?"

"Until I figure out what to do."

"About me?"

"About everything. Your husband produced a body so we would stop looking for you and close the case. I need to find out why."

"Please don't refer to him as my husband."

"You're married to him."

"I despise him."

He held her gaze for several beats, then went into the bathroom and raided the medicine cabinet of toiletries. "How were all those transactions handled? The house, the car."

"Under assumed names. I bought the car in South Carolina from an individual. It's registered there. Cato doesn't know any of this. I'm sure."

"Well, I'm not," he said, dumping the

double handful of bathroom items into the duffel on top of the clothing. "I don't like it."

He checked his closet for anything he might have missed and might need, then took a pistol from the top shelf. Along with a box of bullets, he added it to the duffel bag and zipped it up.

Then he looked around the room, wondering if this was the last time he would ever see it. But he had no time for entertaining sentimental thoughts. He picked up Elise's slicker and draped it over her cuffed hands.

"Where are we going?" she asked.

"I don't know yet. But I can't keep you here. You're good to me only as long as you stay dead. Take off your shoes." She toed off the sneakers without question. He put them in the pockets of the slicker, then hastily wiped up her wet footprints with a bathroom towel. "If anyone comes looking for you, I don't want them to see your footprints."

"Who would come looking?"

"You friend Savich, maybe."

"Savich is not my friend. He for sure wouldn't be if he knew I'd seen him kill Napoli."

Leaving that alone for the moment, Duncan hefted the strap of the duffel bag onto

505

his shoulder and took Elise's hands, pulling her along behind him as he went down the stairs. "I parked my car out back in the alley." He led her through the dark house to the rear door in the kitchen.

He pulled it open cautiously and scanned the enclosed garden. Like the rest of the city, his walled backyard was saturated from the recent rains. Tops of plants were bent low from the weight of the water. He detected nothing out of the ordinary and no movement other than raindrops splashing into puddles.

He took her shoes from the coat pockets and placed them on the floor then guided her bare feet into them. "Okay, let's go." But when he tried to pull her through the door, she resisted. He turned back. "What?"

"Do you finally believe me?"

He stared into her shadowed face for several moments, then said, "Do you have a birthmark partially covered by your pubic hair?"

She gave him a pointed look.

He said, "It was dark. I could have missed it."

"I don't have a birthmark."

"Then I'm close to believing you."

As he got into his car and started the motor, he thought to check the fuel gauge. More than half full. Good. He was reluctant to make another stop before getting the hell out of Dodge.

But there was one thing he must do. He plucked his cell phone off his belt and called DeeDee. She answered immediately. Without even an opening hello, she said, "How was it at the morgue?"

"Cold."

"You know what I mean."

"Judge Laird was still there."

Because he was lead detective on the case, Gerard had asked him to take that duty while DeeDee was sent to the pier where the body had been discovered to interview the men who'd discovered it. He summarized his brief conversation with the ME and with Laird, aware that Elise was also listening from the passenger seat of his car. He concluded with, "The judge is very torn up."

"Well, that's that, I guess," DeeDee said with her typical practicality. "As you said earlier today, it would be over when her body was found."

"Yes, that's what I said."

She hesitated, then asked, "How are *you?*"

"Fine. But I wondered if you could cover for me if I take a couple days off?"

DeeDee expressed concern for his mental and emotional state and told him she didn't think it was a good time for him to be alone. She suggested he see a counselor and discuss his conflicts regarding the late Mrs. Laird.

He couldn't talk openly about it, not with Elise sitting on the other side of the console, but he told his concerned partner that a few days away from the office were exactly what he needed.

"I just need some downtime, DeeDee. I want to hang out, get my head straight, then I'll be right as rain and raring to get back to work. I'll call you in a day or two." He said good-bye before she could ask where he was going for this self-prescribed downtime.

"I wonder who she was," Elise said as he ended the call. "The woman in the morgue wearing my wristwatch. Who was she?"

Duncan had a good guess, but he kept it to himself. There was much he needed to learn before he could trust Elise entirely. "She was a blonde. Approximately your size. And Judge Laird was awfully convincing as the grieving husband. If I hadn't seen you in the flesh, I would have believed he was weeping over the mutilated corpse of his beloved wife."

As they approached the Talmadge Bridge,

they both tensed and stayed that way until they had crossed it. South Carolina's state highway 17 was a dark, narrow, and dangerous road notorious for fatality collisions, but Elise visibly relaxed once Savannah was behind them. She tucked her feet beneath her hips and turned in her seat toward him. He noticed her shiver.

Believing it to be impossible, he asked, "Are you cold?"

"Do you mind turning on the heater?"

He was sweating, but he turned on the heater.

She laid her cheek against the headrest. He could feel her studying his profile while he kept his eyes resolutely on the road's center stripe. The windshield wipers were fighting a noisy but losing battle against the volume of rain. She said, "You could get into a lot of trouble, couldn't you?"

"I'm already in a lot of trouble. I was in trouble when I left the morgue, knowing it wasn't you under that sheet."

After a lengthy pause, she said, "You were in trouble long before that, Duncan."

When he dared to look at her, she was asleep.

She was still sleeping when he brought the car to a stop. He extinguished the headlights and got out. The rain had decreased somewhat but was still falling steadily. His shoes crunched on the oyster-shell driveway as he rounded the hood of the car. She stirred when he opened the passenger door.

"We're here."

She sat up and blinked. "Where?"

"I'm getting wet."

"Oh. Sorry." She got out, a bit awkwardly because of her cuffed hands. "Whose house is this?"

"It belonged to my grandmother."

The small house was built on stilts, a precaution that had kept it from flooding numerous times. He preceded Elise up a set of steep wood steps. "Careful, they're slick."

He found the key under the flowerpot where it was always left, then unlocked the door and held it open for her. "When my grandmother died it became my mom's," he said. "But Mom had a near-drowning experience when she was a kid and never gets near a body of water larger than her bathtub. Dad comes here to fish sometimes, but not that often. I'm free to use the place anytime I like, but I rarely do."

"Why don't you use it? It looks charming."

"In the dark it does. In daylight you can see the wood rot, the peeling paint, rusty hinges. It's practically surrounded by water, so it's a pain in the ass to maintain."

When he switched on a table lamp, he saw that she was smiling at him. "You love this house."

Her small and perceptive smile, her tone of voice, made it a warm, fuzzy moment. This was definitely not the time for warm fuzzies. Brusquely he said, "I used to spend a lot of time here in the summers."

She moved to the nearest window and parted the curtains to look out. "Where are we?"

"Lady's Island. That's Beaufort over there."

For the most part, the town across the water was dark, but a few lights twinkled through the rain and on the rippling surface of the channel.

Turning away from the window, she took in the details of the room. "It's small," he said, sounding more defensive than he intended. He was thinking about the mansion she shared with Cato Laird. "Kitchen," he said, pointing. Only a peninsula of cabinetry separated it from the living area. "It isn't stocked. I'll go out for food in the morning. Bedroom. Bath there."

She moved toward the open door of the bedroom and peered inside. When she came back around, she nodded toward the piano, which was much too large for such a compact room, an indication of its importance. "Your grandmother's?"

"She loved piano. The one at my town house belonged to her, too."

"Do you play?"

He heard himself saying, "Sometimes," and realized that was the first time he'd ever willingly admitted it.

She studied him for a moment, then asked, "Will anyone look for you here?"

He shook his head.

"Not even Detective Bowen?"

Again he shook his head.

"Have you ever brought anyone here before tonight?"

The answer was no, but he didn't want her to know that. Already she was learning personal things about him, which, in their present circumstances, she didn't need to know.

As though to convey that to himself as well as to her, he yanked the telephone cord out of the wall jack with more flourish than necessary, then wound it around the instrument. "Do you have a cell phone?"

"It was left behind in my handbag."

"You've had days —"

"I've had no one to call, Duncan. Besides,

512

if I had a phone, you would have felt it when you searched me."

Reminded of touching her, he turned abruptly and went out, taking his grandmother's telephone with him. He clumped down the steps to the car, where he locked the telephone inside the trunk and got his duffel bag from the backseat. When he returned, Elise was standing in the bathroom door. "I can't use it. . . ." She held up her hands.

He unlocked the handcuffs and removed them. She thanked him, then slipped into the bathroom and closed the door.

He set the duffel bag on the floor and opened it. After quickly loading the spare pistol, he placed it on top of a knickknack cabinet, far enough back where his guest couldn't see it. She couldn't get to it without standing on something.

When she emerged from the bathroom, he sailed a pair of boxer shorts and a T-shirt in her direction. She caught them against her chest. "Since you don't have a change of clothes and yours are damp, you may be more comfortable sleeping in those."

"Thank you."

"You're welcome."

He went into the bedroom and took a quilt and pillow from the closet, then carried them into the living room and threw them on the couch. He took off his shoes. "I'm beat."

"If you want to take the bed, I'll be fine on the sofa," she said.

"And have Grandmother's ghost haunt me forever?" He shook his head. She smiled, but as they gazed at each other across the short distance that separated them, her smile gradually faded. "Aren't you going to ask me about Cato and Savich?"

"In the morning."

"There's a lot to tell."

"In the morning."

"All right. I'll explain everything then. Good night."

She turned into the bedroom, but he stopped her. "Elise?"

It was the first time he had ever addressed her by her first name, and it surprised them both.

"There is one thing I've got to know," he said. "And I'll know if you lie to me."

"I won't lie to you."

"Have you slept with Savich?"

"No." She replied immediately and without equivocation. His need to believe that one thing must have been telegraphed to her by his piercing gaze because she repeated it softly and emphatically, *"No, Duncan."*

He felt as though a fist that had been squeezing his heart had relaxed its tenacious grip. "Sleep tight."

At eight o'clock the following morning, Judge Cato Laird's press conference was about to be televised on all the local stations. He was already in position on the podium, under the glare of lights, waiting for it to begin. With him was Chief of Police Taylor. Sound technicians were adjusting microphones. Reporters from print and broadcast media were milling about, chatting with one another while vying for the best vantage points.

Savich, watching on his silenced TV, dialed a telephone number. He saw the judge react to his vibrating cell phone, saw him reach for it and lift it to his ear, saw his lips form the word when he answered with a brusque, "Yes?"

"Good morning, Judge. I called to extend my condolences."

Cato Laird recognized his voice instantly, of course. Savich watched as the judge's expression changed from that of a bereaved husband to a man who'd just swallowed a raw egg. Savich imagined his sphincter clenching. The judge nervously glanced around to see if anyone was within earshot. He moved away from the police chief, who was talking to a uniformed officer.

"Your upper lip is damp with perspiration, Judge," Savich said. "You may want to dab some makeup on that before the press conference begins."

The judge looked toward one of the many TV cameras focused on him, realizing that Savich was out there, watching him. "Hello, from TV land," Savich said, enjoying himself immensely.

"Thank you for the call," the judge said for the camera, then turned his back to it.

"I assume the cadaver met with your approval?"

"Yes. She was perfect in every regard."

Savich laughed. "With a fortuitously placed birthmark."

"That certainly helped at this critical time."

"Glad to be of service, Judge. You'll find her dental records in your mailbox at home, labeled with your wife's name, of course. How fortunate for us that we have such a harmonious quid pro quo relationship. You needed a body."

"Yes. Detective Hatcher is an extremely thorough investigator."

"And Elise was proving to be a nuisance even in death. She wouldn't surface. Luckily I had a stand-in waiting in the wings, a woman who needed killing as much as Elise."

"I've always relied on your willingness to help, as well as your seemingly endless supply of resources."

Savich chuckled. "Happy to oblige." He saw Laird glance uneasily toward Chief Taylor, who discreetly tapped his wristwatch.

The judge said, "I so appreciate your call, but they're ready to get under way here. I really must run."

"Do not hang up on me, Cato." Savich saw the judge's shoulders tense at his imperious tone.

"I wouldn't think of it, except that I'm pressed for time," he said tightly.

"Napoli had only seconds to call me from the backseat of Elise's car when she returned to it. But everything went according to plan. I was to pick him up on the Talmadge Bridge. Until I arrived, he would pretend to be a stranded motorist with a broken-down car." He chuckled. "When I arrived, he looked a sight. He told me your dearly departed put up an admirable struggle before he sent her over the wall."

"I didn't realize that you'd spoken with him."

"Briefly. *Very* briefly. Before I killed him, I wanted assurance that the problem of your wife had been taken care of once and for all."

"Thank you again for that attention to detail. I'll be certain to return the favor."

"I'll be certain that you do. However, I didn't kill Napoli strictly as a favor to you, Cato." He paused, subtly alerting the judge that the tenor of the conversation was about to shift. Finally he said, "Your hired gun Napoli mailed me a set of those interesting photographs."

There followed a telling silence broken only by Laird's rapid breathing. "I can explain those."

"No explanation necessary, Cato. It's clear that those pictures of Elise and me were to be used if ever you felt like double-crossing me."

"Not at all, not at all," he said hastily and in an undertone. "Please have no worry about that."

"I'm not worried," Savich said smoothly. "Our partnership remains as solid as ever. You and I don't have a problem. As long as Napoli was telling the truth, that is."

"The truth about — ?"

"Elise's death. It wouldn't have been out of character for Meyer Napoli to go to his maker with a lie on his lips. She may not be dead at all."

"Not possible."

"Don't be a fool, Cato. Anything's possible."

24

Duncan crept out of the house, leaving her asleep. He was taking a chance that she would skip out while he was gone, but he didn't believe she would, and if she did, she couldn't get far.

When he returned, she was sitting on the sofa, her legs tucked under her, wrapped in a quilt he remembered from his childhood, watching the small TV that had belonged to his grandmother.

Arms loaded with sacks of groceries, he pushed his way through the door and nudged it closed with his elbow. Elise glanced up at him and nodded toward the TV. "Cato."

He delivered the groceries to the kitchen then joined her to watch the televised press conference. He wondered how Judge Laird had pulled off the gaunt, ravaged visage of a mourner. Had he been fasting for several days so his neck would look scrawny poking out of his collar? The dark circles around his eyes could either be cosmetics, or he simply hadn't allowed himself to sleep much since her disappearance.

Whatever he'd done to prepare for the part, he'd done it well. If you went strictly on appearance, you'd say this guy was shattered over his wife's death, that his bereavement was so extreme, it was unlikely he would ever recover.

The script was spot-on, too. No doubt well rehearsed. As Laird completed one thought and segued into another, he raised his head and squinted into the television lights — a first. Always before he'd been very comfortable in their glare.

"Despite my personal tragedy . . ." He paused to cover his mouth with his fist and clear his throat. "Despite my personal tragedy, I've been overwhelmed by the support of friends, colleagues, and, indeed, strangers. I wish to acknowledge the tireless efforts of the Savannah-Chatham Metropolitan Police Department, the Chatham County Sheriff's Office, the U.S. Coast Guard, the many men and —"

With an angry motion, Elise turned off the TV and tossed the remote aside, then bounded off the sofa and began to pace. "You missed the best part," she said. "About how my life was cut tragically short. Often misunderstood, I was another candle in the wind."

"He said *that?*"

"Quoted the lyrics." She retrieved the quilt from the floor where it had fallen when she stood up and pulled it around her. "He'll play the sorrowful widower to the hilt, but I wouldn't expect anything less from him. He's —"

"Are you hungry?"

She broke off the tirade, looked at Duncan, and nodded.

"Because I'm starved. All that," he said, motioning toward the TV, "can wait till after we're fed."

He was anxious to hear everything she had to tell him. On the other hand, he dreaded it, because it would mean dredging up everything they'd left behind in Savannah last night. "Can you cook?" he asked.

"Yes."

"Good. Because I can't. I'll make the coffee, but don't expect it to pass any taste tests." He went into the kitchen and began removing the grocery items from the bags.

"I'll be right back."

She scurried into the bedroom and closed the door, presumably to dress. Duncan would just as soon have her stay in his boxers and T-shirt. From the glimpse he'd had, she looked good in them. Great, in fact. And he fancied the thought of cloth that had been worn against his skin now rubbing against hers.

He was scooping coffee into the paper filter when she returned wearing the shapeless jeans and shirt she'd had on last night. "How much water did you use?" she asked.

"Eight cups' worth."

"Then that's enough coffee." She surveyed the staples he'd bought and nodded with approval. "This will work. Mixing bowls? Pots and pans?"

In fifteen minutes they were seated across from each other at his grandmother's table, eating scrambled eggs that he declared were the best he'd ever had.

She laughed. "You're just hungry." When she realized that he was holding his fork poised above his plate and staring at her, she said, "What? Have I got food on my face?"

"No. It's just . . . that's the first time I've ever heard you laugh."

Her smile relaxed. "I haven't had much to laugh about."

He nodded, but let the subject drop there, and dug back into his breakfast. "No kidding, this is good. My grits always look and taste like wet cement."

"You can't cook at all?"

"Nope."

"Who normally cooks your breakfast?"

She was casually spreading butter on a slice of toast, but he recognized a loaded question. "I usually grab something on the way to work."

"Always? I thought there may be a . . ." Her eyebrows lifted eloquently.

"No. Not even a . . ." He matched her strategic pause. "No one who stays for breakfast."

Her chest lifted on a quick breath before she resumed buttering her toast. A few minutes later when she pushed aside her empty plate, he remarked, "You were hungry, too."

"Very."

"I think you've dropped a few pounds."

"It's the clothes. I bought them too large."

So not to draw attention to that body while playing dead, he thought.

She picked up her coffee mug and studied the gay daisy pattern on it. "Tell me about the grandmother who lived here."

"Well, she actually lived in Savannah. This was a weekend getaway until my grandfather died, then she moved out here permanently. She thought the town house was too big for her to live in alone. Three stories were two too many, so —"

"*Your* town house."

He admitted it with a nod. "She deeded it over to me. Which was more generous than any of us realized at the time."

"Those old town houses are prize real estate now."

"If I were trying to buy it, I couldn't come close to affording it. Not on a cop's salary. I thank Grandmother every day for her generosity."

"She must have loved you very much."

"Yes," he said with a slow and pronounced nod. "She did. I can't blame any of my shortcomings on a love-deprived childhood."

"Good parents?"

"The best."

He received the expected reaction when he told her that his dad was a minister and that he'd grown up in a parsonage, never missing a Sunday of worship unless he was sick. "Go ahead, ask," he said.

"Ask what?"

"What happened to you? Why didn't you turn out better than you did? Why didn't the religious training take?"

"It took."

Her voice was soft, but direct, and it made

his heart thump against his ribs.

"You're a decent man, Duncan. Even when you're being tough, your basic goodness comes across. You feel things deeply. You try and do what's right."

"Not lately." He looked at her meaningfully.

"I'm sorry," she said softly.

"Don't be. They were my choices to make."

She went back to studying the daisies on the coffee mug. "Did you always want to be a policeman?"

"No, I decided that my junior year of high school." She looked at him inquisitively, an invitation to explain. "A good friend I'd grown up with was brutally raped and murdered."

"How awful," she murmured.

"Yeah. Even worse, it was generally believed — although nobody said it out loud — that the culprit was probably her stepfather. But he owned a car dealership and two radio stations. He was president of the Rotary Club. No one dared touch him, not even the police, who conducted a sloppy investigation. They eventually assigned blame to a retarded kid. He was sent to a state institution and locked up for reasons I'm sure he never understood."

"You've been railing against the injustice of it ever since. So you became a policeman to right wrongs."

"Naw," he said flippantly. "I just like pushing people around and playing with guns."

He expected a smile, but her expression remained solemn. "If you hadn't been *you,* Duncan, I wouldn't have trusted you enough to ask for your help."

He let that lie for a moment, then said, "I figured it was because of what I said to you the night of the awards dinner."

Carefully, she set the coffee mug on the table and stared into it. "That, too. I used what I . . . what I thought might work to get to you. I did what I had to do." She raised her head and looked him in the eye. "Not for the first time."

They were getting to the heart of the subject now. Again, he wanted to postpone it. He stood up and began clearing the table. She washed, he dried. They worked side by side, but silently.

When the chore was done, she said, "Can we go outside? I'd like to look at the water."

In the early hours of the morning, the rain had stopped. The sun was out and everything had that washed-clean brilliance about it. The air was clear. Colors seemed more vivid. The sky was boasting a deep blue that hadn't been seen for days.

He walked her out onto a fishing pier where he, his dad, and his granddad had often fished. When he told her that, she smiled. "You were lucky."

"Not at fishing," he said with a laugh. "The men of my family are lousy fishermen. We just enjoyed being in each other's company."

"That's why you were lucky."

They sat down on the edge of the rough wood pier, dangling their feet over the side, and watched the boats moving in and out of Beaufort's marina. He waited a time, then said, "You weren't so lucky?"

"In terms of family? No. It's a classic case of total dysfunction. My father left before I was born. I never knew him. My mother married a man, had a baby boy by him, and then he left, too. More accurately, she ran him off.

"Although she was never diagnosed, my guess is that she was bipolar. To my half brother and me she just seemed . . . mean. Unpredictably she would fly into rages. I won't bore you with the ugly details."

After a short pause, she said, "My half brother and I survived by sticking together. Our fear of her forged a bond between us. I loved him. He loved me. We were all each other had.

"When I graduated high school, I began working at various jobs, with the short-term goal of getting my brother through high school and then setting us up in our own home.

"But, lacking supervision, he got in with a bad gang at school. Started doing drugs. Committed petty crimes. He was in and out of juvenile detention." She turned toward Duncan. "Familiar story?"

"All too familiar. Typically it doesn't have a happy ending."

"This one doesn't. One day my brother ran away. He left a note under the windshield of my car while I was at work."

"What work?" he asked curiously.

"Video rental store. The owner practically turned it over to me to manage. I did all the ordering, inventory, classifying, bookkeeping, even cleaned the restrooms. I couldn't wait to go to work every day."

"To clean the restrooms?"

She smiled. "Small price to pay. Because basically I got paid to watch movies."

"You like movies?"

"Love them. So that job was heaven for me." Her smiled dissolved as the bad memories crowded out the good ones. "In the note my brother left, he said he had his own plans for his life, and those plans didn't coincide with mine. It broke my heart. But that's the way it was. He was gone and I didn't know where to start looking for him."

She threw back her head to look up at the sky and laughed at herself as she touched the nape of her neck. "It still feels funny. I keep forgetting my hair isn't there."

"I'm beginning to like it."

"Liar."

"No, really." They shared grins, but then he prompted her to continue. She told him that her half brother had been gone for about a year, without a word from him, when her mother was diagnosed with cervical cancer. Elise assumed responsibility for her health care.

"Even though I was working and looking after her, I was also enrolled in art and film classes at the junior college. Things were tough, but going fairly well." Gazing out across the water, she sighed. "Then I finally heard from my brother. It wasn't good news. He was on his way to prison for drug dealing. Hard stuff."

Duncan tensed. "Savich?"

"Savich. He had taken my impressionable brother under his wing. He caught on fast and showed an aptitude for the trade. Savich paid him well. Well enough for him to buy a house, the one where we . . . where we met that night."

"Do they know that house exists? Savich? Your husband?"

"I don't know. I don't believe so."

He doubted it, too. Had Napoli known where she was that night, he wouldn't have had to ambush her in her car. He had tracked her only as far as her automobile. "Your brother was convicted of dealing," he said, prompting her again.

"Well, not exactly. That was the charge, but the case never went to trial. Savich advised him to plead guilty at his arraignment. His court-appointed lawyer disagreed, but Savich held sway. He said if my brother showed remorse, he would get a light sentence and possibly even probation without incarceration. So he pleaded guilty."

"And?"

She took a deep breath. "And he got sentenced to fifteen years at Jackson."

"Shit." The state prison in Jackson was a maximum security prison and housed death row. Only the most hardened criminals were sent there. "His priors must have been —"

"This was his first felony, Duncan."

"Then why such a stiff sentence?"

She looked at him levelly. "Because occasionally one of Savich's dealers has to be sacrificed. Otherwise, Judge Cato Laird's leniency would arouse suspicion."

"Cato Laird's leniency?" Duncan's eyes narrowed. "Wait, are you saying —"

"Savich and Cato are partners. They've been working together for years."

It hit him like a thunderbolt. "Laird goes light on Savich's mules."

"And gets well paid for it."

"Son of a bitch!"

"Savich has dozens of dealers. They can't escape arrest one hundred percent of the time. So when one of them gets arrested and winds up in Cato's court, he usually finagles a way to have the charges dropped. Or he favors the defense attorney during the trial. If he can't maneuver an acquittal, he gives the dealer a light sentence, sometimes probation. Soon, the dealer is back on the streets, making Savich money. Savich pays off Cato, and considers it a cost of doing business. Everybody's happy."

"Son of a *bitch*," he repeated, loud enough to draw frowns from two older ladies walking their dogs along the pier. "It's been there right in front of us all this time and we missed it!"

"Don't be too hard on yourself or the narcotics officers," Elise said. "There's never any direct contact between them. Cato never mentions Savich. Never. He did to me only once, and that was when he explained to me your outburst over Savich's mistrial."

"Which makes a hell of a lot of sense now. They were going through the motions, knowing the goddamn outcome the whole time."

"Probably," she agreed. "Make no mistake, it's a very slick operation. No one would suspect the setup because Cato is smart enough to sacrifice a scapegoat now and then."

"Like your half brother."

"Who realized he'd been sacrificed and decided to expose their game. But before he could, he was killed. It was only his second day in prison. He died in the shower —"

"With a bar of soap stuck in his throat. Your half brother was Chet Rollins."

She looked at him with surprise. "You knew him?"

"Oh yeah," he said tightly. "I never met him, but I know who he was."

"We had different fathers, different last names," she explained. "But in every other regard, he was my brother. Savich and Cato killed him."

Quietly he said, "And yet you're friends

with Savich and you're married to Cato."

"Not because I want to be!" she exclaimed. "They don't know of my connection to Chet."

He searched her eyes, her expression, but could find no deceit there. "Okay. Tell me the rest of it."

She took a moment to collect her thoughts. "Before being whisked off to prison, Chet wrote a letter and gave it to his attorney to mail to our mother."

"Your mother? Not you?"

"That was for my protection. He knew I would be the one who actually read the letter. But if anyone came looking to see whom he had contacted, they would find a terminally ill old woman who posed no threat."

"It was a tell-all letter."

"Yes. He explained how Cato and Savich were in cahoots and how they had set him up, and others before him. He asked for my help to expose them, but stressed absolute secrecy. He had talked to some people, hinted —"

"What people?"

"The Savannah PD narcotics officers who'd busted him. But he hadn't struck his deal yet. He hadn't been guaranteed any protection. He was scared because he knew of others who had tried to turn snitch and died for it."

"How well I know."

Pensively she stared at a sailboat as it glided past. "I was ready to drop everything and rush to Chet's rescue, talk to the police myself. But before I could even leave for Jackson, Mom was notified of his death. She was practically comatose by then. I doubt she ever understood that he was gone.

"Chet was buried without ceremony by the state. I hated that, but I knew that if I made myself known and claimed his body, I'd have no chance to avenge his murder. And I was determined to get vengeance on the two men who were responsible."

"Why didn't you take Chet's letter to the state attorney, the FBI, the officers he'd initially talked to?"

"They hadn't responded immediately. Obviously they were mistrustful of a con who'd pleaded guilty, then after being sentenced claimed that he'd been set up. Would a letter to his sister have been believed? Would *you* have believed it?

"And who was I to trust? Cato and Savich were miles from the prison shower room that day. They had facilitators within the system, but I didn't know who they were. If I raised a hue and cry but failed to bring them to justice, how long do you think I would have lived?"

He knew she was right on all points and told her so.

When she turned her head toward him he saw tears in her eyes. "Not that I was afraid of dying. I just didn't want to die *then*. Chet had loved me and had depended on me to look after him from the day he was born. I swore that if it was the last thing I did, I would make Cato and Savich account for his death."

She brushed the tears from her eyes, then shielded them by raising her hand against the sun. "It's getting hot."

"You need some different clothes." He stood up and extended his hand down to help her up. "Let's go shopping."

He knew if he drove around awhile, he would find a Wal-Mart sooner or later. He drove slowly through the shaded, picturesque streets of Beaufort, in no particular hurry.

"This is a lovely town," she said. "They make a lot of movies here." She expanded on that for five minutes, practically without taking a breath.

When she finally wound down, Duncan said, "You're pretty smart on the topic. How'd you learn all that stuff?"

She blushed at the compliment, but shrugged off her encyclopedic knowledge. "Movie trivia."

She returned to her story by telling him about her mother's death. "Her mind actually gave out before her body did. Anyway, as soon as I had settled all that, I quit my job, vacated my apartment, and moved to Savannah.

"I felt I would have a better chance of breaking into Savich's underworld than I would into Cato's social circle. Chet had mentioned in his letter that Savich hung out at a club called the White Tie and Tails. I got a job there."

Duncan had the air conditioner on, but she lowered the passenger window and let the warm wind blow on her face. "I never danced onstage. I didn't do lap dances. I never left with a customer. I served drinks. That's all."

"I didn't ask."

"But you wondered. Everyone does." After a reflective pause, she said, "Some of the clientele, you'd be surprised, were very nice. Sweet. Almost . . . I don't know, embarrassed or apologetic. Of course others were loud and drunken, obnoxious and vulgar. I hated them. But I stayed on and eventually came to Savich's attention." She looked across at Duncan. "Not in the way you're thinking."

"He liked you for your mind?" he said sarcastically.

She laughed softly. "Actually, yes. The club operates almost entirely on a cash basis. The manager was pocketing several hundred dollars a night, and it went unnoticed. I gave him the choice of turning the bookkeeping over to me, or my exposing his embezzlement to Savich, who's a silent partner. The club manager was stupid, but smart enough to know that he wouldn't live long if Savich learned of his stealing. The first option had much more appeal. So he went to Savich with a request for an assistant and told him I seemed to have a head for money management. Once in the position, I devised ways to cut expenses and increase profits."

Duncan stopped for a traffic light and noticed her staring wistfully at a group of children on a playground. She waited until the light changed before continuing. "Eventually I earned Savich's respect and trust. As much as Savich trusts anyone. I certainly didn't trust him, and I despised him for what he'd done to Chet. I could barely stand to be near him, but at least he doesn't disguise himself. With Savich you know what you're getting.

"By contrast, Cato sits in that courtroom every day and judges other people. He wears the robe. He bangs the gavel. He looks stern, and wise, and righteous, an advocate for the laws of the land, the commandments of God. His hypocrisy is sickening. To me, he's by far the guiltier of the two."

Duncan had found the Wal-Mart and had pulled into a parking space, but neither of them made a move to leave the car.

"Getting Savich will be easy for you now," she said.

"Somehow I doubt that."

"But this time you have an eyewitness," she argued. "I saw him commit cold-blooded murder."

"Napoli," he said. "Tell me again what happened on the bridge."

"I forgot where we left off."

"Pick up where you managed to get Napoli's pistol away from him."

"I yanked it out of his hand and threw it over the wall into the river."

"Huh."

"What?"

"Nothing," he said. "I was just wondering . . ."

"What?"

"Why you didn't just shoot him with it?"

25

She took offense, her eyes turning bright with anger. "I shot Trotter because he gave me no choice. He fired first. But I had Napoli's pistol. Do you think I would shoot an unarmed man? Even now, you believe me capable of that?"

He looked away from her. "Back to the bridge, you took off running."

"Answer my question, Duncan."

He responded just as testily. "I'll answer your question when I have answers to all of mine."

She stared at him for a long moment, but finally tamped down her anger and continued. "I ran for my life. Even wearing only one shoe, I managed to outrun him. When I glanced over my shoulder, he turned around and was running back toward the car. I suppose he gave up trying to catch me on foot and planned to chase me in the car. Just then I became aware of an approaching vehicle."

"From which direction?"

"From town. I was running in the opposite direction, toward Huchinson Island. I thought, thank God, help has arrived. I was about to turn back and flag down the driver. But when the car pulled even with mine, it screeched to a halt and Savich got out. I was stunned. He was the last person I expected to see there. I ducked into the shadow of the tower."

"Why? You and Savich are friends. Okay, acquaintances," he corrected when he saw she was about to object. "Why didn't you shout his name, run toward him with arms waving?"

She thought about it, then answered slowly, "I don't know. The . . . the purpose with which he was walking toward Napoli. His expression. His being there in the first place. I knew it couldn't be happenstance."

"How long did it take you to reason through all this?"

"Seconds. But I didn't reason it out. Instinct kept me from revealing myself."

He thought about that, then said, "Okay. He didn't see you?"

"No. I'm certain of that or I *would* be in the morgue. He stepped over the wall dividing the lanes and walked over to my car, where Napoli was sitting half in, half out the driver's seat. They exchanged a few words."

"What few words?"

"I couldn't hear what they said. But I heard the gunshot. Savich stood there looking at Napoli, I suppose to make certain that he was dead or soon would be. Then he leaned into the car.

"That's when I moved. I climbed down the ladder there beside the tower and crouched down on that thing underneath the bridge."

"Weren't you afraid? I've been on that ladder. It's scary as hell."

"I didn't stop to think about it. I was more afraid of Savich."

"Okay, so you're hiding under the bridge."

"Less than a minute after the gunshot, he closed the car door. Seconds later I heard another car door close. His. I thought I heard him drive away, but my heart was pounding so loud in my ears I wasn't sure.

"But I couldn't stay there forever, so I took a chance and climbed back up. There was no sign of Savich or his car. I ran to my car, looked in at Napoli, and knew he was dead. I didn't stop to think twice. I didn't even think to retrieve my purse. I ran." She stopped, took a breath, and looked at him. "You know the rest."

"How long did all this take?"

She frowned thoughtfully. "Hard to say. It seemed to take forever, an eternity, but I suppose it was only a few minutes, maybe three or four, from the time Napoli forced me out of the car until I ran off the bridge."

"And there were no other vehicles on the bridge?"

She shook her head.

"Why didn't you call the police?"

"We've been over that, Duncan. I had no proof. You hadn't believed anything else I'd told you."

"Then why did you come to me last night?"

"I hoped that you would be so glad to see me alive . . ." She let that thought trail off, then said, "But you didn't believe me last night, either. Not until you saw another woman's body that Cato claimed as mine."

He couldn't argue with that. He sat for a moment, thinking.

Savich had leaned into the car to place Napoli's feet inside. He had also retrieved Elise's wristwatch, which Napoli had been told to take from her for later identification. He had closed the car door, returned to his car, driven away. The whole thing could have taken ninety seconds or less. The puzzle was taking shape, but there were still pieces missing.

"You've explained how you won Savich's confidence. When and how did you place yourself in Cato's path?"

"You don't have to put it delicately, Duncan. I placed myself in his bed. When I failed to glean anything incriminating from Savich, I considered how best to get close to the judge. I'm sure you and Detective Bowen heard some juicy gossip about our courtship."

He didn't bother denying it.

"Probably most of it is true," she said. "I lured him. I had to marry Cato in order to get inside his house, inside his head. But, as I learned, he's scrupulously careful. He never leaves behind a trace of his connection to Savich. No notes, bank deposit slips, receipts of electronic transfers, nothing.

"Twice recently he's caught me meddling in his study. The night of the awards dinner. Then again the last night I was at home, shortly before you called and told him to bring me in for questioning the next day.

"All the time we've been married, I've pretended to be an insomniac so I would have a reason for going downstairs at night while he's sleeping. I've searched every room and closet of that house, thoroughly, numerous times, always being careful to cover my tracks."

"What were you looking for?"

"Any scrap of evidence. But months of marriage to him turned into years. I was beginning to despair that there wasn't any evidence to be found. I wanted so badly for it to be over, I guess I got careless in my haste. Cato was becoming suspicious. He tried to hide it, but for months, I'd had the feeling that he was on to me, that somehow he knew what I was doing.

"The thought of it terrified me. He and Savich would be ruthless against anyone who exposed them. I didn't want to die. More importantly, I didn't want to fail. But I sensed that I was running out of time. When Trotter appeared, I knew that Cato had struck preemptively."

"What did Trotter say to you?"

"You knew I lied about that, didn't you?"

"I knew."

"Trotter looked at me, startled, and said, 'They didn't tell me you were beautiful.' " She paused. The statement resonated in the close confines of the car. "When he said that, I knew he was no burglar. 'They' had sent him to kill me."

"Poor Gary Ray. You would've looked like

a vision to him. Blond and beautiful in your nightie. I'm sure he was asking himself why your husband wanted to kill *you*."

"Just as you did," she reminded him gently.

"Just as I did."

"You were right to doubt me, Duncan. On the surface my life looked perfect. I was living the Cinderella story. But inside that house, when I was alone with him, I could scarcely breathe. I had to endure his touch, and I hated it. Hated him."

Duncan couldn't endure the thought of Cato touching her either, so he redirected his thoughts. "Afraid of what you knew, or suspected, Cato hired Napoli to kill you. But Napoli subcontracted the job to Trotter, who bungled it."

"Cato expected me to die that night in the study, leaving him to continue his lucrative partnership with Savich, worry-free."

Duncan thoughtfully tugged on his lower lip. "One thing doesn't gel with me. Savich. What did he think when you married his partner in crime? Didn't he suspect something fishy?"

"He would have, but I made my own preemptive strike. When I started seeing Cato, I went to Savich and asked him, as a favor, to do a background check."

"What?" he asked on a laugh. "On Cato?"

She laughed, too. "I asked Savich to learn what he could about the judge's history. Were there ex-wives, children, legitimate or otherwise? Health records, financial statements, tax returns, things like that."

"Making it appear you knew nothing about the man."

"Exactly. By doing that, Savich didn't suspect that I knew about their arrangement. And to assure he wouldn't become suspicious, from time to time I'd ask him for a favor."

"Such as?"

"I would ask him to check out a woman that Cato had been particularly friendly toward. Was he seeing someone behind my back? I'd ask him to investigate a company that Cato was investing in. Was it reputable? Was the investment legal? Stuff like that."

She paused, then said, "I made my last request of him the morning after Trotter was shot. I went to his office and asked him to nose around, see if there was any talk in the criminal community of the judge having hired someone to kill me. I wanted to see what his reaction would be. He didn't blink."

Duncan was thinking that either she was very brave, or her relationship with Savich was friendlier than she wanted him to believe. He remarked on her courage.

"I wasn't brave, Duncan. I was desperate. I knew Savich would call Cato the moment I left his office. I hoped that by learning of my suspicion, Cato would be disinclined to try again soon to have me killed."

"You've seen Savich since that meeting, Elise," he said, carefully gauging her expression. "At the White Tie and Tails."

"That's right. The day we were all at the country club. You refused to believe me. I thought . . . I was afraid that you were betraying me to Cato."

"I didn't."

"I know that now. I didn't then. I went back to Savich to ask if he'd heard anything. Were my fears justified? He placated me, assured me that he'd heard nothing on the street except that my husband adored me and would rather die himself than to have one hair on my head harmed."

"Dismissing you."

"More or less, because he knew Napoli would take care of me soon." She asked, "How did you know about my meeting with Savich?"

He told her about Gordie Ballew. "I found out about his so-called jail suicide right after the judge produced the incriminating photos of you and Savich."

She shook her head with misapprehension. "You mentioned photos last night. What photos?"

He explained them, but she still appeared perplexed. "I suppose when Napoli was following me for Cato, trying to catch me with Coleman, he stumbled upon me with Savich."

"Bet he peed his pants. Pictures of you with Savich would be more valuable to your husband than any shots of you and the baseball player. Those photos of you and Savich were Napoli's trump card."

"By the time he played it, he was dead."

"True. They didn't serve him too well, but they served Cato's purpose. He used them to convince us, the police, that you were a lying, conniving female, possibly in bed with a noted criminal, killer of two men, and that when you realized the jig was up, you jumped off the bridge. He had us believing it."

"You included?"

"Me especially."

She gave him a long look, then said huskily, "Is that why you were crying last night? Because you thought I was dead?"

He didn't want to go there. Not right now. "Do you still have the letter your brother wrote you from prison?"

"In a safe deposit box in a bank in our hometown. I placed it there before I moved to Savannah. I'm the only signatory."

"Good to know." He reached across her, opened the glove box, and took out a pair of sunglasses. "One of the stems is bent, but put them on."

"Nobody's looking for Elise Laird anymore."

"I'm not taking any chances."

When they got inside the store, he gave her some cash. "I realize it's not as much as you're used to spending."

She frowned at him as she accepted the cash. "Thank you. I'll pay you back. What are you going to do while I'm shopping?"

"Sit over there in the snack bar, have a strawberry pop, and start planning how we're going to nail these bastards."

She got a cart and left him to do her shopping. He claimed one of the booths in the snack bar and sat there sipping a fizzy strawberry drink, while entertaining fantasies of Savich and Cato Laird being led away in chains on their way to the rack. Whatever the hell a rack was.

But he also took out his cell phone and called DeeDee.

"Hey!" DeeDee exclaimed, obviously glad

to hear from him. "I didn't expect you to call today."

"How're things?"

"My hair's frizzy. Worley's a cretin. You know, the usual."

"The other things."

"Did you happen to catch Judge Laird's press conference this morning?"

"Must've slept through it," he lied.

"The man's a wreck."

The son of a bitch had fooled even DeeDee, the most perceptive individual Duncan knew.

"We're tidying up all that. Dothan made a positive ID with Mrs. Laird's dental records, then performed the autopsy. She drowned. And get this, she did drugs."

"No way."

"Yep. If she was moonlighting for Savich, she also sampled the goods. Dothan found traces of several controlled substances, but they didn't kill her, so he's released the body for burial, no word on when or where yet."

"Anything new on Savich?"

"Nothing except those Kodak moments with the late Mrs. Laird."

"He got to Gordie."

"About that," she said, "you forgot to mention your tussle with him at the detention center."

"Slipped my mind."

"Like hell. The gossip reached the Barracks this morning. Depending on which source you believe, either you got rough with Savich and exchanged heated words —"

"Or what?"

"Or it was violent and both of you wound up in the ER."

"Does Gerard know?"

"He forgave you. Any one of us who had bumped into Savich so soon after hearing about Gordie would've reacted the same. The captain has had somebody questioning jailers about his suicide, but nobody knows nothin'."

"Not surprising." He took a sip of his drink, a calculated stall. When he felt that sufficient time had elapsed, he said, "I've been thinking, DeeDee."

"Wait, let me grab a pen and pad." She was back in a nanosecond. "Okay."

"I want you to find out if Meyer Napoli had any connection to Savich."

"You mean besides the photographs?"

"Yeah, I mean a personal connection. One-on-one. It's probably a long shot, but you never know."

"Napoli was hardly in Savich's league. He

said so himself — why would he need Napoli?"

"Just nose around, see if anything pops," he said. "Start with Napoli's secretary. She'll cooperate because she liked her boss and wants to know who killed him."

"You think Savich —"

"I said it was a long shot."

"Okay, I'll call the secretary. Exactly what am I looking for?"

"I have no idea. And something else . . ." He paused, as though thinking. "It could be beneficial to run some backgrounds on the people we know Savich has hit. Gordie Ballew's history we already know. But what about Freddy Morris and that Andre Bonnet whose house exploded? Maybe if we scratch around in their backgrounds, we'll find someone who knows something, overheard something about Savich that we could build evidence around. At least stack up enough to get a search warrant. What do you think?"

He'd known this would be a tough sell and could imagine his partner's untended eyebrows forming a frown above the bridge of her nose. "I guess," she said with an apparent lack of enthusiasm. "What do you expect to find?"

"I don't know. Won't until we find it." He

hesitated for a strategic time, then sighed. "Aw, hell, I guess I'm grabbing at straws. Skip it. I'll do some more brainstorming."

"Is it still raining where you are?"

"The sun's out."

"Here, too. Steam is rising off everything. It's too bloody hot to breathe." After a telling pause, she asked when he was coming back.

"Coupla more days."

"How do you feel?"

"Good, actually. Slept late. Went for a long run this morning. Really cleared out the cobwebs. That's when it occurred to me to check out these guys again. But if you don't think it'll do any good —"

"I didn't say that."

"As good as."

"No, I'm on it," she said grudgingly. "It's something, anyway, and we've got nothing else cooking."

He had counted on her being glad that he was refocused on Savich this soon. He felt guilty for manipulating her. But only slightly. "Good. Start with Freddy Morris and work backward. Parents, siblings, ex-wives, girlfriends, best friends. Somebody may be dying to unload on us about Savich."

"We talked to most of those people already, right after the hits."

"Wouldn't hurt to revisit them, widen the circle."

"Okay."

He pretended not to hear the reluctance in her voice. "And don't forget Chet Rollins. The guy that got hit in prison."

"The Irish Spring execution."

"Right."

"That wasn't our case," she said. "The investigation was handled in Jackson."

"So maybe the detectives there missed something."

"All right. I'll check." She hesitated, then asked, "Are you sure you're all right?"

"Couldn't be better."

"You sound funny."

"I was yawning." He spotted Elise rounding the end of an aisle and coming his way. Time to wrap this up. "In fact, I think I'll take a nap," he said to DeeDee. "Don't forget to call Napoli's secretary. Get back to me as soon as you learn something. Bye."

Before DeeDee could say anything more, he clicked off and switched his cell phone to courtesy mode. If DeeDee called back, and he wouldn't put it past her, his phone would vibrate instead of ring.

He slid out of the booth and went to meet Elise. He glanced at the items in her cart.

"Find everything you need?"

"Who did you call?"

"The office."

"Why?"

"Habit."

"Did you talk to Detective Bowen?"

"Got her voice mail. Left a message that I was relaxing, enjoying the time away."

"When are you going to tell her that I'm alive?"

"When I've figured it all out. What did you buy?"

Her eyes were still on the phone he had clipped to his belt, but then she smiled wryly and answered his question. "I won't be a fashion plate, but I'll be clothed and groomed. How was the strawberry pop?"

"Want one?"

"I don't want my lips and tongue dyed red."

He wiped his mouth. "Are they?"

"You look like Dracula." She laughed. "Maybe it'll wear off soon."

They paid for her purchases — Duncan doing his best not to analyze the panties and bras as they moved along the conveyor belt — and drove back toward Lady's Island. They stopped at a roadside stand to buy fresh shrimp for dinner. "I *can* boil water," he said as he passed the package to her through the passenger window.

After returning to the house, they went for a walk. Strolling the narrow lanes of the island, shimmering in the afternoon heat, he felt as though they should be holding hands. But he didn't reach for hers, and she didn't touch him.

When they returned to the house, she excused herself to take a shower. Duncan sat on the front steps in the shade, sweating profusely and telling himself he needed the solitude in order to plan his attack on Savich and Laird, when actually he was escaping the sound of the shower and mental images of Elise in nothing but suds.

Eventually she joined him on the steps, bringing with her a glass of iced tea for each of them and the scent of sweet-smelling soap. Her hair was still damp, sticking up in places. Blond strands were beginning to shine through the temporary brown tint. Catching him looking at it, she self-consciously raised her hand to it. "It'll grow back."

"Maybe you should leave it short. It's . . ." He was about to say sexy, and amended it to "fetching."

She was wearing some of her recent purchases, a pair of apple green shorts that came just above her knees, and a white

T-shirt, the vague outline of her new bra beneath it. Nothing fancy. Nothing in the least provocative. He wanted to rip everything off her. With his teeth.

Standing suddenly, he asked if she was finished in the bathroom and when she said yes, he went straight into the bathroom, stripped, and got in the shower, the shelf of which was now cluttered with shaving cream in a pastel can, a pink razor, shampoo and conditioner, and moisturizing body wash. Hanging from the shower nozzle was a round sponge thing made out of lavender netting.

"Damn bunch of crap," he muttered as he picked up the plain ole bar of soap.

But the damn bunch of crap aroused him. He didn't even turn on the hot water tap.

When he came out of the bathroom, she was sitting on the sofa watching television. "What's this?" he asked.

"A classic-movie station."

"It's in black and white."

"Doesn't matter."

"Who's that?"

She frowned at his ignorance. "Natalie Wood, of course."

"Huh." He sat down on the opposite end of the sofa. "What's it about?"

"She and Steve McQueen had a one-night

stand, which he barely remembered, but she got pregnant. She tracks him down and asks him to help her get an abortion — the movie was made when abortions were done illegally in back rooms.

"Steve McQueen has to come up with the money to pay for it, which isn't easy, but he finally does and makes the arrangements. Except when they get to the appointed place — this creepy, cold, empty building — they can't go through with it.

"She becomes hysterical and starts screaming. He — he'd been waiting out in the hall — barges through the door and yells at the abortionist, 'If you touch her, I'll kill you.' Then he holds her while she's crying. That's my favorite scene. That, and the one right after when they're riding in the back-seat of a taxi and he puts his arm around her, and she falls asleep on his chest."

Duncan stared. "Amazing."

"It's a good movie."

"No, I mean you. How did you remember all that? How many times have you seen it?"

"A dozen or more." Surprising him, she reached for the remote and switched off the TV.

"Don't you want to see the ending?"

"It's a fairy tale. It ends happily."

"Don't you believe in happy endings?"
Turning toward him she said, "Do *you?*"

26

"I used to," he said. "I'm not sure I do anymore."

Despondently she leaned her head against the sofa's back cushion. "I'm not sure I do anymore, either. I think I was terribly naive, perhaps foolish." She smiled but it was with self-deprecation. "Maybe I'd watched too many movies. My plan was to marry Cato, so I could find evidence against him, which I could hand over to the authorities. He would be convicted and sent to prison.

"I would have my vengeance for Chet, and Cato's criminal career would be over. He would no longer be duping the trusting public who vote him into office." She took a deep breath and let it out slowly. "Then I would be able to begin again. Clean slate. Make a fresh start on another life."

She gave a rueful laugh. "But I didn't plan on *this*. I didn't make a contingency for his catching on before I could expose his crimes." Looking over at Duncan, she said, "How is this going to end?"

"I don't know yet. We've got no evidence. Nothing except your say-so, and that's not good enough."

"I realize that. Besides, I'm officially dead."

"You will be for sure if either Savich or Laird learns you're alive. I can't hide and protect you forever."

"Chet's letter?"

He frowned. "Still iffy. Too much room for a good defense attorney to maneuver."

"So what are we going to do?"

"First I've got to know the court cases that Laird threw out for Savich. Case numbers, who the offender was, what he was charged with. That will take some research. Delicate research, because we can't tip our hand while we're doing it.

"We also need to locate more sacrificial lambs, like Chet. If we find some who've been languishing in prison long enough, growing more bitter by the day, they may be willing to deal with us for a reduced sentence, maybe even for time served. But we've tried that tack before."

"And they die."

"And they die." He stood up and began to pace. "You said there was no paperwork,

562

phone records, receipts, canceled checks, bank books."

She was shaking her head. "There's a safe in the study, but Cato never gave me the combination to it."

"We'll get into the safe if we ever get a search warrant. But we must show probable cause to obtain a warrant. What about his office at the courthouse?"

"He wouldn't dare keep a record of transactions like that in his office, would he?"

"Doubtful. And again, we'd need a search warrant." He socked his fist against his open palm. "How does Savich pay him?"

"I would guess Cato has a bank account somewhere out of the country. The Cayman Islands, maybe. We went there on a trip once."

"You're probably right, but digging into those records involves the Feds, all kinds of red tape and legal —" He stopped midsentence.

"What?"

"Legal procedures," he said absently. "I need to think about that some more."

"Okay, I'll make dinner. You think."

He tried, but it was hard for him to concentrate while she moved about the kitchen. He was seated at the table, a tablet in front of him, pen primed to take notes.

But he was easily distracted.

Elise reaching for something on the top shelf, lifting her T-shirt and exposing a band of skin.

Elise bending down to get a colander from a lower cabinet.

Elise's breasts at his eye level as she walked past.

His frustration increased in proportion to his distraction, and it made him angry. Eventually he gave up the pretense of working and set the table. She served dinner. She must have sensed the dark mood that had settled over him because she didn't initiate conversation. They ate in virtual silence.

Finally she said, "Good shrimp."

"Fresh off the boat."

"Would you like more French bread?"

"No, thanks."

"Salad?"

"I'm fine."

"Are you sure?"

He tossed an empty shrimp shell on the plate in the center of the table now heaped with them, and popped the meat into his mouth. "Yeah, why wouldn't I be?"

"I don't know. You're being awfully quiet."

"I'm thinking."

"Oh." She ripped a paper towel from the

roll he'd brought to the table and cleaned her hands. "I was thinking earlier today."

"About what?"

"I was thinking that if I'd gone to the police with Chet's letter as soon as I received it, you and I might have met then."

"But you didn't, did you?" He ripped off a paper towel and wiped his mouth. "Instead you got chummy with Savich and made your bed with Cato."

She looked as though he'd slapped her. But once she'd recovered from her initial hurt, she got angry. "That's right."

"Yeah, yeah, you did what you had to do. Used what you had. And we all know what *that* is. You used it first with Cato Laird, then with me. Probably Savich, too, even though you've denied it. That's a real lucky charm for you. It works every time, doesn't it?"

She scraped back her chair. "You can be a real bastard."

He stood up just as quickly. "But at least I'm not a —" He caught himself before he said it, but the unspoken word hung there, trapped in the tension between them.

"Don't back down now, Duncan. Say it. At least you're not a *whore.*"

She picked up her place setting and carried it to the counter, slinging disposables into the trash can, clattering the rest in the sink. He did likewise. They were careful not to touch or even to look at each other.

By the time they finished cleaning up, he was regretting what he'd said. He carefully folded the dish towel, then for ponderous seconds studied the faded stripes woven into the muslin, silently cursing himself for being a son of a bitch and a hypocrite.

Turning to her, he said, "I'm tired. I'm worried. The strain got to me. I didn't mean anything by what I said."

"Oh yes, you did."

"Elise."

She backed away from the hand he extended toward her. "I don't want to talk about it anymore. I'm sick of it. All of it."

Her expression was the cool, closed mask she'd showed him at the awards dinner. Without animation or excitement for a sentimental, romantic movie. Without hope for a happy ending.

Saying nothing more, she went into the bedroom and soundly closed the door behind her.

He awoke to the sound of birds chirping somewhere close. It was still early. The sun wasn't fully up. He rarely woke up in time to see a sunrise, but he'd gone to sleep unusually early. After trying to wrestle his way through his jumbled thoughts and conflicting emotions, he'd given up and allowed his eyes to close. That's the last thing he remembered. His sleep had been deep and dreamless.

He threw off the light quilt and stood up, stretching to work the cramps out of his muscles. He thought about going for a run while it was reasonably cool, but decided he wasn't awake enough yet. He would wait awhile and then go. After Elise was up.

The bedroom door was closed, as it had remained since she'd disappeared through it last night.

He pulled on his jeans. He used the bathroom and conscientiously put the seat down. He wondered what people did at this time of the morning if they hadn't been called into work or they weren't exercising. Reading the newspaper? Watching the morning talk shows? He didn't have a newspaper and he didn't want to disturb Elise by turning on the TV.

Coffee. He would make coffee and go light on the amount of grounds.

But in the midst of the process, his hands fell still. He stared out the window above the sink. The water was calm this morning, almost like glass, undisturbed save for the small wake of one lone fishing boat.

Why had he become so mad at her last night? If Elise had been successful at collecting evidence against Laird and Savich, would he have acted like a jerk and condemned her as he had? Or would he be lauding her courage, commending her for making such a tremendous sacrifice to her personal happiness?

Was he actually blaming her for failing at what he himself had been unable to accomplish? With all his training and advanced degree, with the support of the police department behind him, he hadn't brought these criminals to justice, either.

And he hadn't denied himself a personal life in order to do it. Elise had.

But he hadn't been so much angry as jealous. That's what it boiled down to. He'd become angry because he couldn't stand the thought of her with Cato Laird. With any man. Except himself.

He didn't think about it, he just left the paper filter and the empty carafe on the counter and walked to the bedroom door. Without hesitation, he opened it.

She was lying with her back to him. When the door hinge squeaked, she raised her head from the pillow, then rolled onto her back and looked toward the door. Seeing him, she came up on her elbows. "Is something wrong?"

"No."

She glanced toward the window. "What time is it?"

"The sun's not quite up."

"Oh."

And then there was silence except for their breathing while they stared at each other across the dim room. Duncan walked to the side of the bed. She smelled of warmth and sleep. She was wearing the new pajamas she'd bought yesterday. Under the thin cotton tank top her breasts lay soft.

His voice a harsh whisper, he said, "Did you fake it?"

For several moments, she looked at him with dazed puzzlement, then her eyes cleared with understanding. "Yes."

His heart plummeted.

"Every time while I was married." She gave a small shake of her head, adding huskily, "But not with you."

He dragged in a deep, restorative breath. Never breaking eye contact, he unbottoned his jeans and pulled them off, then stepped out of his boxers. He pulled back the light covers and got in beside her, stretching out above her, trapping her head between his hands.

He lowered his forehead to hers, resting it there, inhaling her scent. "You're married to him."

"Legally. But I'm not his *wife.*"

She angled her head and touched her mouth to his, tentatively. He made an inarticulate sound of surrender and sank into the kiss. His fingers burrowed in her cropped hair, but the passion was tender, not turbulent.

For a long time they kissed, sometimes deeply and wetly and sexily, sometimes just the mere brushing of their lips. Eventually he raised his head and gazed down into her face, now flushed with more than sleep.

"Let me . . ." She pushed him away so she could remove her tank top and matching shorts, then pulled him back down to her. Skin to skin, they sighed with pleasure as his mouth melded with hers once again.

His sex was hard, probing her middle, and by the time the lengthy kiss ended, they were restless, wanting more. He levered himself up so he could look at her. She was the stuff of dreams. He brushed his fingertips through her pubic hair, trailed them around her flat navel, up to circle her breasts before settling on one.

He gently reshaped it, then took her nipple into his mouth and made love to it.

She covered his hand with hers in a gesture of offering, while her other hand cupped the back of his head and held him close. He was guided by her sighs, told what she liked by her soft groans, and learned what she best responded to when her hips came off the bed and she gasped his name.

He kissed his way down her torso and nuzzled the delta between her thighs. Sliding his hands beneath her hips, he scooped her up toward his face and pressed it into the soft hair. He spoke her name, God's name, love words, swear words.

Finally, his lips damp with her, he raised himself above her, and kissed her mouth as he sent his penis deep into her. He thought he had remembered. He hadn't. It was better than memory. From tip to root, she gloved him. Snug and hot. Woman. Elise.

When he started to move, he pressed one of her thighs toward her chest to increase the friction and her pleasure. Her fingertips caressed the small of his back, lower over his butt cheeks, flirted with the crevice, driving him mad.

His strokes grew faster, deeper. He wanted to hold back, make it last. But his climax was racing toward him. He slid his hand between their bodies, applied his fingertip to her in tight, slippery circles.

Her body arched. She called his name and clutched him to her.

He emptied himself into her, thinking: How could anything that felt this right, this perfect, possibly be wrong?

They lay face-to-face, heads sharing the pillow. His penis was limp in her hand, but each time her thumb glanced the tip, it sent a frisson of sensation through his entire body.

"I couldn't fight it anymore," he said.

She gazed at him a bit sadly. "Will I be something you regret?"

He hugged her closer, whispering into her hair, "No. *No.* No matter what happens, I'll never regret this."

They kissed. When they pulled apart, he said wryly, "I had my nerve coming to you this morning after what I said to you last night. Why didn't you tell me to get the hell out and leave you alone?"

"Because you might have."

"You didn't want me to get the hell out and leave you alone?"

"Shamelessly, no."

They exchanged affectionate smiles. His hand was cupped between her thighs. He squeezed gently. "It's not only about this, Elise."

"No?"

He gave a negative motion of his head. "Maybe the first time I saw you, yeah. But even after discovering who you were, and thinking I'd probably never see you again after that awards dinner, you stayed in my mind. You haunted me. The night Trotter was shot, I realized why, and it was more than the obvious. You looked . . . solitary. Alone. Sad."

She touched his cheek.

"Here you were, a rich lady of leisure, with a handsome, influential husband who worshiped the ground you walked on. It didn't make sense to me why you would look so unhappy and . . . Jeez, I just realized the right word. Afraid. You looked afraid. And, even though I was investigating you for a possible crime, my first instinct was to help you."

"It certainly didn't seem you wanted to help when I came to your house that morning."

"I was scared."

"Of me?"

"Big-time scared. Because for all my honorable posturing, I also wanted you naked, like this. Don't smile. That's quite a conflict for a cop."

"I'm only smiling because I'm glad you

have me naked, like this. But I don't make light of the conflict. That conflict is a measure of the man you are. If you hadn't been conflicted about me, I wouldn't have fallen in love with you."

His head went back several inches. He looked at her with an unspoken question. She nodded. "I said as much that night in the old house. Weren't you listening?"

"I was listening. I thought you were speaking generally."

"No," she said. "You were as much a surprise to me as I was to you, Duncan. I thought the years with Cato had destroyed that part of me. I thought I would never feel attraction for another man. Then you spoke to me at the awards dinner, and you took my breath."

"I took your breath? Really?"

"Hmm. And you have every time I've seen you since. I was desperate for your help, Duncan. But I was equally desperate to be with you." She leaned forward and kissed his chest, took a love bite out of his pectoral, then did something incredible to his nipple with her tongue.

He grew hard in her hand, but he angled away from her. "We can't," he said unevenly. "We're oh for two on safe sex, and I don't have anything to use."

Like a cloud moving across the sun, sadness dimmed the lambency in her eyes. "It doesn't matter." She paused, drew a deep breath. "Cato made clear that he didn't want a child. He insisted I have a tubal ligation before we were married."

Duncan lay perfectly still, assimilating that.

"I agreed to it because I certainly didn't want his child. I didn't think beyond getting vengeance for Chet. I thought being childless was a small price to pay." A tear slid from the corner of her eye and rolled down her cheek. She touched his lips. "I may have been wrong."

He pulled her tight against him. As he cradled her close and pressed her face into his neck, he thought he might yet have to kill Cato Laird.

Recognizing the complicated classical piece he was playing on the piano, Elise smiled even before she opened her eyes. He didn't play "sometimes," as he had told her. If he played Mozart that expertly, he played often. What else about Duncan Hatcher didn't she know?

She knew he was an excellent lover. Her body ached, but deliciously so. They'd made love for hours, leaving each other only for calls of nature, and once for glasses of iced water, which they'd drunk only to revive themselves before indulging in more.

There were also long interludes of conversation, some of it the lighthearted banter of lovers. They exchanged information, the getting-acquainted kind of facts that new lovers find fascinating about each other.

However, a lot of their discussion was much more serious. She resented each time Cato's name was spoken, but she sensed Duncan's urgency to strike hard and soon. He laid plans. She listened, argued, wished aloud that they could simply go away together, leave Cato and Savich to the devil.

But he couldn't walk away from his responsibilities.

She couldn't abandon her vow to avenge Chet's death.

They knew this. They also knew they might not survive the inevitable showdown. This fear went unspoken, but it was there, as real and powerful as their desire. The uncertainty of their future increased the fervency of their lovemaking. They engaged hungrily, their passion tinged with desperation.

And there was something else. As serious to her as the fear of losing him was the fear that he still harbored doubts about her character. Once when she'd pulled back, he blinked her into focus, gasping, "Why'd you stop? I mean, if you want to stop, that's fine. But why did you start if you didn't —"

"I did."

"Okay." His question stood. She wouldn't meet his eyes until he laid his hand against her cheek and forced her to look at him.

"Because of what you said last night, Duncan. I don't want you to think that I was like this with him. It wasn't the same."

"Elise," he said on a soft groan. "You are here. With me. Now. That's what matters to me."

Freed to love him as she wished, she had. She turned warm now at the memory of how sensually she had prolonged his pleasure, how he'd moaned her name as his hands bracketed her head, how full and rigid he'd become before her tongue nudged him over the brink and he came.

Then he had gathered her against him, her back to his front. He kissed the nape of her neck. "Rest," he suggested in a drowsy voice. Reaching around her, he covered her breast. They lay quietly for a time, then he idly brushed her nipple with his fingertips.

"How am I supposed to rest with you doing that?"

"Sorry." But his hand wandered down

over her hip, along her thighs, between them.

When he pushed his fingers into her, she sighed his name.

"Shh," he said. "You can sleep if you try."

She tried. For about sixty seconds. Then she murmured, "Keep your thumb still."

"Okay."

But of course he didn't and soon she was clamping down on his hand in the throes of a dreamlike but all-consuming orgasm. It subsided and she relaxed against him, whispering, "Cheater."

His chuckle was the last thing she remembered before drifting off to sleep.

She wondered now how long she'd slept. Looking toward the window, she guessed by the position of the sun that it was midafternoon. As she got out of bed, he ended Mozart's Sonata in C Major and began playing another classical piece.

After the first few bars, she identified the tune and her heart constricted. Quickly, she pulled on her pajamas and went to the door. There she paused to watch him as his hands moved fluidly over the keys, never missing a note, playing with the same level of intensity with which he made love.

She went to him and combed her fingers through his hair. He turned his head and smiled up at her, but continued to play.

"Für Elise," she said.

"Für Elise." He built to the crescendo, his arms and shoulders as involved as his hands, then let the tempo and volume gently coast back down to the final poignant notes. He removed his hands from the keys and took his foot off the pedal. When the last reverberation died, he swung his right leg around to straddle the short bench and placed his hands on her hips, pulling her toward him.

"Beautiful, Duncan."

"No," he said, nuzzling the cleft between her breasts. "Beautiful Elise."

"You lying son of a bitch!"

They both started at the sudden and unexpected voice.

DeeDee Bowen was standing in the open front door, glaring at them. Furiously, she kicked the door closed; it slammed shut behind her. "You *do* play the piano."

27

"Apparently your talent extends to resurrecting the dead."

The piano had kept them from hearing the approaching car and DeeDee coming up the steps. Not that it mattered. This would have been an ugly scene in any case, but at least if Duncan had been alerted to her arrival, he would have had a few seconds to brace himself for the inevitable storm. He would have had time to put on his pants. As it was, he'd been caught in nothing but his drawers, and was damned lucky at that.

Elise slipped into the bedroom and closed the door. DeeDee stared after her, then her irate gaze swung back to him. "How long have you known she was alive? From the night she disappeared?"

"Night before last." Trying to defuse her, he calmly explained finding Elise in his bedroom after DeeDee had driven him home from Smitty's. "I was holding her at gunpoint, DeeDee, thinking everything you're thinking right now. Then Gerard called and told me that Judge Laird had positively identified her body at the morgue."

Elise returned, dressed. She passed him his jeans. He thanked her and pulled them on. "To have done that, Laird has to be dirty."

"He was overwrought, wrung out," DeeDee countered. "In his distress, he made a mistake."

"He didn't make a mistake."

"The dental records —"

"Matched the teeth of the corpse. The X-rays may have been labeled with Elise's name, but they weren't her X-rays."

DeeDee ruminated on that while eyeing Elise up and down. "You look awfully rosy-cheeked for someone who's supposed to be dead."

"I believe you wish I were."

DeeDee's own cheeks turned pink. "I just don't like being dicked around. And before Duncan went soft in the head — and hard in the crotch — over you, he didn't like being dicked around, either."

"That's enough, DeeDee," he said.

"Not by a long shot," she fired back. "I want to know what the hell is going on, or

I'm calling Gerard and telling him about your little scam, or whatever the hell this is."

"I'll explain everything if you'll calm down, sit down, and listen."

Looking mutinous, she clumped to the sofa and plopped down. He moved an armchair closer to her. Elise sat on the piano bench.

Duncan began by asking DeeDee how she'd found him. "If you found us, others might."

"I called your mother."

"My *mother?*"

"I told her you'd gone away for a few days of R-and-R after the Laird fiasco, which she'd read about. Not that she or anyone knows the full scope of the story," she added, shooting Elise a hostile glance. "I told her something important had come up and I needed to see you, told her I couldn't reach you by cell phone, and asked if she had any idea where you might have gone to relax.

"She gave me the phone number here, but I never could get an answer. I called her back — by now she's worried about you. She gave me directions and I volunteered to drive up here and check on you."

"You could have kept calling my cell."

"You ignored the calls."

"I would have called you back."

She glanced toward the bedroom then looked at him sourly. "When you got around to it."

He ignored that. *"Did* something important come up?"

She removed a folder from her oversized handbag and passed it to Duncan. "Your hunches of yesterday were correct."

Elise reacted with surprise. "Yesterday? What hunches?"

"Duncan asked me to check out some things."

Elise looked at him. "You did? You talked to her? You told me you'd left a voice mail message."

"A white lie," he admitted uneasily. Then to DeeDee, "Napoli's secretary?"

"Paid off like a slot machine. She distinctly remembered sending Savich an envelope by certified mail. She even gave me the receipt, signed by Savich's secretary. The guy with the perfect coif and false eyelashes? Anyway, Napoli gave his secretary the envelope sealed and ready to mail, but she believed it contained photographs."

"Let me guess," Duncan said, turning to Elise. "The photographs of you and Savich. The same ones he sent to Cato. Double-dipping as usual. Except it pissed off Savich enough to kill Napoli."

DeeDee jumped as though she'd got an electric shock. "Excuse me?"

Duncan turned to Elise. "Tell her."

Elise gave DeeDee a detailed but concise account of what had happened on the Talmadge Bridge, including seeing Savich shoot Napoli. When she was finished, DeeDee looked at Duncan. "You believe that?"

"I do now that I know Napoli was stupid enough to try and blackmail Savich."

Looking both affronted and puzzled, Elise said, "You didn't believe it until now? You didn't take my word for it?"

He had no time to address that before DeeDee said, "There's more. You suggested I run background checks on the men we know Savich has hit. Unnecessary busywork to keep me occupied, no doubt. But, as it turns out, not a waste of time." She paused, looking smug. "Guess who's related to Chet Rollins?"

"Elise is his half sister."

His knowing that took some of the starch out of DeeDee's posture, but it only increased the animosity with which she regarded Elise. "You heard him asking me to check out Rollins's background, so you covered your ass and told him before I could."

"Actually, Elise didn't overhear me asking you to do that."

"*Why* did you ask her to do that?" Elise asked, raising her voice. "Why, Duncan? Unless . . ." Her perplexity turned to anger. "You wanted to be sure I was telling you the truth," she accused. "That's it, isn't it? After everything, you still don't trust me."

"Go figure," DeeDee muttered sarcastically.

"Put yourself in my place, Elise," he said. "I had to be certain."

They shared a long look, which he was the first to break. He turned back to DeeDee. "What else did you find?"

She hitched her chin toward Elise. "She and Savich go way back. They were cozy friends long before she married the judge."

"We weren't cozy friends."

"I've seen the pictures," DeeDee said hotly. "The ones you killed Napoli over."

"Savich killed Napoli."

"How convenient to blame it on a reputed criminal," DeeDee said, coming to her feet. "I don't believe your bridge story any more than I believe you shot Gary Ray Trotter in self-defense."

"It's true, DeeDee."

She spun around to Duncan. "How can you —"

"Sit down."

"She —"

"Sit down!" He waited until she was once again seated and silent, although still fuming. "Trotter wasn't there that night to burglarize their house. He was there to kill Elise. He'd been hired to kill her. By her husband."

Her dismay apparent, DeeDee looked from Duncan to Elise, then back to Duncan.

Taking advantage of her momentary speechlessness, he said, "Remember the night in Smitty's, I told you Elise had come to me early in our investigation with a story I didn't believe?"

"That's the story?" DeeDee asked with a chortle of disbelief. "The judge hired Trotter to kill his beloved, beautiful trophy wife? How many blow jobs did she give you before you started believing that?"

He heard Elise's gasp of outrage, but he remained fixed on DeeDee. With more restraint than he knew he possessed, and than his partner deserved, he said, "Do you want to hear this or not? If so, apologize to Elise. If not, there's the door, and I'll find another partner."

"Partner? If you ally yourself with her, you'll be lucky to have a job."

He stood up. "You can let yourself out."

"Okay, okay," DeeDee said. "I want to hear the story." He looked at her hard, reminding her of the condition under which she would hear it. She sighed, looked at Elise, and grumbled an apology.

Duncan returned to his chair and began talking. It took a half hour for him and Elise to explain everything. DeeDee asked frequent questions, questions Duncan expected because he had asked them himself.

"Who was the dead woman in the morgue?"

"My guess would be Lucille Jones," he replied. "She was of similar height and weight. On paper, her and Elise's physical descriptions would be interchangeable. Savich needed to get rid of her. Laird needed a body so we would close the case. Savich told Laird about the distinguishing birthmark. All he had to do was pretend to recognize it, and nobody could dispute it."

Except you. That's what DeeDee's look said, but she didn't say it out loud.

"A few days after Elise's disappearance, when her body failed to surface, Judge Laird and Savich must have got nervous. Savich thinks, how lucky is this? I've got a woman whose disposal would serve two purposes. So he drowned Lucille Jones in the river, probably weighted her down so she wouldn't be found for several days, and when she was, she would be a mess and identifiable only by her birthmark and dental records."

"DNA."

"He could have kept strands of hair, which Cato Laird would provide to Dothan, saying they came from Elise's hairbrush. Elise had left the house that night without any jewelry, which was a break for them. Fewer details to worry about."

"What about her clothing?"

"Elise was wearing a tank top and skirt that the judge had brought home as a gift that night. They procured a matching set. Maybe even had Lucille Jones buy them herself."

"What if Napoli *had* pushed Mrs. Laird into the river, or what if she *had* jumped? Weren't they afraid two bodies would surface?"

"Laird would claim whichever was found first, so we would close the case on Elise. Then if the second body surfaced, it would in fact be that of prostitute and drug user Lucille Jones. Or Elise would have been an unidentified Jane Doe. In either case, nobody would be looking for Elise Laird, the judge's wife. She would be dead, positively identified by her husband and dental records, and probably cremated."

DeeDee gnawed the inside of her cheek, looking at them in turn as she tried to absorb the facts as well as the hypotheses. Homing in on Elise, she said, "You married him in the hope of gathering evidence you could take to the DA and blow the whistle on him and Savich. Is that the gist of it?"

"Yes."

"So where's this evidence?"

"If I had any, Cato would already be in prison. None of this would have happened."

DeeDee looked at her with incredulity. "Are you saying that after almost three years of living with the man, you haven't gathered one scrap of paper, recorded one conversation, nothing?"

"If I had something, I wouldn't have stayed with him."

"Yeah, it's such a rotten palace he's set you up in. I can see why you'd hate it there."

Elise came off the piano bench and bore down on her. "I *hate* Cato Laird. He had my brother killed with no more thought than he would swat a housefly. And I had to sleep with him. Pretend to make love to him. For years," she said, her voice quaking. "But I was willing to do it if, at the end of it, Cato would pay."

"Okay, okay, I get it," DeeDee said. "But one more question. Why did your husband bother with Napoli? If he was too fastidious to kill you himself, why didn't he just ask his pal Savich to do it?"

"I've given that some thought," Duncan said. "Savich would have been expedient and thorough. But while Elise's body was still warm, Meyer Napoli would have crawled out of the woodwork waving those photographs of Elise and Savich to every reporter on the East Coast.

"He would have spilled the beans about her relationship with Coleman Greer, about how Cato had hired him to follow her. Cato would have come under scrutiny and would have been made to answer for all that. And so would Savich. But by using Napoli, Cato set himself up to look like the injured party. He got rid of Elise as well as his black-mailer."

DeeDee came to her feet, massaging her forehead. "All right, I have the big picture, but where does it leave us?"

Duncan nodded toward Elise. "We have an eyewitness to Napoli's murder."

"Get real, Duncan. She won't make a credible witness."

"We've got the certified mail receipt for

the envelope Napoli mailed to Savich. That's a direct connection."

"Still doesn't place Savich on the bridge that night. We've got even less on Judge Laird. In fact, we've got no evidence that he's guilty of any wrongdoing except falsely identifying a body, which could be chalked up to confusion brought on by abject grief, and a mix-up at the dentist's office." Turning to Elise, she asked, "How long do you intend to play dead?"

"Until it's advantageous for me to reappear."

"In the meantime," DeeDee said to Duncan, "are you going to stay here and play house with her?"

Her tone of voice grated on him, but for the sake of time and energy he decided to let it pass. "Elise and I have come up with a dozen plans and rejected them all."

"You've been talking police strategy with *her?*"

Ignoring the slight, Elise said, "It's occurred to me that maybe I never found any evidence on Cato because it simply isn't there."

"You think Savich keeps their books?" Duncan asked. She raised her shoulder in a shrug. He felt a familiar tingle in his gut that said she might be on to something. Tugging on his lip, he began to pace. "If we get Savich, Laird will topple as a matter of course."

"How do you figure?" DeeDee asked.

"Yes, Duncan, how do you figure?" Elise said. "Cato isn't going to 'topple' easily. He isn't going to slip up and make a mistake. He hasn't in all the time I've been married to him, and he's not going to now."

"Somehow we'll get him."

"Somehow, but *how?* You didn't get him for having Chet killed. He got away with it. And if I had died, either in the home study or on the bridge, he would have got away with killing me, too." She divided a vexed look between him and DeeDee. "Wouldn't he?"

Neither of them denied that she was more than likely right. "He would have," she said adamantly. "You know it, and so do I."

"I'll figure out something," he said.

"But what?"

"I don't know yet."

"When?"

"As soon as I can."

"Meanwhile, I've got to stay dead?"

"I don't know, Elise. I'm working it out."

"He must be brought to justice, Duncan."

"I agree." He sliced the air with his hand as though to cut off her next argument.

Lowering his volume, he said, "But of the two fish, Savich is bigger. If we can get the judge to help us nail Savich —"

"How are you going to do that?" Suddenly her expression radically changed. Backing away from him, she said, "Please don't tell me you're going to offer Cato clemency in exchange for giving up Savich."

He averted his gaze from her. "I don't think I'll have to go that far."

"He'll never confess."

"I'll twist his arm." He gave a weak grin, but Elise wasn't amused. "Look," he said with diminishing patience, "I'd like to beat a confession out of the son of a bitch. I've got more than one reason to lay into him, but —"

"I hope you don't mean that literally," DeeDee said.

Whipping around to her, he snapped, "You don't have to come along."

"What? This has become personal? It's no longer about enforcing the law, it's about *her*?"

That was the second time she had used the pronoun in reference to Elise, making it sound like a slur both times. "I'm a cop," he said tightly. "Cato Laird conspired to have a man choked to death on a bar of soap. If he goes to jail, I've done my job, and I can sleep nights."

"In her bed."

The silence that ensued teemed with anger. No one spoke for several moments, then Elise said, "I don't think you'll have to get physical with Cato. When he sees me alive he'll —"

"You're staying here."

She turned to Duncan. "Like hell I am."

"You're staying here, Elise. Out of sight, safe, until Cato Laird and Savich are both locked up."

"But —"

"No buts," he said stubbornly. "I can't deal with this and protect you at the same time."

"I must be there when Cato realizes he's been caught," she exclaimed. "I want to see his expression. I've waited years to get vengeance for my brother's murder. I won't be denied that."

He shook his head stubbornly. "You'll have your day in court. I promise. But you've got to stay in the background for now and let us take it from here." She was on the verge of arguing further when he added, "If something happens to you, we're up shit creek again, and we never get the bastards. You're crucial to our case against Savich. Equally crucial to the case against

Laird for Chet's murder and everything else. You stay out of sight until the time is right to spring the trap on them. I'm sorry, Elise, but that's just how it's gotta be."

DeeDee had been listening in silence and with evident satisfaction to his exchange with Elise. She finally spoke. "I hate being the one to remind you that so far you've got no trap to spring."

He outlined his plan to DeeDee. She responded with a decided lack of enthusiasm. "I don't know, Duncan. It doesn't feel good to me."

"The gloves have to come off, DeeDee. It occurred to me yesterday that we're never going to nail these guys using strictly legal methods. We can't play by the book and expect to convict them. They know all the loopholes in the legal system. They know how to beat it. The only way we're going to get them is by bending a few rules."

"Which rules?" she asked worriedly.

"I'm just saying . . ." He let the sentence trail off and got no more specific than that. "You're gonna have to grant me some leeway. Are you in or out?"

"I'm in," she said, but with uncertainty. Then, "Of course I'm in."

He looked at Elise and gave her a tender

smile. "You must agree that this is the best way."

He didn't put it in the form of a question, effectively giving her no choice other than to agree. After a long hesitation, she nodded.

Duncan decided to leave his car with Elise. "Use it only if you must," he instructed as he handed her the keys. "Stay in the house as much as possible. When you have to go out, keep a low profile. You cannot be seen until this is over." With affection, he ran his hand over her spiked hair. "Can't have any Elise Laird sightings reported, okay?"

"Okay."

He reinstalled the house phone and told her that if he called, he would let the phone ring twice, hang up, then call right back. "Otherwise, don't answer. Use it only on an emergency basis. I can't stress that enough." He also gave her the extra pistol he'd hidden above the knickknack cabinet.

"It's easy to use." After acquainting her with the pistol, he put it and extra ammunition in an accessible place.

When the time finally came for him and DeeDee to leave, Elise's distress was plain. "I'm afraid."

"You'll be fine."

"I'm not afraid for myself. I'm afraid for *you.*"

"I'll be careful." He rubbed her arms reassuringly. "DeeDee will be at my back."

Close to tears, she whispered, "Please be careful."

"I promise I will. You, too. Don't take any chances. None. Understand, Elise?"

"I understand."

They clung to each other as they shared a lengthy good-bye kiss. When he finally pulled back, he gave her a look rife with meaning. "Remember everything we said this morning."

"Every word."

He touched her lower lip. "I'll see you soon." Then he turned away quickly and ushered DeeDee out the door.

They discussed the plan on the drive back to Savannah. As they crossed the Talmadge Bridge and turned into the downtown area, DeeDee tried one last time to dissuade him against implementing his plan of attack before clearing it with Captain Gerard.

"It's dangerous and crazy to try and go this alone, Duncan."

"I'm not alone. I've got you."

"We could bring in Worley, a couple of others who —"

"No. Me, Laird expects the worst from. Better if it looks like I've reached my limit, flipped out, become a loose cannon."

She covered several city blocks before she said, "Are you absolutely, one hundred percent positive that Elise Laird didn't cook up this elaborate story and screwed you until you believed it?"

He shot her a hard look. "To what end? You yourself said she's got a cushy nest. Why would she want to destroy it, unless what she says is true?"

"I'm only saying it's a little strange that in all the time she's been married to Cato Laird, she hasn't collected one shred of evidence that he's anything other than a devoted husband, upstanding citizen, and honest judge."

"We'll get the evidence. Eventually."

"If you say so."

"Once we have Savich, it'll be easy."

"Mrs. Laird —"

"Don't call her that."

"She didn't agree with your priorities."

"In the end she did. Stop at my house."

"What for?"

"I need to change clothes. I don't want to meet the judge in T-shirt and jeans."

"We're not 'meeting' him, Duncan. We're abducting him."

28

Cato Laird felt so good it was difficult to keep his posture stooped and his expression aggrieved.

"Work is my tonic," he'd said to those who expressed shock and concern when he returned to his office so soon after the tragedy that had befallen him.

He explained that aside from the healing he would derive from plunging back into work as soon as possible, he had a responsibility to the community. The criminal justice system was backlogged enough. He wouldn't allow his personal tragedy to create a heavier workload for his colleagues.

Yada, yada. People ate it up.

Leaving the Chatham County Judicial Center, he waved good-bye to the security officers and, for their benefit, made it appear as though he had barely the strength to push open the heavy glass door.

But his footsteps were light as he made

his way across the parking lot. The sun was low. He noticed what a tall, trim, and impressive shadow he cast on the pavement. Then another shadow joined his, equally tall, trim, and impressive. Simultaneously he was addressed from behind by a friendly voice.

"Hello, Judge."

He turned just as Duncan Hatcher closed a strong hand around his biceps. The detective was smiling, but it was a cartoon character's smile — that of the wolf up to no good. "How's it hanging, Your Honor?"

"As well as can be expected, thank you."

"When's the funeral?"

"Under the circumstances, I've decided to forgo the customary service. I'm keeping the observance private."

"Are you having the body cremated?"

"Your concern is touching, Detective. But, as I said, I'm keeping these matters private."

Hatcher's lupine leer vanished. "Get in the car."

During their exchange, Hatcher had practically been dragging him toward his Lexus sedan, where Detective Bowen stood waiting, door open, motor running. "Good evening, Judge."

"You broke into my car?"

"Part of the extended service now provided by the police department," she said. "Driving home VIPs after a hard day at the office."

"A judge who's tough on cops and soft on criminals gets special treatment," Hatcher said.

Cato tried to wrest his arm out of the detective's grip, knowing before he even tried that it would be futile. He looked around for help, but the parking lot was deserted. "Let go of me."

"As soon as you get in the car."

"I'll have your job for this, Hatcher."

"Possibly. Probably. But not before I sing loud and clear for all to hear the sad ballad of the late Mrs. Laird's alliance with professional criminal Robert Savich."

So far, that had been kept out of the media. The judge wanted to keep it that way. He stopped struggling.

"Ah!" Hatcher said. "I see you know that tune." He tightened his grip. "Now get in the car, or I'm going to break your arm, and actually nothing would give me more enjoyment."

Hatcher's eyes said he wasn't bluffing. Obviously DeeDee Bowen thought the same. She was looking at her partner with consternation, and maybe a little fear.

"You'll go to jail for this." Despite the

threat, Cato got into the backseat of his sedan. Hatcher scrambled in behind him. Detective Bowen got into the driver's seat, conscientiously buckled her seat belt, then drove them out of the parking lot.

Cato didn't know whether to be relieved or concerned by the direction she took. He would have expected them to go toward either his home or the police station. Rather, they were going toward the river.

Within blocks of the courthouse, the trendy eateries and shops of the Market Square area gave way to run-down project housing, warehouses, and failed industries, most of them vacated and derelict. Boulevards narrowed into rutted streets lined on both sides with chain link fences topped by concertina wire. The car jounced over railroad tracks.

On their left the Talmadge Bridge loomed large. Beyond it was the Georgia Port Authority's sprawling complex. Cato knew there were armed guards at those gates, but little good they could do him at this distance.

No one spoke until Hatcher said, "Here."

Detective Bowen pulled the car to the side of the street and stopped, but left the engine idling.

The judge looked at their surroundings,

then turned toward Hatcher beside him. "Very effective."

"You think so?"

"Deserted. Laden with menace and implied threat."

He wasn't so much afraid as irritated. For all his bullying, Hatcher wasn't going to harm him. But how dare he think he could get away with subjecting Judge Cato Laird to such roughhousing. The detective wasn't only brash, he was also a fool.

In any case, it was time to turn the tables. He gave Hatcher a knowing smile. "Tell me. Assuage my curiosity. Did you fuck my wife? Or did you just want to?"

It was amusing to watch the detective's features tighten and nearly solidify. Cato laughed softly. "Don't castigate yourself too harshly, Detective Hatcher. Elise had that effect on most every man she met. Even a decorated officer of the law like yourself wasn't immune to her charms. You're not at all unique. And you're not nearly as tough as you pretend to be."

He didn't see it coming. Hatcher moved with such speed that he didn't realize what had happened until the blinding pain shot up from his groin and he heard himself scream.

"Is that tough enough for you?" Hatcher

asked as he cruelly twisted the fist that was tightly squeezing the judge's testicles.

In spite of himself, the agony brought tears to his eyes and he actually whimpered.

"Let me tell you what makes me both tough *and* unique, Judge," Hatcher whispered, so close the judge could feel his hot, angry breath on his face. "I'm the guy that's gonna rip off your balls right now if you don't cooperate with us."

From a distance, drifting toward him through a red fog of agony, he heard Detective Bowen say, "Duncan, don't —"

"Shut up, DeeDee!" he barked. "I told you I was going to do this my way."

"But you can't —"

"I can. I *am.*" His grip tightened, gave another twist.

"What do you want?" Cato didn't recognize the thin voice as his own.

Gradually Hatcher's fist relaxed and then he let go. "Now that I have your undivided attention, you'll do well to listen."

Cato, trying to catch his breath and will away the pain, glanced toward the front seat. Detective Bowen was watching them with obvious anxiety. She didn't agree with her partner's tactics, but she wasn't going to cross him by interfering.

"We think you're dirty, Judge."

"What?" He looked back at Hatcher, too quickly, he guessed by the smile that appeared on the detective's face.

"We know you're a crook, we just don't yet know the extent of your criminal activity. And you know what? I don't even care."

Cato's breathing had almost returned to normal, but, all the same, he thought it best to keep quiet.

"I've got nothing on you," Hatcher said. "But I've finally got something on Savich, and it's him I really want."

The judge looked from him to DeeDee, then back to Hatcher. "We all want Savich."

"I'm glad to hear you say that. Because tomorrow he'll be arraigned for doing Napoli."

"Meyer Napoli?" Even if the judge said so himself, his exclamation of surprise sounded genuine.

"Oh, right. I forgot to mention that," Hatcher said. "We've had an eyewitness come forward who saw Savich pop Napoli on the Talmadge Bridge."

"You're serious?" He addressed the question to Hatcher, then looked at his partner for confirmation.

She said, "Very serious, Judge. The witness also saw Napoli push Mrs. Laird over the wall into the river."

"So Elise didn't . . . didn't jump? She didn't end her own life?"

"It appears not," DeeDee replied.

He ducked his head and dropped his voice to an emotional huskiness that also sounded authentic. "That's good . . . good to know."

"Savich came along just after Napoli did his dirty work for him," DeeDee continued. "Apparently Napoli was blackmailing Savich with those photos of him and Mrs. Laird, same as he was blackmailing her and planned to blackmail you. Savich killed him."

"And when the son of a bitch is brought into your courtroom tomorrow for his bond hearing," Hatcher said, "you'd damn well better be in a hanging mood. That hearing should set the tone for his murder trial. Or we're going to start looking for a reason why not."

"I don't understand why you felt it necessary to stage this . . ." He motioned out the window at the daunting surroundings. "Whatever this is."

"Because I wanted to make it clear to you that I'm tired of being jerked around by the justice system — i.e., by you," Hatcher said. "The last time we had Savich in your court, you let him walk."

"I was compelled by —"

"Save it, Your Honor. But remember the conviction in your voice just now. That's good. Very . . . judicial-sounding. Tomorrow, you deny Savich bond. He goes to jail and he stays in jail until his trial. You arrange it to preside over his trial, and you don't give him or his lawyer Stan Adams a single break. Not on jury selection, not on any motions they may file, not on bathroom breaks. Nothing goes their way. Do we understand each other?"

"You've got no problem," Cato returned smoothly.

"Actually we do," DeeDee said, shooting a worried glance toward Hatcher. "Our eyewitness isn't the most credible —"

"Credible enough." Hatcher's terseness effectively silenced her. "We have an eyewitness. We can nail Savich if *for once* you favor us instead of that murdering bastard. I don't want a mistrial, not even if the jurors are reading the newspaper and watching a live broadcast of the trial on their cell phones while sitting in the jury box.

"I'm not going to be satisfied with anything other than a conviction and a sentence that will put him away for the rest of his life. I'll leave whether or not he gets the death penalty to the jurors."

The judge divided a look between them,

ending on Hatcher. Although he despised the man, he felt like kissing him. The blustering idiot didn't realize he was solving Cato's problem: how to end his partnership with Savich without fearing retribution.

He'd recently come to the conclusion that their arrangement had run its course. He'd made a fortune off it, more money than he could ever spend, although he would have a happy retirement trying.

Not that money was the reason he'd entered into the agreement. The initial allure had been the thrill of the secrecy, the danger of getting caught. He'd loved having an ongoing flirtation with disaster.

But it had become almost too easy. The excitement had waned. Their partnership was a vulnerability no longer worth the risks. But to end it would have placed his life in peril. Savich ended partnerships, his partners didn't.

Savich would be imprisoned for life, if not executed. If he called foul and began telling tales about crooked judges, who would listen? All men on death row had a gripe and a grudge, and nobody paid any attention to them, especially when the gripes were aimed at the judges who'd sentenced them.

It was all he could do to keep his expression appropriately somber when he made his pledge. "Savich will get what's coming to him. I'll see to it."

Hatcher stared directly into his eyes as though testing his trustworthiness. Finally, apparently satisfied, he glanced at Detective Bowen and nodded. Without a word, she made a three-point turn and drove back toward the courthouse.

Despite his throbbing testicles, Cato could barely keep himself from humming.

The anteroom was empty, Kenny nowhere in sight.

The door to Savich's private office was ajar. The room was dark except for a small lamp that cast a disk of light onto his desk. His sleek head was bent over paperwork. The part in his hair was so precise it looked like an incision cut by a scalpel.

Sensing he was no longer alone, he reached beneath his desk, where a pistol was secreted, then raised his head and looked at his unexpected guest.

His brilliant eyes widened marginally, but the surprise was quickly shuttered behind the impenetrable blue gaze that was the last thing many had seen in this life.

He said, "I heard the elevator and thought you were Kenny."

"I look nothing like Kenny."

He smiled, his teeth glaringly white in his dusky face. "Your sense of humor is intact. A good commentary on the afterlife."

Elise pushed open the door and walked into his office. "I'm all too alive."

"So I see. And looking reasonably well. Although I can't say I approve of the new hairdo, and the outfit leaves much to be desired."

"You don't seem all that shocked to see me," she said.

"I deal in absolutes, Elise. The accounts of your death were sketchy, speculative, and inconclusive. Did Napoli push you from the bridge? Did you jump after killing him? All very muddled." He raised his hands. "Who knew what to believe?"

They looked at each other for several moments. Finally she said, "You haven't offered me a seat."

"Forgive me." He motioned her into the chair facing his desk. "I guess I am a trifle shocked. Would you like something to drink?"

"No, thank you."

Both were wary, curious, edgy in the presence of the other because neither could predict the outcome of this meeting. She alone knew the purpose of it.

"Is your husband still in the dark?" he asked.

"You mean, does Cato know that I'm alive? No."

"I see."

"You don't see at all."

He flashed a smile. "Too true. I suppose you have a good reason for remaining dead. I'm bursting with anticipation to know what that reason is. Where have you been?"

"For the last three days, with Duncan Hatcher."

He was taken aback, then gave a burst of laughter. "Delicious. Positively delicious. The last time I saw him, he was at wits' end. I teased him about his crush on you. I thought it was unrequited." He arched his eyebrow eloquently. "I guess not."

Laughing again, he said, "I can understand why he would want in your pants. But for the life of me, I can't imagine what you find attractive about him. Granted, he has a certain animal magnetism. Those shoulders. The square jaw. But he's so tiresomely good, Elise," he said with a shade of pity.

Then his smile turned reptilian. "Or rather he was. Until he met you. No wonder he began behaving irrationally. He'd been waging war on his lust, and it seems lust won out over duty." He licked his lips as though savoring the taste of Duncan's fall from grace. "How does it feel, Elise, to have a man give up his soul for you?"

"Duncan didn't give up anything for me."

"A pint or two of his self-righteousness, surely."

"Temporarily, maybe." She lowered her gaze to her hands, which were clasped in her lap. "He wants you more than he wants me."

Savich leaned forward, resting his forearms on the edge of his desk. "I'm not following."

She raised her head and looked at him. "You are what he desires, Savich. No one holds a place in his heart like you do. There's no room in it for anything or anyone else. He has devoted himself to destroying you . . . one way or the other."

He studied her for a moment, then stood up and came around the desk. "Yes. One way or the other. Stand up, Elise."

She did so with hesitation and, guessing the reason for the request, held her arms straight out to her sides. "You think Duncan sent me here? He'd kill me if he knew I was here."

"Forgive me my suspicious nature." He patted her down, then raised her top to check her brassiere for hidden microphones.

She stared at him coldly as he pressed his hands against her.

He flashed a grin, then lowered her top and returned to his chair behind his desk. "It's no news flash to me that Duncan Hatcher has wet dreams about my capture."

"But now he has a way to make it happen."

"Oh?"

"I survived Napoli and made it off the bridge that night . . ."

Since that much was obvious, he waited expectantly for the rest of it.

"But not before I saw you shoot him point-blank."

"Ahh." He leaned back in his chair, appearing not at all upset by the bold revelation.

"Based on my eyewitness, Duncan is on his way here to arrest you."

"Is he?"

"He's meeting with Cato now, threatening reprisals if Cato goes easy on you and lets you leave his courtroom a free man. Then he's coming after you."

Savich kept his gaze trained on her as he ruminated on what she'd told him. "By warning me, you're betraying Duncan Hatcher."

"That's right."

"Lovers' quarrel?"

"Duncan and I have different goals. He wants you."

"And what do you want, sweet Elise?"

"I'm here to offer you a deal."

"This conversation becomes more bizarre by the moment. I'm intrigued. What sort of deal?"

"If I testify to what I witnessed, you'll be convicted of murder."

"Or?"

"Or I'll recant the story I told Duncan. I'll claim that I shot Napoli in self-defense, as I did Trotter."

"Hatcher didn't believe the self-defense scenario then. He would find it even harder to believe you now."

"I'll say that's why I made up this story about you, because I knew he wouldn't believe me. In any case, without my eyewitness account, Duncan has nothing on you. No hard evidence with which to charge you. Without me, he can't get you."

He sat perfectly still, his eyes unblinking as he stared at her. Long moments passed. Finally he said, "This is an incredibly generous offer, Elise. By recanting, you not only make an enemy out of your new beau, you also risk incriminating yourself."

"I'll accept the risk, if you'll accept my offer."

He eyed her shrewdly, knowing that such an offer wouldn't come free, or even cheaply. "What do you want in return? It must be something awfully important to you. Something you want very badly."

"Yes. And it's yours to give."

"Ask."

She leveled a look on him. "Give me Cato."

As DeeDee relinquished the key to the Lexus to the judge, she avoided making eye contact, as though that would somehow distance her from what had taken place. On principle, she agreed with Duncan. But his rough handling of the judge was unacceptable. He had crossed a line. And Elise Laird was the reason.

They watched the judge drive away, then returned to her car. "That went exactly as planned," Duncan remarked cheerfully as he got into the passenger seat.

"Have you lost all sense of what we're about, Duncan?"

"We're about getting Savich and then this asshole judge."

"Getting them by any means, fair or foul?"

"We've tried fair. It didn't work."

"He could have you arrested for assault."

"He could. He won't. He'll cover his ass and protect his reputation." He checked his wristwatch. "We're even ahead of schedule. We'll easily make it to his office before he leaves. Let's go."

"Now?"

"Sure, now. What'd you think?"

"I thought you would follow procedure," she exclaimed. "Get an arrest warrant. Consult our superior officer. Remember Captain Gerard? Worley? We're not vigilantes. We're police officers. We need backup and —"

"No," he said, cutting her off emphatically.

They glared at each other across the car's console. She was the first to relent and try another tactic. "You've lost your perspective, Duncan. Please stop and think about what you're doing."

"I have thought about it. I've thought about it until I'm sick of thinking about it. It's time to act."

"I agree, but we need to act responsibly and legally."

"Fine," he said curtly, "if you're too squeamish for this, I'll do it alone. If the shit comes down —"

"When the shit comes down."

"Okay, *when* the shit comes down, you don't want to be standing under it. I asked for this. You didn't. Being a loyal partner only extends so far. I'm officially relieving you of any obligation to me. Leave and go with a clear conscience. But I'm going to do this, and I'm going to do it my way."

He turned and reached for the door handle; she grabbed his sleeve. "Damn you, Duncan! You know I can't let you barge in on Savich alone."

He flashed her a brief smile. "Okay, then. Let's go."

They drove in silence. When they were a block from Savich's machine shop, Duncan unzipped a gym bag at his feet, took out a .357 revolver, and tucked it into the waistband of his trousers.

DeeDee looked at him with surprise. "Where'd you get that?"

"My house when I stopped to change clothes."

"Where's your nine-millimeter?"

"This fits my purpose better."

"How so?"

He never answered. Instead he made a strangled sound of utter disbelief.

DeeDee followed his gaze.

His car, which he'd left with Elise Laird on Lady's Island, was parked outside Savich's building.

29

Elise?" Duncan said, his voice a croak.

He turned toward DeeDee as though seeking an explanation. She knew her expression must have read *I told you so,* but she refrained from saying it.

The building was dark. There were no employee cars in the parking lot. But a light was on in Savich's second-story office window. Looking up at it, Duncan angrily muttered, "Son of a bitch." Before DeeDee came to a full stop, he opened his car door and jumped out.

She clambered from the driver's seat and trotted after him. "Duncan, wait!"

He kept walking. "This doesn't change anything."

"It changes everything." She lunged for him, but he flung off her hand. "Please let's regroup and talk about it."

"I'm over talking."

Hearing another car pulling into the parking lot, they stopped, turned, and recognized Savich's secretary behind the steering wheel.

Duncan started jogging toward the building's entrance, calling to DeeDee over his shoulder, "Get him before he can alert Savich."

"Duncan!"

He didn't even slow down.

"Shit!" DeeDee wavered for several seconds, then sprinted toward the car, where Kenny was nervously juggling his cell phone.

"Cato?" Savich repeated.

Elise nodded.

His eyes glittered with amusement. "You want your husband removed so you'll be free to live happ'ly ever after with your hunky detective?"

"Don't concern yourself with my reasons. It's your situation you should be concerned about," she said. "Cato won't help you in court as he did the last time. To protect himself, he'll let them throw the book at you. Duncan is seeing to that. Tomorrow you'll be arraigned for Napoli's murder. Following that formality, you'll be taken immediately to superior court for your bond hearing. Cato will deny the request. You'll go straight to jail, and you won't live another free day. Not for your entire life."

"Unless you recant your eyewitness testimony."

"That's right. You see to Cato's destruction. In return, I didn't see you kill Napoli."

"Define 'destruction.' "

"I want him out of commission. I want the life he knows and enjoys to be over. I'm indifferent as to how you bring that about," she added coldly. "Now, do we have a deal?"

Savich's smile remained in place, even as he raised the pistol he'd been holding in his lap and aimed it across the desk at her.

Her heart jumped to her throat. "What are you doing?"

"Exercising another option, Elise. Why would I accept your deal when I can simply kill you here and now and be done with it? It's more efficient to kill an eyewitness than to make a deal with one." Taunting her, he added, "Shame on you for not thinking this through more carefully. Before coming here you should have considered this alternative."

"I *considered* you my friend."

"Your mistake. Add it to your many. The first and primary one being that you underestimated us."

"Us?"

He frowned. "Honestly, Elise, this playacting has become tedious. Cato and I know that *you* know about our working arrangement." Leaning forward, he asked, "Do you know why it's worked so well for so long? Because neither of us is a fool, and one is as cautious as the other. We, unlike you, don't make mistakes."

"Cato made one," she said smartly. "Napoli proved to be an unreliable assassin."

"True. Had it been my decision, I'd have been more swift and sure."

"To get rid of me."

"You were getting too nosy, too curious. You were making us both very nervous."

"How . . . how long have you known?"

He chuckled. "From the beginning. You thought you were so clever, ingratiating yourself to us. Playing the honest and trustworthy employee to me. Being the perfect sex toy for Cato. Sweetheart," he said, dropping his voice to a sympathetic whisper, "almost from the very start we knew you were related to Chet Rollins."

"You never indicated —"

"No, but then we wouldn't, would we? See, we carefully check out the people who get close to us, Elise. We're acutely paranoid, but that paranoia has proved to be a sound policy."

"What gave me away?"

"You didn't fit the mold. You were so eager to work at the White Tie and Tails, and yet you went against the stereotype. You aren't a natural hustler, and it showed. In a business where a girl's earnings depend on getting cozy with clients, you remained aloof and detached. Naturally, that aroused my curiosity, then my suspicion. I didn't have to dig very deep to find your connection to Chet Rollins."

She felt the weight of Duncan's handgun in her purse in her lap, and wondered if she could get to it before Savich shot her. She had no doubt that he would. Eventually. Right now, he was enjoying himself too much.

"When I told Cato about your kinship with Rollins, he panicked. He thought you might have hard evidence against him related to your half brother's demise. He wanted to . . . dispose of you right away, have you meet with a fatal accident on the highway after you left the club one night. But I talked him into waiting. You intrigued me. I wanted to watch and see what you did next.

"It soon became apparent that you had nothing on us except your suspicions. That you were after information, evidence," he said, whispering the last word like it was a secret between them. "When you didn't get it from me at the White Tie and Tails, you moved to the country club. With the express intention of meeting Cato. Am I right so far?"

She didn't reply, but she didn't have to.

"Here's where the story takes an interesting turn. Up to this point, you were just a name to Cato. A threat. He wanted you dead. But after meeting you, he decided he preferred you alive. He thought what better way to keep an eye on you than to marry you, have you under his roof where he could watch you day and night, have you accountable to him. And, of course, he would have your delectable body at his beck and call. He could fuck you to his heart's content."

She flinched, which caused him to smile.

"Poor Elise. All those nights you spent with Cato were for nothing. You were never going to find anything near him linking the two of us because, as with all my partnerships, I'm the bookkeeper."

She glanced at the computer on the credenza behind his desk.

He chuckled. "You'd never crack the firewalls, my dear, even if I let you try. The cruel irony is, if it was evidence you were after, you married the wrong partner. And now, you've made another unfortunate mistake." His mouth formed a moue of regret. "It really is a shame I must kill you. Such a waste of beauty and —"

The hand aiming the pistol at her shattered in a spray of blood.

Savich bellowed in pain. His pistol clattered to the floor. Duncan, coming from behind her, vaulted the desk. He grabbed Savich's ponytail, twisted his head to the side, and slammed it onto the desk. His cheekbone cracked upon impact, causing him to roar in outrage and pain. Duncan jabbed the barrel of his pistol against Savich's temple, hard enough for the metal to create a depression in his skin.

Never taking his eyes off Savich, he shouted, "DeeDee!"

"Coming!"

Her voice echoed from the far side of the building and Elise heard running footsteps approaching. She bolted from her chair, but collided with the woman detective as she barreled through the door.

"Cover her," Duncan ordered.

DeeDee Bowen, pistol drawn and aimed at Elise's chest, backed her into the wall.

"Where in God's name have you been?" Duncan barked.

"I climbed the fire escape and came

through a window," she answered, panting. "How'd you get up?"

"Stairwell." He took his eyes off Savich long enough to glance at Elise. "She's probably got my pistol."

Elise dropped her handbag to the floor. "It's in there."

"Kick it away."

Elise did as DeeDee instructed. The detective knelt down and felt the handbag until she located the gun, then stood up. "We're okay," she told Duncan.

"What about the secretary?" he asked.

"Handcuffed to the car door," DeeDee replied. "He's not going anywhere. I've called for backup."

"Backup? How long ago?"

"What?"

"How long ago?"

"Uh, just before I ran up here. Why?"

"Shit!" he hissed.

Elise took a step forward. "Duncan, I —"

"Shut up! You've got nothing to say that I want to hear, Mrs. Laird. The best thing you ever did for me, the *only* thing, is provide enough distraction for me to get to this piece of shit." He ground the barrel of the pistol against Savich's temple. "How does your gun hand feel now, Savich?"

Despite the pain he must be feeling, Savich's voice was remarkably calm. "Is this about Meyer Napoli? If so, you've got a problem. Nobody's going to believe Elise, you know. She'll make an unreliable witness."

"Yeah, I learned that the hard way," Duncan said, shooting her a look of pure hatred.

"So you're wasting your time," Savich said.

"Hell if I am."

"Very well." He sighed with resignation. "Arrest me. I'll spend the night in the comfort of the hospital."

"Un-unh," Duncan said. "I didn't come here to arrest you. I came to get a confession, and I'm not leaving without it." He pulled back the hammer on his revolver.

Savich laughed. "Oh, I'm scared."

"Your confession or your brains, Savich. You get to choose, and there's no door number three."

"Duncan," DeeDee said with uncertainty, "what are you doing?"

"Did I stutter? I'm going to get a confession from him. Either that, or it's going to get messy in here."

"You'd never pull that trigger, Hatcher," Savich said with infuriating condescension. "We both know that."

Duncan fired at the carafe on the edge of

the desk, shattering the crystal into a thousand shards. Water splashed across the desk and onto the floor. Drops splattered on Savich's face. In the small office, the .357 just as well could have been a cannon. The deafening blast caused a concussion in the room.

DeeDee recoiled, but she kept her pistol aimed at Elise. "What the hell?" she shouted. "Wait for backup, Duncan. They'll be here soon. We'll take him in, we'll —"

"If you've got no stomach for this, DeeDee, you can leave and take Mrs. Laird with you." His eyes and his pistol were still trained on Savich. "This is between him and me. I won't be made a fool of again. Not by her, not by her husband, and for goddamn sure not by you." On the last word, he poked the pistol barrel against Savich's skull, bumping it against the bone. "Give it up, Savich. Freddy Morris. Andre Bonnet. Chet Rollins. Gordon Ballew. Sound familiar?"

"Fuck you."

Duncan fired the pistol again, this time at the cabinet across the room, shattering the glass door. Then he shot out the globe of a wall sconce. The acrid smell of cordite filled the office. The noise was unbearable, but DeeDee could be heard above the reverberation, yelling, "Duncan, stop this! This isn't the way! You've lost your head over *her!* This is about *her.* You're angry over *her.*"

He paid no attention. Bending down, he placed his lips directly above Savich's ear. "Tell me what I want to hear or you're going to die."

"You would never do it."

They all heard the wail of sirens approaching, but the sound didn't deter Duncan.

"Are you sure about that, Savich? Are you willing to bet your life on it? 'Cause that's what you're doing. I've got two bullets left. Count 'em. Two."

"Duncan, for God's sake," DeeDee pleaded. "Don't do it! You'll ruin your career. Everything. Your life."

"My life comes down to this." He cast a bitter glance toward Elise. "I've got nothing to lose. Not anymore." He dug the pistol into Savich's temple. "Is this the way you killed Freddy Morris? Did he stink of fear the way you do?"

"I didn't —"

Before he even completed the denial, Duncan fired the pistol into the desk. The wood splintered, leaving a jagged hole inches from Savich's nose. "That leaves one."

"You're boring me, Hatcher," Savich

replied drolly.

"Tell me you did it, or your brain is mist!" Duncan yelled.

"Duncan, no!"

"DeeDee, I told you —"

"You can't do this."

"Yes, I can. I can kill him. Easy."

"No." DeeDee's voice cracked with desperation as she whipped her pistol away from Elise and aimed it at Duncan. "I won't let you."

"What are you —"

"Drop your weapon, Duncan!"

"You wouldn't —"

"Oh yes, I would."

He stared at her aghast. "You'd shoot *me?*"

"I swear I will."

The sirens grew louder. Tires screeched. Car doors slammed. Yet inside the office, time seemed to stand still.

"I can't let him go," Duncan said.

"For the last time, drop your weapon."

"You'll have to shoot me first."

"Don't make me do this," DeeDee cried, tears in her voice.

"I'm gonna take this bastard."

"Drop it, Duncan!"

"No freaking way."

"Duncan, don't!" DeeDee shouted.

"See you in hell, Savich."

"All right, all right," Savich screamed. "I . . . I did Morris."

No sooner were the words out of his mouth than several uniformed officers, led by Detective Worley, barged into the room. "Shame on you, Savich. I think that means you're in a world of hurt."

The uniformed officers eddied around the desk and surrounded the criminal. Duncan tucked his pistol into his waistband, saying, "He needs an ambulance." Then he rushed across the room to Elise and wrapped his arms around her. "Are you all right?"

She leaned against him and nodded shakily. "I didn't expect him to pull a gun on me."

"Christ, I should never have agreed to let you do this. If I'd been a few seconds later —"

She placed her fingers on his lips, so he wouldn't complete the thought. "But you weren't. I knew you'd be here."

He hugged her tighter, then let her go abruptly and rounded on Worley. "You took fucking long enough! DeeDee was about to shoot me, and I was afraid she would while I was stalling and running out of bullets."

"Hey, there was traffic," Worley said defensively. "I was standing by, waiting for her call, just like you told me to do."

DeeDee was looking at all of them with astonishment. But especially at Duncan. "Just like you told him to do? When? What the hell's he talking about? What's going on?"

Worley shifted his toothpick and said, "She's ticked, all right. Have fun explaining, Dunk. I gotta follow up on that search warrant you asked for. Should be ready soon." He stepped out of the office to use his cell phone.

DeeDee hadn't taken her eyes off Duncan. "When did you call him?"

"From my house when I picked up the six-shooter."

"You never intended to pull this off, just the two of us?"

He shook his head. "No, but I wanted you to think so."

"Why?"

"In order for Savich to be convinced that I'd gone over the edge, *you* had to be convinced I had."

"So you used me."

"I relied on your professional integrity and adherence to the rules."

"That sounds like bullshit."

"It is bullshit," he admitted. "I used you."

"How could you not trust me?"

"But I did, DeeDee. I trusted you to do

632

the right thing, and you did. I knew you'd call for backup. I had Worley standing by, ready to roll."

She nodded toward Elise. "What about her?"

Duncan bent down and retrieved Elise's handbag. "He searched me, but thankfully he didn't check my bag," she said as he withdrew a small tape recorder and passed it to DeeDee, who stared at it with bewilderment.

"My grandmother's. But we checked it out and it works." He turned to Elise. "I arrived in time to hear him talking about his partnership with Laird. What about Napoli?"

"That's why he was about to kill me. He said it was more efficient to kill an eyewitness than to make a deal with one. Just like Napoli, I was a loose end he needed to tie up. It's all on the tape."

"Wait," DeeDee said, holding up her hand. She was gaping at Elise with awe. "You came here and told Savich that you witnessed Napoli's murder?"

"That was the plan. Duncan was against it."

"That's putting it mildly."

She gave him a soft smile, then said to DeeDee, "It was the only way. You mistrusted me from the start. Rather than try and persuade you otherwise, I talked Duncan into staging what would look like a double-cross. We counted on you believing that I had betrayed him to Savich."

DeeDee assimilated that. "The argument between you two over who was the bigger fish, Laird or Savich, was also staged for my benefit?"

"As well as my heavy-handed encounter with Laird," Duncan said. "Not that I didn't enjoy having him by the balls."

"How'd you know I would show up at your grandmother's house today?"

"My mom left me a text message on my cell. She was second-guessing telling you where I was. I knew you'd show up. Elise and I had discussed how we would play it out when you did."

DeeDee still looked resentful over being left in the dark, but there was also grudging admiration in her expression as she sized up Elise. "By coming to see Savich alone, you laid your life on the line."

"Which I was willing to do. I have a stake in this, too, remember. My brother."

"Yeah, but that took guts," DeeDee said. "And frankly, I thought . . . well . . ."

"I know what you thought. And I understand."

"All the same, I owe you an apology."

"Not really. I'd given you absolutely no reason to trust me."

DeeDee acknowledged Elise's graciousness with a brusque nod, then turned to Duncan. "As for you, *partner,* you're an asshole."

Before he could take issue with that, he noticed that another officer was reading Savich his rights. "Hold on. I want to do the honors."

Savich was still seated in his desk chair. He'd been handcuffed, but someone had wrapped a handkerchief around his bleeding hand. He was in obvious pain, but Duncan, thinking of the victims he had either terrorized or murdered, wasn't moved to pity. He felt nothing except supreme satisfaction as he Mirandized him.

Savich sneered. "You never would have fired that sixth bullet."

"Now, Bobby," Duncan said in a singsong voice, deliberately using the diminutive of his name, which he knew Savich loathed. "You didn't sound so confident about that sixth bullet a few minutes ago when you were screaming like a girl."

"That confession is worthless to you. It was made under duress. This cowboy act of yours was for nothing."

"Wrong. But in any case, I would have done it just for fun."

"You wanted to impress your new girlfriend." He slid a glance at Elise, then gave Duncan a sly smile. "Does she let you come in her mouth?"

Duncan's eyes narrowed dangerously. "You know what, Savich? You're still pissing me off. And, you may be right. That confession may not hold up in court. Besides that, it looks to me like you're trying to escape."

He whipped the pistol from his waistband, aimed it at the bridge of Savich's nose, and pulled the trigger.

30

The following afternoon, Robert Savich still appeared as shaken as he'd been the previous night when he was hauled out of his office in handcuffs. After a brief stop at the ER, he'd spent the night in the detention center, no doubt shivering on his cot, reliving that split second when he'd experienced the mortal terror he had inflicted on so many others.

"Orange isn't his color," DeeDee remarked.

She and Duncan were sitting in the gallery of the superior court room, watching with interest as Savich was escorted to his place at the defense table for his bond hearing. Earlier in the day, in another court, he'd been arraigned for the murder of Meyer Napoli. Not surprisingly, on behalf of his client, Stan Adams had entered a plea of not guilty.

During his previous trial, conducted in

this same courtroom only weeks earlier, Savich had been dressed to the nines each day. Today he looked like a different man, wearing the orange jail jumpsuit and sneakers without laces. Despite the thick bandage on his right hand, he was shackled. His ankles were connected by chains to the bands around his wrists. His hair hung loose. The diamond was missing from his earlobe.

"Yeah, but ain't he a pretty sight?" Duncan stared at the man's profile, willing him to turn and look at him, knowing that Savich wouldn't. Duncan had won. Savich couldn't endure his victory.

"Stop fidgeting." DeeDee clamped her hand over his knee to keep it from bobbing up and down. "Why are you nervous?"

"I'm not nervous. More like excited." Feeling the weight of his partner's stare, he turned his head toward her. "What?"

"It's real, isn't it? The thing between you and her. It's like . . . the kind of thing that counts."

"For me, definitely. For her, hopefully." He looked toward the bench, now empty, but where Cato Laird would soon begin presiding over the courtroom with his customary arrogance and aplomb. "She's gotta get past this. Start living as herself, not as his wife. It'll be an adjustment. She's lived on guard and in fear for a long time. It may take a while before she's entirely free from all that."

"Well, I just want you to know — not that you need my permission or even my approval — but, I'm cool with it. With the two of you together, I mean."

He turned and smiled down at her. "Thanks."

"Just in case you wondered."

"Thanks," he repeated. He glanced at his wristwatch. "They're late getting started."

She nodded toward Savich, who appeared not to have moved since he was seated. "He's trying to pretend he isn't here."

"But he is. He's had his last day of freedom, and he knows it."

"You can bet he hates being treated like a common criminal."

"He's common enough," Duncan said. "When I pulled the trigger, he messed his pants."

"Can't say as I blame him. I nearly did myself. Lucky for him you had left the last chamber of the revolver empty. Why did you? Because you figured it would come down to that last pull of the trigger?"

"Exactly," he said. "And if that bullet had

been loaded, I'd have killed the son of a bitch."

"All rise," the bailiff intoned.

DeeDee, dumbfounded by Duncan's last statement, came to her feet a bit more slowly than did everyone else in the courtroom as Judge Cato Laird strode in and assumed his seat.

He glanced over the assembly, his gaze alighting briefly on DeeDee before shifting to Duncan. Their eye contact lasted for several significant seconds, then he proceeded.

"Mr. Adams, you're representing Mr. Savich?"

"Yes, Your Honor." Stan Adams stood up.

"He's been charged with the murder of Meyer Napoli."

"To which he's entered a plea of not guilty. Before we continue, Your Honor, I submit that the restraints on my client are unnecessary and request that they be removed for the duration of these proceedings."

"These proceedings won't take that long, Mr. Adams. Your request is denied." For effect, he banged his gavel.

Duncan noticed that Laird avoided looking directly at Savich.

"Mr. Nelson," the judge said, "you're

representing the DA's office?"

"Yes, Your Honor." Mike Nelson came to his feet behind the prosecutor's table, but not before glancing meaningfully at Duncan, whose heart had begun to beat hard and fast.

"Your Honor," the prosecutor said, "Robert Savich has also been charged with conspiracy to commit murder in the death of Chester Joel Rollins."

Attorney Stan Adams turned his head so quickly, his neck popped audibly, but Duncan's eyes were trained on Cato Laird's handsome face. The judge was smiling slightly, poised to speak, when his brain processed what his ears had heard.

His smile faltered. He blinked several times. He looked at Duncan, whose stare conveyed all the enmity he felt for the man. It also conveyed what he wished he could stand up and shout: *And you thought I had you by the balls* yesterday.

He saw the judge swallow. "Uh, Mr. Nelson, this is a bond hearing. That's not the . . ." He stumbled, tried again. "That's not the case before —"

Stan Adams was back on his feet. "Your Honor, what is going on here?"

"I'm trying to ascertain that for myself, Mr. Adams. Mr. Nelson, the case you . . .

uh . . ." As he stammered, his attention was drawn to the rear door of the courtroom. Duncan watched his features turn slack with dismay, then appear to melt as though made of wax, until his entire face was sagging heavily.

Unsteadily he came to his feet and leaned upon the podium for support as Elise made her grand entrance, flanked by Bill Gerard on one side, Worley on the other. Gerard's countenance, normally affable, was stony with resolve. Worley's toothpick was at a particularly jaunty angle, like he'd just told the dirtiest joke ever.

As for Elise, she looked confident and poised. "Hello, Cato."

"Elise!" he cried. "How . . . This is . . . My God!"

"Stop pretending, Cato. You're anything but overjoyed."

Upon seeing Elise, supposedly a dead woman, astonishment had rendered Stan Adams silent.

Duncan left his seat and stepped into the aisle just ahead of Elise and her escorts. Without breaking stride, he went to the side of the judge's podium and stepped behind it. Taking the judge by the arm, he literally dethroned him and pulled him from behind his bench.

"Cato Laird, you're under arrest for the murder of Chet Rollins. You have the right to remain silent."

"Elise, what . . . What is this?" He waved his arms in an attempt to throw off Duncan. The wide sleeves of his robe flapped like the wings of a grounded crow. Duncan deliberately articulated his words as he read him his rights.

The judge's dismay turned to anger. "Gerard, what is going on?"

"Just like Detective Sergeant Hatcher said. You're being arrested for conspiring to commit murder."

"This is outrageous!"

Elise stepped up to him. "You had my half brother killed, Cato. He was going to expose you and Savich, so you silenced him."

He looked beyond her at Gerard. "She's delusional."

But Gerard said nothing as Elise went on, undeterred. "At the time, Chet was the only person in my life who loved me. The only person I loved. And he died naked and in fear on a cold shower floor, slowly choking on a bar of soap."

Cato looked around frantically, seeking an ally. None was to be found. Everyone in the courtroom was riveted by the drama being played out. Some were regarding the judge

643

speculatively. Others had already made up their minds about the truthfulness of Elise's accusation and were looking at him with contempt.

He shouted, "This woman is unstable! She's a liar. She killed a man in our home, and I, like a fool, protected her from prosecution. She's been pretending to be dead, for crissake."

He pointed a finger at Duncan. "Yesterday, he . . . he kidnapped and assaulted me. She can tell you," he said, pointing wildly at DeeDee. "They've all turned against me. They hate me. You can't believe anything they say!"

Elise continued in a calm, clear voice. "For years you've been taking money from Savich in exchange for favorable rulings. Lenient sentencing. Sometimes you dismissed cases and declared mistrials."

She produced the USB key that had been taken from Savich's computer during the search of his office that had followed his arrest. Despite his claim of having firewalls that couldn't be cracked, they had been last night by the department's computer experts.

"All your transactions are recorded on this. Savich was invoiced by your family's shipping company for its transport services. But he was charged a usurious rate, sometimes twice what other clients were charged for the same service. The overage he paid went into your private account in the Cayman Islands."

The judge's face had turned red with fury. He confronted Gerard. "You can't treat me like this!"

"Yeah, I can."

"I want my lawyer."

"You'll get your phone call, Judge."

Looking past the others, the judge snarled at Savich, "Did you set me up?"

Savich shouted back, "You were going to feed me to these dogs."

Stan Adams told him to shut up.

Ignoring the advice of his attorney, Savich said, "It's her you have to thank for this," and motioned toward Elise with his head. "Her and her boyfriend Hatcher."

"Be quiet!" Adams grabbed Savich's arm and tried to yank him into a chair, but he stumbled on his chains and fell to the floor.

Duncan gave Cato Laird a nudge. "Say good-bye to your bench. You've made your last ruling."

"You son of a bitch," the judge said, spraying spittle. "You lied to me. You . . ." He divided a wrathful look between him and Elise. "You *are* fucking her, aren't you? Well, have her. You deserve the bitch. You deserve each other."

Duncan's eyes drilled into those of the judge and he held his arm in a bone-crunching grip. Lowering his voice to a menacing pitch, he said, "I advise you to leave this courtroom now, before you say something for which I'll be forced to hold you in contempt."

Recognizing the words he'd said to Duncan, Cato lunged toward him and Elise. Two uniformed cops rushed to Duncan's assistance, and it took the three of them to restrain Laird. Feral sounds issued from his throat. The blood vessels in his forehead looked ready to burst.

Elise didn't recoil. In fact, she stepped closer to him. Suddenly the judge ceased his struggles and became perfectly still except for his raspy breathing.

"What Savich says is true, Cato," she said. "I set you up. But you have only yourself to blame. From the day you were born, you were handed every advantage that could possibly be granted to a person, and you abused them all. What a sick, selfish individual you are. As well as criminal.

"I'm sure you realize how unpopular you'll be among the prison population. You'll have enemies already in place, anticipating your arrival. That means every day for the rest of your life, you'll be looking over your shoulder, living in fear, like Chet did.

"Fear will be your constant companion, Cato. Every minute of every day, you'll have to be on guard against ambush, rape, torture. Execution." She took a deep breath, then added softly, "May God have mercy on you. I have none."

Duncan admired her restraint. In her situation, he wouldn't have been nearly that eloquent. But then, she had waited a long time for this day. Maybe she had known exactly what she would say to him if ever given the opportunity.

She turned her back on Cato Laird. Duncan relinquished the judge to the policemen and moved up beside her, taking her elbow. She'd won the respect of Gerard and Worley during the long and detailed telling of the whole story last night. They preceded her and Duncan up the aisle like bodyguards.

They were about halfway to the exit when the shot rang out. Acting on instinct, Duncan dove to his right, knocking Elise to the floor and covering her with his own body.

Screams and warning shouts echoed in the courtroom.

"Stay down!" Duncan yelled at her. Then

in one fluid motion, he rolled onto his back and came up into a crouch, aimed and ready to fire his drawn weapon.

But the threat was over. There had been only one casualty.

EPILOGUE

The November day was sunny but cool. A breeze rippled the surface of the channel between Beaufort and Lady's Island. It was a good day to be outdoors, but Duncan and Elise preferred getting their fresh air through the open window while they languished in bed.

They'd arrived late the previous evening. It was the first time they'd been to this house since they'd departed it separately, he with DeeDee, she alone in his car on her way to confront Savich.

The intervening four months had been turbulent. They hadn't discussed when they might return to Lady's Island, but they seemed to tacitly agree that they wouldn't come back until they could celebrate the end of their ordeal, until their return marked a new beginning.

Yesterday afternoon at 4:38 — Duncan had checked his wristwatch when the verdict was read — Robert Savich was found guilty of murdering Meyer Napoli.

Adams had argued for three days that Elise be disallowed to testify.

He'd spent the next four trying to discredit her testimony.

But the jurors weren't fooled by his blustering and courtroom posturing. They believed Elise. When they retired to the jury room, no one was taking odds on Savich being acquitted.

Duncan had helped the DA's office prepare its case, but from the sidelines. Officially he was on suspension until the end of this month. Since Elise had been integral to the case, they'd seen each other regularly, but not as often as Duncan wished.

She had steadfastly refused to move into his town house. "You're in enough trouble as it is with the police department," she'd said.

"I've already admitted to sleeping with you during an ongoing investigation. I'm taking my punishment like a man. So what difference does it make now if you're living with me?"

"I'm the reason for your suspension. How would it look if I was living with you during it?"

"I don't care."

Quietly she said, "I do."

That had ended the argument, most effectively. Because he realized it wasn't only his disciplinary suspension she was taking into account, it was her recent widowhood.

For days following the scene in the courtroom that had ended with Cato Laird's grisly suicide, the story had dominated the media. You couldn't turn on a TV or pick up a newspaper without getting another account of the stunning events that took place that afternoon in superior court.

Several witnesses had seen Cato wrestle the pistol from the holster of one of the policemen escorting him from the courtroom. Each had a version of how he'd placed the barrel in his mouth and pulled the trigger before any of the surprised officers or horrified onlookers could stop him.

The story was repeated for weeks, told from different perspectives, but always summarizing with the same gruesome outcome.

As details of Laird's criminal activity were disclosed, they were explored and editorialized upon. News junkies couldn't get enough, and the media fed their voracious appetites.

Public opinion of the judge was generally one of outrage over his duplicity and the misuse of his power and position. The widow who had exposed him was regarded with sympathy and admiration.

But Elise had shied from the publicity. It wasn't a celebrity she welcomed. Her triumph was small and simple, but meaningful to her — she was able to exhume her brother's coffin and give it a proper burial in a decent cemetery. Chet Rollins had been no saint, but he hadn't deserved his horrible death. Perhaps he'd found peace. Elise had.

Now, her limbs were tangled with Duncan's in a tableau of lassitude after a night and a morning of lovemaking. He rubbed his cheek against her belly. "You need a shave," she said drowsily.

"Later. Right now, I can't move."

"Hmm." She combed her fingers through his hair, whispering, "I don't want you to move."

Nevertheless he nibbled his way up her torso, until he reached her mouth. The long kiss that followed was sexually evocative. When they finally pulled apart, her eyes remained closed. She murmured, "I only thought I didn't want you to move."

"You like that, scratchy beard and all?"

"Scratchy beard especially."

"Then you should marry me."

Her eyes sprang open. "I can't."

"You don't have to answer right away," he said wryly. "Give yourself some time to think about it."

"I can't marry you, Duncan."

He settled himself beside her, propping his cheek on his fist. "Why not?"

"Because I love you."

"Hmm. Well, see, usually it works the other way. If you love someone, you want to marry him."

"I do love you." She said it like a holy vow, a pledge.

Matching her solemnity, he said, "Then I fail to see the problem."

"No children, for one."

He whisked his thumb across her delicate cheekbones. "Tubal ligations can be reversed."

"Not always successfully."

"If not successfully, we'll adopt kids. Or do without kids."

"But you wouldn't want to."

"What I wouldn't want is to do without *you.*" He laid his hand against her cheek. "You're the one thing I must have in my life."

"I have nothing to contribute to a partnership, especially not to one as important as a marriage."

She had taken nothing from Cato Laird's

house, not even her personal belongings, and had actually become angry when his attorney called to give her the bad news that there was no mention of her in Cato's will.

"As if I ever wanted to touch anything that he had owned," she'd said as she hung up on the attorney.

Duncan would never have influenced that decision, but he was glad of it. He wouldn't have wanted her to keep anything that had come from Cato Laird.

"I've been living on what little I'd saved before my marriage to Cato," she said now, "but that will soon run out and I'll have to find some kind of work."

"If you could wake up tomorrow and be doing the thing you've always wanted to do, what would it be?"

She stared into near space for a moment. "Remember I told you that before I moved to Savannah, I was taking classes in film?"

"Movies are a passion. You practically quoted that sappy chick flick to me."

She frowned at his terminology, but continued her thought. "Not too far from your house, there's an old movie theater."

"Across from Forsyth Park? It's been there since the thirties. Hasn't been in operation for years."

"I was thinking it could be restored," she

said hesitantly. "Very nicely. Make it a theater for classic movies only. *Giant, Lawrence of Arabia, Doctor Zhivago.* Big, epic movies like that. Or film noir. Tracy and Hepburn. There's an endless list of film festivals. It could host premieres. There could be a wine bar off the lobby, not just your ordinary concessions. It could also be rented out for special events or programs, charity fund-raisers, corporate parties, conventions. Think of the convention business it could draw.

"Remember when we were in Beaufort talking about all the movies that are filmed around here? Well, maybe if a film crew was working nearby, the director, or a couple of the actors, would come and lecture, especially if it was a fund-raising benefit. Can you imagine if an Ang Lee or Lasse Hallström . . ." Noticing his smile, she stopped. "What?"

"You're right. You've got nothing to contribute."

She recognized it for teasing. "You think it's a good idea?"

"Only thing, am I gonna have to wear a tux to all those 'events'?"

She laughed softly, but her smile faltered. "It's just an idea. It would take a lot of money to do it the way I envision."

"I'm not entirely without connections and resources. We'll find investors, we'll get the money." He tugged a strand of her hair, which was back to its natural color and had grown out to chin length. "Any more objections to my proposal of marriage?"

"Your friends and family."

"You don't like them?"

"Duncan, be serious."

"Okay. Sorry. What about my friends and family?"

"How would they feel about your being permanently linked to me?"

"Well, you've inspired DeeDee to stop perming her hair and start plucking her eyebrows. Those are damn strong endorsements. My male coworkers grumble behind my back about my undeserved good fortune."

"To be with a topless waitress."

"To be loved by the woman who was brave enough to confront Savich alone. Believe me, none would breathe a slight against you around me. But they for sure as hell would say nothing improper about you within DeeDee's hearing. And anybody who would isn't my friend, so his opinion doesn't matter to me."

"But your parents' opinion does. You love them. They love you." She turned her head away from him. "I would be their worst nightmare."

"You're right." He sighed. "Mom's in a tizzy. I don't remember her ever being this upset with me." He placed his finger beneath her chin and turned her face toward him. "I called today and told them we'd be there for dinner tomorrow. Mom was furious because I hadn't given her enough advance notice. She had wanted to paint the dining room before I brought you home for the first time."

"Home?" Her eyes reflected a childlike hopefulness that pierced his heart with love. All his life, he'd taken for granted the people who had cared about him, loved him without qualification. She'd never had that kind of security. He would love her enough to make up for that deficiency. And more.

"They don't condemn me for what I did?"

"They're in the forgiving business," he said with a smile. Then, turning serious, he stroked her cheek. "But what is there to forgive, Elise? What was your big sin? *Savich* is evil. *Cato Laird* was evil. Not you."

By the time he finished speaking, tears were shimmering in her eyes. She pulled him to her, rubbing her lips against his, whispering, "I love you, Duncan. Love you with all my heart and soul. Love you. Love you."

He gathered her beneath him and pressed into her, his smile against her lips. "I'll take that as a yes."